LIVING
OUTSIDE
THE LINES

HELEN LAPAKKO

LIVING OUTSIDE THE LINES

iUniverse books may be ordered through booksellers or by contacting:

iUniverse
1663 Liberty Drive
Bloomington, IN 47403
www.iuniverse.com
1-800-Authors (1-800-288-4677)

ISBN: 978-1-4917-9270-4 (sc)
ISBN: 978-1-4917-9271-1 (e)

Library of Congress Control Number: 2016904774

Print information available on the last page.

iUniverse rev. date: 04/28/2016

Thank you to my friends and family who
have loved and encouraged me.
And a special thanks to my husband David for all
his editing advice, and my dear friend Karen for
listening to my many stories over the years.

Contents

Prologue

Disconnected Lives

I'm from an ivory tower of disconnected lives,
Where whiskey makes a river of so many lies,
My mother wore her bruises outside and in,
I hid in my stories, until I met him

His father was a hustler; his mother walked the streets,
He knew how to love me and he knew how to cheat,
He was always gamblin' down on one knee,
He knew how to throw those dice with such ease.

Now I'm on those streets where chaos rules the day,
Don't know where I'm going I got no place to stay.
In all the noise and people I see walking by,
Do they know that I'm here? I look up with a sigh.

And see the disconnected tower where whiskey overflows,
No one stops and sees my bruises from the blows.
They're not on the outside; they hide deep within,
I'm the one who sees them cuz I know where I've been
I'm from and ivory tower of disconnected lives

Real Life Stories

My brother, at ten-years-old, literally dodged a bullet. He was sitting up reading; his eyes were getting tired, so he turned out the light, pulled up his covers, and lay down to sleep. Five minutes later, a bullet came through the outside wall of his bedroom and traveled across the room, entering the wall right where his head had been five minutes earlier. The bullet continued through the bathroom walls and ended up in my parents' bedroom, rolling under the bed, where it was found later. He sat up in bed, his face covered in plaster, and walked into my parents' bedroom. The bed was empty. My parents weren't home; they had a habit of putting us kids to bed, then going out somewhere without telling anyone or leaving a note to let us know where they were. I was three at the time, sleeping upstairs with my five-year-old sister. My brother walked upstairs and woke us up. My sister screamed when she saw him. She thought he was a ghost because his face was white from the plaster, and he had just woken her up from a deep sleep. I rolled over and fell back asleep.

My mother "dodged a bullet" the year after I graduated from high school. My father's abusive, alcoholic temper tantrums, brought on by his inability to cope with his bipolar disorder, beat my mother down until she stopped eating. We kids would lay awake listening and go to school blurry eyed after a night of his yelling. My mother began to hide bottles of alcohol in the washing machine so we wouldn't see her drinking. Her skin turned a sickly yellow color; her liver turned the whites of her eyes the same color. She was skin and bones before my older brother got her to the doctor. My mother was hospitalized and almost died. When I went to visit her at the hospital she didn't know who I was. She had five blood transfusions that finally turned her around. She eventually returned home and we had part of our mother back; I think the rest of her was left at the hospital, because she was never quite the same.

When I was twenty, I took a year off college and moved to Milwaukee, where I dodged a bullet. One night I was waitressing at the Crazy Horse restaurant, my car was in the shop, so I needed a ride home after work. The salad girl, Daneeka, said her boyfriend could give me a ride home. After work we waited outside; her boyfriend pulled up in his Cadillac. I got in the back seat with Darnell, a friend of Daneeka's boyfriend. He smiled at me and we made small talk. Suddenly Daneeka told her boyfriend to make a left turn, saying she had to get something from her sister's house. When he pulled over, she asked me to come with her to help carry it. So we got out and walked around the side of the house. She took my hand and told me to run. We ran down the alley away from her boyfriend's car. Along the way she told me her boyfriend had shown her a gun, so she wanted to get away from him. We ended up in a pool parlor on Capitol Drive, where her ex-boyfriend worked. We hung out there for a couple of hours.

When it was about three in the morning, I decided to walk home. My place was only about a half a mile down Capitol Drive. Daneeka stayed there with her ex-boyfriend. I went out the door of the pool hall and turned left. After walking two blocks I noticed a car turn the corner up ahead. It was a Cadillac coming towards me down the street. I kept walking, *thinking nothing of it*, until the car pulled over. The driver of the car leaned over and pushed open the passenger door, pointing a gun at me. It was Darnell. With the gun pointed right at my chest, he told me to get into the car. I wondered whether I could run for it, but the gun was staring at me and I knew I wasn't faster than a bullet. So I sat in the car, leaving the door open with one foot planted on the street. He told me to close the door, that he wasn't going to shoot me. He said if he wanted to shoot me, he could have done it while I stood on the sidewalk, or while I sat with the door open and one foot on the street. I thought about that for a minute, staring at the gun now pointed at my head, and closed the door. I said if he wasn't going to shoot me than why didn't he just give me the gun. He sat there for thirty seconds, lowered the gun, and gave it to me. He asked me why Daneeka and I had ditched them. I told him Daneeka was threatened when her boyfriend showed her the gun. He ended up driving me to my apartment that I shared with my boyfriend, Mack. I left Mack a few days later because he hit me. I lived on the streets for a couple of weeks until I met Janey, a new waitress who was hired at the Crazy Horse where I worked. We became friends and we got an apartment together, spending our weekends selling old record albums on the street corner by the University of Wisconsin.

When I graduated from college in criminal justice studies, I worked in corrections. My years growing up had trained me for this career. So nothing or nobody surprised me anymore. I had learned that I needed to have enough strength to lift a car, enough compassion to forgive all people. I needed the courage to face the darkest shadows, and the intelligence to keep studying and learning what the world had to offer. I was a survivor and I'd been trained to "dodge bullets."

~

This book is a collection of fictional stories, a few based loosely on real life experiences. The majority are stories of characters I have created. I love these characters. They have lived with me over the years. I have heard their voices of courage and strength. I have felt the pain of their struggles, and learned from them the compassion to love myself. They have woken me up in the middle of the night to write down their words, so their voices could be heard. I have watched them grow and develop while they were "living outside the lines."

SECOND STORY WINDOW

The Old Man

One day I was walking, down the road
I saw an old man, carrying a heavy load
He said just follow me, I know where to go
I'll bring you to the place; you need to know

We walked together, along the path
He told me stories; he made me laugh
He said just follow me, and you will see
The place that you, were meant to be

Soon the old man, sat down by the road
He said I'm tired, of carrying this heavy load
He said come rest with me, let's sit a while
I think its time for you, to find your smile

Then the old man, took my hand
And said look around you, at all this land
This is the place, where you belong
This is the place; you will grow strong

Now I'm walking down, the country path
I sing my songs, sometimes I laugh
I laid down my heavy load; I rested awhile
I laid down my heavy load, and I found my smile

Chapter 1

Alex sat in her wheelchair, her brown hair pulled back into a ponytail, staring out the window onto Main Street. *I love being on the second floor,* she thought. *I can see everything from up here in my private little world.*

"Alex, I have to go now. Why don't you get the books we checked out from the library and study?"

"OK, Mom, see you after work."

Her mom left and Alex had the apartment to herself. She glanced around the living room of their two-bedroom apartment. The old familiar couch, chair, and floor lamp gave her comfort. *Something from before,* she thought. Her eyes rested on all the unpacked boxes yet to be opened. The boxes made her feel like a stranger in her new home. She wheeled herself to her bedroom and looked in. She relaxed. It looked like her room in the old house. The bed was in the same corner, she had insisted, the dressing table with her mirror, and her favorite bookshelf with all her favorite books was right by her bed. *It feels like my old room*; the thought made her feel safe and warm as she turned and wheeled back to the living room.

She looked out the window, watching the shopkeepers arriving, turning on their lights, opening their doors, getting ready for the day's business. There was the redheaded lady with the colorful fingernails opening up the hair place, Doris's Hair Boutique. *I wonder if she's Doris. Here comes that guy with the big mustache—it's soooo bushy.* Alex giggled whenever he walked by, his hips swinging a little. *You can tell he works in that clothing store Little Town Attire,* she said to herself. *I wonder where the white-haired man who walks with a cane is? His hardware store is still closed. I wonder if he's sick?* Just then she heard whistling and saw him walking down by Little Town Attire.

Here comes that crabby man, the one who runs the café downstairs. He's really late today. Suddenly Alex could smell eggs, bacon, and hash browns sweeping up from the café beneath her. She wheeled herself over to the kitchen tucked in the corner. She said out loud, "Mom forgot to take the toaster from the cupboard and the bread so I can make toast; now what am I going to eat?" Frustrated, she opened the refrigerator and got out some orange juice and milk. Then she heard a noise in the hall. She rolled to the door, opened it a crack, and saw the crabby man from downstairs. She started to close it, steeled up her courage, and opened the door all the way.

"Excuse me," she said quietly. He seemed to ignore her. She cleared her throat and said louder. "Excuse me." He turned, scowling from under his bushy eyebrows. *Wow, his eyes are so blue.* "My mom forgot to get the toaster and bread down so I can make toast for breakfast. Could you reach them for me, please?"

The man just stared at her, like he was thinking, *how dare you ask me to do something for you.* But then he seemed to notice the wheelchair, blinked a couple of times, and said, "I suppose. Where is it?" as he pushed past her chair into the apartment.

"Up over the counter in the cupboard," she said, wondering why he was so crabby. Before she knew it, she added. "You were late today—are you OK?"

He turned and stared at her. "What's it to you?" Then he opened the cupboard and got out the toaster and bread and put it on the counter. "Here you go. Now I'm busy." He charged for the door, but before he went out, he turned, looked at her with a puzzled expression.

"Thank you," Alex said.

"Yeah," he grumbled, head bent into his shoulders as he closed the door.

Just about the time the toast was ready, she heard footsteps in the hall and a light knock on her door. She opened it, and there was the crabby man, with a plate of hash browns and eggs. He pushed his way in.

"Here," he said. "Toast is not breakfast. You eat these too." He put the plate on the counter and started out.

Alex watched him. "Thanks. By the way, what's your name?"

"Frank," he barked and rushed out.

Alex ate the eggs and hash browns; they were delicious. Then she got her books from the library: Basic ideas of Algebra, Science and Our World Today, and Language Arts through Literature. Pretty soon the smell of burgers, grilled onions, and french fries sneaked in under the apartment door from the downstairs café. Alex's stomach growled. *Boy I'm hungry.* She heard noises outside in the street, so she wheeled over to the window. There were four children about her age. Instinctively she drew back, not wanting them to see her. They were laughing—three boys and a girl. One boy was so handsome, with dark curly hair and a loose, cocky walk. The other two boys were blonde with freckles. The girl wore a baseball cap jauntily backwards over flowing long brown hair. She looked at them and their legs as they walked, and then she looked at her lifeless legs—and she remembered. She brushed a tear away, *I'm hungry.* She wheeled into the kitchen, where she made herself a peanut butter and banana sandwich, and brought it over to the window to watch. There were two elderly women chatting busily as they strolled down the street, stopping at windows to glance at the latest display. There was a mother whose three-year-old boy was holding one hand, while she carried a baby with the other. Her ponytail had pulled loose, and hair straggled into her face. Alex saw the café door below her open up and out came Frank. He stopped a moment to glance at the sky and then her window. She started to wave. He quickly looked away and walked across the street to the hardware store.

The four children she had seen before came out of the café. The girl tickled one of the boys and ran down the street. The three boys took off after her. Alex looked at their legs and how they moved with such power. She remembered that feeling of almost flying, so free, the air tossing her brown shoulder length hair back behind her. Then she felt the wheel next to her hand and she came back to her apartment and her chair.

Alex saw Frank coming back across the street with a box in his hand. He walked into the café and soon she heard footsteps in the hall by her door. Then it was quiet. About five minutes later, there was a knock. She went to the door, unlocked it, and opened it a crack.

It was Frank. "Do you play checkers?" he growled at her, opening the door and walking in.

"I . . . I have played checkers," she said, puzzled.

"Well here, I got this." Frank placed a game of checkers on the table. "I need a break from that café down there, and you look like you've got nothing to do, so let's play."

Frank sat down at the kitchen table, opened the box, and started setting up the checkerboard. Alex just sat there, wondering what her mom would think, not sure she wanted to play with this crabby Frank guy or if she should be afraid. After all, she didn't know him.

He looked up at her. "C'mon—I'm not going to bite." He bent over the board. Alex wheeled herself over.

"You've got black, so you make the first move," Frank barked.

Alex moved her checker, and the game started. Soon, one game became four games. She won one and lost three. Suddenly Frank said, "Got to go. See you tomorrow." He got up and left, taking the checkerboard with him.

Alex realized she had enjoyed playing, even though Frank maybe said eight words the whole time.

Alex went to the window and saw the shadows lengthen. Pretty soon her head started to nod and she fell asleep. Her screaming woke her up—that, and the noise of the crash in her head. She opened her eyes and it took a moment for her to realize where she was—the apartment above the café. She watched as her mom walked down the street, thinking how pretty her mom was with her long brown hair, that always looked like it needed to be combed because she was always rushing around. She was surprised at how tall she looked and how thin she'd become. As her mom got closer, she saw Alex and waved as she turned into their building.

"Hi, Mom. How was your day?" Alex asked when her mother came in the door.

"Exhausting. I had to drive to Overton and Shoreland and show farms. There were more people at the showing than I expected. So it was busy. Then two people made offers. I'm sorry—you don't want to hear the boring details. Look, if you don't mind, I want to lie down for a while before fixing dinner. Is that OK with you?" her mom asked, looking beat.

"Sure, go ahead," Alex said. Alex turned on the television, looking sad and lonely, being careful her mom didn't see.

Chapter 2

"Time to get up, Alex. I've got to go, and we need to bathe you today." Alex's mom was standing in the doorway.

"Mom, it's still dark outside," Alex mumbled as she struggled to get both eyes open.

"I know, but I've got to show some property way over in Porterville. So c'mon, you know bath mornings take more time. Wake up." Alex's mother said, walking over to the bed.

She helped Alex sit up and got her into the chair, slipping off Alex's nightshirt as she sat. "Here's a towel to keep warm," Alex's mom said, as she wheeled her out of the bedroom, into the bathroom and the shower stall.

A half hour later Alex was up, dressed and in her chair. Her mom was ready to go.

"OK Alex, you're all set. I got the bread and toaster down for breakfast. I'll be back from work, later today, so I'll bring supper home with me. How does pizza sound? It might be as late as 7:00 p.m. Do you think you'll be all right?" She looked concerned. "Look honey, I'm sorry, but we need the money, and . . . Look, I've got to go. Study today. Get your math done. We'll go over it tonight. Bye." She kissed Alex on the top of her head, hesitated a moment, then turned to leave.

"I'll be fine, Mom," Alex mumbled as her mom went out the door. Now freshly bathed and dressed, wide-awake, Alex looked at the clock, 7:00 a.m. *It's sooooo early. No one will be on Main Street until 8:30.* She felt the long day stretch out in front of her. She rolled into the bedroom, got a book from her shelf, sat by her bedroom window, and read until noises from the street roused her. The smells of bacon, coffee, and hash browns made their way up the steps, into her apartment. Her stomach started to rumble. She went into the kitchen, got out the peanut butter, and put two pieces of bread in the toaster. Then she heard footsteps and a knock. She answered the door. It was Frank. He pushed into the room, smelling of pancakes and eggs, and placed a plate on the table.

"Here, toast isn't enough for a growing kid." Frank rumbled out.

"Thanks, that does smell good." Alex's mouth watered.

Frank started out, stopped, turned, and looked her up and down.

"I never asked, what's your name?"

"Alex."

"Alex? That's a boy's name."

"Well, really it's Alexandra, but it got shortened to Alex."

"Well, I'm going to call you Alexandra. How about checkers later?" Frank asked. Before she could answer him, he was out the door. She found herself feeling happy at the thought of checkers later and a little guilty because she hadn't mentioned Frank to her mom.

Alex rolled over to the window with her breakfast and looked out. Doris's Hair Boutique's light was on. So was Little Town Attire's. And here came the gray haired man with his cane to open up the hardware store. Then she noticed some activity in the old cinema/roller rink building down the way. *I wonder what they are going to do with that building?*

She spotted the dark curly-haired boy skateboarding down the street, weaving around people, laughing. *Oh, he's soooo cute.* Then the girl with the baseball cap yelled to him from across the street, and he made a daring journey through slow-moving small town traffic. Oh, how she envied that girl in the baseball cap. *Oh, to have him as my friend.*

Alex sighed, turned away from the window, and got her math book. She sat at the kitchen table and worked. Before she knew it, the smells from downstairs gradually changed from eggs and hash browns to hamburgers and fries. She looked at the clock. It was just about lunchtime. She rolled over and looked in the refrigerator.

"Eggs, bologna, and peanut butter," she muttered to herself, "borrrring." She closed the refrigerator, and steered her chair over to the window. The street was busier today because of the town's annual sidewalk sale. There were children buying juice at the Little Grocer down by Doris's Hair Boutique. Even Doris's had hair supplies on the sidewalk for sale. There were a lot of people down at Little Town Attire, especially moms and their babies. She noticed why—there was a whole table that looked like baby stuff: toys, rattles, baby clothes, and bottles.

She saw a group of kids turn the corner on skateboards, having to stop because the sidewalks were too crowded. She turned to listen—*was that a knock on the door?* The knock was louder.

"Who's there?" Alex asked.

"It's Frank, open up."

Alex opened the door. Frank was there, a plate of something in one hand and a box of checkers in the other.

"I've got a dental appointment later so I thought we could play checkers while we ate lunch. Hope you like burgers and fries?" Frank walked in with the two burgers on a plate with a mound of golden brown french fries.

Alex got a plate from the counter and helped herself.

"Wow, I'm so hungry and nothing here looked any good. Thanks, this is exactly what I wanted," Alex said smiling at Frank. They settled in at the kitchen table and played checkers. After losing two games and winning one, Frank sat back and looked at Alex.

"So, what does your mom do all day?"

"She sells real estate in the Southeast Region," Alex said.

"She sure is gone a lot," Frank said, looking at Alex.

"I know, but we need the money." Alex looked down at her legs. "For, you know."

Frank looked at Alex's legs and then at her face. "What do you do up here all day, anyway?"

"Oh, I watch out the window and study. I'm behind in school because of . . . Well, anyway, so I'm trying to get caught up before school starts in the fall."

Frank leaned forward, looked at her legs again, started to say something, and then changed his mind.

Alex asked, "So are you married or have any kids?"

Frank looked up at her through his bushy eyebrows and stared at her a good minute before he said, "Not now." He started laying out the checkers for a new game.

"Got to leave in 20 minutes, let's get in one more game." Frank grumbled.

At two o'clock, Frank slid his chair back. "Got to go," he said, grabbing the checkers. "See you," and he was out the door.

Alex looked at the clock. *Five hours 'til Mom gets home.* Suddenly she felt tired. She rolled over to the window to feel the gentle breeze coming in, put her head back, and closed her eyes and slept.

When her mom got home that night, Alex was reading her social studies book and writing a report on the American Indians.

"Hi, Alex, how was your day?" she asked putting down her purse and the pizza she brought home. "I made a sale today!"

Alex's mom danced around the room. "I made a BIG sale, a farm! We'll celebrate after dinner. I'll go down the street to

Shakes and Cones Etc. for ice cream. Hey, what's this? This is a plate from downstairs. How'd that get here?" Her mom found the burger plate Frank had left.

Alex swallowed nervously, her mom always warned her about strangers. "Well, you know that crabby man from downstairs? He brought it. His name is Frank, and we've sort of become friends. We play checkers."

"How did that happen? He just suddenly came to the apartment?" Alex's mom looked very angry. "I don't think Alex . . ."

Alex's words rushed out. "Mom, you forgot to put the toaster and bread on the counter yesterday. I was hungry and I couldn't reach it. I heard Frank in the hall and asked him to get it for me. He did. Then he stopped by later with a checkerboard."

Alex's mom looked angry, and then slowly her face softened. "I'm sorry I forgot to put the toaster and bread on the counter. I'm glad he got it down for you. Do you like him?"

"Yeah, I do. He's nice in a crabby sort of way."

"I'll have to introduce myself and find out more about him, especially if he's going to be coming here. Let's eat the pizza and then I'll go get ice cream. On the way back, I'll stop downstairs and meet this Frank.

After they ate their pizza, Alex's mom left for the ice cream cones. When she got back she said. "Here, Alex, Rocky Road, just like you asked. I left word for Frank to come up here when he gets in."

Alex and her mom sat over by the window, licking their ice cream cones.

"We really should unpack these boxes sometime," Alex's mom said, glancing at all the boxes stacked up in the living room. There was a knock at the door.

Alex's mom got up and opened the door.

It was Frank.

"Hi, Frank, come on in and sit down. I'm Julie Saunders. I hear you've become a welcome visitor for my daughter."

"Yes, ma'am, I like to play checkers, and I noticed she was here with time on her hands, so we play."

Frank sat down on the edge of the couch cushion.

Alex's mom asks, "So, you own the café?"

"Yes, It's been in my family for years. I inherited it from my father."

"It's always busy down there; the food must be good." Alex's mom comments.

Alex chimed in. "Oh, it is Mom, the burgers and fries are the best."

The three sat and visited for a few minutes. Then Frank got up and said, "Got to go, it's closing time downstairs. It was nice to meet you, Ms. Saunders."

"Please, Frank, call me Julie."

"OK, well, I'll see you later."

Frank walked quickly to the door and left. Alex turned to her mom. "Do you like him, Mom?"

"Yes, Alex, he seems nice, though a little rough around the edges. Now let's take a look at that paper you're writing about the American Indians and at your math homework."

Chapter 3

Frank's visits became part of Alex's routine in the afternoon. His breakfast delivery varied. Sometimes Frank brought it; sometimes a woman named Mabel did. Alex began to feel safe in her new home with her new friend.

A couple of weeks after the pizza night, Frank and Alex were just finishing their third game of checkers when Frank blurted out, "I'm not one for prying, but where's your dad?"

Alex, taken aback, couldn't move or speak, looking down at her legs. She began to tremble slightly and wanted to run out of the room.

"What?" she asked, not quite believing what he had said.

"Your dad, where is he?" Frank didn't seem to notice her discomfort.

"I think I'm done playing checkers today. My stomach feels a little off," Alex said quietly.

Frank looked puzzled as he put away the checkerboard. "You don't want to talk about your dad, huh?"

Alex didn't answer. She just pushed herself into the bedroom and closed the door. She heard Frank leave. Then the tears burst through in big sobs.

When Alex's mom got home, she found Alex asleep in her chair. "Alex, honey, I'm home, wake up."

Alex stirred, rubbed her eyes, tried to take a moment to realize where she was, what time it was, and who was standing over her.

"Dad, is that you?" She said drowsily.

Alex's mom started, like a ghost was in the room, then shook it off. "Alex, honey, wake up."

Finally Alex was fully awake. "Hi, Mom. I think I dreamt dad was here. How was your day?"

Her mom quickly turned away. "It was busy as usual. I'll get supper now. In fact, I need to go back after supper to finish up some paperwork that I need for tomorrow morning."

After supper was over and the dishes were cleared, Alex's mom left. Alex went over to the window, turning off the living room lamp so she could see outside better. Main Street looked different at night. With the streetlights turned on and the neon lights decorating some of the windows, it all looked so festive, a quiet little parade to watch whenever she wanted. The ice cream place looked packed, people steadily going in and out. *Ice cream tastes so good on these warm summer nights. Oh, there's that boy and the girl with the baseball cap. Only she's not wearing the baseball cap tonight.* "She's pretty," Alex whispered to herself. "They're holding hands."

Alex felt sad all of a sudden and rolled over and turned on the TV. She sighed and thought, how suddenly life can change.

Just as she was wondering when her mom would be home, she heard a knock. She opened the door.

"Oh, hi Frank, c'mon in."

"Is your Mom home?"

"No, she had some work to finish up. What's that you got?"

Frank showed the pie to Alex, as he placed it on the counter. It's cherry pie left over from today. I thought you and your mom might like some."

Alex went into the kitchenette and got a plate. Then she served herself a piece of pie. "Are you going to have a piece, Frank?"

Frank looked around, hesitated a second, and said. "Sure, just a sliver, though." They sat down at the kitchen table. "Look, I'm . . . I'm sorry about earlier, your dad and stuff. I . . . I . . . anyway, I'm sorry."

They sat a few minutes in silence. Then Alex said very quietly, looking down, "He's dead. He was in an accident and was killed."

Frank said, "Oh, I didn't know. I'm sorry . . ."

"It's almost a year since the accident. He was . . ."

Alex heard the door open and her mom came in. "Oh, hi Frank. What's this? Oh, cherry pie, my favorite." She set down her purse and she dished up a piece and sat down with Alex and Frank. "Did I interrupt something?"

Frank studied Alex a minute and said. "No, nothing. I was just getting ready to go. See you tomorrow, Alex, for checkers. " Frank got up and left.

Alex's mom asked, "Are you OK?"

"Yeah, I'm fine, just a little tired. Why don't you finish your pie and help me get into bed?"

Her mom looked at the clock. " I didn't realize it was so late."

Alex's mom got her into bed, turned out the light, kissed her lightly, and whispered, "I think about him too sometimes," and left the room.

Chapter 4

Frank came the next morning and brought Alex some breakfast: hash browns, eggs, and a caramel roll with melted butter.

"Come in Frank, can you bring it over here?" Alex was watching out her window.

Alex asked Frank, "Do you know what's going on in the movie/roller rink building?"

Frank sat down and looked out the window at the building. "Some kind of a movie theatre with a café in it, a newfangled idea from the city. Look, I won't be here today for checkers. I've got to do something."

Frank looked at Alex. "Will you be OK?"

"Sure, if you bring me the checkerboard, I'll just practice. Besides, Mom said she might be home early today, since it's Friday."

Frank got up. "I'll go get the checkerboard, and then I'll be by tomorrow afternoon for checkers."

"Sounds good, thanks Frank."

After Frank brought the checkerboard and the apartment door closed, Alex sighed. The day suddenly seemed long and empty. Alex spent a lot of the day by the window. It was one of those summer days you wanted all the windows open, to let in the wonderful fresh summer breeze. *I wish I was out there running and skateboarding, like last summer before the accident.* She shuddered and shook off the feeling of dread and focused on the street outside. *There's the girl with the baseball cap, I wonder where she's going?* Alex watched a girl with long blond hair come out of the hardware store.

The blond haired girl yelled. "Hey, Alex—over here."

Alex's heart pounded. *How did she know my name? How could she see me?'* Then Alex saw she wasn't looking her way, but she was looking at the baseball cap girl down the street. *Baseball cap girl's name is Alex, just like mine? That feels kind of strange.*

15

The Alex down on the street ran to meet her blonde friend and they walked away, arm in arm, laughing. *Just like me and Trish,* Alex thought. Alex closed her eyes remembering . . . *me and Trish climbing trees, me and Trish sliding, me and Trish laughing at Jason and Tyler at the corner drug store, me and Trish skateboarding everywhere. Me and Trish . . .* Alex felt a tear rolling down her cheek. She opened her eyes. *This has to stop. Don't think about it. Think about something else. Quick. Think about, what, what can I think about? What?* She felt panic rising. Then there was a noise outside. She looked out and saw a child who had fallen and hurt his knee, screaming at the top of his lungs. Then she saw "Doris," or the woman she thought was Doris from Doris's Hair Boutique. *Doris got her hair cut, and now she's a brunette.* Alex began to relax, and watched all the activity.

Pretty soon the smells from the café came up, and she knew it was lunchtime. Alex went over to the refrigerator. *Mom made me some tuna salad with noodles,* Alex opened the refrigerator. *I love tuna salad with noodles.* She dished up a big helping and went over to the kitchen table. She ate her lunch and started on her math homework. Soon she was lost in numbers.

Then she heard the door and looked up, 4 pm. *Wow, I've been working a long time.*

"Hi Mom."

"Hi Alex. Guess what, I stopped and rented a couple of movies for tonight. I thought I'd go down to the café and get us some burgers, fries, and milk shakes and make it a regular old movie night."

Alex's mom put down her purse and the movies and saw Alex's homework. "You sure have been working hard today, Alex. Let's go over your math, and then get your social studies report, and I'll look that over too. What else did you do today? Did Frank stop by?"

"Well, he brought breakfast. But then he said he couldn't play checkers. I heard a lot of noise down the hall, so maybe he had to fix something in the café. So I just sat at the window this morning and studied this afternoon. I'm glad you're home early, Mom." Alex looked at her mom, wanting her to come and hug her.

Her mom just said, "I'm glad to be home. It's been a busy week. It would be nice to relax tonight and hang out together, especially since tomorrow I've got to go to the office in the morning and also Sunday afternoon, three showings for people coming from out of town." Alex's mom sat down at the table. "So, let's take a look at your homework."

Alex got out her homework. Her mom looked at the math, and then read through her social studies report. "Nice job, Alex. You are really getting caught up with your schoolwork. Now I think I need to lie down and rest awhile before I go get our supper for tonight."

"OK, Mom." Alex went over to the window. "I'll just watch outside a while. I'll wake you in an hour." Alex's mom went in her room and closed the door.

Alex watched the grey-haired man with the cane lock up the hardware store and head home. Little Town Attire's lights turned off, so she knew in a few minutes she would see the man with the funny walk. She saw a little boy running with a pop bottle, and heard his mom yell, "Jimmy, walk with that bottle!" Of course, Jimmy fell and the pop and glass went all over the sidewalk. Luckily, Jimmy had no cuts, just tears at the lost pop. The street was getting quiet, people going home for supper. Alex heard children yelling from way off. *It must be a softball game*, she thought. She closed her eyes and listened . . . *she was shortstop; Trish was first baseman. A hit right to Alex—she threw to George, out at 2nd base—George threw to Trish, out at 1st base, a double play. She could hear the crowd cheer.* Then there was a crash. Alex jerked awake. *I must have dozed off.* Looking at the clock, she could see that it was 5:30 pm.

"Mom—it's 5:30—time to go to the café. Mommm!"

"OK, Alex, I'm waking up."

She heard her mom yawn and get up. "OK, I'm going down now. Do you want a cheeseburger or a regular burger? And what kind of malt?"

"I want a hamburger, fries, and a strawberry malt."

Alex's mom left. Alex's dream was still with her. *Why didn't Trish call me at the hospital? Why didn't she come to say goodbye? Why doesn't she write back to me?* Alex felt tears burn her eyes.

Stop this, she thought, wiping at her eyes. "Let's see what's going on outside."

The café was busy, the door opening every five to ten minutes. Shakes & Cones Etc. was busy, too, people coming out with hot dogs and shakes, walking down the street on this nice warm summer night.

Oh there's "baseball cap Alex" and that cute boy. They had just come out of Shakes & Cones Etc. with coney islands and a shake. They walked over to the sidewalk bench and sat down.

They look so happy, Alex thought. *I wonder where Mom is? It must be busy downstairs.* Alex went over to look at the movies her mom had gotten: "The Natural" with Robert Redford, "Beverly Hills Cop" with Eddie Murphy—two oldies. *Ah, here's a new one: "Men in Black" with Will Smith.*

Finally, she heard her mom.

Here we go, Alex." Alex's mom came in and over to the couch. "Come here—I'll set up a tray for your chair."

Alex went over and pretty soon she and her mom were tucked in for the night with movies and food.

Chapter 5

Alex's mom got up early the next day, so Alex was up early too. When her mom left for work, Alex watched the rest of "The Natural." She was finishing her lunch when there was a tap at the door.

"Who is it?" Alex asked.

"Frank."

"C'mon in—the door's not locked."

Frank came in looking very strange, Alex thought. *He's smiling—I think that's a smile.* Alex wasn't sure, but his face didn't look so crabby.

"Ready for checkers?" Frank asked.

"Sure," Alex said, realizing how much she'd missed playing.

They played for a half hour, Frank with a funny look on his face.

Alex couldn't take it any longer. "What's wrong? What's going on? You're hiding something."

"I have a surprise for you, but I'm not sure how to tell you."

Alex, impatient now, said, "Just tell me."

"Well, I . . . I fixed the freight elevator. I know the regular elevator broke down after you moved in and the landlord said they couldn't fix it. Then I remembered the freight elevator I used to use to store things up here on the second floor for the café. I've got it in good working order now."

Alex hadn't heard Frank speak this many words at one time since she met him.

"Ya . . . so, why are you telling me?" Alex asked confused.

"Don't you get it? I fixed the elevator so you could go outside in your chair. You can go up and down the street you always watch."

Alex looked horror stricken. *Go outside? Out there where everyone would see her? Would know? Would stare? No way, she thought, no way!*

Frank saw Alex's face. Confused, he asked, "What's wrong?"

"I can't, Frank. I mean I can't go out there. They'll see my legs. No Frank. I can't go out there. I can't, Frank, I can't!" She screamed out the last "I can't." She buried her face in her hands and started to cry. Big sobs, big whole body sobs. Frank just sat, shocked at her reaction, not wanting to move, not knowing what to do. Alex cried and cried. Finally, Frank slowly got up and put his hand gently on her shoulder.

"It's OK, Alex, it's OK." He kept whispering, over and over, "It's OK."

Finally, Alex grew quiet.

"You don't have to go out, Alex." He said gently. "Not until you're ready, not until you want to."

Before he knew it, he and Alex were hugging. He gently rocked her, this crabby man, with a gentleness he forgot he had. Soon Alex was relaxed and quiet.

She looked up at Frank. "I don't want to talk, Frank. Can we just play some more checkers?"

"Sure, Alex, sure."

Frank lost two games and won three before they heard her mom come in.

"Hi, you two—I see you're playing checkers. Maybe I can play the winner."

So Alex, Frank, and her mom played checkers 'til suppertime.

Frank got up. "I've got to go. It will be busy downstairs. It's Saturday night—roast beef special, you know. See you later."

After Frank left, Alex's mom turned to her. "What happened while Frank was here? You look like you've been crying."

Alex wanted so badly to tell her mom. Tell her about her feelings, about her legs, about the wheel chair, about everything. But she knew her mom wouldn't understand. Or even worse, her mom didn't really want to hear it.

"It was nothing, Mom, really—I'm all right."

Her mom seemed relieved and got up. "It's time to get supper on the table. What are you in the mood for?" She opened the freezer and the refrigerator. "I can make chicken, tacos, or salmon."

Alex said, "Tacos, let's have tacos. Can I help?"

"Sure you can. Why don't you get out the broccoli, cheese, lettuce, peppers, and the tortillas?" Alex felt good, working along side her mom in the kitchen. She felt close to her.

After dinner was fixed and eaten, Alex helped her mom clear the table and clean up the kitchen. For the first time in a while,

Alex felt a sense of normalcy, a sense that things hadn't changed completely.

At bedtime, Alex asked, "Mom, I know this sounds silly, but would you lay in bed with me and tell me one of the old bedtime stories?"

"Sure, honey, move over."

Alex glowed in the warmth of her mother's company.

Chapter 6

The next day, Alex's mom left right after lunch. Alex went to her window. There was a light drizzle coming down. The sky was gray—the kind of gray you knew would be there all day. No one was out on the street. Alex sighed. *Now what am I going to do?* She saw the unpacked boxes, went over, and opened the closest one to her. It was photo albums. She lifted out the top album and opened it. There was her mom, smiling at the camera, holding a new baby: her. There was Alex, in all her newborn glory. She turned the page, and there was her dad, his black curly hair, brown eyes, and a smile that warmed your heart. Alex looked at the pictures, turning page after page, devouring the snapshots with her eyes, feeling full. Tears of joy trickled down her cheeks as she remembered her dad: how he smelled, how it felt sitting on his lap, how it felt when he tickled her, how it felt to play catch with him. The joy became an aching inside, knowing that she'd never see him again.

Suddenly she threw the picture album across the room, angry that he left her forever, and left her in a wheelchair because her legs wouldn't work anymore. Anger burned inside her. She pounded the arms of her chair, yelling at the top of her lungs. Eventually she quieted down and felt drained and exhausted. A peace came over her, and she felt her father in her heart, and she knew how much he loved her. She rolled over to the window and sat for a long time, watching the rain.

Alex was still sitting there when her mom got home.

"Hi, Alex—kind of a wet and dreary day, isn't it?" she said as she walked into the living room to sit down.

"I don't know—it feels kind of cozy to me. How did the showings go?" Alex asked.

"Fine. What happened? Why is the photo album on the floor?"

"Oh, I was going to unpack the box, and then I saw the photo albums and started looking through them. There were pictures of dad and I . . . I . . . ."

"Alex, I don't think you should look at those. It's too soon—let's just focus on now, OK?" She went over and picked up the album and put it back in the box.

She looked around at the other boxes. "Oh, look here—let's unpack this box. It's games. Maybe we can find your favorite, Monopoly. We can play tonight. What do you think, Alex?"

"OK."

They started unpacking the boxes, putting the games in a bookshelf under the living room window. When they were finished, Alex's mom started fixing supper: chicken, baked potato and a salad. After supper they cleared the table and set up the Monopoly game. Alex chose the shoe and her mom chose the car. Pretty soon Alex owned Boardwalk and Park Place with a hotel on each. Her mother owned all the utilities. They spent the next two hours playing until her mother called "uncle" because Alex had almost all her money.

"That was fun, Alex, now it's time to crawl into our beds and get some sleep."

Chapter 7

The next morning, Alex woke up with a warm glow. It had been a while since her mom had spent as much quality time with her as she had this weekend. Plus, Frank would be by for checkers, and he said he'd teach her how to play chess. Alex was sitting by the window when her mom opened the door to go out; Frank was standing there about to knock with a fresh plate of cinnamon rolls.

"Frank?" Alex's mom said questioningly.

"Here, take a warm cinnamon roll with you, Julie."

Alex's mom picked up a nice big one with lots of frosting and put it on a napkin Frank handed her. "Thanks, Frank—you sure do spoil us."

Alex's mom left. Frank brought the plate of cinnamon rolls over to Alex. Hi, Alexandra, how are you today?"

"You know, I feel great today. The sun's out—it's a beautiful day. Are you still going to teach me chess?"

"You bet. I'm going over to Howard's Hardware to get a chess set later."

"Howard. Is that the gray-haired man with the cane?"

"Yes, that's him. Enjoy your cinnamon rolls, I'll see you around two o'clock." Frank got up to leave.

"OK, see you later." Alex turned and looked out the window.

"Doris" was unlocking the door to the Hair Boutique. Howard was turning the corner and heading down to the hardware store, so she knew that Little Town Attire would be open soon as well. The building with all the construction workers was quiet today; there was a big grand opening sign hung across the door. The movie/café was opening in a week. Alex thought, *it's been a while since I've been to a movie.*

Suddenly a picture of her old neighborhood formed in her mind. *The white house with the green shutters . . . she was walking out the front door. Trish, Tyler, and Jason were in the car. Trish's mom was driving them to the movie theater. That big city where her home was, and now it's this small town. At least it will have a* movie *theater soon.* Alex got tired of watching out the window. No one was out yet; it was so quiet. She looked at all the unpacked boxes, wheeled herself over, and read the labels. *Here's one that will be fun to unpack, "Knick-knacks and stuffed animals."* She opened it and found her angel collection. She placed it in her lap gently and brought them into her bedroom. *Let's see—I think I'll put them on my dresser.* She worked all morning, arranging knick-knacks in her room and in the living room. By the time she had fixed and eaten her lunch, Frank was knocking on the door.

"Hi Alexandra, I got the chess set!"

"Great, I'm ready to learn." Alex said.

Frank explained the different pieces and how they moved on the board.

After they played a game of chess Frank looked up at Alex, "I don't think I ever asked you, where did you move from?"

Alex said, "St. Paul. Mom said she needed a change. She wanted to start over where no one knew us. I think she just doesn't want to be faced with any of her memories. She even got mad at me yesterday when I was looking at the photo albums. At times, I think she has trouble looking at me now that I'm different. I think she's afraid of me sometimes, or I make her sick or something. But this weekend was different. We actually spent time together like we used to. She relaxed with me."

Looking at Frank, she asked, "Frank, I once asked about your wife and children. Where are they?"

It was Frank's turn to look uncomfortable. Finally, he said quietly, "They died in a car accident."

Alex touched Frank's hand. "I'm so sorry. Was it very long ago?"

"About ten years ago. I don't really want to talk about it. Let's put away chess and play checkers for a while." Frank put away the chess pieces and brought out the checkers. After they played a couple of games, Frank sat back and looked at Alex, studying her. Alex saw him looking at her.

Suddenly he blurted out, "I'm glad you moved here." Then he got up quickly and said, "It's time for me to go back downstairs. Why don't I leave the checkers and chessboard with you? See you tomorrow."

He was out the door a few seconds later. Alex looking after him, feeling his friendship surround her. She got out the chessboard and spent the rest of the afternoon studying the board and the pieces' different moves.

After a while, Alex heard her mom's footsteps, then the key.

"Hi, Alex," she said, putting down her briefcase and walking over.

"What's that you've got there? Chess? I haven't played chess since before you were born. Your dad and I used to play a lot." It slipped out before Alex's mom realized it.

"You and dad played chess?"

"Yes, that was before you were born, before he started working such long hours, before his drinking got so bad."

"Do you ever think about him, Mom? I mean, we never talk about him."

"Alex, it's hard for me. I have so many different feelings."

Alex and her mom just sat there remembering.

"I'd better get supper started. Roast beef always takes a while." Alex's mom got up and started fixing supper.

After their supper was eaten and the dishes were done, Alex and her mom watched TV. Alex's mom seemed kind of distant.

"I'm tired," her mom yawned. "Do you mind if I get you in bed early so I can go to bed?"

"Sure, Mom."

They went into Alex's bedroom and got her wheelchair by the bed. Alex put her arms around her mother's neck and her mom lifted while Alex leaned forward toward the bed. Something happened, and Alex fell flat on the floor.

"Sorry Alex—I don't know what happened."

Alex grabbed the bedpost and tried to pull up while her mom pushed from underneath. Alex slipped again and fell. Suddenly Alex's mother started crying and yelling.

"Damn it, Alex. C'mon help me here! I can't do this alone." She took a few deep breaths, then blurted out. "Oh, damn you, Jim. Damn you all to pieces. Look what you've left me with, you drunk! Your drinking--why couldn't you stop? Now you're gone, and you've left me with it all. Look what you took from us, from

Alex. Just look at her legs. Do you see her?" Alex's mom yelled, her hands clenched into a fist, shaking them at the ceiling. Then her hands were covering her face. She started to sob, and her body crumpled and she sat on the floor. Alex stared. She hadn't seen her mom cry at all since the accident. She hadn't heard her mom's anger or her desperation. She reached over and patted her mother's hand. Soon her mom's sobs quieted down and she began to relax.

She looked at her daughter propped up on her elbows watching her. "Oh, Alex, I'm so sorry. I'm so, so sorry. I love you so very much, Alex. I'm so, so sorry."

Alex felt uncomfortable. She didn't want her mother to feel sorry for her. She didn't want anyone to feel sorry for her. That's why she didn't want to go out. She didn't want to see pity in anyone's eyes. Then she saw her mother's eyes. It wasn't pity she saw—it was anger, but not at her. And in the anger, she felt her mother's love.

Alex's mom laid down next to Alex. They hugged and she kissed the top of Alex's head and stroked her face. "Alex, I'm so angry this happened to you. I'm angry with Jim, with God, with everyone. You deserve the best the world has out there. I don't want you to hide yourself away. Alex, I'm so sorry it's taken me so long to see you. So long to face the anger and the grief of all that's been lost."

Alex started to cry. They hugged and cried, lying on the floor together for a long time.

"It's going to be OK, now, Alex. It's going to be OK."

For the first time in a long time, Alex knew it would be too. Alex and her mom finally got Alex onto her bed.

"Move over, Alex, I'm sleeping in here with you."

Chapter 8

In the morning, Alex woke up feeling lighter than she had in a long time. Her mom was gentler in her touch while exercising Alex's legs and giving her a shower. Her mom's eyes were different. They didn't have a curtain covering them up; they were open and full of love.

"Well, Alex, you have a good day today. Why don't you ask Frank to come over tonight and have supper with us? I'll get some steaks."

"Great idea, Mom. I love you."

"Alex, I love you too." She went over, hugged and kissed Alex, and then was out the door.

Alex sat at her window feeling so happy. She felt light as a feather. The sky outside was a brilliant blue, and the sun was bright—no clouds anywhere. A gentle breeze came in, tickling Alex's arms and neck. All her people were there: "Doris," the man with the big mustache, and Howard, all opening their doors for the day's business. Suddenly she saw something that made her draw in her breath.

A wheelchair. She couldn't believe it. Another wheelchair. She saw it just as it turned the corner and out of sight.

Who's that? She thought. *I've never seen a wheelchair before. I wonder if it is a boy or a girl, if they're young or old.*

Alex, for some reason, felt very excited. There was a knock.

C'mon it, Frank. Oh, hi Mabel, it's you." Mabel came in with eggs and a caramel roll.

"Here you go, sweetie. Frank said he'd be by after lunch."

"Thanks, Mabel."

Alex ate her breakfast by the window, watching for the wheelchair.

When Frank finally came after lunch she was anxious to tell him what she saw.

"Well, Alex, are you ready to try a game of chess?"

"I sure am. Say Frank, earlier today I saw a wheelchair turn the corner. Do you know who it could be?"

Frank thought a minute and said, "No, I haven't seen a wheelchair here in town. It must be a visitor or something. Do you want me to check around for you?"

"Would you, Frank? Thanks. Say, by the way, my mom was wondering if you could get away and have supper with us tonight?"

Frank sat for a minute, thinking. "Yeah, I think I can, if you guys could wait until 7 o'clock to eat."

"Great, I'm sure we can wait. So, let's play chess."

Frank and Alex played two games of chess. Alex lost of course, but it was still fun. Frank stood up. "I've got to go, Alexandra. Tell your mom I'll bring dessert tonight. See you later."

After Frank left Alex decided to go through the box with the photo albums. *It's time to find a place for these.* She took them out one by one, paging through memories and friends. She looked around the room. *The bookcase in the corner of the living room would be a perfect home for these photo albums.* Alex put them on the shelves and felt happy; *they are now part of our new life.*

Alex heard her mom open the door. "Mom, come and see what I did."

"Alex, that is just where those photo albums belong—great job. Now I'm going to change clothes. What did Frank say about dinner tonight?"

"He said he could be here around 7:00."

"Well, let me change my clothes and then you can help with dinner prep."

When Frank arrived at 7:00 the table was set. There was a large bowl full of salad, warm rolls in a basket, baked potatoes on each plate, and the steaks were broiling in the oven.

Frank said, "Smells great in here, I'm starving." Frank held up a pie. "And I brought some dessert, a nice freshly baked peach pie.

Alex's mom smiled at Frank. "Thanks Frank, I'll take that and you just relax and have a seat—would you like a glass of wine?" Alex's mom took the pie and put it on the countertop.

Frank looked uncomfortable. "No, I don't drink anything with alcohol. Water is just fine."

Alex's mom said, "I also have a nice bottle of sparkling cider, let's have that."

Frank smiled. "That sounds great."

Alex's mom got the sparkling cider from the refrigerator and poured it into three wineglasses and put them on the table. Then she served the steaks.

The supper was delicious and everyone belonged to the "Clean Plate Club."

Alex watched Frank as he helped her mom bring the dishes into the kitchen. *Wow,* she thought, *I didn't realize how good looking Frank is. His dark unkempt hair and blue eyes look really good on him. I think my mom thinks so too.*

Alex began to smile and asked, "Mom, I'm tired. I don't think I want any dessert. Do you mind putting me to bed early? I'd like to read in bed for awhile before I go to sleep."

Alex's mom looks at Alex. "Sure. Frank, I'll be right back. Maybe you wouldn't mind making us some coffee. It's there on the kitchen counter." Alex and her mom went into Alex's bedroom.

"OK, Alex what's going on?"

"Nothing, I'm really tired. Plus I thought it'd be nice and if you and Frank had some time alone to get to know each other better."

"Alex . . ."

"Come on Mom, I get to see him all the time. I want you to get to know him too. I really like him."

Alex's mom helped her with her pajamas and got her into bed. "Sleep tight."

Alex's mom was smiling when she left.

Alex thought, *I wonder if he'll kiss her.*

Chapter 9

A couple of days later, when Frank came for chess, he seemed excited about something.

"What is it, Frank? You've got something to tell me. What is it?"

"Alexandra, you can read me so well. I found out this morning. You know that movie/café that's opening this weekend?"

Alex nodded yes.

"Well, I found out who owns it, a family that lives this side of Shoreland. They are new to this area, and they have two children—a daughter ten, and a son twelve. The son's in a wheelchair, his name is Joe. It must have been him you saw."

Alex looked thoughtful. *Someone else about my age in a wheelchair?*

"So, what do you think, Alex?"

Alex looked at Frank. "It feels kind of exciting to know I'm not the only one like me here."

"Want to meet him?"

"Oh, Frank, I don't think so. Not yet, anyway."

Frank smiled. "I don't want to push you, but I'll bet he'll be at the movie/café grand opening, and you could ..."

"Frank, I don't know if I'm ready. Let's drop it for a while and play some chess. I found a chess book in one of these boxes and I've been studying it—I might have a chance to beat you." Alex kept thinking about this new boy, and the opening.

They set up the chess set and played two games. Frank sat back and looked at Alex. "Alex, you almost beat me. You're getting tough. Say, I'm kind of hungry. How 'bout you? Should I go down and get some fries?"

"That sounds great. Maybe we can split a malt—a hot fudge malt."

Frank left to get their snack. Alex rolled over to the window and stared at the movie/café. They were showing "Independence

Day" for the grand opening. She sat there thinking about what it would be like to be out there, with everyone staring at her legs. Could she do it?

Frank came in with the fries and a shake and came over to Alex at the window. They sat and ate.

"Frank, do you want to see a picture of my dad?"

"Sure."

Alex went to the bookcase and grabbed a photo album to show Frank. She turned to the pages with her dad's pictures. "That's my dad."

Frank studied the pictures. "The look on his face when he looks at you—he really adored you."

"Yeah, I was daddy's little girl. He took me to baseball games and basketball games. For football, we usually watched at home with my mom. She'd make cheese logs covered in chili powder that we ate with Ritz crackers. Sometimes there were sardines too. Those Sundays were so fun. But then dad's drinking started to get in the way. If his football team lost, he'd get angry and mean. If they won, he'd sing and be funny. But he was usually drunk by then."

Alex is quiet a moment, then continues. "The night of the accident, he and Mom had a big fight. Dad came home drunk. I was late for a school play rehearsal. He was supposed to take me, because Mom was giving a Pampered Chef party. I remember getting in the car. I was so scared, and he was so drunk and angry. When he pulled out of the driveway, he scraped along the rock ledge. When he started down the street, he kept hitting the curb. I started crying, told him to stop. I wanted to get out." Alex had tears rolling down her cheeks, but she kept going. "He told me he was fine, and to quit being such a baby. Then we were on the freeway ramp. The next thing I knew, I was in the hospital, and Mom told me dad was gone."

Tears kept rolling down. She looked up at Frank. "I loved him so much, Frank, and my last memory of him was so ugly. He was mean and drunk. Usually he was so fun, and cuddly. It just doesn't seem fair, Frank." Alex's tears were gently rolling down, tears of remembering.

Frank handed her his handkerchief. "Here Alex." She took it, wiped her eyes, and looked at Frank. Tears were rolling down his cheeks.

"Frank, you're crying."

"Oh, Alexandra, I am so sorry, you have lost so much." He leaned forward and encompassed Alex in a hug. They sat there a few minutes.

Alex started to pull away. She dried her eyes and sat up straight.

"Frank, let's put away the chess set and play some checkers, maybe here by the window."

Frank looked at Alex and said, "Sure, Alexandra, whatever you want."

Frank brought over a TV tray and set up the checkerboard.

The two of them sat there playing in their new found intimacy.

After a couple of games, Alex looked up and saw Frank's face. "Frank, what's wrong?"

Frank tried to compose himself, wanting to tell her his own secret, but not wanting to burden her. He put his face in his hands for a minute and then looked up at Alex. "Alexandra, I think I should go. I . . ."

Alex concerned said, "No, Frank, tell me. Please, I consider you as one of my best friends. Please, Frank."

Frank sat staring out the window, struggling with himself. Alex saw a tear starting to slide its way down his cheek.

Then he said quietly, "Alexandra, I was driving the car when my wife and son were killed. I was drunk. I don't remember how it happened. But I hear their screams all the time. I haven't touched a drop of alcohol since."

He buried his face in his hands again and cried. Alex moved close to him, leaned towards him, and put her arms around him. They sat there a long time. The shadows lengthened, and the room got darker. Alex handed back Frank's handkerchief. He blew his nose and looked up.

"I'm sorry. I don't usually talk to people about such things, but your dad and you—it just got to me."

"Frank, I'm glad you told me. Remember, we're friends."

Frank looked at her. "Yeah, we're friends."

Frank got up and looked at the clock. "It's late—I've got to get back downstairs."

He turned and left. Alex could almost see the heaviness of the burden he carried on his stooped frame. She knew he probably didn't talk to people much about himself.

Chapter 10

It was Saturday morning. Alex woke up, looked out her window, and thought about the grand opening tonight. The thought caused her body to fill with anxious excitement.

"Mom—help me up. Mom!"

Alex's mom came in, rubbing her eyes. "Alex, it's only 7:00 o'clock. It's Saturday."

"I know Mom, but I can't sleep. I want to watch out the window."

"All right, c'mon." Alex's mom helped her change into her clothes and then got her into her wheelchair.

"Thanks, Mom." Alex wheeled out to the living room window. She looked outside. The air felt electric. "Mom—Mom!" Alex called.

"Yes, Alex, what is it now?"

"Mom, I need to talk to you about something. You know, Frank fixed the freight elevator."

Alex's mom looked puzzled. "Yeah, so?"

"Well, he fixed it so I could go outside in my wheelchair and go up and down Main Street.

Alex's mom looked funny. "So why haven't you mentioned this before?"

"Mom, after the accident I was in the hospital so long and when we went home, I remember everyone staring at me, at my legs. The look in their eyes—I hated it so much. I swore I'd never go out again. Even my friends, they couldn't ever look at my legs. They acted so weird. So I didn't want to use the elevator and go outside. It scared me."

"Oh, honey, it was such a shock to your friends. They were afraid, just like I was. Looking at you brought up feelings in them. Fear, loss, anger, and shock—you were different to them, they didn't know what to say or do. They can't face their own feelings, so they can't face you. Honey, it's them and their feelings, it's not you. It's hard for me sometimes, because you're still you, but you're different. What should I say to you? How much should I push you? I don't know what's best for you anymore. At least, I'm just not as sure as I used to be. It's only been the last couple of weeks that I felt the Alex I used to know is here. The Alex I used to know wouldn't let a wheelchair stop her from doing what she wanted."

Alex looked at her mother and felt relief. Her mom did know and understand. Suddenly Alex felt a familiar sensation in her body. It was the feeling she used to get when it was a tie game, bottom of the 9th, and she was up to bat, with two outs and two strikes against her. This feeling would surge through her, and she would hit a home run, right over the fence. She felt it now.

"Mom, I'm going to that grand opening tonight. Will you come with me?"

"Alex, yes—of course I will." Alex's mom had tears of joy welling up in her eyes.

"Can I ask Frank, too?"

"You sure can."

Later that day, Frank stopped by while Alex and her mom were unpacking more boxes. "Alexandra, are you going to the Grand Opening or not?"

"I'm going Frank, but you have to come with us too—please?"

"I wouldn't miss it for anything."

"Maybe after the movie we can go to Shakes and Cones Etc. for ice cream and I can go up and down the street like everyone else." Alex said excitedly.

Frank looked at Alex's mom. "Should I come by and pick you ladies up at 5:30 p.m.? We can circle Main Street once before we go to the movie. By the way, Joe will be there." Frank winked at Alex; Alex's mom looked puzzled.

"Who's Joe?"

"Didn't Alex tell you? Well, I'll see you later." Frank left.

"Who's Joe?" Alex's mom asked, eyeing Alex.

"Well, the other day I was at the window and I saw a wheelchair. It turned the corner and out of sight before I saw who was in it. Then Frank found out for me. His family has a farm this side of Shoreland and they own the new movie/café."

Alex's mom looked thoughtful. "This side of Shoreland . . ."

"Yes, they have two kids, a girl ten and a boy who's twelve. He's the one in a wheelchair like me."

"You know Alex, I think I sold them that farm. It was my first sale. They said they had two kids, but I only met the girl. The boy was at some sports camp."

"Sports camp? But he's in a wheelchair."

"Maybe that's not the family, but I don't know of any other farms that sold recently in that area. Oh well, we can find out tonight. I think I'm going to unpack the last of these boxes."

Alex looked out the window. The street seemed so festive. A lot of people walking: the woman with the ponytail, and her two children; little Jimmy running as usual, his mom yelling at him to walk; the two women looking in the shop windows. Alex saw the four friends she'd seen before; the other Alex was walking with the cute curly haired boy and his two blonde friends. They were pointing at the movie/café and talking.

"A wheelchair," Alex breathed out.

"Alex, did you say something?"

35

"Mom, it's him, the boy in the wheelchair. Here he comes!"

Alex's mom went over to look. "Oh, he's cute, Alex."

He looked tall even sitting in the chair. His hair was dark and a little long, curling up by his ears. He looked up towards the window.

"Oh, Mom, look at him." Alex's heart was pounding. "This is ridiculous—I feel like an idiot drooling over someone I've never met; he's probably a jerk."

"Alex, I don't think so—look at his smile. His face holds so much joy in it."

"It does, doesn't it, Mom."

Chapter 11

Alex felt like the afternoon just dragged by.

"Mom, what should I wear?"

"How about your jeans with that green top? You look so nice in green, it brings out the green in your eyes."

Alex felt like she was going to a party. Before she knew it Frank was knocking at the door.

"Alexandra, you look so pretty," Frank said looking her up and down.

"Hi, Julie—wow, you look pretty too. Boy, I'm lucky to be going out with two pretty ladies. Time to go—are you ready, Alex?"

Alex felt butterflies tickling all through her insides. "I'm ready."

Frank pushed her through the apartment door.

"Wow, I don't think I've been out of that apartment for two months, since we first moved in." Alex looked at everything around her. She noticed Frank and her mom look at each other and smile. The freight elevator was old and noisy but they were down in no time at all.

Alex couldn't believe it; they were going through the café. Now they were going through the café door. She was down there on the street she had watched like a storybook for weeks. *She could imagine herself sitting up there watching herself and saying, "Oh, look at that pretty girl in the wheelchair with her mom and that nice man who owns the café." She almost waved up at her window.*

Alex rolled down the sidewalk; a few people looked at her legs, but mostly they just smiled and said "Hi." The two elderly women were awfully nice. Jimmy bumped her chair as he ran by, the man with the big mustache was locking up when they went by. *Boy, he is so short,* thought Alex. Further down "Doris " was coming out of Doris' Hair Boutique. "Hi Jenny," Frank said, "Have you met Alexandra and Julie Saunders?" Alex thought to herself, *her name isn't Doris, it's Jenny.* Alex was introduced to Howard in front of the hardware store, and then they were at the movie/café.

She heard her mom say, "Oh look, there's the Larsons, the people I sold the farm to. The ones I told you about with the two children." Alex's mom went over to the Larsons.

"Hi, John, Marilyn, how do you like the farm?"

"Oh, hi, Julie, we love it and so do the kids. We've always had a dream to live in the country with horses."

"Say, did I hear this place is your venture?" Alex's mom asked.

"Yes, one reason we came down here was we inherited this building a couple of years ago. When we came down to look at it we got all sorts of ideas and decided to move down here, plus we found out there's a great camp near here for our son. Have you met my children? Joe and Maggie, come here." A ten-year-old girl with short blonde hair came bouncing over and behind her was the handsome boy she and Alex had seen earlier in his wheelchair. "Joe and Maggie, this is Julie Saunders, the one who sold us the farm."

"Nice to meet you, Maggie and Joe." Alex's mom motioned to Alex who was talking to Frank. "Alex and Frank, come here, I want you to meet someone."

Alex came over, pink brushing her cheeks, Frank following behind.

"Alex and Frank, this is Mr. and Mrs. Larson, their daughter Maggie, and their son Joe. This is Alex, my daughter and Frank is a good friend of the family."

Alex and Joe smiled at one another. Alex felt a thrill run through her. *Oh look how he's looking at me,* she thought.

Then Alex said to Joe, "Hi, when did you move into the farm?"

"About a month ago. Are you from around here?" Joe asked.

"No, we moved in a couple of months ago from St. Paul," Alex responded.

Joe said, "We lived in Minneapolis before here. It sure is different being in the country, so quiet and so dark at night."

Alex smiled. "I know, one of the first things I noticed was no airplane noise. We live here in town over the café so it's not as dark for me. Do you have horses, chickens, and cows on your farm?"

"Yeah, we have four horses, lots of chickens and a few cows. My mom and I started an organic vegetable garden. It's been a lot of work, but I love being outside," Joe said smiling at Alex.

Alex sighed. "It sounds wonderful."

Joe looked at Alex. "You'll have to come visit sometime." Just then the line started moving into the theater. Joe's parents called to him. They needed to get in and make sure everything was set up.

"See you inside," Joe said to Alex as he wheeled away.

"I think he likes you, Alexandra," Frank whispered in her right ear. Alex's smile widened another quarter of an inch.

"You think so?" Alex whispered back.

Frank, Alex's mom and Alex went in and found a table; Alex noticed that Frank and her mom were holding hands. There was a large movie screen on one wall, table and chairs in rows formed in a semi-circle. They found one right in the center. The café served burgers, hot dogs, and fried chicken baskets. They ordered and the lights started to dim. Alex became aware of movement on her right.

Joe moved up next to her. "Mind if I sit next to you?" He chuckled, looking at their chairs.

Alex's mom looked over at Alex, and then whispered to Frank. "Doesn't she look beautiful tonight?"

"Yeah, she looks just like a princess, glowing with anticipation."

When the movie was over and the lights came on, Joe turned to Alex. "How 'bout you and I roll over to Shakes & Cones Etc. and get some ice cream?"

"Can I, Mom?"

Alex's mom smiled. "Sure. Go ahead."

Alex and Joe left, went across the street, got their ice cream, and stopped by the sidewalk bench.

"So do you like sports?" Joe asked.

Alex, excited, said, "Yes, I played on a softball team for years. I just love softball."

"Me too. Have you ever been over to play at the sports camp by here?" asked Joe.

Alex looked puzzled. "What sports camp?"

Joe answered, "There's a camp where people like us, you know with disabilities, go and play all sorts of sports. They are part of the Special Olympics program."

"No, I didn't know about that. You mean there's a way I can play softball and bat again? Oh Joe, how exciting!"

"I was there for four weeks this summer."

Alex and Joe talked excitedly, sitting by the sidewalk bench.

Alex thought to herself, *if I were sitting in my window, watching right now, I bet we'd look just like the other Alex and the dark curly haired boy when they sat here with their coney islands and shakes.* Alex sighed. *Yeah, how suddenly life can change.*

Chapter 12

"Alex! Alex!" Alex's mom stuck her head out the window of their apartment.

"What Mom?" Alex and Joe were on the sidewalk in front of the café, eating ice cream cones from Shakes and Cones, Etc.

Alex's mom answered, "You got some mail. It's from Trish. Do you want me to bring it down?"

Alex, surprised, said, "No, I'll read it later."

Joe looked at Alex, waiting. "So, are you going to go to softball camp with me the last week of August?"

Alex made a face. "I don't know, I haven't done anything like that since my accident. I think I'll be a real klutz. It was hard enough for me just to go down Main Street the first time."

"Alex, we all felt like klutzes the first time at camp. You'll catch on quickly. The other day when we played catch, I was impressed at how well you threw the ball. No offense, but you don't throw like a girl, you throw like a boy."

"You really think so? OK then, I'll go. It really helps to know you'll be there too and at least I know that one person won't laugh at me."

Alex and Joe finished their ice cream cones.

Alex saw a girl walking down the street with her baseball hat on backwards. "Joe, that's the other Alex I told you about."

The girl with the baseball cap turned to Joe. "Hi, Joe."

Joe looked at the "baseball cap" Alex. "Hi, Alex. Are you going to the soccer game tomorrow night?"

The "baseball cap" Alex looks at Joe and then Alex. "Yes, I think it's the last game of the season."

Joe introduced her to his new friend. "Alex, I'd like you to meet Alex."

"Baseball cap" Alex looked at Alex. "Hey, are you new in town? Is your name really Alex or is it a nickname?"

"We moved in here May, I live over the café. My name is really Alexandra."

"Wow, so is mine. Well, you guys, I've got to get going. So Alex we'll have to hang out sometime. See ya."

Alex turned to Joe. "So, how do you know her?"

"Her little brother is my sister's age and they play on a park board summer soccer team. So I see her at games. She'll be out at the softball camp in August. She is an assistant to the assistant coach." Joe looked down the street. "Here comes my mom."

A white van pulled up; Joe's mom got out of the van and opened the doors. She pulled out a ramp. "Hi, Alex."

"Hi, Ms. Larson."

"I'll call you when I get home, Alex." Joe went up the ramp and into the van.

Joe's mom looked at Alex. "So I guess we'll see you and your mom later. I'm making my famous ribs." She closed the van door and got into the driver's seat.

Alex watched as the van drove away and then turned her wheel chair around and pushed open the door leading to the freight elevator. Frank was in the hallway.

"Hey Frank, when are we going to play some chess? I missed our game yesterday."

Frank picked up a crate of groceries for the kitchen. "Tomorrow, I'll come by in the mid-afternoon."

"OK, see you then." Alex wheeled her chair into the freight elevator and pushed the button for the second floor. When she got to her apartment her mom was waiting by the front door.

Alex's mom smiled. "Here's your letter."

Alex took the letter from her mom. "I can't believe it, Trish finally wrote to me."

Alex went and sat by her window. She read the letter from Trish. "Mom, Trish and her mom want to come visit us. Can they come next weekend? Please? Call her mom and arrange something."

Alex's mom walked in and sat down next to Alex. "Sure, we can give them a tour of our town. Take them to lunch at Frank's café. I'll call her in a while."

Alex looked at her mom. "I'm excited to show Trish around. I really like it here."

"Me too, Alex."

Alex quietly asked, "So by the way, what's happening with you and Frank?"

Alex's mom hesitated a moment then says, "I don't know, for right now we're just friends. I enjoy his company—he can be so funny at times—but I do have a full plate right now. So I'm comfortable keeping it at just friends for awhile."

"You know Mom, I think I'm ready to have photos of dad in our apartment. We can put them in frames and hang them on the walls; pictures of just him and some of our whole family together. He is a part of who I am; I loved having him as my dad. Most of my memories of him are good; the bad ones are fading away."

"You're right, Alex, this apartment needs pictures of our whole family. I miss your dad every day, I think mostly of the good memories too, they certainly outnumber the bad ones. Having Frank around helps; he can be so supportive."

Alex chuckled. "I can't believe that I used to call him that 'crabby' man from downstairs."

Alex went over to the bookcase, got a photo album, and went back to the place by her mom. "By the way, Mom, I decided to go to the softball camp with Joe at the end of August."

"I'm glad to hear that, Alex."

Alex opened up the photo book, "Let's look through here and pick out some pictures to put in frames. And with Frank around maybe we'll be adding more."

THE RED SHOES

We stand and she takes my hand,
She leads me out into the sunshine
My heart is filled with laughter and jelly beans
As we walk away from the shadows
And the room with the darkened windows

Little four-year-old Maria and her mom walk in the back door. Maria has on her new red tennis shoes. She takes off across the kitchen running.

"Boy, these shoes are fast, Mommy! I love them; they make me run fast. Don't you think so, Mommy? Mommy!"

"Yes Maria, but it's late. You need to settle down, go to your bedroom, take off your shoes, and put on your pajamas. I'll be in to tuck you in after I check in with your dad." Maria takes off running to the bedroom.

Maria's mom gives a big sigh, exhaustion filling her body as she goes into the living room. Her brown hair shows a few strands of gray and her hips are two inches wider than they were last year.

A few minutes later Maria's mom goes in to check on Maria.

"Maria, what are you doing? I said get on your pajamas and take off your shoes."

Maria is jumping on her bed. "But mama, look how high I can bounce with these shoes on. I can almost touch the ceiling."

Angrily, Maria's mom grabs her arm. "Stop jumping! Now take off those shoes and put on your pajamas. I'll be back in a minute."

Maria sits on the edge of her bed, with tears in her brown eyes. She takes off her shoes. She quickly puts them under her pillow before her mother comes back, and then puts on her pajamas. She crawls under her covers and lays her head on her pillow.

Her mother walks in. "Good night Maria. Remember, we are going to your favorite cousin's wedding tomorrow. Sleep tight now and don't let the bed bugs bite."

"Good night, Mommy." Maria rolls over, hugging her new red shoes hidden under her pillow, as she falls asleep.

The next morning Maria wakes up, takes her shoes, and pulls them on her feet. She jumps to the floor, loving the way they feel. She runs into the kitchen where her mom is making breakfast.

"Mommy, look at these shoes, they make me run so fast. I bet you can hardly see me run by."

"What? Oh, yes Maria—they're nice."

Maria takes off and runs into the living room. "Mommy, watch me run, see how fast I'm going."

"Maria, don't run off, your breakfast is ready. Maria!"

Maria runs back into the kitchen breathless. "I'm not hungry Mommy."

Maria's twelve-year-old brother, Sean, slouches into the kitchen wearing his pajama pants and T shirt, frowning at Maria who is running in circles. "Knock it off, Maria. Mom, I'm hungry, is breakfast ready?" Sean sits down to eat.

Maria runs out of the kitchen, and down the hallway into the living room. "Look at me, I'm flying."

Later that morning everyone is getting ready for the big wedding. Maria is running back and forth in her bedroom. Her mom is laying out her green dress for the wedding.

"Mommy, I just love Joannie and Bill. I'm so excited to see Joannie dressed like a princess in her white, sparkly dress and Bill will be her prince. I can't wait to show them my red, very fast shoes."

"Maria, what are you saying? I can't hear you; you keep running around. Please stop."

Maria takes off into the kitchen, snagging her dress that's lying on the bed with her little finger. It falls on the floor.

"These are the fastest shoes ever. See me Mom? Can you see me?"

"Maria, come back here." Maria's mom walks into the kitchen looking for Maria. "There you are, come on, we need to change your clothes for the wedding."

"Mommy, did you see how fast my shoes went? Did you see me?"

Maria's mom leads Maria back to the bedroom. "Now take off those shoes and put on your patent leather ones."

Maria's mom yells out the bedroom door. "Sean, are you almost ready?"

"Mommy, I just love these new shoes."

"Yes, Maria, I know, now take them off. We need to leave for the church in a few minutes. Where is the dress I laid out on the bed?" She looks on the floor. "Oh, here it is. How did it get on the floor?"

While her mom is looking at the floor, Maria takes off again, running into the kitchen. "Mommy, these shoes are the fastest shoes I've ever owned."

"Maria, where are you now? Get in here this minute so I can change your clothes."

Maria comes running into the bedroom. "I'm never taking these shoes off again, they make me fly!"

Maria's mom grabs Maria as she runs into the bedroom. "Maria, please stand still." Her mother begins unbuttoning Maria's pajamas. "Let's get off these flannel pajamas—that's right. Now, put on your new pretty dress. Then I'll brush your hair."

Maria puts on her dress. "Boy, I love that these shoes are red, they're magic and they make me faster than an airplane." Maria starts twirling around.

"Maria, what are you doing? Come here let me button up your dress and take off those god-awful shoes!"

Maria stops twirling and stares at her mom with tears welling up in her eyes. "Mommy, these shoes are beautiful, I love them. They are magic, I fly when I run now, didn't you see me?"

"Maria, why do you have to be so difficult? Fine—wear the shoes, see if I care. Now come here and let me button up your dress. We are going to be late."

At the wedding, Maria watches her cousin Joannie as she parades down the aisle. Joannie's blonde curls bounce as she walks. She smiles at Maria as she goes by, her blue eyes sparkling. Her pearly white dress trails behind her.

Maria sees Bill, the handsome dark-haired Prince, waiting at the altar to take Joannie's hand.

Maria stands up, staring. "Mommy, isn't she beautiful?" Maria lets out a sigh. "It's like a fairy tale."

At the reception, Maria runs faster than ever before to show Joannie and Bill her magical shoes. "Joannie, Bill—look at my new shoes!"

Joannie watches Maria. Maria's brown eyes are sparkling over her freckled nose, her brown hair is flying behind her; she is smiling as she runs over to Joannie and Bill.

Joannie looks down at Maria's shoes. "Maria, those shoes are soooo fast. They look magical. I just love your new red shoes."

Maria runs around Bill and Joannie.

Bill smiles at Maria. "Joannie's right, Maria, those are the best shoes ever. Let's get a picture of you kissing the bride." Bill calls over to the wedding photographer, "Hey Jim, can you bring your camera over here?"

Jim walks over with his camera. Everyone watches as he takes a picture of the little four-year-old girl, standing on her tiptoes, kissing the bride, wearing her fast, magical, red tennis shoes.

MADDIE'S WORLD

Arms Reaching to the Sky

I see a little girl, arms reaching to the sky
I see the loneliness, hiding in her eyes
Her long brown hair, blows in the breeze
I see the little scabs, covering her knees
Well, she moves so fast wanting someone to see,
A person to watch her as, she climbs her trees
But when she turns around, no one is there
No arms to catch her as, she falls through the air

As she grows older, her arms fall to her sides
The sadness is still there, hidden in her eyes
She makes lots of friends, running the streets
Hiding her eyes from, everyone she meets
She learns as a little girl, how to hide
All those feelings she, has in her eyes
Love doesn't come easy, her heart's hidden in the trees
Waiting for someone to, see what she sees

What is she looking for? What does she need?
Why is she always, looking at me?

Chapter 1

"Mommy! Mommy! Please don't let him put me in here again. Mommy! Mommy?" Little six-year-old Maddie stands and faces the closet door; she tries the door but it's locked. She is wearing her usual dirty jeans, and hand me down T-shirt her mom bought her at the thrift store. She can hear her mother and her boyfriend talking in the next room. Maddie reaches up, pulls a string, and a light bulb turns on, giving off a dim light. There are a couple of jackets hanging in the closet that tickle her arm. Her tangled, uncombed, blonde hair catches on a button. She pulls it loose, leaving a strand of hair. It hurts her head; her green eyes start to tear up. She sits down and begins to rock and sing.

"Jesus loves me this I know. Cuz the Bible tells me so . . ."

After a minute, Maddie stops rocking and listens; she can hear music in the next room.

~

Ricky sits on the couch with a box of Ziploc sandwich bags on the table in front of him. He is measuring white powder and putting it in individual baggies. Under the table a couple of white bricks are sitting in a cardboard box.

The apartment is in a run-down brownstone on the south side of Chicago. It is small with a living room, kitchenette, a bath, and two bedrooms. The wallpaper is missing in places, showing the sheetrock underneath. The wastebaskets are overflowing with discarded take out containers.

"Rickie, why do we gotta lock her in there again? She won't get in the way?" Maddie's mom, Lizzy, is standing in the living room, looking toward the bedroom where Rickie just locked Maddie in the closet.

"Forget it, Lizzy. Remember what happened last time? I had that prime powder all measured and ready to bag and BAM!— she knocks it on the fuckin' floor. A thousand dollars worth lost to the floorboards. It's just for a little while. She'll sleep. Now come on, help me bag this stuff." Ricky looks Lizzy up and down with a smile and licks his lips. "Hey, give me some of that. Come on you sweet thing, pull up that skirt and . . ."

Lizzy walks over pulling up her skirt and straddles Ricky's lap. Lizzy giggles and then moans as Ricky grabs her.

~

Maddie looks around her closet. Still sitting down, she sees something on the wall next to her, a black ant. "Hey, little ant, how are you today?" Maddie puts her finger on the wall by the ant. "Here, do you want to ride on my finger? Come on, I'll bring you up higher on the wall so no one can step on you."

Maddie watches as the ant goes down to the floor and underneath the closet door. "Don't go little ant. Please, don't go."

Then she sees a spider web in the corner by the door. "Hey little spider, that's so pretty. What are you building?"

Maddie looks at the spider and starts singing:

> *"Little spider works so hard, making a play yard.*
> *It's so shiny and bright, a bed to sleep in tonight*
> *Is it gold or candy, something you made for me?*
> *Will it melt on my tongue? Oh, it looks like so much fun"*

"I like your house. If I could pick a house, I think . . . I think I'd want a shoe, a brown shoe with a high heel on it. It would be leather and have little holes for laces. I would sit inside and slide down the soft slippery stuff into the toe. Oooo, I love the way the slippery stuff feels on the backs of my legs. And if someone comes and looks in the shoe, I can slide into the toe. I'll make myself real small, and lie flat on the soft cushion. No one can see me in there. The shoe will protect me from the rain, and thunder, and lightning, all that bad, scary stuff. When everyone is gone and it's quiet, I can crawl back up on the heel, stand on my tiptoes, and look outside through the little holes. I can see everyone out there but they can't see me."

Maddie stops and listens. The music in the next room is softer. There is a knock on the apartment door; then she hears Ricky's voice.

~

Ricky, standing at the apartment door, says, "Hey Donny, my man, come on in . . . whassup . . . I haven't seen ya down on the corner lately, your old lady got ya on a fuckin' leash or something?"

Donny walks into the apartment and nods to Lizzy. "Hey Lizzy. Yeah, I got her knocked up and she's not feeling too great. Anyway, I was in the neighborhood and I thought I'd . . ."

"Donnie, you heard right. I'm flush. How much you want? Lizzy, lay out a couple of lines for my friend Donnie here."

Donnie and Ricky walk over to the table where Lizzy is measuring out lines. Lizzy takes a rolled up dollar bill and snorts one. Ricky says angrily, "Hey, what the fuck you think you're doing, Lizzy? Save some of that stuff for the paying customers."

Ricky looks at Donny. "Go ahead Donny, try out the goods."

Ricky sits down on the couch and pats his lap. "Come here Lizzy, I need some of your love stuff." Lizzy sits down on Ricky's lap, while Donnie snorts a line.

"So Donnie, how much you want . . . ?"

~

Maddie stands up and stretches in her closet and her stomach growls. She yells loudly. "I'm hungry Mommy! Mommy, I'm hungry!"

There is no response from the next room. Maddie sighs, sits back down again and looks at the spider. "Do you have anything for me to eat? Oh, don't worry; I won't eat you. I'm not like that.

Freddie, my friend at school, he ate an ant once. It made my tummy hurt to see him do that. I had to go to the nurse because I threw up. The nurse was nice. She smelled like cotton candy, the kind that melts on your tongue all sweet and sugary. She made me lie down. Then she looked at my face. I didn't want her to look at me. I had this dirty Band-aid by my eyebrow. You know when you take the paper off and the Band-aid sticks together and makes those little wrinkles? Well, my Band-aid was wrinkled like that; she saw it and started to take it off. I didn't want her to. She asked me what happened. I told her I fell and hit the stairs. She mumbled 'stairs my foot' and walked away. I wanted to cry, I didn't want her talking about my secrets. I don't like it when people say my secrets out loud. You won't say anything will you?"

The music and voices start to get louder in the next room. Maddie stops and listens. She hears Donnie leave and the apartment door close.

~

"Lizzy, watch what you're doing when you're bagging that stuff. You gave Donnie way too much for what he was payin'."

There is a loud knock on the apartment door; Ricky answers it. "Yo, Bennie. Come on in. How the fuck you been? I haven't seen you around lately. Hey Lizzy, show our friend the goods." LIzzy picks up a baggie and shows him.

"What do you think, Bennie? You buying . . . ?"

~

Maddie looks around the closet and lies down on her stomach. She looks closely at her spider. Her knees are bent and her feet are kicking back and forth in the air.

Maddie sees something. "There's another spider. She's bigger than you. Is she your nana? I have a Nana. I like to be with her but Mom says she puts poison in my head. So I can't go there anymore. My nana tells me stories about a little girl named Betsy. She has a friend who lives across the street named Tacy. I wish I had a friend. Will you be my friend? Oh, this floor is so hard. It reminds of the time my nana brought me to church and we sat on a hard bench. There was this window that had glass with all different colors that made a picture. There was a baby and his mom held him in her arms. I wish my mom held me like that. The baby's name was Jeepers . . . no Jesse . . . no . . . Jesus. He grew up and had long hair like Ricky's. But He's not at all like Ricky. His eyes were nice . . ."

Suddenly the voices in the next room get very loud and scary. Maddie stops talking and listens.

~

In the living room, Ricky and Lizzy stand up in front of the couch, Bennie has pulled out a gun.

Ricky looks at Bennie. "What the fuck you doin'? Bennie, put that away. That's not funny. Don't be waving that gun in my face . . . man, you're fuckin' crazy."

"I'm fuckin' crazy, Ricky? What do you mean I'm fuckin' crazy? Man, that stuff you got there belongs to me. I found out you held out on me that last deal we did together. You fuckin' cheated me out of . . ."

Ricky reaches out his hand with his palm up to stop Bennie. "What the fuck, slow down man . . . wait a minute. You got it all wrong. Man, that's just not true. Sit down; we can work something out. Come on, let's talk. Lizzy, why don't you give Benny some . . . ?"

Bennie shouts, "Shut the fuck up Ricky, and stop whining! You're not going to talk your way out of this one. Word on the street is you're looking for someone to get me off your fuckin' back; well I decided to beat you to it. Maybe this will make you think differently . . ."

Bennie points the gun at Lizzy.

Lizzy gives Ricky a terrified look. "Ricky . . . ?"
Suddenly there is a gunshot.

~

In the closet Maddie covers her ears.

~

Ricky stares at Lizzy on the floor; she is holding her stomach, and blood is seeping out through her fingers. "Fuck man, you're crazy, Bennie. What did she ever do to you? What the fuck you doin'? . . . Bennie . . . man, don't do it. You can have everything, if that's not enough I'll get you some more. Fuck Bennie, please don't do this . . . ?" Ricky holds up both his hands like he can stop the bullet.

There is another gunshot.

~

Maddie sits up in the closet and starts rocking, still covering her ears. "Yes, Jesus loves me. Yes, Jesus loves me . . ."

After a minute or so she slowly uncovers her ears. Everything is quiet. No music, no voices.

She calls out, "I'm so hungry. Mommy! Can I come out now? I'm real hungry. Mommy!"

When there is no answer, Maddie lies back down and looks at her spider.

"You found a fly. I wish you could share it with me; only I don't like flies. The last time I was in here I missed two days of school. I remember when the door opened, I had trouble opening my eyes. It was like someone put their thumbs on my eyelids and I couldn't open them. Oh, I wonder how much longer? You look tired, maybe we should just take a little nap."

Maddie lays her head down and closes her eyes. Soon she is sound asleep.

~

The quiet apartment starts to fill with the sounds of sirens getting closer and closer. Two Chicago policemen pull over, Nate, tall with blonde hair and Ed, short with black hair. They get out of their car, and run into the apartment building, their guns are drawn.

"Ed, the apartment door is standing open . . . " Nate starts walking in.

"Nate, be careful—the shooter could still be in there."

Both policeman hold up their guns and clear the rooms of the apartment. When they walk back into the living room, they holster their guns.

Nate takes one look and says, "Oh my God, what a mess. These two look like they are in bad shape." Nate grabs his walkie talkie off his belt and calls for an ambulance. Lizzy moans. As Nate bends down to take her pulse, Ed steps out into the hallway. Nate can hear Ed talking to someone.

Ed comes back in the apartment. "Are they still alive?"

The sound of an ambulance's siren fills the air.

Nate answers, "He's gone . . . but she's still got a pulse, it's faint.

"The neighbor said there's a six-year-old kid that lives in this place, named Maddie. I'll take a look." Ed walks into the room where Maddie's closet is and looks around. Maddie wakes up at the sound of his footsteps.

Ed calls out. "Hello, hello, Maddie?"

Maddie stands up. "I'm in here! Can you let me out, please? I'm really hungry." She looks down at her spider. "I'm sorry Mr. Spider, you'll be OK in here without me. It's safe."

Ed unlocks the closet door and opens it. He sees Maddie in the closet shielding her eyes from the light. Ed picks her up in his arms. She lays her head on his shoulder. He starts to bring her into the other room.

"Ed, what are you doing? Don't bring her in here now . . ."

Ed whispers in Maddie's ear. "Maddie, can you do me a favor and just keep your eyes closed? Let's see how long you can keep them closed. I'll count and if you can keep them closed until I count to thirty, we can stop and get an ice cream cone. OK, Maddie?"

Maddie whispers, "OK."

As Ed and Maddie leave the apartment building, an ambulance pulls up, with its lights flashing.

Chapter 2

Ed pulls up to the police station; Maddie is just finishing her vanilla ice cream cone with sprinkles. Maddie gets out of the squad car and walks into the police station holding Ed's hand.

Ed looks down at Maddie. "There is a woman here who would like to talk to you for a while." Maddie looking around, slowly walks down a hallway to the conference room. Ed opens the door, and Maddie sees a woman with short brown hair and glasses. She is sitting at a table, talking on the phone, and writing something on a piece of paper. Maddie seems to hesitate a moment. She looks around at the bare, gray walls and the windows.

Ellen looks up, then says to someone on the phone, "I can't right now." She puts her hand over the phone. "Hi Ed, I'll be with you in a minute."

Ellen takes her hand off the phone. "What? I need to talk to someone here . . . no, it can't wait. I'll call you back later."

Hanging up the phone, Ellen looks at Maddie and sees a small, thin girl with uncombed blonde hair, dirt smudged on her cheeks, a torn T-shirt, and baggy jeans. She is wearing blue sneakers, with holes in the toes.

Ed squeezes Maddie's hand to reassure her. "This is Maddie, the girl I called you about."

"Hi, Maddie. My name is Ellen; I'm a social worker. Are you hungry or thirsty? Can we get you something?"

Maddie looks around her and seems not to hear what Ellen is saying.

"Maddie, come in and sit down. Ed, why don't you go out and get us a couple of cans of soda?"

Maddie reluctantly lets go of Ed's hand and takes a seat in a chair at the table. She looks around her and then under the table. "Can I . . . I mean, would it be OK if I . . . well if I sit under the table?"

"Under the table? I don't think you'd be comfortable . . ."

"Please? I really just have to . . ."

Maddie gets up and sits cross-legged on the floor under the table; facing the wall with the windows. Ellen watches her and then gets up and sits under the table next to Maddie.

Ed comes back with some cans of soda and looks around him. "Ellen?"

Ellen waves her hand out from the table. "We're down here Ed, under the table." Ed bends down and looks at Ellen and Maddie.

Ellen says, "Don't ask. It's a good thing this table is tall and I'm short."

Ed hands Ellen the soda cans, and says, "See you later, Maddie."

Maddie watches Ed walk out the door.

Ellen asks, "Are you thirsty?"

"I'm a little thirsty."

Ellen holds up the soda cans. "Well, here you go. Do you want Sprite or Coke?"

Maddie takes a can and looks at it. "Is it safe? I mean, are you sure it's safe to drink?"

"Of course it's safe. Why wouldn't it be?"

"My mom always says to check the cans . . . you know . . . look inside before you drink. Just in case . . . " Maddie stops talking.

59

"Just in case what, Maddie?"

"Well, sometimes Ricky, he's my mom's boyfriend, he puts things in the cans."

Ellen looks at Maddie. "Like what?"

"Needles or matches. He tosses them in, if the can is open, to throw them away. Once my mom picked up a can of Coke and started to drink, then she said ouch. When she took the can away there was blood on her lip. So are you sure it's safe . . . to drink?"

"It's safe, Maddie, I promise. You can even open it yourself."

Maddie slowly opens the can, takes a sip, and then looks up and sees the window. She suddenly becomes agitated and restless. "Where's my mommy? When can I see my mommy? She always tells me not to stay out after dark and look at the window—the sky's getting real dark. The last time I stayed out after dark she . . . well . . . she got mad . . . and well . . . I have this doll, she's so pretty. She has long blonde hair and blue eyes that close. Her lashes are long and black and she has freckles all across her nose and cheeks. My nana says the freckles are 'angel's kisses.' My nana likes angels. She says I have one on my shoulder all the time, watching over me, and my angel reports to . . . Jesus. He's this guy with long brown hair and He has the nicest eyes I have ever seen. I feel like I could tell Him everything. He looks at me kind of like you're looking at me now . . . this pop is good." Maddie takes another sip.

"Maddie, I . . ."

"My nana says pop is bad for my teeth, it makes them fall out. Mommy says that's a tail from a wife or something. Anyway, I lost two teeth last month. I was afraid to drink pop again, but then, Freddie at school lost a tooth too. He says it's our age. We lose teeth to get more teeth, that are bigger." Maddie takes a sip of her soda.

"Honey, can you tell me about your momm . . . ?"

Maddie looks around. "My mommy is probably worried about me. I should go now . . . Mommy will be mad and well, the doll I was telling you about, with the freckles. When I was late my mommy got angry and she took my doll and she cut off all her hair. So I better get home soon. Please, won't you take me back home in that car with the siren? I really need to go, now, please."

The phone starts to ring. Ellen reaches up and puts the phone next to her under the table. She answers it and listens. "How is her mother? Do they know . . . ? Yeah, I'll ask her. I'm not sure. I'll let you know."

Ellen hangs up the phone. "Maddie, that was about your mommy. She's very sick. She is in the hospital right now. The doctors are trying to make her better. What about your daddy? Do you ever see your daddy?"

"I don't have a daddy. Once I called Ricky daddy and he slapped me. He said no one wanted to be my daddy. So I guess I never got one. My mommy took me to the park once. We had so much fun. She pushed the swing I was on and I felt like I was flying. She sang me a song, '*Birdies fly up in the sky.*' Then we went down the slide. I remember I liked that because she sat me in her lap. It felt so good. I was laughing. Then Ricky came and my mommy seemed to forget about me . . . I want to see my mommy, please, can't I go and see her now?" A couple of tears roll down Maddie's cheeks.

Ellen puts a comforting hand on Maddie's knee. "Maybe tomorrow honey. Right now we need to find somewhere for you to stay and . . ."

"How about my nana?"

"Where does she live?"

Maddie thinks. "She lives in Eagle . . . Eagle . . . something. She has a big house. It has two bedrooms and a bathtub and a stove. I had never seen a stove till I went to my nana's. Mommy always cooks on something she calls a hot plate. Nana's house smells so good, like bubble gum all pink and sweet. Her living room has pictures all over the walls. Some of my mommy when she was a little girl and she even has a couple of me, when I was a baby. There's a picture of that man Jesus I was telling you about, He's walking on water. I asked Nana why doesn't He ever fall in? I liked His face. I like your face too. I like my nana; she holds me on her lap and tells me stories. When she talks, she tickles my arm with her fingertips. I get goose bumps. Mommy won't let me go there anymore, she says Nana's mean. She's not mean . . . and my nana knows things. One time I was sitting on Nana's lap and I told her . . . I told her . . . never mind."

Maddie takes a sip of her soda and starts squirming around.

Ellen watches Maddie. "Why do you like sitting here, under the table?"

Maddie looks around at the table legs. "I can feel the lines around me. The lines can keep things out, scary things. It's like wrapping my winter coat around me, it feels safe and warm."

"Do you feel safe and warm now, Maddie?

"Well . . . yes . . . I . . . guess . . . so. If I tell you something will you promise you won't go away?"

"Sure, honey, I won't go away."

Maddie runs her finger along the floor. "Well . . . my nana and I had just made these cookies with chocolate chips in them. I had two in my hand; they were so warm. I took a bite and it was full of chocolate chips, it tasted so good I shivered. Nana pulled me on her lap and told me the story of "Beauty and the Beast." She talked about the shadows that scared Belle when she was in the forest trying to find her father. When she talked about the shadows, I thought, my nana must know about the shadows that I see in the middle of the night. So I told her about them. I told her about the angry, growling voices and the big monster hitting my mommy. Sometimes the big monster hit me too. I'd pull my covers up over my head to keep those shadows away. I had never told anyone before. She listened, and rocked me and tickled my arm. She cried. After that my mommy wouldn't let me go back there again. She said Nana didn't want to see us anymore. I shouldn't have talked about the shadows. You won't send me away because I told you, will you? I think my mommy must be missing me; I should go see her. She might need me to get her something to drink. Please, can't I go see her? Please. She might get mad . . . " Maddie's voice gets more and more anxious.

"Maddie, your mommy's asleep right now, the doctors and nurses are taking good care of her. If she needs anything to drink they'll get it for her. You can maybe see her tomorrow. But right now we need to find a place for you to stay. I thought maybe we could call your grandmother and see if . . . ?"

"But Mommy said that Nana . . ."

"I know what your mommy said. But it sounds like your grandmother loves you very much. Wouldn't you like to stay with her? Why don't I give her a call? What is your grandmother's name?"

Maddie relaxes a little and takes a sip of her soda as she thinks. "Nana."

Ellen smiles. "Does she have a last name? Does she live here in town?"

"I don't think she's too close. We took a big bus to go see her before. I think Nana is her last name."

The phone beside Ellen rings. She answers it looking at Maddie. "Hello. I haven't had a chance. I'm just getting to it now . . . I know, but she's scared . . . I can't . . . OK, I'll ask her."

Ellen hangs up the phone, looking at Maddie. "Maddie, honey, I have one more question I need to ask you. Do you remember what happened earlier today? Did you hear any . . . ?"

Maddie puts her hands over her ears and starts to rock and sing.

"Jesus loves me, yes, Jesus loves me . . ."

Ed opens the door and walks in seeing Maddie with her hands over her ears. "Ellen, can I have a word with you?"

Ellen gently pats Maddie on her back. "Maddie, I'll be right back."

Maddie continues to rock. Ellen gets up from under the table and walks over to Ed.

Ed asks, "I have good news and bad news, which do you want first?"

"Give me the bad news first."

Ed says very quietly, so Maddie can't hear. "I just heard from the hospital, Maddie's mother didn't make it. But the good news is, when I was looking through missing person's, I found out that about six months ago a missing person's report was sent out fitting the description of Maddie's mother and of Maddie. It's from Madison, Wisconsin; it was filed by her grandmother. I just talked to her and she has been frantically trying to find Maddie. She's on her way here now."

"Oh, Ed, how am I going to tell Maddie about her mom?"

"Why don't you wait until her grandmother gets here?"

Ellen says gratefully, "That's a great idea. I'm so glad to find out there is someone who will be here for Maddie. She is so scared. Thanks."

Ed starts to leave. "I'll check in with you later."

"Actually, Ed, could I ask for one more favor? Could you go out and get a couple of hamburgers and some fries? Maddie must be hungry."

"No problem, I'll go right now."

Ellen goes and sits down next to Maddie. Maddie has stopped singing and rocking and is watching Ellen. Ellen puts her arm around Maddie, who relaxes and rests her head on Ellen's shoulder and sighs.

"Maddie, we found your grandmother. It's going to be OK. You're going to be just fine. She'll be here in just a little while. You're going to be just fine . . ."

After eating a hamburger and some fries, Maddie falls asleep on a cot in the conference room. Ellen finds a blanket to put over her. A few hours later her grandmother arrives at the police station. After she shows Ed her ID and signs some forms, he brings her to the conference room, where Ellen is sitting with Maddie, writing reports.

Ellen watches Maddie's grandmother, a pretty, full figured woman in her mid-forties with short auburn hair, as she walks into the conference room. Ellen motions for her to sit down at the table. "You must be Maddie's grandmother, Patricia. She talked a lot about you. I'm Ellen. She fell asleep a couple of hours ago. She has been through a lot."

Maddie's grandmother sits down and looks anxiously at Ellen. "Do you know how Lizzy is doing? Do they know who did this?"

Ellen says softly, "I'm sorry to have to tell you this but Lizzy passed away a few of hours ago. We think it was a drug deal gone bad. We don't have a suspect yet and Maddie doesn't know about her mother. We thought it would be better coming from you."

Maddie's grandmother, in shock, sits there, shaking her head; tears begin to slide down her cheeks. Then it sinks in and she puts her face in her hands and cries. Ellen slides over a kleenex box and sits quietly waiting, letting Maddie's grandmother have some time to process everything. After a few minutes, Maddie's grandmother pulls herself together, and dries her tears.

She looks over at Maddie and then back at Ellen. "I'm so glad I found Maddie. I have been worried sick about her and Lizzy these last few months. When I saw them last, Lizzy and I had a bad argument; I thought I might never see them again."

Ellen looks at Maddie's grandmother and says gently, "Maddie wasn't able to talk about what happened today; she is too traumatized. So I made you a list of names and phone numbers of excellent therapists in Madison who deal with trauma in young children."

Maddie's grandmother takes the list and stands up. "Thanks, I know Maddie and I will both need help dealing with all this. And thanks so much for being with Maddie until I could get here."

Ellen stands up and walks over to Maddie's grandmother. She puts a hand on her arm. "Maddie is such a creative, wonderful little girl. She is strong and smart; I know she will get through this with your love and support. You are very important to her and she is lucky to have you."

Maddie's grandmother looks at Ellen. "I feel lucky to have her too. She is a very smart and creative little girl. Her first six years have been so chaotic and unstable. I can't imagine what she has seen or been through, so I will definitely be calling a counselor from your list. I am so happy to finally be able to bring her home and give her the love and stability she needs. I left all my personal information with Ed. May I bring Maddie home now?"

"Yes, we'll contact you when we find out more about what happened and if we have any questions."

Maddie's grandmother, with tears in her eyes, walks over to where Maddie is sleeping and picks her up. Maddie responds by putting her head on her grandmother's shoulder. She is still sound asleep.

Maddie's grandmother stops on the way out and looks at Ellen. "Again, thank you so much for everything."

Chapter 3

Maddie wakes up and looks around the pink bedroom, with ruffles on the edge of her bedspread. She sees a white rocking chair in the corner with a doll dressed in a blue jumper. On the wall is a picture of her, when she was four, sitting on her grandmother's lap, and a picture of her mommy too. Outside the bedroom window is an apple tree with lots of leaves, and green apples that look ready to pick. When Maddie's grandmother walks by the bedroom she hears a noise in Maddie's room. When she opens the door she sees Maddie sitting up in bed looking around her with a puzzled expression; her blonde hair is dirty and snarled. Maddie's grandmother wonders if she will be able to get a comb through it.

Maddie looks at her grandmother. "Nana, I'm at your house. How did I get here?"

Maddie's grandmother walks in and sits on the bed. "I picked you up late last night in Chicago and brought you home with me. You slept the whole way."

"Oh." Maddie looks around her. "I just love this bedroom and the apple tree outside my window. I'm so glad to see you,

Nana, I've missed you so much." Maddie gives her grandmother a big hug.

Her grandmother kisses the top of her head. "I know, honey, I've missed you too."

"Nana, where is Mommy? Is she coming too?"

Maddie's grandmother pulls Maddie onto her lap. When she's settled in, she looks at Maddie, and holds her tight. "Maddie, your mother was in the hospital and they did everything they could for her, but she didn't make it. She died, Maddie."

Maddie starts crying. After a few minutes she looks up at her grandmother. "Nana, I was so scared. There was all this yelling; Ricky was talking to a very angry man. Then I heard a couple loud bangs, like a balloon popping or a firecracker going off. Then it was so quiet. I called to my mom, but she didn't answer, I guess she couldn't hear me. So, I just laid down and fell asleep, until that nice policeman found me. By then it was getting dark outside and I missed my mommy."

"It's all right, Maddie. I'm here now and you're going to be living here with me." Maddie cuddles into her grandmother and relaxes. They sit there for a couple of minutes; then her grandmother says, "I think today we need to have a 'fun' day. But before we eat breakfast, why don't you get in the bathtub and I'll wash your hair. After breakfast we can go to the neighborhood hair salon for a new haircut. Then we can shop for some new clothes. We can go out for lunch and maybe go to the Children's Museum. How does that sound?"

"Can I get clothes that have sparkles? Can we go to the malt shop in town and get hamburgers, French fries, and a shake?"

"Yes, Maddie, we can do all those things today."

Maddie starts to get up from her nana's lap, then stops and sits back down. "Nana, I miss my mommy."

"I know Maddie, I miss her too." Maddie and her grandmother sit a few minutes. Then her grandmother says, "I have an idea—after breakfast we can get out the photo albums and you can pick out pictures of you and your mom. We can make a collage to hang in your room. Then we can have our fun day. How does that sound?"

Maddie smiles. "I made a collage at school once of kittens. I hung it in my bedroom."

After Maddie's bath, they go downstairs to have breakfast and get the photo albums out. An hour later they have a collage of pictures of Maddie and her mom. They hang it in her bedroom, right between the picture of Maddie and her nana and her mommy. Then Maddie gets her hair cut, picks out clothes with sparkles, and has lunch at the malt shop.

The following week Maddie's grandmother gets Maddie enrolled in school. Then she calls Denise, a counselor from the list Ellen had given her. She likes Denise and makes an appointment for Maddie on Wednesday after school.

On Saturday they have a small memorial service for Lizzy at Maddie's grandmother's church. Maddie sits in the wooden pews. She looks around the small church and sees the stained-glass window of Jesus walking on water and her mother's picture sitting on the table with flowers.

"Nana, I love this church. I remember sitting here before and looking at that picture of Jesus. It makes me sad to see my mommy's picture up there, but also I think it will be OK, because her picture is sitting by the picture of Jesus. He'll take care of her now. Won't He, Nana?"

"Yes, Maddie, He will be with her."

After the service, Maddie gets into her grandmother's car, and says, "I love my new school. I made a friend yesterday. I really like Denise—she told me that I'd make friends at my new school, and she was right. And Denise helps me feel safe too. Like you do." Maddie sits for a couple of minutes, looking down at her hands, tears escape down her cheek. She quietly says, "But . . . I still miss my mommy."

Chapter 4

Maddie is dancing around the large living room. She looks out the four long windows and sees the big backyard which is almost an acre of land. Beyond the backyard is a nature center. The nature center is surrounded by more homes like hers.

Maddie's long blonde hair is pulled back into a ponytail. She is wearing her favorite T-shirt with a sparkly heart on it and jeans. "Nana, I'm so excited. I just love birthday parties, especially my own. I invited nine kids because of course I'm turning nine years old. Did they all say they were coming?"

"Yes, Maddie, they will all be here."

Her grandmother's house is decorated with balloons of all colors: pink, green, blue, yellow, purple, and red. Streamers are hung along the ceiling. The dining room table is set with colorful plates, napkins and silverware. A birthday cake sits in the middle of the table, waiting to be eaten by ten hungry girls. The doorbell rings.

Nana walks to the door and opens it; a parade of parents and girls begin to come in the front door. Soon the living room is full of giggling girls talking a mile a minute. The girls spend the afternoon playing games: pin the tail on the donkey, dropping clothespins in a bottle, carrying spoons with eggs on them in a relay race. Suddenly a big balloon, floating on the ceiling, pops. Maddie jumps a mile and gets a funny look on her face and runs out of the room. Her grandmother starts another game and then goes to find Maddie.

She walks upstairs, goes into Maddie's bedroom, and looks in the closet. There is Maddie, curled up in the corner, eyes wide, tears falling down her cheeks, looking out the closet door. Her grandmother comes in and sits down next to her. "It's OK, Maddie, it was just a balloon."

"I know that, now, but not when it popped . . . I wet my pants, Nana."

Her grandmother looks down and sees Maddie's wet pants.

Maddie leans against her grandmother trembling. "It sounded so loud and I thought I heard Ricky's voice. I was so scared."

Her grandmother puts her arms around Maddie until she calms down. "I'll get you a change of clothes but then I should go downstairs and see how our guests are doing. Will you be OK? Do you want to come down when you're ready? Or do you want me to tell your friends you got sick and threw up?"

"I can get my own clothes; I'll be down in a few minutes. If they ask where I am just tell them I had a upset stomach but it's OK now."

Her grandmother leaves and Maddie gets up and starts changing her clothes. She sees the collage she made of her mother and herself. "Hey, mom, I'm nine years old today."

Then Maddie goes down and joins her friends. They play a couple more party games and soon Maddie's grandmother announces it is time for food. "OK everyone, go sit in the dining room. I'll bring out the hamburgers and hot dogs. There is a cooler by the table so choose which kind of soda pop you want."

Sara, Maddie's best friend, walks up to Maddie and whispers. "Are you feeling OK?"

Maddie whispers back very quietly, "I just had a touch of diarrhea, it was something I ate. I'm fine now."

Then Sara and Maddie join the other girls at the table. After they have eaten, the girls gather back in the living room and sit in a circle. There is a bottle on the floor. Maddie spins the bottle and whoever it points to brings Maddie their present. Soon there are a pile of presents and a garbage bag full of wrapping paper and ribbons. When the doorbell rings, everyone is sitting at the dining room table finishing up the birthday cake.

When all the girls are gone, Maddie turns to her grandmother. "Nana, will you read me the Betsy, Tacy book you got me for my birthday?"

"OK, but first, why don't you run upstairs, take a nice warm bath and put on some comfy clothes, while I clean up the living room and dining room?"

Maddie runs upstairs and takes a bath. Twenty minutes later Maddie and her grandmother are cuddled together on the couch.

"Thanks for the party. I am so glad you're my Nana. I feel so cozy and warm when I'm with you."

"Me too, little one." Her grandmother kisses the top of her head.

Maddie's gets a funny look on her face. "Did you give my mom birthday parties like this?"

"Yes, honey, I did."

Maddie sits a minute. "Nana, I think that maybe I want to see Denise again. I have questions about things, like how long will I be scared like today? And what are things to do to help me when I'm scared, and my thoughts about my mom. Luckily, my friends really believed I got a little sick, so I didn't feel embarrassed. But sometimes I only feel safe if I hide in a closet."

"Why don't I call her tomorrow and make an appointment? You know she told us you might want to check in periodically as things come up. Now, let's read this book, it is a great story about family and friendship." Maddie relaxes and snuggles into her grandmother, a smile on her face.

Chapter 5

Maddie's grandmother walks by Maddie's bedroom and looks in. Maddie is standing there, in her pink pajamas, looking at the clothes in her closet. "Nana, I can't believe I start middle school in a week. I'll have to switch classes, have a lot of different teachers, and I hear there is a ton of homework. I'm so glad Sara and Caitlin are in most of my classes. Now, if I could just figure out what to wear the first day."

Maddie's grandmother says, "Why don't you get dressed, then I can take you shopping for some school clothes. After we're done shopping, we can go out and have lunch at that restaurant you like so much."

A shadow passes over Maddie's face as she looks at her grandmother. "Did I tell you about the new boy who moved here last week? My friends think he is so cool, but there is something about him that I just don't like. He swears a lot and his name is Bennie. For some reason I hate the name Bennie. Anyway, he's in some of my classes too. I wish he wasn't."

Maddie's grandmother walks in and sits on Maddie's bed. "Well, you don't have to talk to him if you don't want to. Why don't you like the name Bennie?"

Maddie puts her hand on her stomach. "I don't know but when I hear people say it, it makes me feel sick."

Maddie sits next to her grandmother.

Her grandmother puts her arm around Maddie. "It sounds like it might be something we should check out. Have you thought about calling Denise to talk about it? You haven't seen her in a while and maybe she can help figure out what's really going on. I can give her a call?"

Maddie thinks a minute. "Yes, I think that's a good idea, especially because I found out he's in my classes. Now let's go shopping. I can't wait to get some new clothes. I hear the Gap is having a sale."

After a fun day of clothes shopping and a lunch at Maddie's favorite restaurant, they walk in the house exhausted.

Maddie's grandmother says, "I think I'll put a load of these new clothes in to wash. Then I'm taking a much needed nap."

"I'm tired too, Nana. Wake me up when you get up." Maddie walks upstairs to her bedroom.

After Maddie's grandmother puts the clothes in the washer, she finds a good book to read, and lays down on the living room couch. She is just dozing off when she hears Maddie screaming. She runs upstairs into her bedroom; Maddie is tossing and turning yelling words that are unrecognizable. Her grandmother sits down and rubs her back, talking quietly with words of reassurance. She notices the collage that Maddie and she made years ago. And she feels anger at Lizzy for the nightmares that still plague her granddaughter six years later. Eventually Maddie calms down and is fast asleep. Her face looks peaceful again.

Two days later, Maddie's grandmother is parked in front of Denise's office building waiting for Maddie. When Maddie gets in the car after her session with Denise, she has a funny look on her face.

"Maddie, what is it? What's wrong?"

Maddie looking uncomfortable says, "I got more of the memory from that day in Chicago. Bennie . . . Bennie is the name of the angry man that Ricky was yelling at. I didn't remember that until Denise and I started talking. Then I remembered Rickie yelling his name before the loud noises. I feel scared again, Nana. It feels like it just happened. Denise called it PTSD or something. I don't want to go to class on Monday and see that boy named Bennie."

"Maddie, he is not the Bennie from Chicago. You have Sara and Caitlin in class with you. We can try to change classes but then Sara and Caitlin wouldn't be in your class."

"I know, I don't want to change classes. I just don't like those memories coming up again."

Her grandmother looks at her. "Well, now you know why the name bothers you, and you can be reassured he is not the Bennie you are afraid of. Maybe I should call Ellen and let her know you remembered Bennie's name. The Chicago police will probably want to know since they haven't closed the case on what happened that day. Then we can leave it in their capable hands. Now, what would you like to do tonight? What would make you feel safe and warm and know you are far away from those old memories?"

Maddie thinks a minute, sighs, then says, "I know, how about you make your lasagna with garlic bread, I'll make a salad. We can curl up in our pajamas in front of the TV and watch a funny movie. And I'll let you put me to bed, so you can tell me one of your bedtime stories."

Maddie's grandmother starts the car and they drive home. She parks the car in the driveway. They get out and walk into the kitchen. Maddie's grandmother puts down her purse and pulls out a sauce pan to boil the lasagna noodles. After the lasagna noodles are ready she adds the sauce, mushrooms, spinach and cheese and puts it in the oven.

Meanwhile Maddie finds a good movie to watch.

"I found a good romantic comedy," Maddie says as she walks back into the kitchen. The phone rings. Maddie answers it, "Hi, Sara, tonight? No, I can't—I've got plans with Nana. How about tomorrow? OK, just a minute let me ask. Sara wants to have a sleepover tomorrow night at her house, can I go?"

Maddie's grandmother takes out a loaf of garlic bread. "Sure, it'll be nice for you to have a sleepover before school starts on Monday."

Maddie turns back to the phone. "I can. OK, see you tomorrow night. Bye."

Maddie's grandmother looks at her. "Good, now lets go up and get our pajamas on. Then we can come down and you can make the salad and by then everything will be ready to eat."

Soon Maddie and her grandmother are cuddled together on the couch in the living room, with trays of food in front of them, laughing and watching the movie. Maddie's bad memories recede with each laugh.

The next day, after Maddie leaves for school, her grandmother calls Ellen and tells her what Maddie remembered.

Ellen says, "That's great. Now, at least, we have a name. I'll give it to the detectives working cold cases; it will give them something to go on. How is Maddie doing?"

"She's doing fine; at times memories get triggered by little things. She still has nightmares once in a while. But she is mostly a happy pre-teen with lots of friends and she loves school."

Ellen's phone beeps. "I've got a call on the other line, I need to go. Thanks for calling. I'll let you know if anything turns up."

Chapter 6

Maddie's grandmother is in the kitchen stirring batter in a bowl and talking on the phone to her friend, Jeannie. There are two round cake pans on the counter, waiting to be filled with batter. "Hi, Jeannie, I wanted to call and talk to you about something. I just heard from Ellen in Chicago. They finally tracked down Bennie, the one who shot Lizzy. What? No, I haven't told Maddie anything yet. Anyway, he is in prison serving a life sentence for a couple of murders that he committed three years ago. I don't know if I should bring it up with Maddie. She has been so happy lately; it seems like turning sixteen has given her more confidence. She still has dreams but they aren't the scary ones she was having before. So, I don't want to set things off again. I'm just not sure if she really wants to know. I thought if she brings up that day I'll tell her. What do you think, Jeannie? . . . you think so, I should wait till she talks about that day herself? . . . I know, she really has turned out to be quite the young lady. I'm proud of her too. Well, I probably should go. Thanks Jeannie, I'm sorry I called so early but I wanted to talk to you before Maddie woke up. Thanks for listening . . . Yes, let's have lunch next week."

Maddie's grandmother hangs up the phone, sighs, and adds some flour to the batter in the bowl she is stirring.

Meanwhile Maddie is upstairs sleeping in her bedroom tossing and turning in her bed. She is dreaming. In her dream she is six and riding in a car with her mother, Lizzy. The car radio is playing a blues piece.

"Mommy, where are we going? Mommy . . ."

Lizzy looks over her shoulder at Maddie who is sitting in the back seat.

"Maddie, oh, my dear, little Maddie I'm . . ."

The music on the car radio gets louder and drowns out Lizzie's voice.

"What . . . what did you say, Mommy . . . Mommmy . . . what did you say?

There is a loud bang like a tire blowing out. Lizzy's voice has a singsong quality to it, ghostlike.

"Maaaaaadie . . . Maaaaaadie . . . Maddie."

Maddie wakes up with a start and sits up. Her heart is pounding. She takes a couple of deep breaths, stands up and stretches. She looks at her birthday banner still hung on her wall from her sixteenth birthday, her Johnny Depp poster, and the collage of her mother and her.

She stops and looks at the collage and thinks, *Mom, what are you trying to say to me,* as goes downstairs and walks into the kitchen where her grandmother is baking.

"Oh, Nana, I had that dream again."

"Which one, honey?"

Maddie gets impatient. "Nana! You know, the one about the car. Mom's driving on the freeway towards the bridge and she is telling me something, but I can't quite hear her because the music's so loud. Then there's the loud bang and the tire blows and Mom is calling me but she sounds so far away. I get the feeling that if we can reach the bridge, maybe I can hear what she is saying. But we always get that flat tire. Oh Nana, I wish I . . . " Maddie is interrupted by the phone ringing.

Her grandmother answers the phone. "Hello . . . Oh, hi Sara. Yeah, she's right here." Maddie's grandmother gives the phone to Maddie. "It's for you dear."

Her grandmother goes back to the bowl that she was stirring and pours the batter into the two round cake pans.

"Hey, what's up? What . . . how do you know? Sophie said she thought he might ask me. Graham really told you that? Yeah, well if Bobby asks you, then we can . . . who said . . . someone nominated me? Did you? Really, homecoming queen . . . me? We gotta talk. Look, I just got up. Why don't I call you after I have something to eat? We can go to the mall . . . maybe look at some dresses. OK, later."

Maddie hangs up the phone, walks over to her grandmother and dips her finger in the batter and licks it off. "Sometimes, I just wish I could hear what she is saying to me."

"Couldn't you hear Sara, honey?"

"Nana, I'm talking about my dream. I just wish I could hear what my mom is saying to me . . ."

"You'll hear her someday, Maddie, when you're ready. Now help me get this cake in the oven. I thought we'd have it later, to celebrate."

"Celebrate what?"

"Didn't I hear you were nominated for homecoming queen?"

"How did you know?"

"Oh, Maddie, you know I have my ways."

As they are putting the cake in the oven, the doorbell rings. Maddie's grandmother looks puzzled, "Who can that be this early in the morning?"

When she opens the door there is a box wrapped with a bow.

"Maddie, there is a package for you."

"Oh, who could it be from . . . ? Oh, I bet I know." Maddie rips open the package. There are several puzzle pieces in the bottom of the box. "Nana, lets go put this on the living room floor. You can help me fit the pieces together."

When they get the puzzle done it says, "Homecoming? Graham." Maddie jumps up and dances around the room. "I thought he might ask me. Now, I have to figure out a way to tell him yes—I better call Sara back and ask her for some ideas. Thanks Nana." Maddie dances out of the room to get the phone.

Maddie's grandmother watches her, feeling happy to see her vibrant teen-age granddaughter dancing around with unbridled joy, proud of how well she is doing facing the complexities in her life.

Chapter 7

Maddie's bags are packed. A TV set is in the back seat of the car, along with some boxes, and her suitcases are in the trunk. Maddie's grandmother is driving down I-94 bringing Maddie to Evanston, Illinois, for her first day of college. Maddie is asleep in the car. She is dreaming and starts mumbling in her sleep. In her dream she hears Ricky.

"Hey Lizzy, Come here and give me some of that love stuff."

Maddie hears her mom giggle and then she hears Bennie's voice.

"Who's trying to be funny, man?"

In her dream, she hears gunshots.

Then she hears Ellen's voice. "Maddie, we found your grandmother, she's on her way. You're going to be fine, honey. You're going to be just fine."

Maddie is moaning and begins talking in her sleep

"Moooommmy . . . Moommmy . . . Mommy!

Maddie's grandmother glances over at her. "Maddie, Maddie, are you all right?"

Maddie wakes up and looks at her grandmother. "Can we pull over a minute? I feel a little shaky."

"Sure, were you having one of your dreams?"

Her grandmother takes the next exit off the freeway, pulls over and parks the car. Then she looks at Maddie.

"Nana, I . . . I could hear that music again. I saw Ricky and Mom and that nice lady, Ellen, the one who gave me soda pop and found you. Then I heard the . . . gunshots . . . then I was with Ellen lying under the table and you walked in dressed in that blue dress with the daisies and the white collar with the lacey edge.

Maddie's grandmother puts her arm around Maddie and pulls her in close. "Are you OK? Hearing the gunshots . . . are you . . . ?"

"I think so, I finally remember that day when Mom and Ricky . . . the gun shots. I heard gunshots, and the voice of Bennie." Maddie shivered. "I've always dreaded this moment.

But it's funny it wasn't so scary because you and Ellen were with me in the dream. I wasn't alone."

Maddie's grandmother turns to face Maddie. "Maddie, I think it's time to tell you something. Ellen called me a couple of years ago and told me that Bennie is in prison serving a life sentence for two other murders he committed. So he is locked away for the rest of his life."

"Why did you wait to tell me?"

Maddie's grandmother takes her hand and holds it. "Honey, these last couple of years you've seemed so happy and carefree. You haven't had any nightmares like you used to. I just didn't want to bring it up and set off any old memories. I thought I'd wait until you brought up that day yourself."

"I guess that makes sense, Nana. I do feel better knowing that he is locked up. I really haven't thought about him since I was in middle school. But now I have all the pieces, I'm glad I know where he is. I wonder why I am having these dreams now, and why did I finally hear the gunshots—there were two of them. Why of all times, why now?"

"It makes sense to me. After all Maddie, where are we heading today? Back to Chicago and to your new home."

"That day when my mom and Ricky . . . well, I felt so alone. I think I knew I wasn't ever going to see her again. I was scared and lonely and didn't know . . . and now. Now I'm going away from you. You'll be so far away. Northwestern is just too far. I should have gone to the college in Madison. Then I could live at home . . . I'm scared."

"Maddie, of course you're scared, and nervous. It's a change and change can bring things up. But really, honey, I'm only a few hours away by car. You loved Northwestern when we visited it. And they have one of the best psychology programs in the country. I'm just a phone call away. You'll make lots of friends. Now relax, put some music on, and close your eyes. We need to get going, we don't want to miss the orientation."

Maddie's grandmother starts the car and pulls out onto the road again and back onto the interstate.

Maddie, looking out the window, says quietly, "I heard gunshots, not tires blowing out, not balloons popping. I heard gunshots."

"Remember what Denise told us? The more you remember, the deeper the healing. You're going to be OK, Maddie. You're going to be just fine. Relax, lay your head back, and listen to the music."

Maddie lays her head back on the seat and closes her eyes. Her dreams start up again. She can hear her mother and the music is playing softly.

"Maaaaaadie … Maaaaaadie … come here my little Maaaadie. I want to tell you … what mama? … what do you want to tell me … ?"

Maddie startles awake and looks around.

Her grandmother asks, "Another dream? You were talking in your sleep."

Maddie looks at her grandmother. "I had the car dream again. Mom's driving on the freeway, the bridge is just ahead. There are tall, beautiful, green trees. Mom's talking to me; I sit up to hear her. The music is playing, only softer. This time we reach the bridge and I hear my mom, I hear what she's been saying. Nana, she's been saying that she misses me and that she loves me so much. She said she is sorry, so very sorry. And then she said something I didn't quite understand. She said she knew I'd go far. It's like she believes in me. I really do miss her sometimes, Nana."

Chapter 8

As Maddie and her grandmother drive onto the campus, they check the street names to find her dorm. They can see Lake Michigan a couple of blocks away, and green grass and trees everywhere. Maddie looks at her grandmother. "Isn't the campus beautiful? And it's so peaceful here but also close to Chicago, where there is shopping and shows."

"I know, I think I'll have to visit often. So we can see those shows and, of course, do tons of shopping."

Maddie's grandmother parks the car in a space by the residence hall where Maddie's dorm room is located. "What floor are you on again?"

Maddie looks at the building. "I'm on the 4rd floor, room 403."

Maddie and her grandmother take a load of bedding and suitcases and walk up four flights of stairs. When they enter Maddie's dorm room, a tall, thin girl with long dark hair, is sitting on one of the beds, writing in her journal.

Maddie looks around the room. The room is about the size of her bedroom at home. But it has two beds, two small desks, and dresser and a night stand. "Oh Nana, this room is so . . . small."

Maddie and her grandmother go to the bed that is empty and set down the suitcases and the bedding.

Amy looks up from her journal. "Hi, Maddie. I got your e-mail. I brought a microwave. Do you have the TV? I thought we could put it over . . ."

Maddie looks around. "This room is so small, how are we going to fit . . ."

"I know; can you believe it? I thought maybe we could bunk the beds?" Amy looks at Maddie's face. " . . . or not. We could put things on top of the dresser?"

Maddie's grandmother looks at the girls and the room. "I think you guys will figure it out. After a while you'll hardly even notice how small it is. Do you want to unpack now? Do you want some help?"

"I think I'd just like to do it myself. Let's go down and get the rest of the boxes from the car."

Maddie and her grandmother go down to get two boxes from the back seat of the car. As they walk back upstairs to her dorm room her grandmother says, "One of these boxes contains your favorite snack foods. You let me know if you need anything else once you unpack."

"Thanks, Nana, for all your help."

Maddie and her grandmother walk into the dorm room and put the boxes down by her bed.

"Well Maddie, if you don't think you need me for anything. I should probably be heading back. You know I don't like driving in the dark."

Maddie walks her grandmother to the door. Her grandmother puts her arm around her. "Amy seems nice—a little talkative, but that's good. You're going to be fine here. I can feel it. So call me tonight before you go to bed and let me know how orientation goes today. You know I'll miss our little bedside chats and our late night check ins. So call me—you know, tuck me in."

"Right Nana, I see through you. Yes, I'll call."

Maddie's grandmother, with tears in her eyes, reaches over and tucks a strand of hair behind Maddie's ear. "I love you."

Maddie turns and hugs her grandmother. "I love you too. Bye."

Maddie watches as her grandmother walks down the hallway, then turns and waves goodbye as she disappears down the stairs. Maddie lets out a big sigh, and goes to her bed. She puts the suitcases on the floor, takes her bedding, and starts making up her bed.

Amy asks, "So, what do you think of Evanston? I think it's awesome. I'm from Iowa—oh, that's right you already know that. They don't have cities like Chicago in Iowa, and we are so close to Chicago. I feel like I'm in a movie or something. I mean is this for real or what? I mean, did you notice all the cell phones? Everywhere I look someone is talking on a cell phone. Do you have a cell phone? I'm going to ask my mom and dad to give me a cell phone for my birthday, which is next month. They wouldn't let me have one when I was in high school. They said it would distract from my studying. But now I'm in college I should be . . . well anyway. The streets here are so crowded, people everywhere. I just love all the people. Don't you? I'm a music major. Back home they say I could be another Christina Aguilera or Jessica Simpson. How about you?"

"Well, I . . ."

"I'm sorry. I'm talking too much. When I'm nervous or excited I just can't shut up. I mean I've already written ten pages in my journal. I'm doing it again. So how about you? What's your major, where are you from, you know all the standard stuff?"

Maddie shrugs. "I'm not sure about my major. This semester, I'm taking English Lit, a theatre class, psychology 101, and some other generals. I'm just undeclared for the time being, I want to explor . . ."

Amy interrupts, "That's a good idea. I'll probably change my major every semester. So where are you from again?"

"Wisconsin . . ."

"Oh, That's right you're a "cheese head.""

"A what? I've never heard that . . ."

As Maddie is talking, a handsome, dark-haired boy comes barging into the room, dressed in jeans and a torn t-shirt. Maddie and Amy stop what they are doing and stare at him.

"Hey, Tony, come on what's keeping . . . ?" He sees Maddie and thinks *look at those eyes, and that tight little body with curves in all the right places.* "No, you are not Tony. You are de-fi-nite-ly not Tony. I must be on the wrong floor. What floor is this?"

Nick is staring at Maddie so intensely; she is speechless. So Amy answers, "It's the fourth floor . . ."

Nick, still looking at Maddie. "Oh, Tony's on the third floor. And your name is . . . ?"

"Her name is Maddie and I'm Amy . . ."

"Hi, Maddie, Amy, I'm Nick, I live on the first floor. Room 111, come down sometime, I'll show you around."

Maddie finishes making the bed and sits down on her bed, trying to break away from Nick's intense stare. She opens a suitcase, and starts putting her clothes on the bed, not looking at him.

"Sure, we'll come down later, won't we, Maddie?"

Maddie ignores her and Nick and continues unpacking.

Nick turns to leave. "I'll look forward to it. Later."

Amy, still looking at the door where Nick had just been standing, whispers, "Wow, he was . . . he was so . . . he was so the type my mother told me to stay away from. Those eyes, that hair . . . he sure had eyes for you."

Maddie, still focused on unpacking, pulls out a picture frame from her suitcase. There is a nightstand between the beds where Amy has put her family's picture.

Watching Maddie, Amy moves the picture of her family closer to her bed. "Here, I'll make some room for your picture. This is my family. That's my brother. He's seventeen and he loves to be kissed. I think he has had a different girlfriend every month since he was in ninth grade. My dad is the greatest. He makes me laugh so hard my stomach hurts. My mom, I already miss her cookies and her smell . . . I'm sorry, I'm doing it again. This is the first time I've been so far away from my family. Oh, look—my pants are still covered with cat hair from Max. How about you? Do you have any brothers and sisters?"

"No, it's just me."

"So, was that your mother? Couldn't your dad come? When my parents dropped me off there was absolutely no room for anyone in here."

"No, that was my grandmother."

Maddie puts her picture down on the nightstand and walks toward the door. "I just remembered I forgot to bring in the TV. It's still in the car. I need to go out and call my nana. I'll be back in a couple of minutes." A few minutes later Maddie walks into the room carrying a TV set.

"Luckily my nana saw the TV in her rearview mirror and turned around and came back. She pulled up to the curb just as I was calling her. I guess we can put it on the dresser."

Amy gets up and helps Maddie with the TV set. Amy looks at her watch, "Oh, we need to hurry, the first orientation session starts in fifteen minutes. I think it said we meet downstairs in the lounge."

Maddie and Amy hurry downstairs to their first college orientation.

Chapter 9

Amy and Maddie, wrapped in big fluffy towels after their showers, walk into their dorm room and stop to look around: The nightstand is between the beds, the desks are against the wall by Maddie's bed and one by Amy's bed, the dresser is across the room with their TV set on it, and on the floor, next to the dresser, is their dorm size refrigerator with the microwave on top. Their bottom desk drawers now hold a variety of microwave snacks.

Maddie says proudly, "I like how we set up the room. It feels so homey."

Amy looks around. "I know, it feels bigger—oh, look at the time. We need to get ready for the party tonight. I wonder why the party is on a Sunday night?"

Maddie picks up her purse. "I don't know, I don't think it's his birthday. Anyway I don't want to stay out too late. We've got that test in the morning."

Amy turns on the CD player and the room fills with music. She grabs her nail polish, sits on her bed, and starts painting her nails.

Maddie walks over to the mirror by her desk, takes her makeup out of her purse, and starts putting on eyeliner, mascara and blush. "I wonder if Nick will be there tonight?"

Amy laughs. "Nick miss a party? From what I hear, I don't think it's considered a party unless he's there."

Amy blows on her nails and says, "I just heard today, he was arrested once, possession of some drugs. Ooh, I wonder what it was? He is soo hot, those black curls around his ears, his eyes the way they look, so mysterious; like he's hiding something way down deep inside and all you want to do is go down there and find out what it is. Secrets, dangerous secrets that seem to pull you closer to ..."

"AMY!!!!"

"Oh, I'm sorry, I just got carried away."

"Are you after him?"

Amy looks shocked.

"Who me? No way, I don't think I'm his type. He wants someone that's ... that's." She looks Maddie up and down, "That's more like you."

Amy starts brushing her hair. "Have you ever noticed when he walks through campus, how all the girls just turn and watch him?"

"Stop it, Amy, he's just a guy, he burps, he acts stupid just like every other boy we've ever known. Was that a knock on the door?"

The girls stop talking. They hear another knock on the door. Maddie looks at Amy and asks loudly, "Who is it?"

"It's Nick. Hey Maddie, are you going to Paul's party?"

Maddie turns and looks at Amy. Amy covers her mouth so she doesn't scream, then says to Maddie. "Answer him."

"Yeah, me and Amy are getting ready ..."

Nick smiles outside the dorm door. "Look, can I come in, I ... ?"

Maddie looks at Amy. "No! Some of us are only half-dressed."

Still smiling, Nick says, "That's OK, maybe I can help you ... ?"

"Go away! Come back in a half hour."

"Are you sure? I mean I could ..."

Both Maddie and Amy say at the same time, "No!!!"

"OK, OK, I'll see you in half an hour."

"Oh my god, Maddie. Are you sure you want to go with him?"

"I can handle him. He doesn't pull me into that, what did you call it, that 'mysterious, secret place.' He is just a guy who thinks he's all that. I think it will be fun. Besides, you're going to come with us, right?"

Amy slips on her jeans. "OK, but once we get to the party you are on your own, Maddie."

A half hour later Nick knocks on the door. "Are you ladies ready? Your chariot awaits."

Maddie opens the door and looks at Nick. "Seriously, did you just say that?"

Nick, Maddie, and Amy walk to Nick's car.

Maddie looks at the car. "This is what you call a chariot?"

Laughing, Nick says, "Hey, give me a break."

Ten minutes later they pull up in front of an old house that has been divided into small apartments. Nick says, "Here we are."

Maddie, Nick and Amy walk into Paul's apartment and look around; it is crowded. In the living room, students are dancing or standing around drinking and smoking. Others are making out on sagging couches. There are chips and dip on a table made of stacked bricks and a sheet of plywood. Beer kegs and twelve-packs of soda are lined up in the kitchen.

Amy looks at Maddie. "I'll see you later; I'm going to go talk to Justin and Tony."

Tony sees Amy approaching and puts his arm around her. "Great party, don't you think? I like the CDs you gave to Paul for the party. Do you want a beer Amy, Justin? I'm going to get myself one."

Justin hesitates, and then says, "No thanks, I think one is my limit tonight. I'm starting a new job tomorrow morning working in the bakery. I have to be there by 5:00 a.m. and then we are having a test in my 9:00 class. I think I need to keep a clear head."

Tony sees Maddie and Nick. Tony yells over to Nick and waves.

"Yo, Nick!" Tony nudges Justin with his elbow. "Now, that's a man who never has a clear head."

Maddie is standing talking with Nick. "Nick, I can't."

"Aw come on, Maddie?"

"No! I've got a test tomorrow, maybe some other time."

Nick calls loudly to Tony as he walks away angrily. "Hey Tony, come on—let's get this party started, you too, Justin."

Maddie just stands there, wondering what just happened.

Suddenly the party seems to slow down and take on a bluish light. Maddie hears her mom's voice. "Maaaaaaaaaaaaddie . . . Maaaaaaaaaaaaaddie."

Then the bluish light fades, the party comes back and she can hear the music playing. Amy walks over to Maddie saying, "What's wrong, Maddie? You look funny."

"What, oh, I'm fine. I just felt a little queasy, but it's gone now."

"Good, let's get you something to drink. Tony got me this beer from the kitchen."

Someone turns up the music and more people start dancing. Nick walks over to Maddie. "Come on Maddie, let's dance." Nick grabs Maddie and they start slow dancing. Nick is using every part of his body. Maddie stiffens up but as the music continues she begins to relax. Nick whispers in her ear.

Later that night Maddie stumbles into her dorm room. She is drunk and starts singing loudly. "Do you love me, now that I can dance. Watch me now."

"Maddie is that you?"

Maddie slurs. "Who else would be coming in your room at three in the morning?"

Amy sits up and looks at Maddie. "Are you drunk?"

Maddie staggers to her bed. "I'm not sure but the room is spinning. I think I better lie down."

"Where did you and Nick go when you left the party? I thought you'd be home hours ago. We've got that test and I thought you said you'd be home early."

"I know, then Nick talked me into going to some friend's apartment, his friend wasn't even there. He kissed me, his lips were so soft; it was the perfect kiss. Like you see in the movies. Just a little tongue . . . yeah, it gave me the shivers, the hair on the back of my neck was standing up, and then he brushed his lips on my neck. I thought I was going to melt into the cushions and disappear. But then I got mad at him. Yes, I did, those lips started to travel to places never traveled before on this body. So I got up and walked home and here I am. I don't think I should see him anymore, I mean, those dark eyes . . . so dangerous . . . when I think of those eyes my whole body . . . Oh shit, I think I need to . . . I think I'm going to . . ." Maddie leans over the bed and throws up.

Chapter 10

The next day Maddie and Amy walk into their Psych class and sit down.

Amy looks at Maddie. "Are you ready for this? You still look a little green around the gills. I wish I had started studying sooner. I'm just going to fail."

"No, you're not. You always get A's. Relax, you'll do fine. And I feel fine."

Justin, a tall, dark-skinned boy with dreadlocks, walks in and sits down next to Maddie. "Hey, Maddie, you didn't stay very long at the party last night. I wanted to get a chance to at least have one dance with you. But then you were gone."

"I know, Nick wanted to show me something on campus."

"Instead of giving me a dance, do you want to study together for our science quiz tomorrow? All those terms to memorize. I need some help."

Maddie smiles. "Yeah, let's. We can quiz each other. I can meet you at the student union at around 3:30."

"Let's make it 5:00 and I'll treat you to a pizza."

"OK, let's meet by the computer lab."

Nick enters and walks up to Justin. "Hey, man, how about letting me sit next to my girl?"

Maddie with a frown says, "I'm not your girl."

Nick stares at Justin. "Come on Justin, my man, be a sport."

Justin looks up at Nick. "Look, I'm sorry, I didn't know she was your girl."

"I'm not his girl! Justin, don't . . ."

Justin gets up and sits in another chair saying, "I'll see you later, Maddie."

Nick sits down by Maddie and looks at her. "Why is he seeing you later? I thought . . ."

"Nick, you are so rude. Who do you think you are . . . ?" The professor enters the classroom, a stack of tests in his arms.

"Shhhh, Maddie, the teach is here to open our heads, fill us with garbage and the newest psychological torture and then see if we've learned anything with his 'amazing' test."

Chapter 11

A couple of weeks later, Maddie is sitting at her desk studying when Amy walks into the room.

Maddie looks at Amy. "Hey Amy, what time is your birthday party tonight?"

"8:00, Tony said that was the earliest he could have it at his place."

"Cool, I'll let Nick know."

Amy looks at Maddie. "I know it's none of my business, but I can't believe you're still seeing Nick after what he pulled."

Maddie smiles, "Well, it really isn't any of your business. But since it's you, I won't take offense. Remember, he did apologize and bring me those flowers. I said I'd give him another chance. I made it clear that I wasn't 'his' girl. He's been pretty good lately. He doesn't claim ownership if I study with Justin or go out for pizza with him. Nick's cool now."

Amy looks at her watch, grabs her purse, and stands up. "Just be careful, Maddie. Anyway, I've got to go. My parents are meeting me downstairs, they are taking me out to dinner. Can you believe they drove all the way here for my birthday? My mom said she needed to do some big city shopping too. So I can't stay out too late tonight because tomorrow we are going shopping. Anyway, see you at the party."

A few hours later, Nick and Maddie walk across the quad to Amy's birthday party, carrying bags of chips. Tony lives in a dorm room with a big living room, kitchen, and three bedrooms. A birthday banner is hanging up on the living room wall. Students are everywhere eating, drinking, and dancing. There's a couple on the couch making out. The three bedrooms are open. Kegs are set up in one room. Food and twelve-packs of soda are on the kitchen counters.

As they walk into the party Nick says, "Look Maddie, let's not stay too long. I got something I want to show you . . ."

"Come on Nick, don't pull that again. We just got here, it's Amy's party. She's my roommate, I can't just leave early."

Nick goes into the kitchen and gets a couple of beers. He hands one to Maddie and then sees Tony and Jason.

Tony says, "Yo, Nick, over here."

Nick walks over to where Tony and Jason are standing with a group of boys. Maddie takes a drink from the beer bottle. She hears Nick whisper to the boys, "Hey, you guys I'm flush, I mean, I got the stuff. How much you want?"

Maddie feels a strange sensation. Nick looks over his shoulder at her. *Then the bluish light is there, the party fading away, familiar music is playing. Maddie thinks she hears Rickie say, 'Hey Lizzy, come over here . . . '* Then Nick speaks louder. "I said Maddie, are you deaf? Come over here."

Amy sees Maddie and walks over to her.

"Maddie, are you OK? You look like you've seen a ghost . . ."

Suddenly a balloon pops from somewhere. Maddie runs out of the party. She jogs through the quad to her dorm room, then opens the closet door, sits down, and starts rocking.

A few minutes later Amy comes running into the dorm room looking for her. "Maddie, where are you? I saw you run in here."

Amy hears a noise in the closet. She looks in. "Maddie? What are you doing in there? Why did you run off like that?"

"Amy, please, just go away. Please?"

"But Maddie, you're scaring me, what's wrong?"

"Please, just leave me alone."

Maddie gets up, pushes past Amy, and runs out of the dorm. She finds herself in the college square. The square is empty. She sits down, covers her face with her hands and begins rocking. After a minute or two she stops and looks up at the sky. "Are you happy, Mom? Can you see what you've created? When will the ghosts go away? Do you know I can't sleep in my dorm room unless I've checked the lock four times? When I'm in the bathroom I break out in a sweat because I can't lock the door. When I'm scared I will go and sit in my closet with the door closed because it's the only way I can feel truly safe. I had to tell my roommate I was doing an experiment for my psych class. Tonight she found me there again . . . I can't stand the shame. I've grown up creating a fantasy world to get through it. I can't even tell my roommate or anyone else about you. I am too ashamed . . . I mean what would I say? 'Oh, my mother, she was a drug dealer who was addicted to men that beat her.' Who is my father, Mom, who? Do you even know? I was locked in that closet so many times, listening to Ricky slap you . . . you crying . . . him saying 'Come on Lizzy, save some for the paying customers.'"

As Maddie is talking, Justin runs into the college square looking for her. He sees her and slows down, walking quietly so he doesn't interrupt her. He stops, standing behind her and waits for her to stop talking.

Maddie continues on her rant. "And that day, I was only six years old and I heard gunshots . . . I tried to crawl into myself so far so I couldn't feel the pain. I wanted to live in an old woman's shoe and crawl in the toe so I didn't have to hear or see or feel what was happening around me. And to think I was starting to turn into you, with Nick; then I was drinking and now it turns out he's into drugs. I don't want to be weak like you. I don't want men like Ricky. Oh, I hate you so much . . . I love you so much. Do you remember the time we went down the slide together? It felt so good to be sitting on your lap and you were smiling, laughing. I loved your laugh, it was light and airy and beautiful.

I loved feeling your arms around me with your breath brushing my ear. It was so warm . . . but then Ricky would come and I was just another rock on the playground. A rock you stepped on or put away in a closet until you needed it for something. Mom, I just wanted you to love me back, to smile at me, and hug me. I just wanted you."

Maddie finally finishes and puts her face back in her hands and cries. Justin, still standing there, isn't sure what to do. Finally he sits down next to Maddie.

"Maddie, are you all right? I've been looking all over for you."

Maddie startled, looks at Justin. "Oh, my God. I didn't hear you come up. You scared me."

Justin looks at Maddie. "Is it OK if I just sit here with you?"

"I don't think I . . . look, I just need to be alone right now."

"Maddie, I won't say anything. I'll just listen. I promise, no matter what you say I won't go away. People say I'm a great listener. And I'm not afraid of stories about gunshots . . ."

"Gunshots—how long were you listening . . . ?"

"A couple of minutes. I was going to leave because I didn't want to eavesdrop, but then I heard you talk about gunshots. And then you were talking to your mother. You seemed so sad, so lonely. I just couldn't leave you like that. Please, can I sit here with you?"

Maddie sits there not saying anything.

"I'm sorry Maddie, I'm sorry I heard, but I'm more sorry to know someone has made you so sad."

Maddie says very quietly almost to herself, "No one else knows."

"No else knows what, Maddie?"

"I have never told anyone about my mother, except my grandmother and a counselor. I could never tell any of my friends growing up; it was too hard and too painful. Plus I was always afraid they would look at me like I was a freak. But tonight . . . at the party . . . Nick . . . the balloon popping, it just came flooding back all at once. It was too much."

"I'm not looking at you like you're a freak."

Maddie looks at Justin. "That's true, you're not."

Very slowly and gently Justin kisses her. After the kiss Maddie sighs and puts her head on his shoulder. Justin puts his arm around her and kisses the top of her head.

Chapter 12

Maddie's alarm goes off at 8:00 a.m. the next day. She wakes up and notices that Amy isn't in the room. She gets out her cell phone and calls her grandmother. "Nana, I'm sorry for calling so early . . . no everything's fine. I was just wondering if you're not busy, could you come visit today? It's Sunday and I only have a little homework and I thought . . . I mean . . . I miss you. We could shop or see a movie? You can? Great. So what time? OK, I'll see you around noon. And can you bring the collage on my bedroom wall?"

As Maddie hangs up her phone, Amy comes in, and for once when she sees Maddie, she doesn't say anything. She quietly goes and sits on her bed avoiding Maddie's eyes.

"Hey, Amy, about last night, I'm really sorry, I just got freaked out and . . ."

"No Maddie, I'm sorry, I shouldn't have tried to force you to . . ."

"No, really, I appreciate you cared enough to leave your own birthday party to find me, it was really nice of you. But I just needed time to work through some stuff."

Amy looks at Maddie. "I know what you mean, Maddie. At home I had this treehouse in my backyard and sometimes when I would get upset, I mean so upset, I couldn't talk, which I'm sure you know, means I must be upset. I mean if I couldn't talk . . . well anyway. I would go sit in my treehouse. One time I think I sat there all afternoon. My brother tried to get me to come down. It just made me angrier. So anyway I'm sorry."

"Oh, don't be sorry—really thanks, Amy. Do you want to go get some breakfast?"

"Well, I just had breakfast with my family and they are coming back in a couple of hours to go shopping. But I could probably go for another cup of coffee at the Pancake House down the block."

After breakfast Amy and Maddie take a walk around the campus. Maddie is starting to feel better. Then she sees her grandmother's car. Her grandmother is looking for a parking spot. Finally she finds one and pulls in. Amy and Maddie run over to her car.

"Wow Nana, you made it in record time."

Maddie's grandmother gets out of the car. "Hi Amy. Well, Maddie, I got the feeling something must have happened."

"Nothing happened, Nana ... well, I mean ... oh, how do you always know?"

Amy waves to someone across the street and turns to Maddie and her grandmother. "Look, there's my mom, we're shopping for my birthday and then going to lunch. I'll see you later." Amy runs across the street to where her mom is standing.

"I always know young lady because I'm your grandmother. Now come on, let's go up to your dorm room, sit down, and then you can tell me all about it. Then we'll go shopping. Oh, and here is your collage."

Maddie takes the collage and walks up four flights of stairs, with her grandmother following behind her panting. "I hope next year you can get a dorm room on the 1st or 2nd floor."

When they get to Maddie's room they sit down on her bed.

"So out with it, Maddie, what happened?"

Maddie looks around. "Wait, I want to hang up my collage. How about over my desk?"

Her grandmother smiles. "That is a perfect spot."

Maddie takes some hanging putty and hangs up her collage.

"Now, I'm ready to talk." Maddie sits down next to her grandmother. "Last night there was a birthday party for Amy and I went with Nick, that guy I told you I've been seeing. When we got there, he said something that sounded like Ricky and I was right back in that closet with the musty jackets, the spider webs tickling my arms, the darkness all around me and then a balloon popped and I freaked out. I ran out and came here and hid in the closet. I was so scared, scared because I was drinking beer and Nick was dealing drugs and suddenly I felt like I was my mother. I was petrified and then my roommate found me. I got embarrassed and ran out and sat on the bench in the Quad. I was so scared; I was back there again. Oh Nana, I don't want to be like my mother."

"You are not like your mother . . ."

"Nana, It's like I'm afraid of myself and what I might do. I mean I was so attracted to Nick and I found out he's a drug dealer, I was drinking . . ."

"Oh my god, Maddie, you are not your mother. You are in college for the first time. There will always be young men, drugs, and alcohol thrown at you. It's what you do that counts. Maddie, you left the party, you didn't stay. Your 'ghosts' helped you realize it didn't feel right. Sometimes the ghosts from your past will come up and shove you so hard it'll take your breath away. The ghosts will help you make the right decisions. Your mother had ghosts but she ran away from them, always going too fast to listen to them. Not you Maddie, you listened and you knew. There is absolutely no way you are your mother."

"My father, Nana, who is my father? I keep wondering, does he even know about me? I really want to know. Every time I bring it up, the subject gets changed. I need to know ..."

Amy comes running into the room. "I'm sorry to interrupt, but I forgot my purse. My mom's downstairs, so I really got to run. Bye." Amy grabs her purse and runs out the door.

"Have fun with your mom, Amy."

Maddie's grandmother looks at Maddie. "Are you sure you want to talk about all this now?"

Maddie settles back on the bed. "Yes, I am. First I want to know more about my grandfather. You've told me the music stories but what about the 'you and him' stories? The real stories—who was he really?"

"Your grandfather was probably the sexiest . . ."

"EEEEOOOOWWW, Nana!"

Her grandmother chuckles. "You asked. Anyway, he was so talented. He could play the guitar like his fingers were just an extension of the strings. And he had this voice that . . . well anyway. We fell in love and I traveled with his band. Then I got pregnant and our life changed. He didn't want to raise a child on the road. So we settled in Wisconsin. I got a job at the high school and your grandfather found a job at the music store. He played in a band on the weekends. Then I got pregnant again, your mom had just turned five. I told your grandfather and he started to change . . . he said the pressure of two children. Well, he'd stay out all night and come home drunk. One night we had the worst fight. I ran away from him and fell down the stairs . . . I lost the baby."

"Nana, you never told me you had a miscarriage."

Her grandmother sits a minute and then says, "Oh honey, I was so sad. I was five months pregnant. After that things were never the same between your grandfather and me. He tried for a while to be a good husband and father. But then the band was starting to tour. Sometimes he'd be gone for two months; part of me was glad. But your mother, she looked up to him so. She was his little girl. He'd bring her home presents from every state he played in. His drinking was getting worse and then he started in on drugs. The worst was cocaine, he'd try to control it, but . . ."

"My grandfather was a drug addict? You never told me that. So maybe my mom got it from him?"

"I don't know honey, I thought I protected your mom from all that back then, but I don't know."

Maddie looks at the collage on the wall. "It sounds like Mom was trying to be like my grandfather."

"Maybe or it was because she missed him. Because eventually he just stopped coming home from touring. The last time your mother saw him he promised he'd be home for her sixteenth birthday. It was going to be the best birthday ever, according to her. He was going to take her to the fanciest restaurant and then to find her a car—she was turning sixteen, after all. She put on the dress he brought her from New Orleans, a yellow sundress with thin straps and a hem too short to matter. She looked beautiful standing there at the front window waiting for him. Her auburn hair fell just so across her face. He didn't show up or call."

Maddie sits quiet for a moment, a tear in her eye. "That is so sad. No wonder my mom . . . I mean my grandfather was a . . . was a . . . oh I really don't like him, what he did to my mom is unforgivable. She was only sixteen, my poor mother."

"I know Maddie. After that your mother just went wild. It's like all those boys were going to fill the hole left by her father. Then just before she graduated from high school, he suddenly showed up. His band was playing in a club downtown. Your mom and I went to see him play. Your mom was so happy to see him. He said he would come and see her the next day, but he didn't show up. Then a month after she graduated she just took off. I didn't see her for over a year. I tried to find her but I couldn't, then she came home. She was five months pregnant and she was hungry. She wouldn't tell me where she'd been. Then four months later you were born. You were the most beautiful baby I'd ever seen. Your eyes were so deep blue and you were bald, not a stitch of hair on that head. And you were fat and pink and so very, very, cuddly . . ."

"She didn't tell you anything . . . nothing about where she'd been? Or who she'd been with?"

Her grandmother takes Maddie's hand. "No, honey, nothing. I kept asking who the father was. But she wouldn't tell me. She said it was none of my business."

"Nana, do you think she knew who it was? I mean was she with so many boys that she just . . . ?"

"I don't know, honey. Your mom was stubborn and good at keeping secrets. Then she took off again. Oh Maddie, I lost so much during those years, but all of it was healed when I found you again."

"Who do I look like in our family?"

Her grandmother laughs. "You know who you look like. We've talked about this before."

"I know but I just want to hear about it again, my eyes are like . . ."

"Your mother's and your mouth. You have your grandfather's thick hair. You're short and petite like my mother's side of the family. You have your mother's temperament, strong, sensitive and smart as a whip. You have my insight into others. I've never mentioned this before because I didn't know if you were ready to hear it, but I think your blonde hair and freckles probably come from your father. No one in our two families was blonde and no freckles anywhere."

Maddie touches her hair. "Like my father's . . . ?"

Her grandmother squeezes her hand. "So honey, just hang on to the good things you got from your mom and know you won't turn into who she became. You are your own person. You let your ghosts help you; you didn't run away. You called me, you reached out. You knew what to do."

"I'm really glad you told me about my grandfather. I never realized that you had . . ."

"Ghosts. Yes, Maddie, I did, but I had you to take care of, it kept the ghosts away. Late at night when you were asleep I'd cry and then I'd pray for the strength to be all you needed. And look at you now, all grown up—enough of this talking, let's go shopping!"

"Nana, you always know the right thing to do or say. Where do you want to go first?"

Maddie's grandmother smiles. "Let's go to Macy's, I heard they are having a one day fall sale. I can get that sweater I've had my eye on in their catalogue."

Maddie says, "OK. Then we can go to that French restaurant you like so well for dinner."

"Great idea. Let's go, Maddie."

Maddie and her grandmother stand up and head for the door.

Maddie looks at her grandmother. "By the way I sent a text to Nick. I told him I didn't want to go out with him anymore. And I think I like this other guy, his name is Justin. He kind of reminds me of you. The way he listens. You'll have to meet him."

"I'd like that. You'll have to bring him home during Christmas break."

Chapter 13

Outside the window everything is covered in snow. There is frost in the corners of the windowpanes. Justin and Maddie sit cuddled together on her grandmother's couch, looking out the windows. A Christmas tree is brightly lit in the corner by the fireplace. Presents are wrapped with brightly colored paper and tied up with ribbons and bows.

"Your grandmother is the greatest! Where does she come up with all those card games?"

"I don't know, I think she makes them up."

Justin and Maddie sit quietly in their own thoughts.

"What's going on, Maddie? You seem a little distant today, a lot of one-word answers. I've been trying to. . ."

"I know, I've been feeling a little weird today. I think it's because of this dream I had last night. It was so real, it keeps creeping into my mind and I feel so . . ."

"Sometimes talking about a dream can take the charge out of it and help it disappear from your mind."

Maddie looks out the window. "That's just it. I don't know if I want this one to leave me. I think I want to put it in a bottle or a jar so I can dream it whenever I want to. It feels almost too precious to say out loud, so fragile."

Maddie's grandmother comes into the living room carrying a basket of laundry. She sits down in the chair by Justin and

Maddie and starts folding clothes. Maddie and Justin sit quietly watching her. She looks up and sees them staring at her. "I'm sorry, am I interrupting?"

"No, in fact I'm glad you're here. I was just going to tell Justin about the dream I had last night. Now I can tell you both."

Maddie's grandmother stops folding the clothes and looks at Maddie. "Oh, I just love your dreams. We've learned so much from them."

"I know. Well, in my dream, I saw a man. I mean, I didn't see his face or anything, just the back of his head. He came into my bedroom, the bedroom I had when I was a little girl. He leaned over, kissed me on my forehead, and said 'Little one, you deserve a whole lot of these.' Then he kissed me again and tucked my blanket around me. When he stood up and turned to leave, I could smell something kind of like green apples."

As Maddie is telling the dream, her grandmother stops folding the laundry and stares at Maddie like she is seeing a ghost.

"I'm not sure what that all means. But when I woke up I felt I was loved. There was this gentle man who tucked me in and kissed me goodnight. I wanted him to stay and tell me a story in the dream, but I looked up and he was gone. I keep thinking there is this man out there, and does he even know I exist. But in the dream he was so real. Nana, what do you think it means?"

Maddie looks at her grandmother. "Nana, what's wrong? You look like you've seen a ghost."

"Well Maddie, as you were talking I . . . I remembered something. Right after you came to live with me, your grandfather's band was in a town nearby. I couldn't believe he was suddenly standing on my doorstep. I almost didn't let him in. But I thought I should tell him about your mother and you. So suddenly I had five hungry men in my house looking for food and a bed for the night. I told your grandfather about your mother; he actually cried. I told him about you and that you were upstairs sleeping. He went upstairs to see you and when he came down he looked haunted. They left the first thing in the morning before you and I were awake. He left a note on the kitchen table that said something like: I'm sorry, I wish I had been a better husband and father. Maddie looks just like her mother. Then he said in the note that Lizzy had traveled with the band when she was eighteen and he wished he had protected her. I never heard from him again. And what is really strange, is your grandfather always smelled like green apples. It was this bar soap he used. I forgot about that night. You don't think . . . someone from the band . . . ?"

"So my dream could have been a memory about my grandfather? I'm just going to hang on to my dream and those feelings. It felt like he loved me."

"But Maddie, your grandfather might know . . ."

Maddie stands up. "Nana, where are your photo albums? I want to see them. Are there some pictures of the band? Maybe we can find someone with blonde hair and freckles."

Maddie's grandmother gets up. "Sit down, Maddie, I'll get them." Her grandmother walks over to the cabinet, opens the door, and pulls out two photo albums. She brings them over to the coffee table in front of Justin and Maddie, and puts them down. Then she sits next to Maddie. They open up the first photo album and there is her grandfather's band. There are five members of the band. A bass player, a drummer, a rhythm guitar player, a lead guitar player and singer who was Maddie's grandfather, and a keyboard player, who also sang backup. There were two band members with blonde hair and a few freckles. One was the drummer; the other was the keyboard player.

Maddie's grandmother looks at Maddie and then the picture, then back at Maddie. "Look at the keyboard player, is there a resemblance or is it just me?"

Maddie and Justin look. Justin gasps. "Look at his ears, and his nose turns up a little, just like Maddie's."

"What's his name, Nana, do you remember his name?"

"I sure do, his name is Keith James. He was the youngest player in the band. I think he joined the band shortly before Lizzy took off for a year. I remember he was a big deal because he was so young and so talented. He might have been just nineteen or twenty when he joined the band."

"That time my grandfather visited, was he still with the band?"

"You know, come to think of it. He wasn't there. I think I remember your grandfather mentioning that he'd just recently quit the band."

"I think I would like to see if I can find him."

"Of course, Maddie, I'll help."

The next morning Maddie sits curled up on the couch in her pajamas and bathrobe, sipping a cup of coffee.

Justin comes in looking for her. "Oh, there you are. I went out for a walk in the nature center and when I got back I went upstairs, saw your bedroom door open . . ."

Yawning, Maddie says, "I don't know when I've slept so late. How was your walk?"

Maddie sips her coffee.

Justin sits down next to her on the couch. "It was refreshing and invigorating. I've loved being here and spending Christmas with you and your grandmother. If I wasn't here with you, I'd probably be sitting at my sister's, bored out of my mind. Do you know why I'm so attracted to you? Besides the obvious beauty and intelligence, it's your fire and strength. Your ability to stand up and face what comes your way, and your desire to find the answers. I love your depth of feeling, the passion I saw in you that night on the quad was so beautiful. You were so alive."

Justin slowly turns toward Maddie. "I told you before my mother died when I was five. But I haven't told you how. In my family no one will say out loud what she died from, so I don't know what to think or how to feel. I have suspected for a long time she did it to herself. I've always thought my father was having an affair with his new wife while my mother was alive. None of this has ever been talked about. I watch you and your grandmother and how you talk about things, even the hard ones. You are so lucky that way. You don't walk on eggshells to keep the secrets from each other. You don't have to always pretend. I love being with you, Maddie, and your grandmother. It feels so real."

Maddie's grandmother pokes her head in the room and says, "We love being with you too, Justin. Now that everyone is finally up, why don't you come in the kitchen and enjoy my homemade caramel rolls?"

"OK, we'll be there in a few minutes."

As Maddie's grandmother goes back in the kitchen, Maddie curls Justin into her arms.

"Justin, close your eyes, relax, let me tell you a story about a very handsome prince." Maddie begins sliding her fingers across Justin's forehead very lightly and playing with his hair. "Let's see . . . once upon a time there was a handsome prince, he had eyes the color of dark chocolate and hair the color of a fine mocha. He walked with a gentle strength that no woman could resist. His voice mesmerized everyone he spoke to. He wandered his kingdom far and wide, looking for that princess who could look into his eyes and see his soul and love him and all his secrets."

Chapter 14

Amy and Maddie are sitting in the student union having lunch. Their table is by the windows and they look out over the campus square. All the tables are full, with students talking excitedly about finals being over soon and their summer plans.

"Can you believe it, Maddie? One week and we will have completed our first year of college."

Maddie plays with her cell phone. "I know, and what an eventful year it has been. Are you going to see Tony this summer? Will he visit you in Iowa or are you getting a summer job here to be by him? Come on, have you decided?"

"I've decided. I'm going home, I just miss my family too much. I told Tony after class today. He says he'll come visit on the weekends. It's only about a six hour drive."

Amy looks at Maddie. "How about you? Did you hear anything yet from the private investigator about your father?"

"Well, actually, I got a call from him right after you left for class this morning. The man, who I think might be my father, lives here in Chicago. My grandmother is on her way. We are going to contact him this afternoon."

"Wow Maddie, that's big."

Maddie looks at her cell phone. "I know, but I'm holding back a little, I'm not positive it's him. We'll probably know soon."

Justin walks in and sits at the table with Maddie and Amy.

"Hi, you two." Justin looks at Maddie. "I got your message—are you nervous?"

Maddie taps her cell phone lightly on the table. "Like I just told Amy, I'm kind of neutral until I know for sure. My grandmother will be here pretty soon."

As Maddie's talking her cell phone rings.

She quickly presses accept. "You're here, OK, I'll be there in a minute."

Maddie stands up. "I've got to go you guys. My grandmother's here and we're going to see the private investigator, and then maybe see the man who could be my father."

A tear escapes from Maddie's eye as she turns to go. Justin stands up and pulls her into a hug. "Here's one for the road. Know I'm with you every step of the way. Good luck. I'll see you later."

Maddie kisses Justin on the cheek. "Thanks. I'll call you."

Amy says loudly, "Good luck, Maddie." Then she sits down with Justin and watches Maddie walk away.

Amy starts talking nonstop. "Maddie told me the story about her mom and stuff. I don't know how she's going to handle this. I mean meeting your father for the first time when you're nineteen. Especially when you were told you didn't have a father. Then realizing when you're older, that you have to have a father, but not knowing who he could possibly be. Your mother's gone and there's no one else who really knows. Then suddenly from a dream you realize that you might know who your father is. And now she's going to meet him. What if it's not him? What if it is him and he doesn't want to see her? What if he sees her and . . . ?"

"Calm down, Amy, she'll do fine. I really think he is her father, and I believe he'll want to meet her. And once he meets her, he will want her in his life."

A couple of hours later, Maddie and her grandmother pull up to a brownstone in an area of Chicago called Wicker Park. After seeing the investigator who gave them the address and phone number, Maddie's grandmother called and talked to Keith James. He was curious enough to meet with them. So now they are here.

"It's OK, Maddie, relax. Try not to let your thoughts run away with you. Let's go meet him and see what happens."

Maddie takes a deep breath. "OK, let's do it."

They walk up the stairs to the door and ring the bell. The brownstone is three stories high and looks like it's been newly renovated, with a front door that is a rich dark green. They hear footsteps, and a ten-year-old boy with blonde hair and freckles across his nose opens the door. He smiles and is missing one of his front teeth. Maddie's grandmother says, "Hi, we're here to see Keith James."

"Yeah, that's my dad. I'll go get him." The boy walks down the hallway, yelling, "Dad!"

"Nana, did you see his face? He kind of looks like me."

"You're right, Maddie."

Maddie's stomach fills with butterflies. Her hands start to tremble; she doesn't know if her knees can hold her up. She grabs her grandmother's hand. Suddenly walking down the hallway is a very good-looking man; he has blonde hair with a few freckles on his nose. She looks into his eyes and she knows for sure he is her father.

He looks questioningly at Maddie and her grandmother. Then he studies Maddie's face, looking puzzled. "Hi, I'm Keith James, do I know you? You look kind of familiar."

"My name is Maddie and this is my grandmother, Patricia. We haven't ever met but . . ."

Keith says. "Well, Come on in."

He leads them into the living room; they walk across the hard wood floors and notice a fireplace along the wall. He gestures for them to sit down on a dark brown leather couch. There is a baby grand piano tucked in the corner of the room. Pictures of Keith playing piano at various venues decorate the walls. Mixed in are pictures of Keith and his son. Maddie and her grandmother get comfortable on the couch. Keith pulls a chair around and sits across from them. He is studying Maddie and says, "So, what is this about?"

Maddie looks at Keith. "Did you ever know a woman by the name of Lizzy?"

Keith stares at Maddie. "That's why you look familiar. You look like the Lizzy I knew years ago, except her hair was auburn. She was the granddaughter of someone in the band I was in. We got involved and I was in love. Then one morning she was just gone. I never saw her again."

Maddie's grandmother clears her throat and begins to fill in all the details about Lizzy's life, the band, the birth of Maddie, and trying to find Maddie's father. As she is explaining everything he just keeps staring at Maddie and starts to get tears in his eyes. A couple tears escape and roll down his cheeks. When Maddie's grandmother has told the whole story she stops. The room is so quiet, thick with emotion and uncertainty.

Keith looks at Maddie. "I didn't know she was pregnant. She just suddenly disappeared from my life and I never knew what happened to her. I can't believe this . . . I have a daughter. I don't know what to do with all this emotion. I'm so sad I have missed out on watching you grow up and being part of your life. I'm angry that Lizzy never let me know about you. I would have married Lizzy back then. I never knew why she left so suddenly. I can't believe she didn't tell me. But mostly, right now, I just want to take you in my arms and hug you and never let you go."

Maddie says quietly. "I want to hug you, too." She gets up and walks over to him. He gets up and they hug, a big making-up-for-nineteen-years-hug.

Then Keith pulls away and looks at Maddie. "My son and I are going to go out for an early supper tonight. Then I have a gig at a small club just around the corner. It's just me singing and playing the piano. Would you two like to come? You could sit with Michael and keep him company while I'm playing."

Maddie looks at her grandmother who gives her an encouraging nod. "Yes, we'd love that."

Keith asks, "Do you like Italian? There is a café on the corner that makes a mean spaghetti and meatballs."

Maddie says, "We love Italian."

"Great, I'll go get Michael. Give me a few minutes so I can fill him in on having a surprise sister." Keith leaves the room.

Maddie and her grandmother sit for a few minutes. Then Maddie says, "Oh, I can't believe this. I have a father and a little brother. I wonder where his wife is?"

When Keith comes back with Michael they leave for dinner. Maddie and her grandmother enjoy the Italian café. After dinner they walk to the club around the corner. The club's entrance is in an alley. It looks like an old time blues hall: dark, dim lighting, candles burning on the tables. Maddie is mesmerized at her dad's performance, his voice is low and rich and his fingers just dance across the piano keys. His songs bring her to tears a couple of times, and make her want to get up and dance at other times. The night feels magical. She never wants it to end. Michael and her grandmother have lively conversations which end with Michael and her laughing.

Later that night, Maddie's grandmother is driving them back to Maddie's dorm. Maddie is looking out the window. "Wow, Keith is really talented, isn't he, Nana? I love Michael, he has such a great sense of humor."

"I know, Maddie, it is all so exciting—our family just doubled, from two to four. Oh, and you were wondering about Keith's wife, well, Michael mentioned something tonight about them being divorced. She lives in California."

Maddie looks at her grandmother. "I can't wait till next weekend. Keith, I mean my Dad—that feels so weird to say. Anyway, Dad is cooking dinner for us next Sunday and he said I should bring Justin too. You are coming for that aren't you?"

Her grandmother smiles. "Of course, I wouldn't miss it for the world."

Maddie looks out the car window a minute. "I was thinking at the dinner I could bring the collage of mom and I. Keith could see pictures of my mom and of me as a baby. What do you think?"

"Maddie, I think that is a wonderful idea. I think he would love to see some of the pieces he missed. In fact, maybe I'll select a few pictures of you as you grew up. The collage only covers pictures of you between one and five."

"Thanks, Nana. That is a great idea."

Chapter 15

After four years of study, Maddie is graduating with a child psychology degree, Justin is pre-med, and Amy has a vocal performance degree. It is a beautiful June day. The sun is shining, not a cloud in the sky. The graduating class at Northwestern University is gathered outside of Ryan Field waiting for the graduation ceremony to begin. Maddie and Justin are standing together waiting for the signal to line up in alphabetical order. Tony and Amy hurry over to them. Amy looks at Maddie and holds up her left hand.

"You are the first to know, Tony and I are engaged. He proposed just before we came here. He brought me down to the shore of Lake Michigan and got down on one knee and everything."

Maddie hugs Amy and then takes a good look at the ring. "Congratulations! Have you two set a date?"

Tony jumps in the conversation. "We are thinking next summer like May or June." Justin looks at Tony.

"We did it again, Tony."

Tony looks at Justin. "Did what again?"

Justin smiles. "Have the exact same idea at the same time."

Tony asks, "What are you talking about?"

Maddie lifts up her left hand.

Amy takes one look and screams. "I can't believe it, we both got engaged the same day. Oh Maddie, you are like having the best sister ever. Did you guys set a date?"

"Not yet. We aren't getting married until I finish my master's program. So probably it will be a couple of years. Justin will still be in medical school. But at least then I can move to where he'll be going to school."

"That's right, you'll have a long distance relationship for a while."

There is an announcement over a loud speaker for everyone to line up.

Tony, Justin, Maddie and Amy all say at once, "See you later," as they rush off to find their spot in line.

After the ceremony, Maddie is standing in the quad waiting for her grandmother, Dad, and brother to find her.

Justin walks over and gives Maddie a hug. "Are you excited to tell them?"

Maddie laughs, "I can't stand waiting any longer. Oh, there they are. Where's your dad and your sister? Have you seen them yet?"

"No, I haven't, but they'll find us soon. Maddie I need to tell you . . ."

Maddie's grandmother rushes up and hugs her. "Congratulations, it is so exciting." Maddie's grandmother pulls away from Maddie and looks into her eyes. "Now, what is it you want to tell me? I can see it on your face. Out with it, Maddie." Maddie holds up her left hand just as her dad and brother catch up to her grandmother.

"I knew it, I just knew it. Congratulations you two."

Maddie's dad says, "Yes, congratulations." Keith and Justin exchange looks.

Maddie looks at her dad. "You don't seem surprised."

Justin speaks up, "I thought that I should ask your dad's permission, out of respect, before I proposed."

Keith quickly adds. "And I immediately gave my blessing. By the way, Justin I got us a couple of tickets to the Cubs game next Saturday. Michael here has something else going on that day. Something to do with girls, I think." Michael blushes. Justin sees his dad and sister walking towards them.

"Here comes my family." Justin introduces them to Maddie's family.

Justin's father looks at Maddie. "Congratulations, you two. I called Justin early this morning and he accidentally told me the news."

Maddie looks at Justin and mouths, "What?"

Justin shrugs.

Maddie's father speaks up, "So, where should we all go to dinner to celebrate?"

After a lengthy discussion a restaurant is chosen; they decide to go to the Stained Glass restaurant which is well known for its fine dining. They all agree to meet there in an hour. Justin goes with his dad and sister to show them around the campus. Keith and Michael decide to go for a walk by the lake.

Maddie and her grandmother start walking back to Maddie's dorm room.

Maddie looks at her grandmother. "I'm kind of upset at Justin. I didn't know Justin had asked Dad for permission or that he told his dad this morning. I thought we were saving it for a surprise today or I would have called you last night."

"I understand, Maddie, I really like that he asked Keith for permission. That is the tradition and I bet it made your father feel honored. I am just so happy for you two."

"I'm glad you understand. By the way Nana, I was accepted into the master's program for child psychology here on campus. The notice got delayed until today. They finally posted it this morning."

"That's great, Maddie. Are you OK with a long distance relationship for a couple of years, with you staying here and Justin moving to Minnesota and going to med school at Mayo?"

"I think we'll be fine. Our programs are going to keep us plenty busy. I'll miss him but we'll see each other on holidays. Plus you and I have a wedding to plan. In two years, when I'm done with school, we'll get married. Then I'll move to Minnesota until he finishes medical school."

Maddie's grandmother smiles. "It sounds like you two have it all figured out."

Maddie and her grandmother walk up the flight of stairs to Maddie's dorm room. The whole second floor is deserted.

"So what now?"

Maddie and her grandmother go into her dorm room and sit down on the bed. Maddie looks around her room. As a senior she was able to get her own dorm room, which was even better because Amy was in the dorm room across the hall.

Maddie smiles. "Well, I'm excited about my internship with Cook County working with the 'families in crisis' program; it will be good for my resume. And Justin is going to be working with Dad on some computer project for the summer. Oh, and we heard yesterday our summer living situation fell through. When Dad heard he offered the top floor of his brownstone to Justin and I until school starts mid-August. He has two bedrooms up there that are being used for storage. We are going to help him clean them out this weekend. We have to be out of our dorms by Monday. It'll be fun to live with Dad and Michael. I think Michael's more excited than we are. It's weird how so many things finally just fell into place. But, Nana, I'll miss coming home for the summer."

Maddie's grandmother looks at Maddie. "I know honey, I'll miss you too. But I love traveling to Chicago and I'll bring a cot and bunk in with you when I'm here this summer. We'll have a slumber party." She looks up at Maddie and sees a tear running down her cheek.

"Oh Nana, so much is changing so fast. I'll be away from you more than I'm with you. And I'll only be visiting home, not living there. Boy, it's just all sinking in."

Maddie's grandmother puts her arm around Maddie. "I know, that's how life works. It kind of sneaks up on you and pushes you forward into these new adventures. You'll be fine. You'll get to spend some quality time with your dad and Michael. I've had you all your life, I don't mind sharing you with your dad." A tear escapes from her eye. "Now, enough of all this."

Maddie's grandmother pulls away, wipes away the tear and looks at Maddie.

"So Maddie, you did it. You graduated with honors. I am so impressed with all your accomplishments. So, tell me, how did Justin propose?"

"Last night, he took me to dinner, a nice place with candlelight and white table cloths. Then we walked along Lake Michigan. He laid a blanket on the beach. He brought dessert, the moon was out, and the water was lapping quietly on the shore. He got down on one knee and told me he wanted to spend the rest of his life with me. He pulled out the ring, put it on my finger, and said, Maddie, will you marry me?"

"Oh, Maddie, how romantic." Her grandmother sits a moment and then sighs. "Just think that fateful Christmas day when Justin was with us for the first time and you had that dream. That day has led us to now. You found your father and your future husband all in that same year."

Chapter 16

It's a couple of hours before the wedding ceremony starts. Maddie is sitting on one of the pews of her grandmother's church, her grandmother is sitting next to her. She loves this old fashioned church with all its wood trimming. The front has a beautiful stained glass window of Jesus walking on water with his arms outstretched. There are white ribbons tied to the end of the pews. White flowers are in vases along the front altar.

Maddie's grandmother takes one of Maddie's hands. "I can't believe it, my beautiful Maddie is finally getting married. You are all grown up and you are marrying the perfect man. Justin and you are made for each other. And I get to watch your father bring you down the aisle and give you to Justin. Oh, Maddie, I love being your grandmother and I've loved watching you grow into this amazing young woman. I know your engagement turned out to be four years instead of two. But you two dealt with your long distance relationship is such creative ways. Now Justin is in his new phase of medical school; it's really lucky he landed his residency in Chicago at Northwestern hospital. That means you can continue working as a child psychologist there. Finally you two are back where you wanted to be. And having your dad and Michael in our lives these past few years has been such a special gift."

Maddie and her grandmother sit a minute looking at the stained glass window.

"Remember Nana, years ago, when you brought me to church, I asked you why Jesus didn't fall in the water? Do you remember what you said?"

Maddie's grandmother looks at Maddie. "I remember you asking the question, but no, what did I say?"

"You said that to Jesus the water was solid and firm and that sometimes in our lives we feel like we are walking through stormy seas with the waves tossing us here and there, but if we concentrate we will feel a stable foundation that is always under our feet. From shifting sand, to turbulent waters, if we go to His reaching arms, we will feel the strength and firmness of His love. Then we too can walk on water."

Maddie's grandmother looks up at the window. "I said that? I guess I do have some wisdom in these old bones." She looks at her watch. "Well, I think it's time to go downstairs and get ready for the wedding. Sara and Amy should be here any minute to get ready with you. Your dad, your brother Michael, Tony, and Justin should be arriving any minute. It's time to dress you in your white dress, fill your hair with little white roses, and celebrate the beautiful woman that you are."

Maddie and her grandmother stand up to go. Maddie turns and looks at her grandmother and takes her hands. "You know, Nana, you have been my solid, firm foundation. It was you who helped me walk on stormy waters and wade through shifting sand. You were always there guiding me and loving me. You've helped me become who I am today." With tears in her eyes she hugs her grandmother and says, "Thank you."

Just as Maddie finishes talking, the door at the back of the church opens. Maddie's father walks in. "Oh, there you two are." Maddie and her grandmother turn and see Keith walking up the aisle. He is dressed in his black suit, minus his tie. He has a big smile on his face.

"I have something I need to give you before the ceremony, Maddie." He walks over and stands next to his daughter. "There is a saying that when you get married you should have 'something old, something new, something borrowed and something blue.'" He hands Maddie a small, square black box.

Maddie opens it and inside is a beautiful necklace with blue sapphires, sparkling in a circle of small diamonds.

"This necklace belonged to my grandmother, I had it cleaned and restored for you. I think this covers 'something old and something blue.'" Keith has tears in his eyes. "I feel so lucky to have you in my life. And I can't wait to walk you down the aisle. Now, can I have the honor of putting on your new necklace?"

He takes the necklace out of the box and fastens it around her neck. He hugs Maddie and kisses the top of her head. "I better go now, before the others come looking for me."

Maddie stands speechless, overcome with emotion, as she watches him walk to the door. She is holding the sapphire pendant tightly in her hand. "Dad, wait!" She runs to him and he holds her while she lets the tears fall. After her tears have freed themselves she looks up at him. "I am so happy you are with me here today. Thank you, for everything, Dad."

Chapter 17

Maddie, now married with two children of her own, has just celebrated working as a child psychologist for eight years. Her practice is joined with other psychologists, who get their referrals from social services, corrections, and the county. Their offices are located in a brownstone that has been converted into separate offices. She looks around and thinks how much she loves it here because her office has a warm home-like feeling. This room, where she sees clients, has a fireplace and lots of windows. She can see her two daughters and Justin smiling at her from a picture frame across the room. She looks at the long, tall table with a small refrigerator under it. She sits a moment, waiting for her next client.

A couple of minutes later, a six-year-old girl is led into her office by a social worker Maddie knows. The little girl looks around at the couch, the desk, the dollhouse and the long table with a small refrigerator under it. Mrs. Nelson looks at Maddie. "Hello, Maddie." She turns to the little girl. "You'll love Maddie, she is really nice."

"Hi, this must be Allison. Hi Allison, I'm Maddie. I thought it would be nice if we spent some time together. Would you like to see my dollhouse?"

"OK, My friend Amelia has a dollhouse. It has lots of furniture in it. Does yours?"

Maddie walks with Allison over to the dollhouse. "Yes, see, it has lots of furniture and cats too."

Maddie turns to Mrs. Nelson. "Why don't you come back in an hour Ms. Nelson. We'll be fine."

Mrs. Nelson waves. "I'll see you later, Allison."

Maddie looks at Allison, who is playing with the dolls in the dollhouse. "Are one of these dolls your favorite?"

"I like the mommy, that other doll isn't really a daddy."

"Really?"

Allison's eyes start to wander around the room. She sees a picture of Maddie's family. She walks over to it and picks it up. "Are these your kids?"

"They sure are. One is three and the other is almost as old as you are. Do you have any brothers or sisters?"

Allison looks at the picture. "No, I like the doll your little girl's holding. I used to have a doll with long, blonde, curly hair, and blue eyes that closed when I laid her down. She had real long eyelashes." Allison puts down the picture and starts to wander around the room still talking. "And she wore a white blouse with a little bow and a red dress over it that was soft. I loved the way it felt on my face when I hugged her."

Maddie smiles at Allison. "Would you like to sit down over here on the couch?"

Allison looks at the table.

"Or we can sit anywhere you want."

Allison says quietly. "Can I sit anywhere . . . like under the table?"

Maddie takes Allison's hand. "Sure, that's my favorite spot."

Allison and Maddie sit under the table. "So, Allison, are you thirsty?"

"I'm a little thirsty."

"I have some Sprite in the refrigerator here."

"I love Sprite."

Maddie opens the refrigerator and hands Allison a can of soda. Allison opens it up and takes a sip.

"So I know why I like to sit under tables. How about you? Why do you like to sit under tables?"

Allison shrugs. "I like to sit under tables when my daddy gets home because . . . I don't know. Did you know soda is bad for your teeth? I lost two teeth on the same day. I thought for sure it was the soda I drank, but then my friend, Tremain. He said it wasn't the pop; it was because I'm getting bigger and I need bigger teeth. Tremain is so smart. So now I drink soda again."

Maddie asks, "Why do you go under the table when your daddy comes home?"

Allison whispers loudly to Maddie, "He's not really my daddy. He said he's more like my uncle because he and my mommy aren't married. I call him daddy anyway because all my friends at school have daddy's that live in their houses."

Chapter 18

Later that night Maddie arrives home late from work. She walks up the steps of their newly purchased two story brownstone, only a mile away from her dad's. She walks in the front door, takes off her coat, and hangs it on the coat tree by the front door. It is late, so the girls are already in bed. She walks down the hall and notices her collage, now in a frame, hanging in the hallway. She smiles, thinking of how far she has come. Then she looks around the living room, with its hardwood floors and comfy furniture. She sees Justin sitting on the couch, listening to her father's newest album.

Justin looks up. "Hey, are you hungry? I saved you some supper."

Maddie walks over and sits down next to Justin. "I think I'm too tired to eat." Maddie sits quietly, listening to the music, looking at the table next to her and the photographs in their picture frames. She turns off the lamp and sighs.

"How was work today?"

Maddie answers, "Fine."

"Maddie, That fine didn't sound very convincing."

"Oh, Justin. I don't know if I want to talk about it . . . it was."

Justin stands up, takes Maddie's hand and leads her under the table by the couch. The table is tall enough for Maddie to sit under, but Justin, being quite a bit taller, has to sit slouched with his head down.

Maddie looks at Justin. "You really know how to treat a girl."

Justin, feeling uncomfortable, decides to lie down, putting his head in Maddie's lap. He looks up at her and says, "That's better. OK, Maddie, come on, out with it."

Maddie starts stroking Justin's hair as she is talking. "There was this little girl that came in today, a new client. She looked so much like me at that age, the way she walked in. She had the same look in her eyes—scared, haunted. She wanted to sit under the table . . . it brought back my own haunted memories. It felt like the first time I was with Ellen. It was like I was in the little girl's body feeling and seeing it all over again. When I asked her why she sat under the table she kept changing the subject. Just like I would have. I hope she'll learn to trust me enough to share that deep, dark place of terror she's holding inside."

Justin takes Maddie's hand. "That little girl is lucky to have you. You've taken your dark place and turned it into a big, safe place . . . a place filled with understanding, like with the kids and me. I love to watch you with our children, the way you hold them on your lap. The way you help them put into words what their tears mean, the gentleness of your touch."

The phone starts ringing. Justin reaches up and takes his cell phone off the table. "Hello, Oh great . . . you can come, Wednesday night will be fine. We'll get the guest room ready. Do you want to talk to Maddie? Oh, OK, I'll tell her."

Justin hangs up the phone and looks up at Maddie. "Nana's coming next Wednesday around suppertime and can stay until Sunday. She is excited to see Keith perform on Friday night at 'The Blues Café.' She sends her love. She said she had to go because her doorbell rang. She has a date."

"What? Nana has a boyfriend? She's seventy-five years old. Are you sure you heard right?"

Justin smiles. "I'm sure. It's someone she met at the senior center where she plays cards once a week. She said she'd fill you in when we see her on Wednesday. Are you going to call your dad? He'll probably want to know she'll be there next Friday night. Oh, wait, isn't it this weekend we're going to the zoo with your dad and brother?"

"Yes, we're meeting them there. We can't all fit into one car. Then after the zoo my brother has a date, so he is going to drop my dad off here. My dad wants to have supper with us and then spend some time with his grandchildren. The girls just love having him around. Sometimes I just can't believe how lucky I am."

Maddie hears a little girl's sleepy voice calling from her bedroom upstairs.

"Mooooommmmy, moooomy I'm thirsty. Mooomy."

Maddie answers, "I'll be right there, honey."

Maddie slides Justin's head off her lap. She grabs a pillow from the couch and gives it to Justin to lie on. "I'll be right back. I love you."

Maddie gets up and walks upstairs to the bedroom.

Justin watches her as she goes, a smile on his face until he hears his other daughter. "Daaaadddy, daaady, I'm scared—will you come and lay with me, Daddy?"

Justin gets up and walks upstairs to his youngest daughter's bedroom to scare away the monsters and tickle her arm until she falls asleep.

THE CORNER HOUSE

Daddy

I hear the sounds late at night,
You and mother's loud angry fights,
I pull the covers up under my chin.
I try to stop the trembling within.

Oh, daddy, protect me.
Oh, daddy, why don't you protect me?
You are my daddy.

Sometimes I daydream you are holding me,
Gently, protectively on your knee,
You stroke my hair & kiss my cute nose,
You tell me you love me way down to my toes

Oh, daddy, you're gone now.
Oh, daddy, why didn't you love
me way down to my toes,
Just love me way down to my toes.
You were my daddy.

I walk by the house at least four times a week. It's a large, sprawling beige house, carved out of big stones and stucco. The kind of house a rich person would own. A house you see and wonder who lives there and what do they do for a living.

One day as I am walking by the house, I see a man; he is stooped down on one knee, pulling weeds and picking up debris from the boulevard. He wears khaki pants and a plain white t-shirt with streaks of dirt and sweat. I'm not sure if he is the gardener or if he lives here. As I walk by him I make some mundane comment about such hard work on such a hot day. He responds that he is helping beautify the city. When he looks up I see adventure in his face, a face that has seen a lot, that knows a lot. Then he looks away and he is again busy at work.

I can't get him out of my mind, his gray brown curly long hair, long for a man in his fifties. I can't forget that feeling of strength, the masculine essence, and the sense of arrival. He has an aura of knowing. He seems so relaxed, so unassuming, so himself.

I walk by his house three more times that week and there is no sign of him. But the fourth day I am rewarded. I see him walk out his front door and I watch as he walks down to the boulevard to examine the new grass coming up where he has cleaned out the weeds. He leaves the front door of his house wide open. I can see through the outer glass door; there is blue and white flowered wallpaper in the front hallway. I watch him turn and pick up some litter from his front sidewalk and then retreat back into his house. Then I notice a big window at the back of the house; through it I can see a roll top desk and chair. Now that I know he lives in the house, I thrill at the thought of seeing him sitting in that chair, working. He must be a writer, I think. He is a bachelor. He inherited this house and spends his time writing and publishing big delicious books, serious intellectual ponderings.

One day I walk by and see something move by the desk and chair; it is a golden retriever, a handsome muscular dog. Ah,

123

I think, so this man is not only a writer but also a hunter, an outdoorsman, a real man's man.

About a month after I start spying on this house with no more clues to the man's life, I am rewarded. In his yard is a woman, a very gray woman, an old, withered, aged vision of a woman. It can't be his wife; I think, jealously, she is too old. I begin seeing her almost every time I go by, pulling weeds in the garden, hanging out the laundry, and walking that big muscular dog. She belongs there; I think with some disapproval, she must be his wife. But as time passes I begin to like her. She also has brown in her gray hair. She really doesn't look that old, I decide. Her small frame is such a great contrast to his large one. Then I notice there are two roll top desks in that room with the large windows. Ah, I think, so they are both writers, working side by side. They probably both travel a lot, sharing in a world of glamour and excitement. She is the perfect companion to his adventurous face.

One day I walk by and the chairs at the roll top desks are cluttered with books. They are doing their spring-cleaning, I think.

I still keep waiting to see him, sitting at his desk working, dog by his side. I want to see his large, massive head and shoulders bent over his desk writing frantically or maybe he poises his pen in the air while he ponders some profound thought.

But the chairs are still full of books the next week when I walk by. Then I see her; she is hanging out the wash, and he is painting the garage door yellow. As I walk by the house watching them do their chores, I feel a pulling inside me. I imagine them inviting me in their house. We sit and have lunch, a meal of cold cuts, croissants, and fresh fruit with a dab of yogurt and mineral water with a twist. I sit at their dining room table and watch them eat. I see them look at each other and I talk to them. They invite me to spend the night in their beautiful home. I go to a bedroom with its fireplace, hot and glowing, to warm the room for me. In the middle of the room is a large four-poster bed with fluffy down pillows and a comforter in soft blues and whites to snuggle into. I throw back the comforter and climb into clean white sheets, soft as cotton to pull up over my body. I revel in all the closeness.

I look over my shoulder at the house as I pass. The woman, who was hanging the wash, has gone back into the house. He is still painting the garage door yellow.

A few days later when I walk by again, he comes out to get his mail. He doesn't see me. He just stands there studying the assorted envelopes and magazines in his hands. He has on the same khaki pants and dirty white t-shirt with holes. In case he sees me, I pretend to study the house across the street, sneaking looks when I can. Then I feel a sudden urge to call out to him, invite him into a conversation. I want him to want to know me. Just as I am about to say something, he turns and goes back into the house.

It has been a week and I haven't been able to go by the big sprawling house. So in the evening, I decide to drive by, just so I can see in those lighted windows. When I drive by, I see a light on in what I think must be the living room. I can picture them both sitting in their easy chairs, probably reading some new volume of literature they will discuss over dinner. I wonder, fantasize what it would be like to come to this house with my family. My husband, my son, and I would come over for dinner. We'd ring the doorbell, and they would answer it. They would invite us in and take my little boy in their arms and kiss and hug him. They would let him know how special he is.

When I walk by their house the next day, my heart is beating so fast, and my stomach has butterflies. Just seeing that large stone house excites me. I know I just have to meet the natives of my private country, my intimate imaginings. I stand across the street staring at it, trying to work up my courage. Then I take a hesitant step off the curb and walk across the street and up the other curb; now I am standing at the foot of the stairs leading to the sidewalk that goes to their front door. I take a deep breath, exhale, and then slowly walk up the steps; one, two, three. The third step is cracked; little ants are busy running in and out with their food. I am at the top of the stairs staring at the front of this massive structure. I start down the sidewalk to the front door, it is just a few feet away; my feet feel like lead not wanting to move. I wonder if they're looking out of the window and see me here and think, "who is she?" I swallow, steel up my courage, throw my shoulders back, and walk directly up to the door. The inside door is standing open, showing the blue and white wallpaper; then I notice a black metal wall-hanging filled with pictures—their family, I think. I can see children smiling from the photos. Now I am standing at the door; the doorbell is inches from my hand. I hear faint music somewhere in the house. I reach my hand up, poised like a gun ready to fire. I hold it on the bell but I can't push—what if they think I'm crazy or maybe they have noticed me too and have wondered who I was? Maybe they are nice friendly people or what if they are cruel, vicious people? Finally with all the courage I can muster and a "who cares" attitude, I push the bell.

I hear footsteps approaching the door. I take a breath and ready myself. It is him, I can see him in the hall mirror. What am I going to say? Why should I tell him I'm here? What story should I use? How will I introduce myself? Then he is there, standing—no *towering*—over me, looking at me with a blank look. A look you'd give a delivery boy, not exactly blank, but more of a look of questioning. He looks at me like he has never seen me before, like I am a total stranger. It shocks me—after all these weeks, I always picture him knowing me too. At least noticing me. But there is nothing there, no spark of recognition. I can't find my voice; I just stand there. He says, "Can I help you?" and waits.

The silence is awkward. I blurt out, "You are not John Olson. I must have the wrong house."

I turn and run so fast. I never look back. I am so embarrassed; tears are streaming down my cheeks. I am choking up with some emotion I can't define.

A month has passed since that forsaken day. I have not been able to look at the house; I avoid going by it. I feel a knot in my stomach even when I am a block away, so I turn and walk in another direction. Finally I decide it is time to confront the house and walk my usual route. I can see it just ahead. I take a deep breath and keep walking. The house is still there. The same sprawling structure, clothes on the line, a newly painted garage door, the front door still stands open showing the blue and white wallpaper. The two roll top desks still sit side-by-side, chairs full of discarded books and magazines. The roll top desks still empty like they had simply forgotten them or maybe they just didn't notice them. I guess I will never see them sitting at their desks writing profound literature. I will not sit at their table to lunch. They are probably not even writers.

To my surprise I don't feel my stomach knot up or my heart beating faster. It is just a house where two ordinary people live with children and grandkids. A house where the man likes to work on his yard and his wife walks the dog and does the laundry. As I look up at the house I begin to realize that their house looks just like all the others on the block, no smaller, no bigger. It is just a beige house carved out of large stones and stucco sitting on a corner that I pass by on the way to where I'm going.

THE SPIDER WEB

Death You Do Linger

Death you do linger, way up in the sky
Why must you linger there, why, oh, why
Please won't you go now, please just fly away
Won't you leave us for a while,
please just let us stay

It is a cold day for August; the whole summer has been colder than usual. My six-year-old son Tommy and I have just returned from a ten-day vacation. We get off the train and my husband, Daniel, and my two year old daughter, Jessica, are there waiting for us at the depot. Daniel fills me in on what has happened during the time we've been gone. Then he mentions his mother, Angela, isn't feeling well and the doctor is running some tests. We get home around 4:30 and I unpack our things. I do a load of laundry, and then our family drives over to Angela's house to take her out to dinner. When I see her she looks tired. I notice her ankles and feet are swollen. As she turns to get into the car, I notice a black spider web with a small black spider on her left shoulder. No one else seems to notice it. We have a pleasant meal at the Red Lobster. Later when we get home and we put the kids to bed, I ask my husband about the spider web and spider; he says he didn't see it. He said it is probably just the light playing tricks with my eyes.

On Monday we pick her up to bring her to the hospital. The doctors want her in the hospital for some more tests. Again when she turns to get in the car, I see the spider web with its spider. It has gotten bigger and more complex. I notice another spider. I look at Daniel, but he doesn't seem to see it.

A couple of days later the tests are completed, the call comes; my mother-in-law has lung cancer, inoperable. They say radiation treatments might help her feel better in the time she has left.

We pick her up later that day and bring her home with a portable oxygen machine. When she turns I notice the black web is even larger and the spiders have multiplied. All the spiders are black and hairy; their legs scurry everywhere building onto their existing web; it is a work of art, with swirls and designs leading here and there, but going nowhere. I am the only one who seems to see it. At night I can't sleep, I think of her home alone with nothing but that spider web to keep her company. My sleep is filled with dreams of patterns and darkness, netting thrown over my head. I startle awake; I feel like I can't breathe.

Over the next week we visit her often. Every time the web is thicker, larger, blacker, more spiders. One day the web is even more intrusive in the space around her. It seems to be getting ready to swallow her up like a cocoon. I can't believe no one is aware it is there. In fact, that day my mother-in-law dictates a letter to my husband to send to her co-workers. It says she has been diagnosed with lung cancer but doctors misdiagnose things all the time. She tells them she is feeling better and will soon be able to stop by the office. As she is talking I notice the spiders start working at an even faster pace; darkness is everywhere.

The following Sunday my husband and I have a date night. Tommy and Jessica are at the Thompson's playing with their children. We decide to bring some dinner to Angela before we go to a movie. We bring her homemade chicken soup my husband made. When we walk into her house with the food I see something sitting in the recliner. I don't see Angela anywhere; in her place is a human-sized black spider, surrounding it is a handiwork of webs, black and thick with smaller spiders crawling everywhere. The spider opens her mouth and a stream of venomous words come out; words of criticism of my husband and shameful stories of how he embarrassed her over the years. My husband's face is covered with the green viscous liquid. I am about to scream when my husband goes over to the spider and says, "Here, we brought you some chicken soup." He pulls up a TV tray for her and gets her a spoon. I am speechless; he doesn't see the spider at all. He doesn't react to the vicious invectives she just threw at him. I turn and go outside and sit in the car. When Daniel comes out, he looks hurt with tears in his eyes, "Boy, the medication she is on sure makes her angry and bitter. I don't know where all that came from." Then he looks at me and asks, "Why did you leave?" All I could say was I wasn't feeling very well and I wanted to go home.

The next day I decide to go shopping and my sister is watching Jessica; Tommy is in school now and Daniel is at work. An hour later I come home with my arms full of shopping bags. My sister and Jessica are sitting at a small table coloring. My sister looks up; there is an intense look in her eyes. I put down my shopping bags. She gets up and gives me a big hug. A warm, strong, protective hug, as she puts her mouth to my ear. Then she whispers, "Angela died." I'm in shock—I can't understand what she is saying, she has to repeat it again. "Daniel just called; Angela passed away at the hospital when they were admitting her into hospice care." I can't believe it. I say, "What? We were just there last night. There was no talk of hospitals or hospice." Then I start to cry grabbing my car keys as she tells me what hospital she is at.

I can't remember driving there, or parking my car. All of a sudden I am walking down the halls of the hospital. When I enter the hospital room I see Angela lying there. The spiders are gone; the dark netted web is gone. All they left behind is this other life form that doesn't look like my mother-in-law. It is stiff and drained of life, the jaw is slack, the eyes are half closed and unseeing. I turn frantically looking for the spider web and the spiders, afraid I will see them on Daniel or myself. But they are gone.

Every day now I seem to look for that spider web filled with spiders hoping that it will be years and years before I ever have to see that black lacework again.

NIKKI

Little Child Within

Oh, little child, write your songs now.
Oh, little child, sing them loud now
Little child sing your songs so clear.

Little child be with me, help me set your soul free.
Tell me all your hopes and dreams
and all your hurts and fears.
You are so loveable and special to me.
I feel your presence here and all your energy.
Come sit on my lap and let me hold you near.
Tell me all your feelings now, I promise I will hear.

Oh yes, little child, write your songs now
Oh yes, little child, sing them loud now.
Little child sing your songs so clear.

Chapter 1

The bell rings as Nikki leaves the school office and walks slowly down the deserted hallway of her new school, looking for her classroom. She notices the dingy white walls, where pictures of students hang, and the blue lockers. As she goes by a trophy case, she sees her reflection. She stops and smooths down her long, light-brown curly hair and notices the freckles across her nose. She is amazed at how tall she looks and thinks, *I always seem to be the tallest girl in my class.* She starts walking again and wonders what it's going to be like here. Will the students make fun of her like at her other schools? Will the teacher look at her funny? She doesn't really mind moving too much; at nine years old, she realizes there is so much to see in this world. Her mother always tells her to "stay open" and experience everything around her. She just wishes it wasn't in the middle of a school year. Finally she finds the room she is looking for, room 203. She likes the number 203 because its total number is five, and five is a lucky number for her. So maybe this school will be different. She walks into the room and sees the teacher, a short full-figured woman with permed brown hair, standing in front of the classroom. She hands the teacher her "new student" form. The teacher takes it and looks it over.

The teacher says loudly, "OK, everyone, settle down." Then she looks at Nikki. "My name is Mrs. Archer. We are about to have a spelling test." She takes a sheet of paper from the desk and hands it to Nikki. "This is a list of the spelling words, look it over. Nikki, you can take the last seat in the second row."

Nikki finds her seat and takes out the notebook her mom made for her with unicorns on the front and mermaids on the back. She looks out the window, then glances at the spelling list. *The words are so easy*, she thinks, as she looks at the other students who are still talking loudly. She notices her neighbor, a short girl with long red hair, stealing looks at her.

The teacher speaks up. "Good morning class, it's time to settle down. We have a new student today. Nikki, why don't you stand up and tell us a few things about . . ."

Nikki's hand shoots up in the air.

"Yes, Nikki?"

"I don't want to."

The teacher looks puzzled. "You don't want to what?"

"Stand up, I don't want to stand up. I'll just sit down and tell you a few things about myself. If that's OK?"

The teacher looks at Nikki. "Well, usually students stand . . . but I guess you can sit if you feel more comfortable."

The students start whispering to each other. Nikki hears a girl next to her say, "What's her problem? She's weird."

Nikki ignores the comment and says, "My name is Nikki Branford. I moved here on Saturday from Chicago. It's just me and my mom and my cat Frankie. Frankie doesn't have a tail because it got caught in an elevator door, so the doctor had to cut it off. I love English, my hobby is music and I collect bottle caps and musical notes. I have a bottle cap from a Mountain Dew bottle that belonged to Julia Roberts. She threw it in the trash can and I reached in and . . ."

"That's quite enough, Nikki." A few students laugh at Nikki. She hears someone whisper. "Did she say she collects musical notes? Weird."

The teacher continues. "Thank you for sharing, Nikki. I'll give everyone fifteen minutes to look over their spelling list before we take the test."

The girl with the red hair whispers to Nikki, "I have a cat too. His name is Lucky because my mom says he's lucky we found him when we did. My name is Shelby because my mom says I was almost born at the beach. You know Shells, Shelby. My mom does that all the time. My brother's name is Andy because she was sucking on a piece of candy when he was born. What are you looking at?"

Nikki is looking at the window. Whispering back she says, "I was watching that musical note sitting on the window sill. I was trying to figure out if it was an eighth note or a sixteenth note. I think it's an eighth note; I'm sure there is only one flag."

Shelby looks at Nikki. "What are you talking about? I don't see any . . ."

Nikki shrugs and whispers back, "Never mind, it's gone now. You have to look quickly or you won't see them. They move fast, especially the eighth notes. Now over the clock is a half note. If you look quickly you might see . . . no, it's gone."

Shelby looks at Nikki. "Is there something wrong with you?"

"No, why?"

"Because you see musical notes?"

Nikki looks puzzled. "Don't you?"

"No." Shelby answers a little too loudly.

The teacher frowns at Shelby, stands up, puts on her glasses and clears her throat. "Everyone put your lists away and please get out a sheet of paper." The teacher watches as the students put their lists away. When they are ready with their pencils she says, "OK, the first word is lunch. I had hot dogs and beans for lunch."

Nikki writes down lunch.

Shelby whispers, "You're kind of weird."

Nikki scratches her head and whispers back. "Maybe you're the one who's weird because you don't see musical notes."

"No one else sees them." Shelby looks around the room checking to see if she's right.

Nikki looks directly at Shelby. "How do you know? Have you ever asked them?"

The teacher looks at Nikki and says firmly. "Please, there can be no talking during a test. I know you're new Nikki, but I'm sure you couldn't talk during tests at other schools. This is your only warning. The next word is window, she opened the window to get fresh air."

Shelby whispers out of the side of her mouth. "No, I've never asked them."

Nikki writes down window and whispers back. "See, you don't really know."

The teacher with her hands on her hips looks at Nikki. "Nikki, no talking, please pick up your paper and come sit here by my desk."

Nikki gets up slowly and picks up her paper, her face red with shame as she walks up and sits by the teacher's desk. Just as Nikki is sitting down, her mother rushes into the classroom; her skirt is bright and colorful, like a gypsy's. The teacher looks up from the spelling list and sees Nikki's mom as she goes over to Nikki and kisses Nikki on the top of her head. Nikki's face flushes an even brighter red.

"Nikki, I said I'd tell you the minute I heard. Well, I got the job so I won't be there when you get home from school. I left you a surprise snack in the refrigerator and . . ."

The teacher, looking very flustered, interrupts. "Excuse me, but you can't just barge into a classroom in the middle of the class. We are in the middle of a spelling test. You can leave a note in the office."

Nikki's mom looks at the class and realizes where she is. "I'm so sorry, I was so excited, and I guess I wasn't thinking. Really I AM sorry. I better go, see you later Nikki."

Nikki hears someone behind her whisper, "Boy, her mother's as weird as she is."

Nikki lowers her head to hide a tear that escapes her eye and is rolling down her cheek. *Not the best start in my new school. I already have two strikes against me,* Nikki thought as she quietly brushed away the tear.

The teacher looks at the class. "Now, where were we? Oh, yes, restless, I can't wait for recess because I feel . . . " Just as she says feel the recess bell rings.

"Please, put your spelling papers in your desks. We will finish the test after recess."

All the students get up and go out to the playground; Nikki is the last one to get out of her seat. She walks slowly to the playground and sits on the bottom step of the stairs, by the door. She pulls out a pencil and some paper and begins writing. A couple of minutes later Shelby comes and sits down next to her.

"Why do you see musical notes? What do you do with them?"

Nikki looks up at Shelby to see if she is making fun of her. Shelby looks genuinely interested, so she says, "I collect them and put them here on this piece of paper and make songs out of them."

"Wow, that's cool—will you show me a song when it's done?"

Again Nikki looks at Shelby's face to see if she is serious. "OK, I'll show you this one when it's done."

"Your mom sure is pretty. I liked her skirt. What does your dad look like?"

Nikki brushes away hair that's fallen over her eye and reaches into her pocket. "I don't know. Do you want a piece of gum, it's bubble gum?"

Shelby takes a piece, unwraps it, and puts it in her mouth. "So where do you live?"

Nikki thinks a minute. "You know the lake at the end of town, where there's a place with lots of docks and boats?"

"Yeah, I know that place, it's my favorite place to fish."

"That's where I live."

Shelby looks puzzled. "I don't remember any houses down by there . . ."

"No, silly, I live on a boat."

"You live on a boat? For real, a real boat? Like a pirate or a gypsy . . . ?"

Nikki interrupts. "No, I just live on a boat. I don't think I'm a pirate or a gypsy. I think I'm Italian or French."

The bell rings; recess is over. Shelby stands up. "By the way, I'm sorry I got you in trouble for talking. I mean we were both talking and I . . ."

"That's OK, I'm used to it."

The girls walk into the classroom and sit down, Shelby in her seat in the back and Nikki next to the teacher's desk.

After school, Nikki walks home slowly, thinking about her day and about Shelby. She thinks that maybe Shelby might want to be her friend.

When she gets home she finds the chocolate cake her mom had made for her. She cuts a piece and puts it on her plate. Frankie, her cat, follows her up the steps to the boat deck. As Nikki eats her cake, Frankie lays in her lap purring as she pets him. "Don't you just love looking at the lake, Frankie? It's so blue and the waves are fun to watch as they splash to the shore."

An hour later Nikki sees her mom walking up the dock, with her colorful skirt and blouse. Her mother is smiling and Nikki can see the dimple on her left cheek, and her short brown curly hair. Nikki and Frankie jump up and run to meet her. "How was your first day on the job?"

Her mom smiles. "Oh, Nikki, I love it. How was school for you?"

"It was fine. I think I might have found a friend; her name is Shelby. She seems interested in my musical notes."

Chapter 2

The next morning Nikki gets to school a couple of minutes early. When she passes two boys on the playground, one of them says to her, "I hear you live on a boat, so are you a river rat?"

"I'm not a river rat. How'd you know I live on a boat?"

"We heard you tell Shelby at recess yesterday. So do you like being a river rat?" The boys start laughing.

Shelby walks up interrupting the conversation. "Go away Mike, go bother someone else." Mike and his friend walk into the school building. Shelby looks at them and then Nikki. "Boys can be sooo stupid. So, have you always lived on a boat?"

Nikki is relieved Shelby came up when she did. "No. In Chicago we lived in an apartment on the twentieth floor. My mom said she felt like she was living in a sardine can with other sardines.

Before that we lived in a house with other people. Mom had a fight with one of them so we moved out."

Shelby looks at her watch. "We better hurry—the bells going to ring any minute." Nikki and Shelby make it to their seats just before the bell rings.

When lunchtime comes Nikki walks to the crowded lunchroom and stands in the sandwich line. Two girls from her class stand behind her in line, whispering together. One of the girls looks at Nikki and asks, "Is your mom a hippy or something? How do you like sleeping on a boat? Isn't it fishy?"

Nikki doesn't like the way the girls look at her when they ask their questions. She feels like they are laughing at her, so she turns around and ignores them. She can hear them whispering and laughing. When she gets her sandwich she brings it over to an empty table and sits down. She takes out her notebook and starts writing. She feels someone sit next to her and looks up. It's Shelby. She puts her sandwich down.

Shelby looks at Nikki's paper. "Hey, what are you writing about?"

"You know, you don't have to sit with me. I know everyone's whispering about how weird I am. They might whisper about you too if you sit here."

Shelby looks around. "I don't care. If you want, we could whisper about them."

"I don't do that. It's a waste of my time, I'd much rather use my time to create things."

Shelby looks at Nikki. "That's why I like you. You are different and seem totally fine being who you are. I want to be more like you."

Nikki smiles. "Maybe sometime I'll bring you to my special place."

"Special place?"

Nikki looks at Shelby, sorry she'd let that slip out. "Never mind."

The bell rings; lunch period is over. Shelby and Nikki clean their stuff off the table and throw it in the garbage. When they get to the classroom they take their seats just as the teacher comes in.

"OK, everyone take out your reading books. Open your books to chapter four. Shelby, why don't you start?"

Shelby finds the page and begins reading. "Sara took off her wet raincoat and hung it in the closet. She felt lonely being the only one home, two whole hours before her mom got home from work. Three hours before her dad got home. She wished Natalie could have come over."

"That's enough. Nikki, why don't you continue?"

Nikki just sits there.

"Nikki, did you hear me? Could you please read the next paragraph?"

Nikki looks up at the teacher confused. "Sure, let's see, where were we?" She turns a page. "Oh, yes, here we are. Sara went into the kitchen to find something to eat. She opened the cupboard door and reached in to get a bag of cookies but when her hand came out it wasn't cookies but a bag of glittering stars, purple ones, green ones, blue ones. She opened the bag and ..."

The teacher says very loudly, "Wait a minute, where does it say that? That's not what my book has, mine says . . ."

Nikki continues reading. "She opened the bag and the stars flew around the room spinning faster and faster until a unicorn appeared with . . ."

The teacher, getting very angry, says, "Stop it. Stop reading; there are no stars, no unicorns. There is just a bag of cookies."

Nikki stops reading, the classroom is very quiet, no one dares say anything.

The teacher takes a deep breath, slowly releases it and says, "Mike, why don't you continue reading?"

Mike starts reading. Nikki has lost interest in the book and starts writing in her notebook.

When school ends for the day, Nikki gets up to leave. The teacher is sitting at her desk. "Nikki, I would like you to give this letter to your mother." She hands Nikki a sealed white envelope with her mother's name on it.

When Nikki's mom gets home that night from work, Nikki hands her the envelope from the teacher. "Is this what I think it is?"

"Yes, I got in trouble for talking yesterday and today when I was reading, the words did that thing they usually do. She got mad because I wasn't reading the right words."

"I'll look at it later. Come on, help me make supper."

Nikki and her mom make sandwiches and bring them up onto the deck of the boat, with Frankie trailing behind them. They sit quietly, eating and watching the water. Shelby feeds Frankie little pieces of what she is eating. When they are done Nikki lays her head in her mother's lap looking out over the lake, Frankie curls up next to her purring. "The kids think I'm weird because I see and catch musical notes and I live on a boat. And now the teacher's mad at me. I'm afraid I haven't had the best start at my new school. It's hard being me sometimes."

Nikki's mom strokes her hair. "The way I see it Nikki, you are unique. That is a good thing. Just remember what I told you before: people seem to be afraid of things that are different from the norm, things they don't understand. You have special gifts. You know and see things other people can't. You were born with it. You got it from your father . . ."

Nikki turns and looks up at her mother. "Tell me again about my father."

"Your father had your gift too but not as strong and his parents pretended he didn't have a gift. He saw music everywhere he went, but he never learned to write it down. It used to frustrate him and his parents were no help. He'd have dreams that a week later would come true. It was something exciting to him, but it scared his parents so they just ignored it. He never understood himself and what he saw. Because of that, he became angry and dark and eventually he shut himself off from the world. He became a hermit and now lives in the mountainous woods in Colorado. He's found peace there without all the people. He loves the animals, they seem to know and understand him. Do you remember anything about him?"

"I remember his hands, they were so gentle and hairy. He had black hair. I remember looking at his hands where the hair came out, the . . . what's the word? Pores, the pores, and I used to wonder what it would be like to climb down the hair into the pore. I wondered what I would see in there. And I remember his voice when he would sing me a song about butterflies and toadstools. His voice was low and rich and comforting to hear."

"That's right Nikki, how do you remember all that? You were four when he left." She kisses Nikki on the head, and looks at her watch. "Time for bed, my little princess."

"Just ten more minutes, Mom? I'll help with the dishes."

"OK, but then off to bed with you."

Nikki and her mom get up and head down to the kitchen. They wash, dry and put the dishes away. "So Nikki, how about a bedtime story?"

They head to the bedroom. Nikki crawls into bed, where Frankie joins her, her mom sits on the other bed in the room. "Don't worry about the teacher's note, Nikki, I'll talk to her. And I was thinking maybe Shelby would like to come home with you after school tomorrow."

"I guess I can ask her, we'll see." Nikki nestles into her pillow. "How about that story now?"

Her mom reads her a story. Soon Nikki is asleep. Her mom smiles and goes back up on the deck to watch the stars.

Chapter 3

The next day at recess Nikki is sitting in her favorite spot on the bottom step; Shelby is sitting next to her. "So when are you going to share your song with me?"

Nikki looks at Shelby. "I suppose I could sing it for you right now. But I have to do it quietly, I don't want anyone else to hear." Nikki starts singing:

Last night I rode the moonbeam,
straight into the sky
I sat on stars and saw so far, with
my very own two eyes
I saw a girl on her bed. Her eyes
were closed real tight
I saw her dreams riding on the
darkness of the night
They brought her to a friendly place,
where people sat a while
A place where she could sing her
songs and everyone would smile

Shelby just stared at Nikki. "You didn't write that."
"Yes, I did, I finished it this morning when I woke up."
"Nikki, that is so amazing, I can never . . ."
"Yes, Shelby, you can. I'll help you. You just have to find the magical place inside you."

The bell rings; recess is over. The girls stand up. "By the way, my mom wanted me to ask if you want to come over after school?"

"I'd love to. I'll call my mom at lunch and see if it's OK."

The girls walk into the classroom and sit down. The teacher walks up to Nikki and quietly says, "Nikki, you can go back to your regular seat next to Shelby."

Nikki grabs her things and goes to her seat. She puts her things in her desk with a big smile on her face. She looks at Shelby, who is also smiling.

At lunch Shelby and Nikki go to the school office to use the phone. Shelby calls her mom and asks if she can go over to Nikki's.

Shelby puts her hand over the phone and turns to Nikki. "Nikki, my mom wants to know your mom's phone number so she can check in with her about today." Nikki reaches into her pocket for a piece of paper that has her mom's work phone on it. She hands the paper to Shelby. Shelby's mom calls back a couple of minutes later.

"Hello . . . I can. Yes, I've sort of met her before; she's really nice. I'll be home by supper time." Shelby turns to Nikki. "I can come over."

When the bell rings for the school day to end, Shelby and Nikki collect their books. The two girls walk a mile to the marina. As they are walking down the dock, Nikki points to a boat. "That's my boat."

Shelby looks down the dock and sees four boats attached to the dock. At the end of the dock is Nikki's boat. It is tall, wide, and white with brown trim. "What kind of boat is that?"

Nikki grabs her hand. "Come on, let's run!" Shelby and Nikki start running down the dock. "It's a houseboat. Our houseboat has an engine and a steering wheel so we can take it around the lake whenever we want to."

Shelby looks around. "Where's the steering wheel?"

Nikki points up. "It's up there on the top deck, I'll show you later. Come aboard, matey." The girls step onto the houseboat and suddenly a purring cat appears and starts rubbing on Nikki's legs.

"This must be the tailless Frankie you talked about." Shelby puts out her hand and Frankie walks over and pushes his head against her hand wanting to be petted.

Shelby's stomach growls. "I'm hungry."

"Well, let's go to the galley, that is boat talk for kitchen."

"Wow, Nikki, your boat is so cool."

When they get to the kitchen Shelby looks around at the two burner stove, the skinny refrigerator, the almost doll sized sink, and the table connected to the left wall that seats four people. "Wow, Nikki, this is almost like a children's playhouse—everything is so small."

Nikki opens the refrigerator. "I know, but it feels like the perfect size to us. Let's see, we have pudding . . . some left over chocolate cake, and we have ice cream."

Shelby licks her lips. "I'll have the chocolate cake. So Nikki, where do you sleep?"

"Right through that door is a bedroom with twin beds, one for my mom and one for me. We even have our own closets."

Nikki cuts two pieces of cake and puts a scoop of ice cream on each piece. She hands one to Shelby. She puts a small scoop of ice cream on a plate for Frankie and puts it on the floor. She grabs her plate and sits next to Shelby.

Nikki takes a bite of cake. "Sometimes when it's hot I sleep up on the top deck. I lie on my sleeping bag and stare up at the sky. I see thousands of stars. Then suddenly I'm not here but I go to this special place. It's where the musical notes come from."

Shelby looks at Nikki. "You talked about this magic place before, what is it?"

"You'll see Shelby, when we have a sleepover. I'll take you with me."

Nikki and Shelby finish their cake and ice cream. Shelby sits quietly for a moment then says, "Wow, listen to the water."

Nikki laughs. "That's not the water. That's the mermaids knocking, wanting to come and visit. But when I call to them they run away. They're shy. Quick, let's run up and see if we can see any."

Shelby and Nikki run up the ladder to the first deck. Nikki lies on her stomach and looks over the side of the boat. Shelby lies down next to her.

Nikki points. "There's one. See, the back fin is bluish green. Oh, she went under the boat. Did you see her?"

Shelby looks hard at the water. "I didn't see anything. My mom says there's no such thing as a mermaid."

Nikki looks at Shelby. "I've seen at least four. You should see them; they have the most beautiful hair. Some have hair that looks as yellow as the sun and others are as red as the clay we use at school. And when they smile, everything becomes still and peaceful."

"Nikki, I don't see any. You're making it up. You're pretending."

Nikki sat up, startled. "I don't pretend. I touched one once, on the back part, where the scales are. When I took my hand away it sparkled. It was full of some glimmering dust. I didn't wash my hands for two days, until my mom made me because I was getting that dust on everything."

Shelby sits up. "I don't want to talk about mermaids anymore. Let's play with Barbies or something."

"Barbies? . . . oh, you mean dolls. I don't have any. Let's go play in the magical forest, where trees talk and flowers sing."

"Nikki, stop doing that, quit talking that way."

"What way?"

"You know, all that magic and fantasy."

Nikki sighed. "Shelby, close your eyes."

"I don't want to."

"Please Shelby, close your eyes and listen." Nikki closes her eyes. Shelby looks at Nikki, closes her eyes, then opens them, closes them again, then opens just one eye.

Nikki sighs. "Shelby, are they closed?"

Shelby closes both eyes. "Yes."

Nikki listens hard. "What do you hear?"

Shelby itches her nose. "I don't know . . . cars on the road."

"Come on, Shelby, really listen. Listen to the water."

"OK, Nikki, let's see, I hear the waves on the shore . . . I hear the breeze. Wow, I feel the breeze but I hear it too. I hear a bee buzzing somewhere and a dog is barking . . . birds are flying . . ."

Nikki whispers. "You hear all that. Now feel it inside you. You are here but there. You are part of all those sounds. The bee hears you breathe, he feels your warmth, the breeze feels your skin and tickles your hair . . ."

"Wow, this is weird, it's like I'm in a world where . . . oh Nikki, I think I saw one of the musical notes . . . I." Shelby opens her eyes. "I don't want to do this anymore. Now you've got me seeing those note things. I'm hungry. Let's have some more cake. Come on." Shelby gets up.

Nikki sighs, opens her eyes and follows Shelby down into the kitchen. She dishes up some more cake and ice cream. Frankie is curled up in the middle of the table ignoring the girls.

Shelby takes a bite of cake and looks at Nikki. "So tell me about how you write your songs."

Nikki looks at Shelby. "I don't want to."

"I knew you were pretending to write them, Nikki."

Nikki takes a bite of cake. "I'm not pretending. I don't want to tell you about it, I want to show you how I do it. But you have to want to come with me, to the magical place. It's a place where you can write your own songs, or paint your own pictures. Whatever your own creative voice is, you can find it there."

"I don't think I could ever . . ."

Nikki interrupts Shelby. "Yes, you can. I'll help you. You just have to find the special place inside you. Like earlier when you were listening."

The girls hear footsteps. Nikki's mom is home from work.

"Nikki! Are you home?" yells Nikki's mom as she steps onto the boat. Frankie hearing her voice, dashes up the stairs.

Nikki, hollers back. "Yes, Mom. We are in the galley. Shelby and I are having some cake and ice cream."

Nikki's mom appears in the galley, Frankie in her arms. "Hi, Shelby, it's nice to see you. Do you want to stay for supper? We're having turtle stew with angel mush?"

Shelby gives Nikki a funny look. " I don't think I . . ."

"Shelby, when my mom says turtle stew and angel mush she is really talking about chicken and dumplings," says Nikki reassuring Shelby.

Shelby looks relieved and says, "Oh sure, I'll call my mom."

Nikki grabs Shelby's hand. "We don't have a phone. Come on, we can go up to the marina and use theirs."

Nikki and Shelby step off the boat and walk down the dock to the marina, a one story building with white paint peeling and a couple of cracked windows, to make the phone call. Nikki's mom starts making supper.

After supper Nikki and Shelby sit up on the first deck.

Shelby dangling her feet off the side of the boat, says, "That supper was really good, thanks for having me over. It's starting to get dark so I think I better go. My mom wants me home before dark. I'll see you tomorrow, Nikki."

Shelby gets up.

Nikki gets up too. "Wait Shelby, I'll walk you to the marina."

After Nikki returns home and helps her mom do the dishes, her mom says, "Let's go sit up on the top deck." The two of them go up to the top deck; her mom sits down and Nikki lays her head in her mom's lap looking up at the sky.

"So, Mom, what group of stars are those?"

"Well, let's see, that's the big dipper where the giant fish lives with the purple scales. On certain nights if you watch long enough you'll see him leap up from the dipper and splash back down again."

"Mom, Shelby doesn't believe in mermaids. She says I'm pretending and I'm not Mom. I really see them."

"I know you do, honey. Give Shelby time, she sounds like she might be someone you can bring with you on your magical, creative journeys. Maybe a week from tomorrow, she can sleep over. It's a Friday night; we have nothing the next day. Ask Shelby for her mom's phone number and I'll give her a call."

Chapter 4

Nikki wakes up to a beautiful sunny day. It is Friday, and Shelby is sleeping over. Nikki eats breakfast with her mother, grabs her backpack, almost trips over Frankie and runs all the way to school. She feels so happy that she has a new friend. She gets to her classroom and sits in her seat next to Shelby. Shelby smiles at her as the bell rings. The day goes by so fast and suddenly it's 3:00 and it's time to gather up their things to go home.

They practically run all the way to Nikki's boat. When they get there, Nikki's mom is standing on the dock. "I'm glad to see you, Shelby. I'm making flying saucers for dinner with lots of tomato and cheese."

Nikki looks at Shelby and mouths, "Pizza." Shelby shakes her head.

After their "flying saucers" Shelby and Nikki get out their sleeping bags and bring them to the top deck of the boat.

Shelby and Nikki are lying in their sleeping bags on the deck of Nikki's boat, looking up at the stars. "Shelby, I'm so glad you're sleeping over."

"I know, me too. What did you say those stars were?" Shelby asks pointing.

"That's Orion, the warrior."

"Wow, how do you know so much about stars? I've heard of the Big Dipper but no one ever showed it to me."

"My mom loves the sky and the stars. We sit up here a lot and she'll tell me stories about each star. Sirius is the brightest star in the galaxy. See there, that constellation is Draco; he is a dragon. There is my constellation, Aquarius, the water bearer. Do you know in ancient times they discovered the astrology constellations lead them on a road through the galaxy? So all the astrology signs are up there. What is your sign?"

"I'm not sure, my birthday is June 5th. What sign is that?"

"You're a Gemini, a sign of the twins. See there you are, up there by the Milky Way, its hard to see you now because its summer. Gemini is seen better in a winter sky." Nikki points up to the sky.

"Wow, that's me, I mean my sign?" Shelby sighs, "I wish my mom knew about stars. All she knows about are computers and web sites and Internets and cell phones. I don't think she ever looks up." Shelby says sadly.

Nikki sits up and looks at Shelby. "Well, are you ready to go with me to my special place?"

"I don't know, Nikki, it seems weird to see musical notes and . . ."

Nikki shakes her head. "You're sounding like your mother."

"Oh, all right, but if I get scared will you bring me back?"

Nikki lies back down next to Shelby. "Of course I will, but I doubt you'll want to come back. Now lay on your back, look at the stars. Now see that real bright one right above us? Stare at it. Now, can you see it's not just white?"

"Yeah, there is blue and red and green . . ."

"That's right, you got it. Now close your eyes and listen," Nikki's says softly.

Shelby and Nikki lie there and listen quietly for about a minute. Then Shelby says, "I hear the water, and a cat meowing, an insect is buzzing."

Nikki whispers. "Shhhh, now just listen and take my hand."

Shelby takes Nikki's hand. They lay there quietly until Shelby says nervously, "Nikki, hold my hand tighter, I'm feeling kind of weird. Ohhh."

Nikki holds her hand tighter. "It's OK Shelby, you're doing fine. Just breathe through your nose—what do you smell? Open your ears—what do you hear? Now open your eyes—what do you see?"

Shelby slowly opens her eyes. Nikki and Shelby are no longer lying on the boat deck, they are lying on grass in the sunlight surrounded by trees and flowers.

"What do you think?"

Shelby looks around. "It's a forest, kind of like the one by the lake." Shelby stops talking because she hears a small wind blowing through the trees that sounds like voices whispering. The trees are moving and swaying. "I hear whispering, Nikki. Do you hear it? I don't see anyone."

Then Shelby hears quiet giggling and laughing. Nikki smiles at Shelby and speaks loudly as she looks around her. "It's OK, you can speak up, Shelby is with me."

Two of the trees—a beautiful maple and a tall apple tree— speak up over the other trees. The beautiful maple tree standing nearby waves its branches and says, "Hey, Nikki, nice of you to come visit. Come on and climb on my branches so I can feel you with me. Bring your friend, Shelby, I have a branch for her too."

The strong, tall apple tree standing next to the maple says, "No, come sit with me, Nikki. Please—I grew some nice juicy apples for you to eat."

The maple tree speaks up louder. "I don't have apples but I have stronger branches so you can . . ."

Nikki raises up her hands. "Come on you two, quit fighting. I'll sit in one tree and Shelby can sit in the other. Come on Shelby."

Nikki starts walking over to the trees, but Shelby stays back. Nikki tries to pull her. "Come on Shelby, you'll learn a lot from these guys—they've been around for hundreds of years."

The maple tree stands as tall as it can. "That's right Shelby— in fact, you look just like a little girl that used to climb me. Let's see, I think it was about twenty years ago. Except her hair was blonde and she had a chipped front tooth."

Shelby climbs up into the maple tree as it is speaking; Nikki climbs into the apple tree, picks an apple and listens.

The apple tree speaks up, "Yeah, what was her name . . . ? Josephine, no Jaclyn . . ."

Loudly the maple says, "It was Jennifer. But we called her Juniper because she had long legs and arms, and hands with these wispy fingers."

Shelby looks at the maple in shock. "That sounds like my mom you're talking about. Her one friend still calls her Juniper. She was here, with you? Did you talk to her?"

The apple tree speaks up. "We tried, but she could never hear us, except this one day. She came and she was crying. I think she lost her dog and her parents couldn't find him and she looked and waited but it had been a week and he hadn't come back. Her parents told her they'd get her a new dog but your mom wanted her old dog and felt her parents didn't understand. She sat on this branch and I tried to comfort her. I think I said something like, I'm sorry, or maybe it was, I hope he comes back. Anyway she turned every which way and said, 'Who said that?' I said, 'me.' Her eyes opened wide and then her mouth. She tried to scream but nothing came out. Then she fell off the branch and broke her arm. She ran away screaming. We haven't seen her since."

Nikki picks an apple. "Hey, Shelby, here's an apple." Nikki throws it to Shelby. Shelby catches it and takes a bite, thinking. "Really. My mom. She fell out of a tree and broke her arm. That just doesn't sound like the mom I know. Hair short, business suits, never laughs, always a cell phone on her ear. I can't imagine her in a tree."

Nikki looks at Shelby. "Hey Shelby, where's your dad? You don't talk about him much."

"Neither do you."

Nikki shrugs. "Never mind, let's play some music. I brought my CD player. Now lean against the tree trunk out of the line of fire."

"What? What are you talking about?"

"When you're here in this place and you listen to music, you don't just hear it but you see it too. Watch."

Shelby leans back; Nikki leans back and turns on the CD player. The minute she does musical notes and rests fly through the forest. She turns it off and they disappear. Shelby looks around excitedly. "Nikki, do that again."

A squirrel climbs up the tree and onto Shelby's shoulder. "Hi, Shelby, remember me, you fed me popcorn after you'd been to the county fair. And you fed me two peanuts complete with shells. That's the best treat anyone's ever given me. You were with your dad. He gave me two of his French fries."

Shelby looks at the squirrel, then Nikki. "Does everything talk here?"

Shelby reaches in her pocket and pulls out a cracker. "Here, I bet you like crackers."

The squirrel grabs it and scampers down the tree. "Thanks, Shelby, I've got to go."

Nikki watches as the squirrel climbs up another tree and disappears into the trunk. "I guess he's storing food away. Well, what do you think of this place, Shelby?"

"It is really something, Nikki."

Nikki sits back and lets out a big sigh. "I know, I come here a lot. It helps me deal with things. Things like moving a lot and my dad being gone."

Shelby looks around her. "Does this place always look the same wherever you go?"

"No, in Chicago it was a park with a park bench and swings, but the trees and music were still there. The music and the trees are always with me. When I'm in school I like to stare out the window at the trees. When I see them I know I'm home. So no matter where I go, if there are windows and trees, I know I'll be safe and I'll feel at home."

"Nikki, did your dad ever live with you?"

"He did till I was four. He didn't like people very much so he lives in the mountains and takes care of animals."

"You miss him?"

"Yes, especially at night. He used to come and tuck me in. He would sit and tell me stories. He'd make them up about animals that talked and pictures that became real and stones that recorded time. Every night was something new, but then one night he didn't come. He just . . . never came back. Anyway after that I made up my own stories at night when I was in bed."

Shelby looks sadly at Nikki. "I wish my dad told stories. My dad, well, he drinks."

Nikki smiles. "So, my mom drinks too, so do I. In fact I've seen you drink too. Milk and soda."

"No, Nikki, I mean he gets drunk and then he, he gets mean. My mom kicked him out last summer. He lives in an apartment across town from us. My mom works even more now. She says she has to so my brother and I have enough food and clothes. . ."

Nikki suddenly looks really excited. "Look, Shelby, look up there."

Nikki points up over the tops of the trees. "What is that?"

Shelby looks up. "I don't know, but it sure is bright."

Nikki puts up her hand to shield her eyes. "Wow, it's getting closer. I've never seen anything like it. It looks like . . ."

"Nikki, I'm scared. I want to go back. Please." Shelby climbs down out of the tree and grabs Nikki's ankle and pulls her. Nikki jumps down off the branch and Shelby grabs her hand. Shelby starts trying to pull Nikki away. "Come on Nikki, please, I don't like this. I want to go, NOW!"

Nikki stands firm not moving. "Shelby it's OK, I know its OK."

"Nikki, you said we could leave whenever I felt scared. Well, I feel scared so let's go."

"Look it's going away from us. It's gone"

Shelby keeps pulling Nikki's hand. "I still want to go back. You promised."

Nikki faces Shelby and grabs her other hand. "OK, we'll go, but first I have to show you one more thing."

Nikki lets go of Shelby's hand, bends down, lifts up a rock, and picks up something under it that sparkles. "Here, Shelby, this is a magic crystal. Whenever you're afraid, hold this in your hand. It will comfort you."

Shelby hesitates, "I don't think that will comfort me, I don't . . ."

Nikki takes Shelby's hand and puts the crystal in it.

"Wow Nikki, it feels so warm." Shelby starts to relax.

"Yeah Shelby, just like our friendship. Come on." Shelby and Nikki walk back over to the trees, and wave goodbye. They close their eyes; holding each other's hands tightly, they lay down in the grass. "OK, Shelby, breathe, smell the breeze, hear the sounds, feel the warm sleeping bag and the wood boat, breathe slow long breaths, and relax. When you feel ready open your eyes." After a few minutes, Shelby opens her eyes just a little; she sees the boat and Nikki lying next to her. She mumbles to Nikki. "I'm so tired," and she drifts off to sleep. Nikki smiles and soon falls asleep too.

Chapter 5

The next morning they wake up with the warm sun overhead. Nikki's mom is in the kitchen singing. They can hear the dishes clattering onto a table.

"Nikki, Shelby, time to wake up. I made your favorite Nikki, toadstools and dragon tails."

Shelby turns and looks at Nikki. "Don't worry Shelby, it's pancakes and bacon."

After breakfast Shelby packs up her stuff and heads home. "Thanks Nikki, for everything."

With Shelby gone, the weekend stretches out in front of Nikki.

Nikki's mom comes up from the galley to the deck. "What would you like to do today, Nikki?"

"Can we take the boat out and have a picnic on the deserted island we saw last weekend?"

"I don't know Nikki, it looked pretty wild."

"But Mom, it had some real tall trees we could climb and sit in. We haven't climbed trees together for a long time. Remember how we used to do it so you could get away? You said it was like taking a mini vacation, sitting high above the world like that, not being part of it, just watching it. You said it gave you persective, no perspir, per . . ."

"The word you're looking for is perspective. You're right Nikki, we haven't done that in a long time. OK, I'll go up to the top deck and start the engine—how about you go and undo the ropes on the dock."

Nikki jumps off and unwinds the lines from around the posts that anchor the boat to the dock. Soon she hears the rumble of the boat's engine and she can smell the gasoline. She steps on board the boat and climbs up the ladder to sit with her mother while she drives the boat. About 20 minutes later they spot the island. Nikki's mom slows down and steers the boat to the sandbar at the end of the island. When she can't go in any further, she drops the anchor. She and Nikki go to the galley and make sandwiches and grab a couple of bottles of water. They step down off the nose of the boat where the water is up to Nikki's waist and wade along the sandbar to the island. They stop and put their sandwiches in their shirts, and the water bottles in their pockets and explore the island. They find the biggest tree they can and start to climb it. Soon they settle on the highest branch that will hold them. They look out over the big lake—sea gulls are diving for fish, and there are a few fishing boats with their lines in the water.

"I kind of feel like I'm in a hot air balloon hovering over the lake, being able to see everything," Nikki says.

"I know, it makes me feel free." Nikki's mom sighs. "It feels so good to be up here, all the problems are way down there. So do you like it here, Nikki?"

"I love living on our boat, I love this big, humongous lake; and having Shelby as a friend is so great. I haven't had a best friend for a long time, not since Lisa, the girl that lived in the house with us. School is OK, I just wished the teacher liked me. At least she doesn't think I should be with the special needs kids, like some of my other schools that thought I couldn't read or something. I do like it here, it's way better than the city."

"I'm glad Nikki, because I like it here too. I found a great job with the arts counsel and I love the boat too, being able at night to sit on deck and look up at all the stars."

Nikki gets out her sandwich and water bottle and starts to eat.

"Mom, do you miss dad?"

"I used to miss him a lot, when he first left, but it was also a relief. He was hard to be around. But I miss how he was when we first met." Nikki's mom sighs and gets out her sandwich. Nikki and her mom sit there for a few minutes, eating and looking out over the water.

Nikki very quietly asks, "Do you think I'll ever see my dad again?"

Nikki's mom sits a moment, then turns and looks at Nikki.

"Nikki, I think you might be old enough now, to hear the real story about your dad. When I first met your dad, he worked at the University doing research on molecular biology, things I never understood. He had his Ph.D. by the time he was twenty-three. He was charming, full of life and always had a smile on his face. He had so much energy. He loved music and always wanted to master it, but never quite could. He wrote poems and short stories in notebooks that he left all over the house. When you were first born he was ecstatic. He was the best father ever, so creative with funny stories that had these charming characters that did marvelous things. You would laugh. You and him were inseparable. He loved you so much. But then his illness began to set in. I saw glimpses of it at times. Then he was diagnosed as bipolar. Which means when he is depressed he has a darkness that makes him seem cruel and mean. He gets too angry, too happy, too sad, and he sometimes will hurt others, or himself. He tried medication but he said it interfered with his research and he hated how his brain felt, so he stopped taking it. Instead he drank too much alcohol and smoked too much marijuana to calm his demons. It got so bad that when he walked in the door I didn't know if he'd be Dr. Jekyl or Mr. Hyde. He eventually had Electric Shock Therapy which slows down the brain and quiets thoughts, and helps to forget things. Sometimes in moments of clarity, he said he knew he should leave to protect us from his darkness."

Nikki looks at her mom. "What are demons?'

"Honey, they were like dark thoughts inside your dad's head he couldn't control."

Nikki moves closer to her mom.

"And Nikki, I know I told you he left us to protect us, and you remember him as being suddenly gone. Well the truth is, there was one night when his darkness got so bad. He hit me, broke my arm, and threatened to hurt you. I got away from him and called the police. I pressed charges so he went to court and was sentenced to a place in Colorado that deals with problems like his. That's when you and I moved and lived with all those people, it was a women's shelter. A couple of years later he escaped the treatment facility and managed to find us. So I fled with you to Chicago. He was caught again and the court sentenced him to the locked unit at the facility in Colorado. Now he lives in a group home connected to the treatment facility. There he continues to get help and they can monitor him."

Nikki's mom looks at Nikki and sees tears running down her cheeks. "Mom, I'm sorry he hit you and broke your arm. I'm glad he isn't with us now. I don't want to know the man you are talking about. I just want to keep hold of my good memories of him."

Nikki's mom puts her arm around Nikki and hugs her. "Remember Nikki, he does love us. He would escape because he wanted to be with us. But he just can't control his illness, so it isn't safe for him to be near us."

Nikki's mom kisses Nikki on the top of her head. "Nikki, this has nothing to do with his love for you. He has given you his gift of 'knowing' and 'seeing' things like you do, he's given you his genius for writing and music. He helped you find that special place inside you when you were little. He did not give you his darkness. He only gave you the best of himself."

"Will he ever get better, mom?"

"I don't know Nikki, but I don't think so."

"Do you think he still remembers us?" Nikki takes the last bite of her sandwich, finishes her water bottle, and sticks it in her pocket.

"I'm sure there is a part of him that does." Nikki's mom sits quietly giving Nikki time to digest everything she has just heard. She finishes her sandwich and water, putting the bottle in her pocket to recycle. Nikki looks thoughtfully out over the water that surrounds them.

Nikki says quietly, "Thanks mom, for telling me the truth about my dad. It helps him become a real person to me, not just a fairy tale that lives someplace far away. I've always wondered about him. Now I know."

Nikki's mom doesn't know how to respond, so she says, "Let's climb down, Nikki, and climb that tree over there—it looks taller."

Nikki feels relieved to do something, so she starts climbing down immediately, saying, "Last one down is a rotten egg."

"Nikki, be careful, I don't want to race down, but I'll race you up the next tree."

Soon the afternoon sun is setting and Nikki and her mom head back to the docks. When they get back they see Shelby standing on the dock. When the boat is close to the dock, Nikki jumps out and runs to Shelby.

"Did you come to see me?"

"Of course, who else do I know here? My mom was wondering if you and your mom would like to come over for dinner tonight?"

Nikki yells to her mom. "Mom! Can we eat over at Shelby's for supper tonight? We've been invited."

Nikki's mom climbs down the ladder from the top deck and looks over at Nikki and Shelby.

"Nikki, would you please tie up the boat?" Nikki grabs the ropes her mom hands her and wraps it around the posts. "Boat is secure, Mom. So what about going to Shelby's for supper?"

"Supper tonight? Sure, I don't see why we couldn't. It would be nice for your mom and I to meet. What time do you want us to come?"

"My mom said you could come anytime after 5:30. I have to go; I'm going to help Mom make shish kabobs for tonight. See you later."

Shelby runs down the dock waving good-bye.

Chapter 6

On Monday morning Nikki and Shelby meet at the corner drugstore to walk to school together.

"I had fun at your house on Saturday night. Our moms are so different from each other, but my mom seemed to really enjoy talking with your mom." Nikki said.

"I know, Nikki, my mom likes your mom too. I haven't seen my mom laugh as much or smile as much as she did on Saturday. Did you see any more musical notes this weekend?"

Nikki reached into her backpack and pulled out a piece of paper. "I wrote this song. I don't have the words yet, just the notes. It's a song about you."

Shelby looks at it, but it doesn't make any sense to her because she doesn't know a lot about notes. "Thanks, Nikki." She gave the paper back to Nikki and says, "I want to go back to that magic place again."

Nikki puts the paper back in her backpack and looks at Shelby. "Come home with me after school. We can go for a while. Why don't you bring the colored pencils you showed me on Saturday night—they are so pretty, so many different colors. We can stop at your house on the way to mine and get them."

"OK Nikki, if you think I'll need them."

"Oh, you'll need them, just wait and see."

They get to their classroom, just as the bell is ringing, and sit down.

Mrs. Archer clears her throat. "Good morning class, let's quiet down now and get started. I have a new lesson planned for today. We are going to start our morning with a writing assignment. Last week we read other people's stories so today we are going to write our own. I want everyone to take out a piece of paper and a pencil." The teacher waits until everyone has their paper and pencil sitting on their desk. "OK, now at the top of your page write 'My Special Place.' I want you to describe your special place and what you like to do there."

Nikki whispers to Shelby, looking very upset, "Shelby, I can't write about my special place. It's my private place that I've only shared with you."

"Nikki, you don't have to share your private place with anyone you don't want to, just think of your second favorite place."

Nikki chews on the end of her pencil, thinking. Then she starts to write. The classroom is quiet, only the sound of pencils scratching on paper.

Thirty minutes later the teacher stands up. "Your time is up, finish your sentence or paragraph." There is frantic writing, and then everyone lays down their pencils. "Now we are going to share them with the class. Who would like to stand up and read their story?"

"Mrs. Archer, do we have to stand up?"

"Yes, Nikki, you do."

"Then I don't want to read mine to the class."

"Why not?"

"I don't like feeling people's eyes staring at me when I read about my special place. I think special places are private places you only share with special people."

The teacher looks a minute at Nikki. "I never thought of that. Well, let's do it this way: when you share your paper, you can sit down or stand up. I'll let you choose. Who would like to share first?"

Michael raises his hand.

"OK, Michael you start."

Michael stands up and starts reading. "My favorite place is a baseball diamond. I love to go there with my friends and play baseball. I love to go with my dad, we have batting practice, and throwing and catching . . ."

Shelby whispers to Nikki. "Are you going to share yours?"

Nikki looking upset, "I don't know."

Soon everyone in the class has shared their stories but Nikki. Mrs. Archer says, "Well, Nikki, it's your turn."

The students, used to Nikki by now, wait quietly to see what will happen next.

Nikki stays seated and clears her throat. "I am not writing about my special place, but I am writing about my special person. My special person is my mother. I like how she dresses in bright colors, and how she explains things to me. I like her stories and how she climbs trees. I like how she looks when she is making me my breakfast. Her hair is messy, and she talks about the dreams she had. I like her hands; her fingers are long and graceful. When she talks they look like dancers dancing with the movement of her words. I like her lap when she sits; it is a welcome place to put my head when I'm tired. I like how my mom is always there."

When Nikki finishes she looks up. She's surprised to see a tear in Mrs. Archer's eye. Then the bell rings. "Great job class, now go out and enjoy your recess."

As Nikki gets up and passes the teacher's desk the teacher asks, "Nikki, can you sit a minute and talk with me?"

"Sure, Mrs. Archer." Nikki sits down by the teacher's desk.

"You confuse me, Nikki. Sometimes I think you are purposely trying to be a troublemaker. Like when we had reading a while ago. You're very smart according to the school records, so I know you can read. It doesn't say anything about being afraid to speak in front of people."

Nikki looks upset. "Oh no, I'm not trying to cause any trouble. It's just that sometimes when I read, letters run around the page and then form themselves into different words than other books. I kind of like my version better."

"That's beside the point, Nikki. I'm just not sure what to do with you. You're smart, you're attentive, you do well on your tests, but you are different. You have your own way of doing things in such an outgoing way that well . . . it feels like you're defying me or purposely trying to . . ."

Nikki interrupts, "No, I wouldn't do that. I mean you're the teacher. My mom says teachers are the most important people, besides mothers. Teachers guide us and teach us and help us grow and become adults. No, I wouldn't, what did you say? De . . . defy you. No, never, I just see things . . . differently ... and I don't always know I'm doing it. And it has always been hard for me to stand up in front of people, because other students seem to whisper about me. I don't like seeing the looks on their faces. Because they usually look like they are laughing at me. If I sit down and talk all I see are the words on the page, or the backs of people's heads. It's just easier."

Mrs. Archer looks at Nikki. "Well, you certainly are unique. I had a good talk with your mom last week. She shared some of your history. I think I understand you a little better. You have a real gift with the way you express yourself, so much honesty, and what you wrote about your mother was beautiful. I'm kind of an 'old school' teacher, but between you and me, you are starting to change me. I am beginning to appreciate how you express yourself."

Shelby walks into the room. "Nikki, there you are. I couldn't figure out what happened to you, I thought you were behind me."

The teacher stands up. "Go ahead Nikki, enjoy the rest of your recess."

After school Shelby and Nikki go to Shelby's house to get her colored pencils and some large paper. They walk along the street talking.

"Nikki, I liked the paper you wrote, it was the best one in class."

"Thanks, Shelby. Are you ready to go to our special place?"

"Actually Nikki, I need to go to there. I like how I feel when I'm there. I feel magical too."

"Are you sad, Shelby?"

"Yeah, I saw my dad on Sunday."

"Oh, well the magic place will help."

When they reach the dock they run all the way down to the boat. Breathless, they climb on board and lay their supplies on the deck. "Are you hungry, Shelby?"

"No Nikki, I'm anxious to go, so come on."

Nikki looks at Shelby. "OK, lie on your back." Both girls lie down on the deck. "Grab your pencils, I'll grab the paper. Now breathe through your nose and out of your mouth. Feel the soft breeze on your hands and fingers, smell the water with its fish and mermaids, hear the wind blowing through the trees, hear the whispers that are far away, listen as they get closer. Keep breathing through your nose and out of your mouth. When the whispers are close, open your eyes."

The girls lay there a couple of minutes. Slowly Shelby opens her eyes. She is laying in a grassy meadow just a few feet from the maple and apple trees.

Nikki says pulling Shelby's hand. "C'mon, get up, we've got lots to do."

Shelby gets up and looks around. "Why are the colors so much brighter today?"

Nikki laughs. "Because you brought your really colorful, colored pencils. Let's go sit over there under the apple tree." The girls sit down under the tree and lay out the big paper.

"OK Shelby, look at the maple tree, imagine it is fall and its leaves are full of fall colors, orange, yellows, reds, browns, etc. When you see the maple tree like that, then stare at your paper."

Shelby studies the tree, then starts to imagine all the colors. She looks at the big paper and suddenly a fall maple tree starts to form on the page.

"Oh, look Nikki, the tree is appearing on the page. But the colors aren't as bright as I imagined."

"Shelby, that's what the colored pencils are for—now finish your picture by coloring it in with the colored pencils. I'll be over here writing." Nikki walks over to the maple tree.

"Nikki, why aren't the trees talking today?"

Nikki looks around her. "I think it's their nap time, I heard them a little when we first got here. Look behind you, you have a visitor."

Shelby looks behind her and scampering toward her is the squirrel she saw when she was here before.

The squirrel jumps on the paper. Shelby yells, "Stop that, don't mess up my picture."

The squirrel jumps off quickly, switching his tail. "Sorry, did you bring me any crackers?"

Shelby reaches in her pocket. "Of course I did. Now here, take these and let me work." The squirrel grabs the crackers and leaves.

After about an hour Nikki stands up and stretches. The maple trees' leaves start to stir and then the apple trees leaves join in. There is a quiet whispering breeze and eventually the girls can hear the words. "Hey Nikki and Shelby," says the apple tree and maple tree at the same time.

The apple tree starts to say something but the maple tree speaks louder and says, "We had a visitor here last night. It came in this amazing bright light, it searched through the forest here looking up in all us trees. When it didn't find you it left."

Nikki looks up in the trees. "A bright light, I saw a bright light just before we left last time but Shelby got scared and wanted to leave. I wonder what it is? I've never seen it before, not here or anywhere else."

Nikki walks over to Shelby and looks at her picture. "Wow, that's beautiful, did you know you could draw like that?"

Shelby looks at the picture and then Nikki. "Not really, but I never really tried. I just got these colored pencils, and mostly at home there are screens, you know computers, TV's, and handheld games. But since I met you I'm not so interested in those anymore.

I like all this way better. How come you didn't play any music today? I kind of like watching the notes fly around."

Nikki shrugs. "I don't know, I just felt like writing. The assignment at school we had about special places, well, I just wanted to come here and write about my special place while I sat in it. Anyway we should get back, my mom will be home soon. But before we do let's climb our wonderful, friendly trees."

The girls run to the trees and climb, the trees talking to them the whole time.

After a few minutes, Nikki says, "I think it's time to go—let's pack up our things, Shelby."

The girls go back and lay down in the meadow, smelling the breeze, the grass, feeling the sunshine on their skin. Before they know it, they hear water lapping on the sides of Nikki's boat.

Nikki walks Shelby along the dock when she leaves for home. "Shelby, who was your friend before I came here?"

Shelby looks at Nikki. "Actually last year my best friend was a boy named Brad. His family moves a lot, so he was here for only a year. Before that I was best friends with my next door neighbor, Lucy, but they moved away a year and a half ago."

Nikki smiles at Shelby. "Well, I'm really glad you're my friend. I love sharing my world with you."

"Thanks Nikki, me too."

The girls hug and Shelby leaves.

The next day in school a girl named Ginny sits down at recess with Shelby and Nikki. "What do you guys do over here on this step?"

Nikki looks at Ginny's face and sees genuine curiosity. "We write and draw."

"That's so cool, I wish I had the talent to do things like that."

Nikki looks Ginny in the eye. "You do Ginny, you just have to find a way to tap into it."

"I don't know, but I sure think it's cool what you do. I loved what you wrote in class about your mom."

Nikki gives Ginny a piece of paper and then a pencil. She writes on the top of the page "mom." "Here, just sit a minute and write a detailed description of what your mom looks like."

By the end of recess Ginny has written something about her mom she is really proud of. Ginny gets up to leave and turns to Nikki. "Thanks, Nikki."

After Ginny leaves, Shelby asks Nikki, "Can we go to our special place tomorrow after school?"

"Sure." The recess bell rings and the girls go back to class.

Shelby and Nikki start going to their magic place at least three times a week, Shelby drawing lots of pictures and Nikki writing songs and stories.

Chapter 7

On a Saturday Shelby comes running up the dock to see Nikki. Nikki is sitting on the first deck of her boat writing music down that she had seen the night before, Frankie is sunning himself next to her.

"Nikki, hey, Nikki."

"Hi Shelby, come on up."

Shelby jumps onto the boat. "I just had to come and tell you what happened last night. I had taken my pictures from our private place and put them up on my bedroom wall to decide what else they might need. My mom came in the room to ask me something, but when she saw the pictures she just stopped and stared. She told me they were beautiful. Then she told me I had my dad's talent. A talent he never used anymore. I didn't even know my dad drew pictures. Then she brought me to the store and bought me an easel, canvas, and paints. So I've been up almost all night painting pictures of our special place. I felt so inspired."

"Wow, that is so great Shelby. I can't wait to see them. So your dad is an artist?"

Shelby looks at the paper Nikki is writing on. "I don't know about that, I think he drew as a hobby. So what are you doing? Is that new music?"

Nikki looks at the music. "Yeah, I keep thinking of that bright light coming to visit my special place, the one the trees said seemed to be looking for me. Last night when I was sleeping I kept hearing this music and there was a soft light coming through my window and on it rode these musical notes and I've been trying to capture them and put them on this paper. I'm finally getting it. It sounds so beautiful. Here, sit down with me, and I'll hum a few measures." Shelby sits down and Nikki begins to hum. As Shelby listens, her face starts to relax and her eyes seem to lose their focus and a warmth fills her.

"Nikki, that is amazing, it made me feel so . . . so . . . I can't find a word for it but I want to feel that again. But I've got to go now; my mom, Andy, and I are going to visit some relatives on a farm near by. See you later." Shelby stands up and hops off the boat and runs down the dock, humming Nikki's new song under her breath.

Later that night Nikki lays in bed and wonders about the bright light she saw and why it came looking for her.

The next week flies by for the girls, seeing each other every day after school. When Friday comes Shelby looks at Nikki and says, "I've been at your place for the last few weeks, so why don't we spend Saturday at my house? I have this place I want to show you."

Nikki thinks a minute. "I think, Saturday will work; Mom and I have plans for Sunday."

"OK Nikki, why don't you come over around 10:00?"

"See you then, bye Shelby."

When Nikki's mom gets home that night, Nikki is doing her homework; Frankie is curled up on her lap.

"Shelby invited me to her house tomorrow—is that OK? I told her we had something on Sunday. We still do, don't we?"

"Yes, we have Jake and his mom from Chicago coming for dinner and a boat ride. They are up here visiting family in the next town over. Jake found a journal of yours he thought you'd want."

The next morning Nikki walks to Shelby's house. Along the way she notices for the first time how quiet the streets are—there must be three or four blocks of houses neatly arranged with picket fences and flower gardens. And there are soft rolling hills behind them. She's never lived in a neighborhood like this. She sees Shelby's house, walks up the sidewalk, and rings the doorbell.

Shelby answers the door. "Come on in, Nikki."

Nikki walks in and looks around. "OK, what do you want to show me?"

Suddenly Andy and Lucky, the cat, come running, almost knocking Nikki over as they head out the front door.

Shelby laughs and says, "Sorry, those two never walk, they are always running."

Shelby's mom calls out from the den. "Shelby, is that Nikki? I'm in the den on the computer, I'll be out in a few minutes."

"That's OK, Mom, Nikki and I are going out to the backyard for awhile."

Still calling out from the den, her mom says, "OK, I'll see you when you come back in."

The girls head out to the back yard. Shelby points, "See that hill, that is my favorite place."

Nikki turns around and looks up at a fairly large hill. "What's that at the top of the hill?"

Shelby smiles. "Those are two very large, flat rocks perfect to sit on. It's like nature made me my very own chairs. Come on, Nikki." Shelby and Nikki start climbing up the large hill. When they reach the top, they each find a rock to sit on.

"Wow, Shelby this is cool, you can see the whole town from up here, and look, there's my boat."

Shelby smiles. "I know, I love it up here, it's a great place to get away. I love to look at the colors, and watch the clouds float by and feel how peaceful it is. It's like this place belongs only to me."

"Shelby, you have a special place too. Do you draw up here?"

Shelby shrugs. "No, usually it's where I go when my dad comes around; I feel safe up here."

Shelby sits quietly.

Nikki watches her face. "Your dad, he makes you sad. Let's go down to your house and get your colored pencils and paper. You draw how you feel, and I'll look at what you're drawing and find musical notes and words that go with it."

"That's a great idea, Nikki."

Both girls run down the hill and into the house. They run up to Shelby's room and get her colored pencils and paper. They also find paper and a pen for Nikki to use.

When they are settled again at the top of the hill, Shelby immediately starts drawing. It is like she can't stop. Nikki looks over Shelby's shoulder and then sits down frantically writing musical notes and words. After a couple of hours they both look up at the same time and say. "I'm done." Then they look at each other and start laughing.

Shelby says, "Wow, that was intense, I can't believe we both finished at exactly the same time." For the next few minutes Shelby looks at what Nikki has written. When she looks up, she has tears in her eyes. "The words are perfect Nikki. Sing the song to me."

Nikki starts singing and when she is done, she sits next to Shelby on the same rock, and puts her arm around her. The girls sit quietly.

Shelby's mom calls up the hill to them. "Shelby, Nikki, it's lunch time, I made you some sandwiches."

"We'll be right down, Mom." Shelby looks at Nikki. "Thanks."

The girls gather up their things and head down the hill.

"I'm glad you understand, Nikki."

Shelby's mom is talking on the phone when they walk into the kitchen. "Just a minute ..." She puts her hand over the phone. "Here's the sandwiches and chips, there is ice cream for dessert. I'd like to visit more but I have so much work to do." Taking her hand off the phone, she starts talking, " . . . yes, I'll have it done by 3:00." She walks out of the kitchen.

"That's my mom—always working, either on the phone or the computer." Shelby and Nikki bring their lunches out onto the patio and sit at a picnic table. When they are done eating they walk into the kitchen. Shelby's mom is just standing there, no phone on her ear, looking at Shelby's drawing and Nikki's song. A tear is rolling down her cheek. She looks up at the girls and whispers, "Beautiful."

Chapter 8

Monday morning Nikki wakes up bright and early. Her mom is already up making breakfast; Frankie is sitting by her feet waiting for her to drop food. Nikki gets dressed and sits at the kitchen table.

"Nikki, I never asked you about the journal Jake found of yours, was it important?"

"It was—it had all the stories in it that dad used to tell me when I was little. I didn't realize I'd left it in Chicago. I'm so glad they came yesterday."

Nikki's mom looks at her. "You remember all his stories? You'll have to read them to me sometime. I'd like to remember them too." Nikki finishes her breakfast. "You'd better hurry, Nikki, or you're going to be late for school."

Nikki grabs her books and practically runs all the way to school. She sees Shelby just as they reach the front door. "Thanks again for Saturday, Shelby."

"No, Nikki, thank *you*. I didn't know we could bring our magical place with us to other places, like my hill. Thanks for showing me how."

The girls get to their classroom and in their seats just as the bell rings.

Mrs. Archer announces to the class. "To graduate from fourth grade everyone has to do a project with a friend, we will share them the last week of school. So I want you to take a moment now and pick a partner."

Nikki and Shelby look at each other and say at the same time, "Let's do our project together."

Everyone looks around and gets a partner.

The teacher speaks up. "Now get your partner and sit together at a desk and come up with an idea for your project."

Nikki pulls her chair over to Shelby's desk. "I'll write the story, you draw the pictures, and I'll use my new music for our final project. The music can be playing in the background, while I read, and you show your pictures. I'm so excited. It's like we've been getting ready for this project for the last couple of months."

"Nikki, that is a great idea—not only can I draw the pictures now, but I can paint them. I'm just loving my new paints. What should we write and paint about? The magic place we visit?" Shelby asks.

Nikki frowns. "I don't know, that place is so special and private. I don't know if I want to share it. I couldn't stand it if someone made fun of me about my special place."

"I know Nikki, let's go to the magic place today after school, maybe it will give us some ideas of what we could do"

"That's a great idea, Shelby."

The day flies by and soon Nikki and Shelby are in the magic place creating together with the trees whispering words of encouragement; even the squirrels join in as a rooting section. Musical notes fly through the forest, while Nikki writes and Shelby draws. Suddenly while they are working, a darkness creeps into the shadows for a moment and Nikki and Shelby shiver. But just as suddenly it is replaced with a beautiful white light, too white to look at directly. It swoops down and Nikki hears a voice, saying words she doesn't understand. Then all at once she is alone with the white light; everyone and everything else disappears. The voice starts saying words she can understand and out of the corner of her eye she can see a man standing in the white light, angelic looking but with no wings.

The voice sounds familiar, low and soft. It is the voice of her father. "Nikki, I came here to give you a message."

Nikki whispers, "Dad, is that really you?"

"Yes, Nikki, my little moonbeam. I love who you have become. You are like me, you see things and know things other people don't. I never understood what those things were. So I became confused, scared, dark, and afraid; I withdrew from the world that didn't understand me. I'm sorry I couldn't be with you because of my illness. I have missed you. I love how you embrace who you are, you are not afraid to show people the real you. You know and see things and you have the gift of putting them into words so other people can understand. I could never do that. My mind would get so confused and I didn't know how to explain things to other people. You have found this wonderful magic place to create in, and you've brought others to share it. You've taught them to feel the creative magic place they have and not be afraid. Nikki, though I can't be with you in body, I am always here watching over you from my place in Colorado. It takes a lot of energy to visit you. But I want you to know that I'm proud of you and I hope you write about this special magic place for other people to see and understand. Don't be afraid to share your special place. Help them Nikki, to understand." The voice starts to weaken and fade.

"Dad, I love you. Please don't go, I want you to stay—Dad."

"Goodbye Nikki, I wish I could stay too."

"Dad?"

Suddenly she hears voices speaking her name loudly. "Nikki, Nikki, wake up, Nikki."

Nikki opens her eyes, notices tears on her cheeks, and then sees Shelby.

"Nikki, where did you go? There was that bright light, and then all of a sudden you were out cold. I couldn't wake you up. You scared me."

"Shelby, the white light is my dad. He spoke to me. That's all I want to say right now. So please, don't ask any questions. I just want to go home."

Soon Shelby and Nikki are back lying on the deck of the boat. They open their eyes and look at each other and hug. Without saying a word, Shelby gets up and leaves. Nikki watches her as she walks down the dock, carrying her colored pencils and paper. Shelby passes by Nikki's mom, who looks sad as she walks down the dock towards the boat.

"Hey, Nikki, how was your day?" Nikki's mom asks when she sees Nikki sitting on the deck.

"It was, um, interesting."

Nikki's mom looks at her and can see something has happened. "Are you all right?"

"Yes—after dinner can we sit up here and talk?"

"I think that's a good idea. I have something I need to tell you too. But for now come and help me with dinner." Nikki and her mom make tacos and cut up fresh fruit. They bring their dinners up on the deck and sit down next to each other. They eat quietly and watch the water lap lazily to the shore. The sun starts to edge its way down and the first glimmer of stars twinkle in the sky.

When they are done eating Nikki sighs. "Mom, Shelby and I went to the magic place today and the 'bright light' I told you about, came. It was dad." Nikki stops and looks at her mom.

Nikki's mom looks very sad.

"Mom, what's wrong?"

"As I was leaving work today I got a call from your father's doctor in Colorado. I am listed as his next of kin. Your father has been in a coma for three or four weeks and they don't think he is going to make it through the night."

"Mom, that's about the time I first saw the bright light in my special place."

Nikki's mom looks out at the lake. "I knew he would come one day. But I didn't know it would be this way." She turns and looks at Nikki. "What did he want, Nikki?"

Nikki tells her mom everything that her dad said. Her mom holds her while she talks and lets her gentle tears fall.

When Nikki has talked herself out her mom says, "I'm glad you had that moment with him. Hold on to it, it's probably all he could give you. I am so happy that he sees you too. That he knows how special you are. He is right, you should share your special, magical place with others. Look what it's given to Shelby. And Nikki, I think he has been trying to find you because he wanted to say goodbye."

Nikki and her mom sit quietly watching the stars, listening to the water lapping at the shore. Remembering the husband and father they once had, tears are rolling down their cheeks.

Early the next morning Nikki's mom calls the doctor in Colorado from the marina. Nikki's mom walks slowly back to the boat, Nikki watches her the whole way.

She sees Nikki and steps up next to her on the boat. "Your father passed away this morning at 4:00 am. I called into work and told them I wasn't coming in today, and I called your school and told them you wouldn't be in either because of a death in the family. In Colorado they are cremating his body and spreading his ashes over the mountain he loved so much. So I thought we could have our own memorial service today. What would you like to do?"

"I'd like to sit with you—read his stories I have written in my journal, take a walk in the woods, and feed the animals in his memory. Then I want to write the words to the song he sent me the other night riding in on a soft light. I'll hum it to you." Nikki hums the tune from the other night and her mother's face seems to relax and her eyes lose their focus.

"Nikki, that's beautiful; if you want I can draw a picture I see when I hear the song."

Nikki and her mom spend the day remembering the good things about her dad: his creativity, his passionate, emotional response to life, his deep concern for animals, and his profound intelligence. The animals in the woods are now well fed. Nikki and her mom laugh and cry at the stories her dad told, the ones she saved in her journal.

Later that afternoon Shelby walks down the dock with a cake she made. Shelby runs up to Nikki, who is sitting on the deck with her mom. "Nikki, I am so sorry to hear about your dad." The girls hug. "I made this cake right after school, so it's still warm."

Nikki takes the cake from Shelby. "Thanks, Shelby."

"Well, I should go. I'll see you tomorrow at school." Shelby runs down the dock. Nikki and her mom get some plates and sit on the deck eating white cake with chocolate frosting.

Then Nikki and her mom separate to take some time, Nikki to write her song and her mom to draw her picture. Later that night when the stars come out, they sit back up on the deck to look at the stars.

"Mom, I finished the words to dad's song that he sent me."

"Sing them to me."

Nikki begins singing:

Why did you leave me? Why did you go?
Why did you leave me? I never will know

Now I can see you surrounded by light.
I feel the greatness around you at night.
Oh, there you are, I see your star
Einstein will teach you all that he knows.
Mozart will make the music flow
Yes, there you are, follow your star

I know you left me, I know you are gone,
But you'll always be with me, inside me's your song.

Nikki's mom whispers through her tears, "Beautiful." Nikki and her mom sit a moment hugging and letting their tears flow.

Then Nikki's mom picks up a sketchpad that is lying on the deck next to her, and flips the cover over to reveal her drawing.

Nikki gasps, "Mom, it's a picture of the night sky with a bright red star flickering. Ghostly outlines of people thread through the stars. It's the words to my song in a picture. It is amazing."

"Well Nikki, let's hang my picture on our bedroom wall and underneath the picture let's put the words to your song."

Nikki and her mom get up and go down to their bedroom. They hang the picture and the words below it on the wall across from their beds. Just as they finish, a soft light comes through the bedroom's small window and lights up the drawing and words and nothing else. Nikki and her mom whisper at the same time, "He's here."

Chapter 9

On Wednesday, Nikki and Shelby get together to work on their project. They are sitting on the deck of Nikki's boat.

Shelby looks at Nikki. "Do you want to talk about what happened yet?"

Nikki hesitates, then looks at Shelby and tells her everything her father had said. "My mother said, he came when he did because he wanted to say good-bye."

Shelby listens with a couple of tears trailing down her cheeks. "Nikki, my dad lives in the same town as me. I don't ever think he'll see me the way your father saw you."

"Keep drawing, Shelby, maybe someday he'll see one of your drawings and he'll understand you better." Shelby and Nikki hug.

"So Shelby, I know what to do our project about. Let's do it about the magic place. It was something my father said he wanted me to do. I'm going to share it in his memory. We will use my stories and your pictures and my songs to bring people into our magic place. We will share it with others."

"Nikki, I'm so happy, I really have wanted to share our special place. Now, let's get working, we have lots to do."

For the next couple weeks, Shelby and Nikki spend time every day after school sitting on Nikki's boat, putting their story, pictures, and music together for their project.

On Friday, Shelby, laying on the boat deck drawing, looks up at Nikki. "It's almost done, let's show our moms the project and see what they think. Tomorrow is Saturday—why don't you and your mom come for lunch? Then after, we'll set up the pictures, play the music, and you can read your story."

"Shelby, that's a great idea, it'll also give us a chance to practice. I'll ask my mom tonight."

The next day Nikki and her mom walk to Shelby's. Her mom is carrying chocolate brownies she made for dessert, and Nikki is carrying her writings and music.

Nikki's mom looks at Nikki. "I am really looking forward to hearing your presentation, Nikki; you two have been working so hard for the last couple of weeks."

"Mom, you should see how good Shelby's drawings are. She is so talented."

"You both are, Nikki. I'm so glad you found someone to share your special place with. You have been so happy."

Shelby's mom has sub sandwiches ready with homemade cole slaw and with Nikki's mom's brownies; they are stuffed by the end of lunch.

"Let's see the project," both Moms say at once.

They walk into the living room where Shelby has set up her easel, Nikki has put her music in the CD player, and there is a place for Nikki to stand and share the story. After the girls finish their presentation they look at their moms, whose faces are beaming with tears trickling down their cheeks. Their moms start clapping and can't stop.

"That is amazing. You girls brought me to a place I've always wanted to visit. A magical place that I once felt as a child and had lost." Shelby's mom hugs Shelby, and says, "You know there was a time I was sitting in a tree and I thought I heard someone whisper. There was no one there, so I got scared and fell out of the tree, breaking my arm."

Shelby says, "I know Mom, the tree told me about it the first time I visited the magic place. I just couldn't picture you climbing trees."

Nikki and her mom start packing up. "See Nikki, what a gift you gave to Shelby. And with this project, so many others can experience some of the magic, the creativity the world has to offer. You've done a great job. I'm so proud of you. Shelby's drawings add such beauty to your music and stories."

The following Monday when Shelby and Nikki get to school, Mrs. Archer looks at Nikki. "Nikki, can I see you a minute?"

Nikki looks at Shelby, then walks up to the teacher's desk. "Ginny showed me something she wrote about her mom; she said you told her how to do it. How would you feel about leading our creative story time on Friday?"

Nikki looks uneasy. "Sure, but do I have to stand up?"

""No, you can sit in a chair at the front of the room if that works."

Nikki shrugs and says, "OK."

Nikki walks back to her seat and tells Shelby.

Soon Friday arrives and it's time for creative writing. After all the students are seated and the bells rings, the teacher quiets the class down and says, "We are starting today with a creative writing project. Nikki, will you come up and get us started? Everyone, please get out a piece of paper and a pencil."

Everyone starts whispering. Nikki hears someone say on the way up to the front of the classroom, "Why is she leading it? Are we doing stories of the weird?"

Nikki sits down in the chair and looks at everyone; soon the whispering quiets down. "I want everyone to close their eyes." Mrs. Archer looks around, making sure everyone closes their eyes. "When I say 'a person who makes you happy,' who is the first person you see? Now open your eyes and write down the name of that person and then write down a detailed physical description." Nikki waits a moment. "Now, look at that name and write down a list of feelings you feel when you look at the name." Nikki waits until she sees pencils start to slow down. "Now, write words that fit that person's personality." Again Nikki waits. "Now take the next ten minutes and write a paragraph about the person you have named."

The class starts writing, not a sound in the room. Mrs. Archer looks at Nikki and smiles. Ten minutes later the students put down their pencils and look up. Then they start talking to each other. Nikki hears one person say, "Wow, I can't believe I wrote this."

Later at lunch Nikki is standing in line with Shelby. A couple of girls come up to them. "How did you do that? Are you a witch or something?" Nikki looks in their eyes and sees sincere confusion and surprise.

"I'm not a witch, I'm just me and I just helped you put your thoughts on paper. They were in there, I just helped you find them."

They look at Nikki. "Well, Thanks." Then they walk away.

Chapter 10

At recess the next day Shelby and Nikki are sitting on the usual bottom step drawing, writing and talking. Two boys walk up; one is Mike. "Nikki, I'm sorry I called you a river rat before. So do you guys want to play foursquare with us?"

Nikki looks at Shelby and then at the boys. "OK." The two girls get up and join the boys for a game of foursquare. Mike looks at Nikki. "You know you aren't really that weird."

Nikki looks at Mike. "Thanks, I guess."

The next two weeks fly by. Finally the day for the presentations arrives. Mrs. Archer brings her students to the auditorium for their presentations. There is an easel set up for the pictures and a podium for students to stand up and read from. As they are walking to the auditorium, Nikki sees a tall, thin man with red hair walking down the hall. "Shelby, is that your dad?"

Shelby looks down the hall. "Yes, why is he here?"

He approaches them and Shelby stops to talk to him. The rest of the class keeps walking.

Her dad says, "Shelby, I saw your paintings, Mom showed me. Is it OK if I come and watch your presentation? Your paintings are so beautiful, they make me want to be a better person and start drawing again."

Shelby smiles and hugs her dad. "Yes," then she runs to catch up with her class.

Soon it comes time for Shelby and Nikki's turn; they get up. Shelby puts her drawings by the easel and stands by it, while Nikki starts her music playing and stands at the podium to read her story. Shelby whispers quickly to Nikki. "Nikki, I think this is the first time you've stood up to read."

Nikki laughs, and then clears her throat. "Today, we will be sharing our special, magical place." Music starts playing over the loudspeakers.

"In my almost ten years I have lived in a lot of places, met lots of people, and have seen many different things. Some have been good, others not so nice. I went to schools that thought I was a special needs student, because they didn't understand me. I had friends who stopped being my friends when I told them about my magical place. I had people look at me strangely because they didn't understand what I was talking about.

In the world, I am open, so mean words or critical eyes make my heart hurt and I bleed tears and I feel the meanness and darkness in people's souls, and it scares me; it makes me start to feel dark too and I don't want to. I just want to love and be loved. The magical place helps me be who I am; I brought Shelby to this magical place and now we want to share it with you."

As Nikki talks, Shelby places a painting of maple and apple trees, with birds singing, and a beautiful red squirrel.

"The trees talk, the birds sing, the squirrels chatter words at us as we sit. This is a squirrel that told us Shelby fed him at the state fair last year. These two particular trees, one apple, one maple, fight over us when we get there. They want us to sit on their branches. The first time Shelby visited the trees they told her a story about her mom when she was a little girl. We love to climb the trees and listen to what they say; trees have so much wisdom."

Next Shelby puts up a painting of large, comfortable rocks you can sit on by a pond. And sparkling on the ground are magic crystals of brilliant colors.

"We love to sit on the rocks and feel the rumble of lives from the past. Under these rocks you can find magic crystals that can heal you with their energy."

Shelby displays an amazing painting of musical notes flying in the air and through the trees.

"When we play music, musical notes soar through the air, landing on branches, on flowers, on my fingers. Words come into my heart that are whispered by everything around me. The music we are listening to right now are songs I created by catching those musical notes and putting them on paper."

Shelby slides a new painting onto the easel. It is a painting of herself with colors pouring out of her fingers and onto the paper.

"Pictures come out of Shelby's fingers filled with colors and shapes, making these beautiful paintings. When we sit here we're not alone. We come to this magic place, because here we are free to love with all our hearts. We are open. We are free. We are able to go inside and see who we really are."

Shelby puts on another painting. It a picture of Nikki and Shelby dancing in the trees with a crown of flowers woven through their hair.

"Today we want to take you to this place, so you can feel the beauty of making things, of listening, of smelling, of seeing, of opening up, and loving and feeling the world around you."

The students start talking and looking at each other. Mrs. Archer frowns and says, "Please, can everyone quiet down?" The students become quiet.

Nikki continues speaking.

"Now, will everyone please close your eyes, and put your feet firmly on the floor. Relax and be willing to let us bring you to this magical place we all have inside. Now listen with your ears, hear the music flying its notes around the room."

Nikki's music continues playing from the loudspeakers.

"Now imagine you smell the green grass and the leaves you saw blowing in Shelby's paintings, feel the leaves blowing in the breeze, imagine the breeze tickles your nose, hear the gentle waves lapping at the shore of the nearby pond. Imagine yourself sitting on the branch of a beautiful maple tree; hear its whispers—what is it saying? Hear the music; see the music flying by—how does it feel to be wrapped in its beauty? See squirrels and birds—hear them chirping and talking. What are they saying? Feel them sitting on your shoulder. Smell the crackers, seeds, or nuts you feed the squirrels. How does it feel to know you're not alone?"

Nikki's beautiful song, the one her father gave her riding the light one night, begins playing. Nikki and Shelby see the students' bodies relax.

"Who are you in this world? What do you want to say? What feelings are stirred inside of you? Now sit there quietly."

Nikki waits a couple of minutes.

"Now feel your feet on the sturdy floor, feel the cushion of the chair you're sitting in, hear the noises in the room, and gradually open your eyes."

The students open their eyes; one girl says to her neighbor. "I heard the tree whisper something."

Another girl says, "I think I saw a musical note." Soon everyone is talking at once about what they have experienced, excitement and wonder in their voices.

Nikki and Shelby, holding hands, smile at the students in the auditorium. "Wow Nikki, you brought them to the magic place for just a moment, and look at them."

"No, Shelby, you showed them what it looks like, I added words and music to your pictures. We did this together."

THE WOODS

I Met Her On a Touring Ship

I remember seeing her that first night,
Her beautiful face held humor and light
She is like a whisper, I have to listen to hear,
She is always in my heart; I keep her near.

I touch her face and look into her eyes,
I brush her hair back and give her a smile
I say so quietly the words she needs to hear
I comfort her soul and take away the fear

Sometimes she snores and sometimes we fight
But in the cold winter months,
her warmth is just right
As she lies next to me, all night long
She makes me feel I can do no wrong

Ellen, a tall woman with a runner's body, walks out the cabin door and looks out onto the calm, blue lake. Her brown hair is pulled back into a ponytail. She takes her first big, deep cleansing breath of the day. She lifts up her arms, one at a time, first the left and then the right. She stretches out all the stiffness of a good night's sleep. She warms up her leg muscles, and then her arms and back. She turns and looks at the big expanse of sparkling water. She yells "bye" to Dave and Joey through the cabin's screen door and takes off for her morning jog.

Meanwhile Dave, a tall dark haired man with a full beard, is attending to their son, Joey. Joey is sitting on a booster chair at the table, in his pajamas. Dave gives him toast, cereal, and chocolate milk for breakfast. When the little, almost three-year-old finishes his breakfast, he gets down from the table. His daddy plays the "I'm going to get you" game, so he can capture him and get him dressed. He puts on Joey's jean overall shorts and striped blue and white t-shirt, leaving his little feet bare. Joey looks at his dad and says, "Stones, daddy."

Dave and Joey walk down to the shore and collect stones in a plastic bucket. They bring the bucket to the end of the dock and throw stones into the lake, a game little Joey never seems to tire of. Dave watches Joey as he throws the stones, noticing his brown curls bounce and his brown eyes sparkle. Dave glances at his watch and thinks about Ellen on her run. He flashes back to yesterday when she came back from her run. She said she had felt a little uncomfortable. She said she wondered if there were bears in the woods. And if there were bears, how could she yell for help when she was alone on a deserted dirt road?

"Daddy, help me?" Joey is saying. Dave sees the bucket is empty. So he carries Joey to the shore to find more rocks. They find little rocks, medium sized rocks, and big rocks. They decide to stand on shore and see how far they can throw them. Joey likes the big ones the best, even though he can't throw them very far. He likes the splash they make. Dave skips his stones along the water. After about ten minutes Dave's arm is tired and sore. Eventually Joey starts to tire of this activity. He says, "Daddy, clothes off, swim." So Dave takes off Joey's clothes and then his own clothes. They jump into the lake in their underwear and splash in the refreshing blue water. After a while Dave gets out to dry off, puts his clothes back on and starts to warm up. Joey "swims" along the shoreline, watching minnows swim just ahead of him. Again Dave glances at his watch and looks down the nearby road to see if he can see Ellen in the distance. There is no sign of her.

Dave can still hear Ellen telling him the story of what happened to her last year when they were up here. She had jumped into his car breathless and trembling, barely able to speak. There had been this man in a car who kept driving by her and slowing down, then looking her over as she ran. He was there every morning. She would start running and about ½ mile into her run there he would be. On the fourth day it was different. Ellen was almost to the one-mile mark and he wasn't around. But as she rounded the bend, his car was there, parked on the wrong side of the road: her side. She had wondered if he was waiting for her. She decided not to find out. She turned around and started running back to where she had come from. She heard him start up his car. The trees loomed up around her and the narrow dirt road began to close in on her. Her heart was beating so hard she could hardly breathe. Fear gripped her and she thought she was going to lose the little breakfast she had eaten. She ran so fast, faster than she ever remembered. She heard his car approaching from behind. Suddenly in front of her Dave's car appeared, the old red station wagon. Dave had pulled up and rolled down his window saying, "I'm going to get some milk at the lodge. Do you want something?" As Dave was talking the man in the car drove by. Ellen jumped into the car with her husband, saying she wanted to go with, relief flooding through her.

Dave looks at his watch again. God, he thinks, she has been gone one hour and five minutes. She never runs that far. He calls to Joey to get out of the lake; he picks him up, gets him dressed, and puts him in the car seat. Dave climbs into the car, starts the engine, and drives down the narrow dirt road. Dense, thick green trees surround them from both sides. Sweat is beginning to form on his forehead. There is still no sign of her. Joey is saying, "Daddy, where we going? Where's Mama?"

Dave can't answer. He is staring down the road, fighting a feeling of panic. He goes past one cabin, a white shoebox with a flat roof. The paint is chipped and the window screens are torn. It looks deserted. He passes a raccoon carcass lying on the side of the road. Its head is missing. A shiver runs down his spine. Another cabin can be seen down the road. It is newly painted, a fresh maroon with white trim. White ruffly curtains hang at the windows, which are dark and empty. Then he sees something lying by the side of the road; when he gets closer, he sees the missing head of the raccoon he saw earlier.

Dave's hands are beginning to shake. What will he do if he can't find her? Or worse, what if he finds her lying somewhere . . . he can't think about that.

He focuses again on the road. Joey is singing and talking about boats rowing or something. Dave notices another cabin. It is a log cabin, with nicely polished rounded logs. Several lawn chairs are set up in front, ready for some social gathering. A large, powerful looking boat is tied up at the dock, bobbing up and down with the rhythm of the waves. Out of the corner of his eye, he sees a wolf standing in the trees watching as he drives by. Then Dave sees something red.

Ellen was wearing red jogging shorts when she left this morning, he thought. He turns his eyes to focus on the red he sees through the pine trees. As he rounds the bend, he sees the red shorts and Ellen; someone has a hold of her arm. His heart begins to race and he feels breathless. As he gets closer to them he sees it's a woman holding Ellen's arm. She is the neighbor from the new cabin he just passed.

Laughing—Ellen is laughing at something the woman is saying.

THE PRINCESS, THE LION, AND THE ROSE

Finding My Way Back Home

I look inside and see those faces
and parts of me I left behind
The little girl with eyes full of wonder,
another who is sad and so afraid
No one could see her special beauty;
no one was there to hold her hand
She lived in a world of imagination,
Creating people who could love and understand

All alone on this journey,
trying to find my way home

It's such a hard path to follow,
when you're lost and so scared
I used to feel the Spirit in me; it
would guide me on my way
My legs feel heavy, my arms are tired,
hands empty, no where to go
Now that voice is quiet inside me,
I can't hear those guiding words

All alone on this journey,
trying to find my way home

Then a bird lands on my shoulder,
singing a song so very sweet
I feel the trees standing with me,
blowing softly a gentle breeze
The sun is warm, it comforts my body,
I can feel the healing rays
Here I am in the beauty of nature,
feeling the touch of Gods own hand

Not alone on this journey,
trying to find my way home
I'm not alone on this journey,
trying to find my way home
Trying to find my way home

In the glen there lives the most beautiful princess. She has long golden brown hair—silky and shiny, thick as a lion's mane, soft curls swirling it like the wind. Her green eyes dance in a field of soft gentle freckles sloping over her nose. A whirl of energy surrounds her wherever she goes. She looks like she is running even when she is really walking. Always a sense of wanting more than is here. An urgency of wonder engulfs her.

One day this beautiful little princess is out picking flowers—yellow daisies, red roses, pink carnations, purple lilacs, wildflowers of every color and shape—until she has the most beautiful, elegant bouquet. She ties a white ribbon around it and holds it in two hands. She begins to dance through the meadow; butterflies and bees, dragonflies and crickets seem to join in her dance. The sunlight feels warm on her face. She can see her home in the distance and she shudders at the darkness in its windows. She dances faster, laughing, twirling, until she is out of breath. Falling into a bed of grass, rolling around, then looking up into the blue sky watching wisps of white clouds lazily floating, aimlessly swimming across the blue.

As she lies there, feeling warm and free, she feels safe, safe from the darkness of the windows and the empty tower. She stands up and brushes off her dress, shaking grass from her hair. Suddenly she sees a black robe, next to the tower, beckoning to her, wanting her to come. The black robe is holding something in its arms, carrying it almost like it is a baby. Only it is too large for a baby. The princess shudders, draws her shoulders up close to her ears, hugs her arms, and runs as fast as she can away from the tower and the black robe.

Where will she go now? The tower is her home. The quiet darkness, a reminder of an emptiness she endures. She runs faster, deeper into the meadow until she sees the woods: tall, majestic trees forming an arch of protection, a path of safety. She walks quietly into the silence of the trees, breathing little breaths until she finally relaxes in this new world. The trees whisper words in the wind: "It's OK—we're here. We're strong—we'll protect you, you're safe here." The princess grows tired. She stretches and yawns and sees a very large tree that resembles a picture she's seen in a book, of a nursemaid, full-bodied, large-bosomed, to rest her head, a woman who sings and rocks and says loving, warm words of acceptance. The little princess crawls into the crevice of the tree, feeling the warmth of the nursemaid's picture wrap around her as she falls asleep. She sleeps long and hard; she dreams of a kitten playing in a field, chasing a butterfly. She watches the kitten grow larger and larger until it is the most beautiful creature she has ever seen. He is golden with a mane so thick, ants get caught in his hair. He roars louder than any thunder she's ever heard. He is surely the King of all Beasts. Still he gently plays with the butterfly, warming himself in the sun.

The princess sleeps and she sleeps, dreaming years away. When she awakes, she feels refreshed and stands up to stretch. The princess feels strange. She is much taller and feels much older. "How long did I sleep?" she asks out loud. The trees whisper back, "Ten years." Now she feels scared and confused. Who is she now with ten more years? The woods suddenly seem darker and colder than before. The playful innocence has left her. The whirl of energy that had encompassed her is still. Now she only walks. The urgency and wonder have been swept away by the long sleep.

She wanders with no particular direction, just slowly going nowhere in particular, except far away from the empty tower with the beckoning black robe. She shivers at its memory, wondering what happened to the nursemaid tree and her youth.

Then she sees it, a glowing light off in the distance. She walks towards it, feeling a warmth from the light. Suddenly just in front of her is the most beautiful white rose, light encircling it like a beacon of praise. The rose is elegant, soft and velvety, unusually large and radiant. As the princess approaches she longs to hold it in her hand, to feel the warmth and the softness. She reaches out to touch the rose, but her arm aches so badly and becomes so crippled; she can't seem to reach it, no matter how hard she tries. She bends over to smell its sweet fragrance and her nose swells up. She tries to get closer but her legs become large and heavy. She aches for that rose. Every part of her wants to hold it and feel it. But try as she may, she cannot. Finally she turns away and sits a distance from the rose, just watching it, feeling the warmth even at such a distance. She sleeps fitfully, dozing and waking until she feels a presence close by. She becomes fully awake; leaving the rose, she ventures toward the presence she feels. It leads her further into the thicket of trees. Branches catch at her hair, tear at her clothes; bleeding scratches appear everywhere on her legs and arms, face and hands.

She hears a voice so low and rumbling, it sounds like a growl; eventually the growl becomes words. "Follow me," it says. The princess looks around to see who is speaking. It is so dark; then before her stands the lion from her dream. The most beautiful, powerful lion she has ever laid eyes on. The lion turns and looks at her. In his eyes, she sees wisdom, gentleness, and knowing. The lion speaks again: "Follow me." And he begins to walk.

The princess follows; a whirl of energy begins to feel its presence. She feels warmth return as she follows this lion. Everything is quiet—even the trees no longer whisper their words of encouragement. Only the lion's soft growl can be heard: "It's OK. Follow me, follow me." They walk through the forest, into the meadow she had once danced in. Suddenly, there in front of them stands the empty tower and the dark beckoning robe. The princess feels afraid, but still follows the lion, who walks straight toward that which she had run from years before. As she gets closer, she shivers. Fear makes her fingers icy cold. Her nose tingles. Her stomach knots up. Suddenly the black robe stands directly in front of her. The lion moves to the side, watching protectively, growling words of reassurance as she looks at the black robe.

Inside the robe is the face of a mother, a father, and in their arms they hold a little child. The black robe enters the empty tower carrying the child. The princess follows, the lion at her heels growling, softly growling. They walk up a darkened staircase, their footsteps echoing in the cave-like space. When they reach the top, there is a room, a circular room and in its center is the white rose—the beautiful white rose. As they approach, the princess feels the warmth and experiences the same sense of awe at the radiance of its beauty. She wants to touch it and feel its velvety softness. The black robe with the mother, father, and child encircle the white rose. The princess watches and a wondrous thing happens. The rose's petals begin to open slowly, one by one. Each time the petals open, more warmth and light fills the room. The brilliance is almost blinding. When the rose is fully open, the mother, the father, and the child climb slowly into the center. The black robe that shrouded them melts away and they look like angels dressed in white, and the littlest angel is a cherub singing sweet songs. The rose begins to close its petals slowly; the music plays deep inside, until the room holds the most beautiful white rose—petals velvety soft, warm energy spreading from the whiteness. The princess and the lion watch. The room is bright with the soft, white light that steadily glows. The princess follows the lion as he leaves the room, walking down the stairs, out into the sunlight. A brilliant picture fills her eyes. The meadow she loves is filled with her favorite wildflowers. She runs and dances; a whirl of energy surrounds her, an urgency of wonder twirls her dizzily in the sunlight. The lion just watches her, lazily growling softly. She turns and looks at her once empty tower with the dark windows and to her surprise, the tower is filled with light; a white radiant warmth surrounds it. A vine of wild white roses covers its walls. Beautiful songs float from its windows on angels' wings.

CONNECTIONS

Mother I See Your Face

Oh, mother, I see your face
So open now and full of grace
I reach out my hand; you reach out yours
Our fingers touch, Oh I just want more

We walk and talk, along the path
You tell me stories; we start to laugh
My heart does sing and I share my songs
My face it glows, as my love grows strong

We start to dance and twirl around
I touch your face and my heart does pound
There's something in your face I see
Oh yes, it is, a part of me.

Chapter 1

In the city of Daegu, located in South Gyeongsang Buk-do Province in South Korea, lives Mai Lee's family. Mai Lee is an eighteen-year-old girl who is very pretty, with fine features. She is thin and stands no higher than five feet tall. She is very close to her grandmother, Sim Chung. So on this particular day in September, Mai Lee, who is very upset, runs to Sim Chung's home. Mai Lee bursts into her grandmother's house, breathless. She is holding her right cheek; tears are in her eyes. She looks around frantically, then realizes her grandmother is probably upstairs in the "quiet" room. She runs up the stairs, slides open the rice-paper door, sees Sim Chung kneeling, and praying in front of the altar. While Mai Lee waits for her grandmother to acknowledge her, she studies the older woman, who is also small of stature but carries more weight than Mai Lee. Her grandmother's black hair is beginning to turn gray. She wears it short, and tiny curls frame her face. She is wearing her usual blouse with a long flowing skirt. After a minute Sim Chung becomes aware of someone standing behind her. She asks, "Who has entered my room?"

"It is me, Halmoni, Mai Lee."

"Why do you interrupt me at so sacred a time, Mai Lee?"

"I'm sorry Halmoni, but I couldn't wait any longer, something has happened. I told Oma and she said she doesn't want a daughter like me under her roof. She—she slapped me, Halmoni, she slapped me. She has never raised her hand to me before. I don't know what to do. Oh Halmoni."

Sim Chung bows once to the altar, gets up and walks across the wood floor to a low tea table. There are flat cushions on the floor around the table for sitting.

Sim Chung sits down on a cushion and says, "Come, Mai Lee, sit with me. Please, you pour us the tea and we'll talk of this urgent matter."

Mai Lee hesitates a minute, then walks over to the table. "Oh Halmoni . . . I'm so sorry."

Sim Chung interrupts Mai Lee, "Mai Lee please, come and sit and pour us some tea, then we will talk."

Mai Lee sits down on a cushion across the table from Sim Chung, her eyes lowered in respect for her grandmother. She takes the teapot and pours tea for Sim Chung and then for herself. Still looking at her teacup she begins speaking, "Halmoni I . . ."

"Drink child. Let the tea center your thoughts, calm your feelings, let its heat give you strength."

The two women sit and sip their tea each in their own thoughts.

After a couple of minutes, Mai Lee starts slowly speaking. "Halmoni, Oma has disowned me. I don't know what to do. I know I have brought shame to this family, but if Omoni had let me marry Jai Cho this never would . . ."

"Mai Lee, do not speak of your mother this way. You are only eighteen. Jai Cho was married when he asked you to marry him. Separation is not divorce. You know all we have is our family name. That would have been a dark shadow on our ancestors . . ."

Mai Lee interrupts, "I'm afraid I have still brought shame to our ancestors. Jai Cho has been gone for three months now. And I . . . I saw the doctor this morning. My suspicions were confirmed I'm . . ."

Sim Chung looks at Mai Lee. "With child. I saw a couple of weeks ago the change beginning in your energy."

Mai Lee asks, "How could you have known? I didn't know. I mean I've been late before. Why didn't you say something to me, Halmoni?"

Sim Chung sighs. "You wouldn't have believed me then. I waited until the time was right. Now the time is right. Be patient Mai Lee, give your Oma time to look inside and find a place for you again. Give her time. She is your Omoni. But now, the baby, what will you do?"

Mai Lee says quickly, "What can I do? I feel the energy thicken in my belly. I know of its presence. A child . . . Halmoni . . . a child." Tears start to stream down Mai Lee's face. "A child . . . but I cannot keep it. Jai Cho is back with his wife. There is no name to put on the birth certificate. The child will grow up with the black mark. The shame of no father will keep the child as nothing more than an indentured servant. This child, my child, will have no name. Oh Halmoni, what to do? Oma has hardened her heart to me. Please Halmoni, please don't turn your humble granddaughter away. There is so little money. I have nowhere to go. When Oma tells Oppa . . . what will I do?"

Sim Chung takes a sip of her tea. "When will this child be born?"

"In June, Halmoni, when the birds' nests are being built in the trees."

"Mai Lee, we must keep our ears open and listen to the words of the women at parties. See if someone is wanting a child, then we can . . ."

Interrupting, Mai Lee says, "Oh Halmoni, with all due respect, I cannot put this child on a doorstep. I cannot leave my baby lying there, abandoned. I've heard something about families in America wanting children. I talked to Kyung Lee who said that Mee Sung went to Eastern Services . . ."

Sim Chung interrupts, "You spoke to someone outside the family before coming to me? Mai Lee, you bring further hurt and shame to this house . . ."

"But, Halmoni, I saw Kyung Lee after I left the doctors. I was crying. She's my best friend. She asked me why I was crying. Halmoni, please forgive me. I didn't mean to bring further shame to this house. Please understand . . ."

"OK child, please calm down. Clear away the confusion. We must decide this matter. My heart will forgive you these indiscretions. You are my beloved Mai Lee who when she was young danced like a butterfly and sang like the morning sparrow. You brought me such hours of joy. Oh, but this Jai Cho was trouble, charming, intelligent, but trouble. I'm sorry of this unhappiness; our whole family must bear this in our hearts. America, you say, it is so far away. How will this child know about their heritage if they are so far away?"

"But I will know where my child is. I can bring her to the Eastern Services agency. I can put my child into someone's arms and know they will find them a good home. These families in the United States want children. I heard they are good homes, homes with love and caring. A home where there is no black mark on them because they will have fathers. This child will have all the privileges and opportunities as other children. My child could be anything, oh Halmoni, my child, MY child. My heart hurts already, like ten thousand arrows are piercing it. I'm so sorry, Halmoni. I'm so sorry."

"Mai Lee, come let's pray and ask for support and guidance on this matter. Then we will listen for the right answer."

Mai Lee and Sim Chung stand up and walk over to the altar.

Mai Lee complains, "If only Jai Cho . . . if Oma was more understanding."

"Stop Mai Lee, don't, we must look at what is. Come, let's pray. We will know the right answer."

Sim Chung and Mai Lee kneel in front of the family altar, they light sticks of incense to clear the negative influences and purify the energy around them, and bow their heads. The candles on the altar flicker behind the red glass.

~

An American family, living in a two-story house in Minneapolis, is waiting for their baby to arrive from Korea. They live on a quiet street with a fenced-in backyard. They have a room upstairs with a crib and it is decorated with wall hangings of pink balloons, teddy bears, and Winnie the Pooh. Jeremy, a handsome, dark-haired man of thirty, is standing looking at photos on the living room table. There is a stroller sitting by the door. His wife Elaine is looking in the stroller to make sure everything is there.

"Are you sure about this, Elaine? I mean what if . . . what if I . . . I mean will I bond . . . you know . . . will I . . . ?"

"Love her? Of course you'll love her." Elaine picks up a teddy bear from the stroller and starts to hold it like a baby as she continues talking. "You'll hold her in your arms and she will be yours. Your heart will open up and wrap around her and bring her into your soul. Your arms will tingle with the warmth of her body. You'll look into her eyes and know she is your daughter. You will feel a connection so deep you will know for certain she is your child."

"You seem so sure Elaine. After all of our losses at trying to have our own, I sometimes feel so beaten up. I mean, it feels so unreal. To think we are really, actually, truly going to have a child, one that will wake us in the night to be fed, and one who I will have to change diapers and make bottles for. One I can teach how to read. Oh, I can't wait to hold her in my arms. But what if . . . ?"

Elaine still staring at the teddy bear says, "What if? What if nothing. She'll be here; nothing is going to stop her from getting here. When she does, we'll take one look at her and know she is our daughter—I like the sound of that, our daughter." Elaine hands Jeremy the teddy bear and sees her watch. "Oh, look at the time. We must leave for the airport. Now, hurry!"

When they get to the airport, Jeremy parks the car, gets the stroller out, and starts pushing it to the terminal doors.

"Hurry." Elaine rushes ahead of Jeremy and opens the door. They get into the security check line, which thankfully is only about a block long. Elaine keeps looking at her watch. "I wish they would go faster."

Finally they get through the security check.

Elaine is almost running. "Hurry Jeremy."

Finally they make it to gate 19, where the plane from Korea is landing. When they get to the gate they see a man with glasses, a white shirt and tie, standing with a clipboard. Elaine rushes over, with Jeremy following behind with the stroller.

The man with the glasses turns to Elaine. "Good afternoon. You must be Jeremy and Elaine Swanson?"

Elaine blurts out. "How did you know?"

The man with the clipboard chuckles, "The empty stroller. I'm from the Children's Agency. My name is Jeff. I have a few forms here for you to sign. The plane is on time and should be arriving at any moment." Jeff gestures to a group of chairs. "Why don't we sit down over in those chairs and go through these forms?"

Jeremy follows Jeff over to the chairs and sits down. He watches Elaine, with her long curly brown hair, her petite body, as she goes and stands at the window watching for the plane. Then he thinks to himself how lucky he is to have her and what a great mother she will be.

Jeremy calls to Elaine, "Elaine, the plane won't get here any quicker because you're watching for it."

Elaine says, "I suppose you're right, I just want to see the plane land."

Elaine walks reluctantly to the chairs still watching out the window. She finally looks at Jeremy and sits down. Jeff hands them a clipboard with three forms that they need to read and sign.

"That's right, just sign here . . . here . . . and here."

The waiting area is beginning to fill up with people waiting for Flight 341.

The airport PA system makes an announcement. "Flight 341 from Seattle is landing and will be arriving at Gate 19 on the Blue concourse."

"Did he say flight 341? Isn't that her plane?"

Elaine jumps up and runs to the window. "Jeremy, there's her plane, she's here. Can you believe it? She's here."

Elaine watches as a plane lands and starts taxiing over to their gate.

Elaine pulls out a photograph, Jeremy gets up, walks over, and stands behind her looking at the picture of Jai Ling.

"Oh, Jeremy, Jai Ling is finally here."

Jeremy reaches into their stroller and finds the camera. "Let me get a picture of the plane." He takes a couple of pictures. "Just think—she is sitting behind one of those little windows."

Elaine, still watching out the window, says, "She's in there right now with that black stick up hair and pudgy cheeks and eyes that see right through you."

Jeremy puts his arm around Elaine. "Elaine, our daughter is here."

Jeff walks up behind Jeremy and Elaine. "I'm sorry to interrupt but there are a few things I must tell you. When the escort comes off the plane you must say Ahn-yang-ah-sa-yo.

That is hello in Korean. After she gives you your daughter, bow and say Kam-sa-ha-mida, which means thank you. Then you . . ."

Elaine, not really listening, interrupts Jeff. "Oh Jeremy, do we have everything? Let's see, the stroller and a bottle with cool water, diapers, and a blanket. Did we bring the stuffed bunny?" Elaine, frantically, looks everywhere in the stroller. "Jeremy, it's not here, where is her bunny? Oh, here it is under the diaper bag."

Elaine watches as the plane pulls up and attaches to the tunnel where passengers walk through to the terminal. Then she sees the first passengers walking through the tunnel. "Passengers . . . here come the passengers!!!!" Jeremy sees a tear escape Elaine's eye. Elaine starts jumping up and down and exclaims loudly, "Oh Jeremy, it's her!!!!"

Chapter 2

Mai Lee is in her grandmother's "quiet" room, kneeling at the altar; her head is bent in prayer. She is wearing a simple, soft green dress. Her hair is pulled back in a ponytail. Sim Chung walks into the room quietly and waits. A couple of minutes later Mai Lee asks, "Is that you, Halmoni?"

"Yes, Mai Lee. I thought you might like to have some tea with me."

Mai Lee lifts her head up, and turns to look at her grandmother, who is dressed in a loose violet blouse and beige pants. Sim Chung's eyes look at Mai Lee with intelligence and wisdom. Sometimes Mai Lee gets lost in those eyes.

Mai Lee finally speaks, "You know what day it is too?"

"Yes, Mai Lee. Come, let's sit at the table and have our tea."

Mai Lee gets up and walks over to the low table with the tea set and sits down on a cushion. Her grandmother sits across from her. Mai Lee pours them each some tea. They take a couple of sips.

Mai Lee speaks up, "Six years, Halmoni, it's been six years, I've prayed and lit her candle. Do you think she wonders about me? Do you think she is happy?"

"I'm sure she does, at some level. I feel her thoughts with us at times. She knows where she comes from. She is proud of her heritage."

Sim Chung pulls up her violet blouse a couple of inches to get something out of her pants pocket. "Mai Lee, I have brought you something."

Sim Chung pulls out a little doll. It is a cloth doll with a porcelain face. The doll is wearing a beautiful Han Bok of red, pinks and greens. "Here, this is your Jai Ling to hold. See her eyes, how they look right at you, almost like they are looking through you. Smart eyes. She has smart eyes like your Jai Ling. This doll was given to your great-great-great-grandmother when she was six. She was the first grandchild born in her family. Jai Ling is my first grandchild. This doll has always brought with it happiness and good fortune. Let it bless my first grandchild, and your first child."

~

A beautiful picture of a Korean countryside is hanging on Elaine and Jeremy's living room wall. A woman stands in the center of the picture wearing a traditional dress; a colorful hanbok. Just below the picture, there is a table filled with birthday presents wrapped in sparkly pink, green, and blue paper. Jeremy is lying on the floor of the living room; his daughter is sitting on his stomach and tickling him.

Jeremy says, laughing, "Janey, stop! I can't take anymore! Please stop!!!"

Janey stops and gets off. "OK, Daddy, when I first got here from Korea my name was?"

Jeremy looks at Janey. "That's easy, it was Jai Ling and now it is Janey Ling Swanson."

"OK, Daddy. How do you say yes and no in Korean? Remember if you're wrong I get to tickle you."

Jeremy rubs his chin thinking. "Let's see. Yes is nay and no is . . . no is . . ."

Janey jumps on top of Jeremy and starts tickling him. "It's ah-ne-o Daddy. Can't you remember your Korean?"

Elaine walks into the living room and says, "OK, you two. It's time to sing and blow out candles."

Elaine is carrying a birthday cake in the shape of a cat, with six candles, one on each whisker. The candles are burning brightly. Jeremy and Elaine start singing:

> happy birthday to you, happy birthday to you
> happy birthday, dear Janey, happy birthday to you.

After they're done singing, Elaine puts the cake on the table next to Janey's presents. Janey gets up and runs over to the cake, leaving Jeremy sitting on the floor. Elaine looks at Janey. "OK, it's time to blow out your candles."

"Let's see I wish for . . . I wish for . . . " She blows out her candles. "You know what I wished for?"

Elaine says, "Don't tell us or it might not come true."

"Oh Mommy, you're so silly. I wished foooor . . . " Janey starts laughing. "I wished for . . . I'm not going to tell you."

Elaine smiles at Janey and says, "Oh, you little tease. Come on, let's bring these presents and put them on the floor by your dad."

Elaine and Janey carry over the presents, put them on the floor next to Jeremy, and sit down. Janey sits on Elaine's lap. "Which present do you want to unwrap first?" Elaine asks.

Janey looks at the presents and picks out the biggest one wrapped in sparkling pink wrapping paper and shakes it. "Oh, Mommy, Daddy, is it what I think it is?"

Elaine laughs. "Well, open it and find out."

Janey rips the paper off the package and opens the box. She pulls out a Korean ceremonial dress, a Han Bok. The dress has pinks, reds and greens and is very beautiful.

"Oh! I love it. It's the one I loved so much at the Soon Hee Korean market in St. Paul. Now I will look like a real dancer."

Janey gets off her mom's lap, stands up, and slips the Han Bok on over her clothes.

"Mommy, Daddy, look at me. Aren't I pretty? Can I wear it to grandma's for the family birthday party? Please, Mommy, pleeeease. I can't wait to show my cousin, Jessica, she'll want one just like it. I know she will."

Jeremy gets up, goes to Janey, and reaches out his hand. "May I have this dance my beautiful ballerina with the sparkling eyes?"

"Do my eyes really sparkle, daddy?"

"Like diamonds, my princess."

Janey and her daddy start to dance together. Elaine sits on the floor watching and smiling. Suddenly Janey stops and runs over to Elaine and crawls on her lap.

"You know something, Mommy. I'm really lucky. I have two moms. I have you and my mom in Korea. I know she loves me; she cried when I left."

Elaine and Jeremy exchange a knowing look and smile.

"Yes, She loves you very much." Elaine kisses the top of Janey's head. "How could anyone not love such a silly girl who teases her mom and dances with her dad?"

Janey jumps up and runs to her dad. "OK, daddy, this is your last chance. How do you say thank you in Korean? I bet you forgot."

Jeremy falls on the floor and Janey crawls onto his stomach and starts to tickle him.

After a full day of birthday celebration at Janey's grandmother's house, Elaine and Jeremy sit down to relax after tucking Janey into her bed upstairs.

Jeremy kicks off his shoes. "Finally, a little peace and quiet."

Elaine puts her head on Jeremy's shoulder. "I know, it was a really busy day. I think Janey loved everything—from the chocolate cake her grandmother made and her favorite meal of cheesburgers and fries, to the presents her cousins gave her. Janey really loved the Barbie Dream House my mom gave her. I'm glad my mom put up the pin the tail on the donkey. The kids really enjoyed that."

They both sit there quietly; five minutes later Jeremy starts snoring.

From upstairs Elaine hears little feet running across the floor then a voice yelling, "Mommy, Mommy!"

Elaine gets up just as Janey is starting to walk down the stairs to the living room, wearing her purple night gown with small white princess crowns printed on it. Elaine goes up the stairs, picks Janey up in her arms, and sits back down on the couch. "What's wrong, Janey?"

"I had a dream, Mommy. There were these people who looked like me and they took me away from you and brought me to their house. They were really nice, but I wanted to go back to my home with you and Daddy. They wouldn't let me and then I woke up. It was scary, Mom. They were nice but I wanted to be with you."

Jeremy wakes up while Janey is talking about her dream. He puts his hand on Janey's arm. "Janey, it was only a dream.

You are here with us and no one is ever going to take you away from us. I promise."

Janey starts to relax. Jeremy stands up and says, "Now, how about I pick you up and carry you to your comfy bed and read to you. I know, let's read your new book, 'the Beauty and the Beast?'"

"OK, Daddy." Jeremy and Janey head upstairs. Elaine goes into the kitchen and makes a pot of tea, brings it into the living room and sits down.

Jeremy walks in shortly after, sits downs, pours himself a cup of tea, and looks at Elaine. "Do you think a part of her is remembering being brought here from Korea, a place where everyone looks like her, to here, where we don't look like her? She was only six months old."

"I know, and remember after she had been here for a week, the social worker came; she was Korean. Janey took one look at her face and started crying, holding on to me tighter, like she was afraid the social worker was going to take her away. It sure does make you wonder, doesn't it?"

Chapter 3

Mai Lee slides open the rice paneled door and enters her grandmother's living room. Sim Chung is sitting on her favorite bamboo couch with colorful cushions, sipping her tea in deep thought. A teapot is on the table in front of the couch. Mai Lee stands and watches her grandmother, waiting a moment to speak.

"Halmoni, do you have a few moments to spare for this humble granddaughter?"

"Mai Lee, you know I always have time for you." Her grandmother looks at her closely. "Your cheeks are flushed. Does this have something to do with Hee Sauk?

You have been spending so much time with him and his family."

Sim Chung pats the cushion next to her. "Come sit next to me and have some tea. Tell me your exciting news."

Mai Lee walks across the room, noticing her grandmother's new oriental rug on the wood floor, and sits down on the couch. She pours herself a cup of tea.

Sim Chung asks, "You have been dating now for what, almost two years?"

Mai Lee takes the tea and says, "Yes, and now he has asked me . . . to marry him."

Sim Chung smiles. "He is a good man. He comes from a well-respected family. He has an important job as a clerk with the Supreme Court. You have done well Mai Lee with this Hee Sauk. Do you love him?"

"With all my heart, Halmoni. But Halmoni I came because . . . well . . . is it OK to . . . well, to keep secrets from your husband? Do I have to tell him everything when I marry? Can I keep parts of myself hidden from him? Is it still honoring him if I . . . ?"

Sim Chung interrupts, "You are thinking about Jai Ling. Mai Lee, you will always be your own person, no one can ever take away what is inside of you. That is yours to hold sacred. It is OK to still love Jai Ling and remember her without having to share it with Hee Sauk. It will feel like a burden on your soul to carry this alone, but love her you will, regardless. Hee Sauk would not understand this indiscretion from before. He is a man of our government, therefore a man deeply embedded in our cultural ways. This part of yourself you must keep secret from him. Maybe someday . . ."

"Oh, Halmoni. I do love him. I do want to marry him. So you think it will be OK? Oh Halmoni he must never find out. He must . . ."

Sim Chung puts down her cup of tea. "No one will tell him. Your family wants the best for you. Your secret, it is safe. Here, Mai Lee, lay your head on my lap. Let me stroke your hair like I did when you were a child."

Mai Lee puts down her cup and lays her head on Sim Chung's lap.

Sim Chung strokes Mai Lee's hair. "It will be OK, my little cherry blossom. It will be OK." She begins to hum 'Arirang.'

~

Elaine is sitting on the couch in her living room, talking on the telephone. Janey is upstairs asleep in her bed and Jeremy is out for his evening walk.

"Hi, Patty. What? Janey's doing fine. She just loves her piano lessons. She practices every day, her favorite song is 'The Entertainer.' She loves to listen to music and watch music videos where the girls are all glittery. And the phone never stops ringing; she has so many friends. She is always so busy. Lately though, the questions she is asking are so hard. She is usually so happy and full of life. But lately at night, in the quiet moments when I tuck her in, the questions come. I know, being nine years old means wanting to fit in and be like everyone else. The other night she asked me, 'How come you are so much older than everyone else's moms? You are at least ten years older than all my friends' moms, except Kaylee, you are only five years older than hers. I wish you were younger, Mom.'"

Elaine sits back on the couch and sighs, "Janey keeps bringing up all the differences. I know right now all she wants to do is be like everyone else. Then last night she said,

'Mommy, I wish you looked like me. I wish your eyes were like mine and your hair was black. I wish you were Korean like me.' I told her that I would be Korean in a minute if I could. I would love to look like her. Then she said, 'Mom, it's hard sometimes when no one in my family looks like me, especially you, Mom.'"

Elaine looks at a picture on the table of Janey at the state fair. "Then Janey said, 'Mom, when we went to the state fair with Tae-suk's family, I liked holding the mother's hand because she looked like me. I pretended I was with their family.' What did I say? I told her I understood why she felt that way. That I liked that my sister and I looked alike."

A small tear rolls down Elaine's face, her voice choked with tears, she says, "Then she asked the question I knew would come soon; she asked, 'Mom, why didn't my mother in Korea want to keep me? Did she really cry when I left?' Both of us had tears by then . . . what did I tell her? Well . . . I hugged her and told her I knew for a fact her mother cried when she left and it was the hardest decision she ever had to make. Then Janey looked up at me and said, 'How do you know, mama?'"

Elaine hesitates then says, "I hope it's alright, but I told her about you, her Aunt Patty, and how you had a child you placed for adoption. She asked me, 'Was she sad mama? Did she cry a lot?' I told Janey how you cried very hard. That it was the most difficult thing you ever did. I told Janey I saw the love you had for your child. I told her how you still think about him, especially on his birthdays. Then she asked, 'Sometimes I wonder what my life would be like if I was still in Korea?'"

Elaine sighs, "The questions are hard. But it feels good to talk at that quiet tuck-in-time. We cuddle. You know sometimes . . . well, I feel . . . promise you won't laugh at me? I can feel when her birth mother is thinking about her.

Watching what you went through helps me understand her birth mother. I told Janey it was out of love. Oh, do you think what I said was the right thing? I mean I hope I didn't say too much. What? How did we end our conversation? Janey snuggled up to me and said, 'Momma, I love this time of night when we can sit and have our girl talk. Guess what, I like Josh; he kissed me on the cheek at recess and told me I was cute. Did a boy ever kiss you on the cheek and say you were cute? Can I get a Korean Barbie doll; I mean do they have any? Can I get my ears pierced? Kaylee did.'"

Chapter 4

Hee Sauk and Mai Lee are walking to her grandmother's house. Mai Lee is pregnant; she looks at Hee Sauk and motions for him to stay on the front porch. "I will be right back, I just need to run into my grandmother's and ask her something. Please, just wait right here."

"OK Mai Lee, but remember we don't want to be late for the performance, the tickets were very expensive and . . ."

"I promise it will just take a few minutes. Just take a seat on the porch. The Daegu Opera house is only three blocks from here, we have plenty of time."

Mai Lee rushes into her grandmother's home. Sim Chung is just walking into her living room carrying a tray with a teapot, cups, and a bowl of sweet Korean rice balls.

Mai Lee says, "Oh, Halmoni, let me carry that." Mai Lee takes the tray from Sim Chung and carries it to the table in front of the couch. "I only have a moment. Hee Sauk is waiting for me on the porch. I had to see you for just a moment."

Mai Lee stops, trying to calm herself.

Sim Chung sits on the couch and pats the seat next to her. "Let Hee Sauk wait. Come sit and have a cup of tea

219

and a sweetened rice cake—you need food for the baby you are carrying. The tea will calm you so your words will come out with more clarity. Where is Kim Lee?"

Mai Lee sits down. "He's with Oma."

Sim Chung pours Mai Lee a cup of tea and offers her a rice cake. Mai Lee takes the sweetened rice cake and eats it while Sim Chung is talking.

"I can't believe your Kim Lee is almost five. Now, Mai Lee, tell me this so important news."

She says quickly, "My due date for this second child has been changed, it's ..."

Hee Sauk's voice calls from outside. "Mai Lee! We must hurry."

Mai Lee calls to Hee Sauk. "Hee Sauk, please be patient, I will be there in a minute."

Mai Lee turns to Sim Chung. "Oh Halmoni, the due date is June 18th, the same as . . ."

"The same as Jai Ling's."

Mai Lee picks up her teacup and takes a sip, then says, "Oh, this is so hard. The last thirteen years I have thought of her every day. I cannot tell Hee Sauk, he would . . . it would be disastrous. Now the birthdate, the connection is so strong. How do I keep the secret any longer, knowing my child with Hee Sauk shares the same birthday as Jai Ling? Oh Halmoni, he would divorce me. He would disown me like Omoni did. He would never have married me if . . ."

"He must not find out . . . yet. Maybe after some years and his love has deepened its roots into your married life . . . maybe. But Mai Lee it will be OK. Trust in your faith, there is a reason the baby is being born on this day. There is a reason, I will pray for you. You go home tonight and light incense on your altar and pray for enlightenment and trust.

Hee Sauk knocks gently on the door. "Mai Lee, we are going to be late."

"Now go, my child. Your husband is waiting."

Mai Lee puts down her teacup, gets up and starts to leave. She stops, rushes to Sim Chung and kisses her on the cheek. Then she rushes out and takes Hee Sauk's arm. They hurry down the street, not wanting to be late for the performance at the opera house. Sim Chung sits and sips her tea, then eats a sweetened rice cake. After bringing the tea tray into the kitchen she walks upstairs to her "quiet room" and goes to the family altar. She kneels down, lights the incense, and bends her head in prayer.

~

Elaine walks into the living room carrying a tray with a teapot and cups. She puts it on the coffee table in front of the couch, sits down, and pours herself a cup. Today she is dressed for comfort in her baggy jeans, and her favorite cotton T-shirt. She looks around the room sipping her tea and notices the laundry basket she had brought in earlier, sitting at the end of the couch. She puts her teacup down, moves the laundry basket closer, and starts folding the laundry. She hears the front door open and thinks, *Janey's home from school*. Suddenly Janey comes bursting into the room looking around and pacing. Elaine looks at Janey's jeans with holes in them, her tank top, and ponytail whipping back and forth as she paces and Elaine thinks, *teenager, my daughter is a teenager.*

"Mom! Mom! Hello, Mom."

"Yes, Janey, I see you and I hear you, loud and clear."

Janey still pacing starts ranting. "Sometimes I just can't stand all this . . . I mean why are people so . . . what is the world coming to . . . I just don't think it's fair . . . oh Mom. I just don't think it's . . ."

"Calm down, Janey. Here have some tea. You look like you need it. It will calm you down enough to at least finish your sentences so I can understand what you are saying."

Elaine pours a cup of tea for Janey.

Janey ignores it and starts pacing faster. "Oh, Mom. It isn't fair. I mean when I was younger the boys on the bus and playground would tease me and call me 'flat face,' 'china girl' or say 'can you see through those eyes?' I knew they just wanted to make me angry. I mean it didn't really bother me. But lately, I get worried that a boy isn't going to like me, because I'm . . . I'm . . . different. I mean I've always felt a little different, you know because I don't look like you or dad . . ."

"But Janey, you have the same color hair as your dad. You have my ears and chin and Aunt Peggie's legs, your . . ."

"Stop Mom, you always do that, but face it, I don't really look like any of you. And today after school the gang stopped at the malt shop. I sat there eating my French fries and listening to every one talk. Sara . . . well she got asked out. I mean Jon has been calling her for a month now about math stuff and today he asked her out. And then Lisa said that Jason called her . . . and Jenny said that Tom called. I just sat there listening; I had nothing to add. And soon it will be summer vacation and I bet no one will call me and . . ."

"Janey, slow down, slow down. You had a boyfriend in first grade, and then again in second and third grade. And two in fourth grade and fifth grade. And let's see, last year in seventh grade Jackson called you and you always told me to say you weren't home. Where is this coming from? I mean who was the boy that kept calling a couple of months ago?"

Janey, still talking fast says, "That was James, a boy I met at Korean camp. He is nice and I like to talk to him but he wants me to be his girlfriend, and I'm just not attracted to him that way. I don't know why, but I don't like to hang out with Koreans too much. I guess inside I feel more Caucasian than I do Korean. I want to fit into my own life. I don't want to feel any more different. I'm just not attracted to Korean boys."

Elaine looks at Janey. "So, where is this all coming from? Why are you all of a sudden . . . ?"

Janey stops pacing and sits down next to her mom. "I don't know . . . I just don't know. I've just been feeling so . . . so . . . different. I'm not Caucasian like my friends are, and I don't know anyone else in my class at school who is adopted. I'm glad I have my friends from Korean Culture camp but they don't go to my school. I just feel like there is no one at my school that is like me. And lately when I'm with my friends they make comments like, 'What's it feel like to be adopted?' or 'Do you ever wonder about your real mother?' I tell them you are my real mother. They can be so dense sometimes."

Janey takes a sip of her tea. "And today in class we talked about genetics. We had to fill out a questionnaire about our genetic history, things like eye and hair color, but also any family diseases, or genetic abnormalities. It felt terrible; I couldn't answer any of the questions. I don't know the medical history of either of my birth parents. It made me feel so alone and different. And then I realize I lived in Korea for almost six months and you lived here. And then I start to think about my birth mother. What would it have been like to be raised in Korea? And lately I've just been feeling so emotional about everything. At times I feel so angry inside, it hurts all over my whole body. But I don't know what I'm really angry about."

"Well, it is your birthday next week."

"I know Mom, and I'll be fourteen years old. And no one is asking me out and I'll be an old maid with no friends."

Jeremy walks into the living room. "Who's an old maid with no friends? Not my Janey."

"Oh Dad, you're prejudiced because I'm your daughter."

"I don't think so. I see the way the boys look at you when we go to your band concerts."

"You think so, dad? I mean, will I ever have a boyfriend?"

"Janey, you will have so many you won't know what to do with them all. I will have to set aside time to interview them and decide which one I will let date my daughter."

"Stop teasing me, dad, I'm serious. No one is ever going to ask me out."

"OK, Janey, I'll be serious. You are beautiful, intelligent and wonderfully creative. Having a boyfriend will never be a problem for you. Your problem is going to be your father, who is going to lock you in a closet until you're 21. So he can protect you."

"Oh, Dad."

"Well, my two favorite girls, I need to get going, the dentist awaits."

Jeremy walks over to Janey and kisses her on the head. "I love you, Janey. I'm going to make sure all those boys treat you right."

He gives Janey a wink and then kisses Elaine good-bye.

After Jeremy is gone, Elaine turns to Janey and says, "You know, your dad is right. Don't you remember last Valentine's Day? The doorbell rang three different times and when you opened the door there was a box of candy and a card from three different secret admirers.

"Yeah well, I never found out who they were. Anyway, I hope you guys are right. I guess sometimes, Mom, I just want to look like everyone else. I want to just blend in and not stick out so much. I mean my differentness always sticks out."

"Being different is hard, especially at your age. I know, I was always different too. I was heavy as a little girl. I'd get teased about my fat legs and I was told I was weird because I was always reading. It didn't feel good. But then I started to like those things that made me unique and different. I eventually wrote a play called 'Murder at Midnight' that the neighborhood kids performed. Everyone loved it. So embrace who you are, Janey, a beautiful and intelligent young lady. That face could launch a thousand ships, just like Helen of Troy. And those eyes of yours that see it all, so bright and . . ."

"Mom, can I meet her someday?"

"Meet who, Janey?"

"Can I meet my birth mom? I want to find her. Mom, do you think if I find her she'll want to meet me? Oh, can we go to Korea and I can see where I was born and maybe meet my foster mother and see where I stayed? And then maybe eventually meet my birth mom. Can I?"

"Well, I know there are tours that go to Korea every summer. I think it's too late for this summer. But next summer would be perfect. I just got a brochure in the mail."

Elaine gets up and walks into the front hall, looks through a pile of mail on the hall table. "Here it is." Elaine picks it up and walks back into the living room, as she's reading it. "Yes, the tour leaves on June 18th—wow, it leaves on your birthday, and returns three weeks later. I do have some paperwork upstairs we can fill out to start the search for your birth mother."

"Oh Mom, can we? How long will it take? Do you think she'll want to meet me?"

"I don't know, honey. But I feel in my heart she'll want to. Do you want to go upstairs and read about your birth in Korea? How old your mom was, where she lived, what she's like? Where you stayed? We can look at the picture of your foster mother. And fill out the paper work."

"OK, and let's bring up some of the chocolate chip cookies you made, to have with our tea."

Janey goes into the kitchen and gets the cookies, while Elaine carries their tea upstairs.

"Janey, about all your anger, I think you have so much going on inside right now. Not having answers would make anyone angry. Try to be patient."

"I know, thanks for saying that. I was just thinking that maybe for my birthday this year, I could do a Korean theme. I'll bring my friends to a Korean restaurant or maybe a costume party where everyone must dress Korean or maybe we can have a Korean style dinner at home with my friends. Yeah, they'll have to use chopsticks and sit on the floor and eat Kimchi. Ooooo, can't you just see Lisa and Katie from next door taking a bite of Kimchi?"

Chapter 5

Mai Lee runs to her grandmother's home. She is breathless from running all whole way. When she gets to the front door, she pauses, takes a deep breath, releases it and slides the rice paneled door open. "Halmoni!"

Sim Chung is sitting in the living room waiting for Mai Lee. "Come in, Mai Lee." Mai Lee walks into the living room and sees her grandmother. Sim Chung smiles and says, "Come, I have made us some tea and I have your favorite snack, ginger candy."

Mai Lee looks surprised. "How did you know I was coming?"

Sim Chung smiles. "I heard your steps on the porch and have been feeling your energy all day. I knew something was happening. So come and sit."

Mai Lee sits on the couch watching her grandmother as she pours the tea. "Thank you, Halmoni, I have felt so distraught all day. I couldn't wait for Hee Sauk and the children to leave. They all went to the Daegu Stadium to watch baseball, so that gave me a chance to get away and come see you."

Sim Chung looks at Mai Lee. "Here have some ginger candy, it will settle your stomach and fill your mouth with sweet goodness."

Mai Lee takes a few ginger candies. She puts one in her mouth and moans with the pleasure of its taste.

Sim Chung, happy, asks, "So tell me, what has happened?"

Mai Lee's words rush out quickly. "Yesterday, I took the children to Haein-sa to see the temple-library in the beautiful mountains. As I was walking up the path, I saw Jai Cho. We gave each other a very slight nod and moved on. My heart was racing. I thought about Jai Ling. I never told him I was pregnant. He doesn't know about her."

Sim Chung takes hold of Mai Lee's hands and looks sternly into her eyes. "You must never tell him. It would do him no good to hear of this. He has his family. It could bring harm to both our families. Let it be, Mai Lee. This again is something you must carry on your own."

Mai Lee looking distressed. "I wanted to tell him yesterday. When I saw his face, it all came back—our time together. I wanted him to know about our child. But you are wise, Halmoni, I know I can never tell him.

Sim Chung pats her lap. "Come Mai Lee, let me stroke your hair so you can release all these emotions you are carrying."

Mai Lee puts another ginger candy in her mouth and lays her head in her grandmother's lap. The tears start to flow as she releases the loss of the past.

As Sim Chung strokes Mai Lee's hair she shares her thoughts with her granddaughter. "I have a very strong feeling that Jai Ling is also being faced with her life and is struggling. The planets are aligned in such a way that we are being forced to deal with our inner dragons and fears. This is good, for bringing light to those places will tame the dragons and lessen the fears. I am here with you, Mai Lee, you are not alone."

Mai Lee's grandmother continues stroking Mai Lee until the tears dry up. "Mai Lee, close your eyes and rest. In a little while you and I can go to the corner café and have some Bulgogi, chop chae and Bibimbop."

~

Janey is getting dressed to go out with her girlfriends. She has tried on at least ten shirts and finally decided on a pink tank top that has some "bling" on it. She has on her new tight skinny stretch jeans and her sandals with a 2-inch heel. She looks at herself in the mirror and decides she needs to wear her hair up. She puts her black hair in a messy bun at the top of her head. With the heels and the bun it makes her look at least 5'2" tall. She smiles and looks at her watch; it's 7:00. Her phone rings. "Hi, Jenny. Yeah, I'm almost ready. I'm glad you got your mom's car. OK, I'll see you in a few minutes."

Elaine walks by Janey's bedroom and looks in. "Who was that, Janey?"

"It was Jenny, she's driving tonight. We're all going to the mall to see a movie."

Janey drops her lip gloss and it rolls under the bed. "Shit," looking at Elaine, "Sorry, I mean shoot."

"So who is going tonight?"

"I don't know, Mom."

"What movie are you going to see?"

"Mom, is this a third degree? What's the matter—don't you trust me? I'm just going out with friends."

"Janey, what's going on?"

"Nothing."

"Janey?"

"Allison met her birth mother last week. She said it was uncomfortable at first but then they spent time together and she sounded so happy. Why haven't I heard anything about my birth mother? Jason broke up with me, my birth mother doesn't want to meet me, oh, never mind. I've got to go. Please just quit asking so many questions. Just leave me alone. You are so nosey. I'm almost seventeen, I'm almost an adult. Quit treating me like a child." Janey hears a horn honking outside her window.

"I've got to go; Jenny's here. I'll see you later. Don't worry about me and please stop asking so many questions. It is annoying."

A few hours later Jeremy and Elaine are pacing the floor of the living room in their pajamas. It is well past midnight.

Elaine stops and looks out the window. "Where could she be? Last year we find out she's cutting herself, then I find alcohol hidden in her drawers. What is happening to our Janey? She has never stayed out past curfew and not called."

Jeremy, still pacing, looks exhausted, his black hair showing strands of gray. "Everything was going so well. What happened? She seems so angry and sad. It has been almost three years and nothing from her birth mother. I don't know what to say to her. I try to think of reasons and tell her why it's taking awhile. Then she blows up at me and says I don't know anything. She's right, I don't. Last night I tried to tease her a little, like I always do to get her to smile, and she just got angry and slammed the door in my face."

"I know Jeremy, this anger of hers, that started in middle school, just seems to be getting worse. I feel like she is always angry with me, like there is something I've done wrong. Even though every time she asks for something I bend over backwards to make it happen, it's just never enough. I feel like there is an itch she has that I just can't scratch. But I don't think she knows what it is either. Nothing seems to help."

The phone rings and both Jeremy and Elaine grab for the phone. Elaine is closer so she answers it. "Hello, yes, this is

Janey's mother. You're who? She's charged with what?" Elaine listens a minute. "OK, I understand. Yes, we'll be there in a few minutes."

Elaine hangs up and looks at Jeremy. "She's at the police station. Janey was at a party that was busted. The cops brought the kids from the party to the precinct to call their parents. They were all drinking and smoking marijuana. Janey could be charged with possession of marijuana for personal use or she might have to pay a fine and take a drug education course. But we can go and pick her up now."

Jeremy grabs his car keys. "Let's go."

Elaine looks at Jeremy. "Aren't you forgetting something?"

Jeremy looks puzzled. "What?"

Elaine says, "Pajamas."

Jeremy looks at Elaine. "Right."

Both Jeremy and Elaine run upstairs and put on their jeans. They leave on their pajama tops, grab a jacket and the car keys.

When they get to the precinct they see the parents of Janey's friends all heading for the door of the police station. No one is talking or making eye contact. The front area by the desk sargeant is crowded; everyone is there to sign out their children. When it is Elaine and Jeremy's turn, they step up, show their ID, and sign Janey out. When they see Janey, her head is hanging down, her hair has come loose and falling over her face, and she won't look them in the eye. They all three climb into the car and drive home.

Janey is sitting in the back seat crying. After a couple of minutes she says, "Mom, Dad, I'm so sorry. I don't know what is happening to me. I swear tonight was the only time I've smoked dope. I just wanted to try it. While I was sitting there in the police station I looked around me and thought this is not me. I think I need to see somebody. I don't feel like myself anymore. I feel so angry and I just want to strike out at someone. I know it's no excuse, but I just keep wondering why I haven't heard from my birth mother. I can't understand how she does not want to see me. And then Jason broke up with me. But, I really seriously don't want to smoke dope or drink anymore. I want you to be able to trust me again. So, I really mean it when I say, I want to see someone. I want to work on all this stuff I just can't seem to deal with."

Elaine turns and looks at Janey. "I understand, honey, you have so much going on in that head of yours. Maybe we can . . ."

As Elaine is talking, Janey's tears stop. Her leg starts bouncing up and down; a tension starts to build in the car.

"Stop it Mom! You don't understand—you never will! You are not adopted, you are not from a different culture. You can never understand. No one in the family looks like me. I look in the mirror and I see a Korean face, but inside I feel like I'm Caucasian. I know I went to Korean culture camp and learned things about Korea. But I haven't been raised Korean, I've been raised Caucasian American. Sometimes I just don't know who I am. When strangers see me they see a Korean girl. They think I speak Korean. They ask the dumbest questions. Like the policeman at the police station who came up and asked me if I spoke English. It is all so confusing. I feel angry at you, because you are not my birth mother. You haven't known me all of my life; there are six months I lived somewhere else. In biology we are studying reproduction and this last week they talked about the baby getting to know his mother's voice because he spends nine months in there hearing her voice every day. So when I was in my birth mother's uterus I heard her voice, her Korean words and when I was born I lived in a Korean foster home surrounded by the language of my mother. Then suddenly as a baby I'm here, in this country where the words and sounds and smells are so different. I just feel so sad and angry that you weren't there with me during that time, and angry at my birth mother for giving me away. In my head I realize it isn't anybody's fault, it's just what is. But it hurts and I don't know what to do with all the hurt and anger."

Janey stops ranting and takes a couple of deep breaths and exhales slowly, trying to calm herself down. "I know you guys love me and you try to understand when I'm in my dark, overwhelmed, lost place. I do love you for it. You guys are trying so hard. But you just don't seem to really understand. I think I need some help working through all the issues that are churning inside of me. I need some help with the hurt and anger and to accept myself. I don't think this is something you can help me with." She stares out the side window of the car and watches as the trees go by, she sees a man walking his dog, and she notices a couple sitting on the front porch kissing.

Janey sighs. "I'll be seventeen in a couple of months. I want to go to college, so I need to buckle down next year and study I know my junior year is important, because colleges really look at those grades. I need to get a handle on all this. It just all feels like too much." Janey starts crying again.

Jeremy pulls over to the side of the road and parks the car. Elaine looks at Jeremy. They both get out of the car and go sit in the back seat with Janey, each putting an arm around her. They let her cry it out.

Then Elaine says, "Janey, I had no idea all this these things were bothering you. I wish I could magically make it all go away; these are all hard issues to deal with. I'm glad you are ready to get help. This next week, while you're grounded, we'll have time to research together and find someone for you to talk to who understands what you are going through. You are not alone in this Janey. We'll talk with someone too. Someone who can help us understand. Tonight has been a wake up call for all of us."

Jeremy and Elaine exchange looks. Jeremy clears the tears out of his throat and looks at Janey.

"Janey, I know I can't understand it all now. But I know it helps to not look at the whole pile of issues—you have brought up a mountain of them. Just slip one out from the pile at a time and work on it. Pretty soon it is no longer a pile—just a few scattered pebbles, with space and time to work them out. Remember we can't change the past or the world out there, but we can change how we react to it. You are still our loveable Janey. I'm glad you finally shared what's been going on with you. That is the first step, to ask for help when you need it and to know you're not alone."

Chapter 6

Sim Chung is in her "quiet" room kneeling at her altar; the incense is burning, and her head is bowed in prayer. Mai Lee has finally found time in her busy day to stop at her grandmother's house. She knocks on the door. When there is no answer she slides the front door open and walks in calling, "Halmoni . . . Halmoni! When she can't find her grandmother downstairs, she rushes upstairs to the "quiet" room.

She slides open the door, sees Sim Chung praying, and stops. "I'm sorry, Halmoni, I didn't realize what time it is."

Sim Chung, whose hair is almost all gray now, bows to the altar and then stands up with some difficulty because of her age. Mai Lee rushes over to help steady her.

"It is OK, Mai Lee. I always have time for my granddaughter."

The two of them sit down on cushions at the low table.

Sim Chung looks at Mai Lee. "I hear in your voice that something has happened. Where are Kim Lee and Sang Hee?"

"They are with Oma. She says she never gets enough of her grandchildren. Halmoni? How do I say this? I have thought of this for so many years. I mean this day, what should I do?"

Sim Chung puts her hand over Mai Lee's hand. "Slow down Mai Lee, you are speaking to an old woman whose mind works at half the pace it used to. What are you talking about? Oh my, my brain is catching up. They have called you, haven't they?"

"Yes, Halmoni. They said she put in a search for me five years ago, but because I moved and my marriage they had trouble finding me. She is coming to Korea. She is coming here to find . . . me. She wants to meet me. Oh Halmoni, my arms ache to hold her, to look into those eyes that see right through you. I want to kiss those eyes . . . but Hee Sauk must not find out and Kim Lee and little Sang Hee must not . . . oh, I want to see her, I ache to see her but what if my family here finds out . . . ? Halmoni . . ."

"Mai Lee, you will see her. I will go with you. Your family does not have to know. It is hard in our culture where adoption isn't talked about; it always has to be such a secret. The shame of a child born out of a marriage keeps it all in the shadows. We will ask this agency that called you. We'll ask for anonymity or confidentiality or whatever it is called. You will see her, Mai Lee; you deserve to see her and she deserves to see you. Fate is willing it or she would not be coming. But you must protect your family here, our culture; it is cruel to this adoption idea. Your husband is so much a part of that culture; we must protect him from this news. I will go with you."

"Oh Halmoni, will you? Omoni will be angry if she finds out."

"It is OK, I am the matriarch here. You will see her."

"OK, I will call them back today. Halmoni, she is coming to find me . . . she is coming to find ME. She has thought of me all these years, twenty years next month. Oh, my God. Halmoni, she is coming to meet me on her twentieth birthday. She is a woman now, my child, is a woman."

Mai Lee gets up and walks over to the altar and kneels down, she lights incense, and bows her head. "Thank you, oh ancestors, for bringing my daughter to me, thank you."

~

Elaine is in the living room pacing and talking on the phone when Jeremy walks in. Suddenly she goes to the couch and sits down. "What?" Elaine listens for a couple of minutes. "Yes, I'll talk to my husband and Janey; we will let you know. I'll get back to you later today."

Elaine hangs up the phone and looks at Jeremy. "They found her birth mother. She moved and then got married, that's why it has taken so long to find her. She wants very much to meet Janey. Let's call Janey; I don't think she is in class right now. Let's see—she has two more weeks of classes, then finals, and then she'll be home for the summer. We can get plane tickets for a month from now. I can't believe we are finally going to meet her birth mother."

Janey a month later, is home from college and is upstairs packing to go to Korea. Elaine and Jeremy are sitting on their couch in the living room. Jeremy is reading the newspaper and Elaine is writing. Jeremy looks over at Elaine, slowly folds up the newspaper, and puts it on the floor. Elaine looks up from her writing.

"Are you OK, Elaine? You have been so quiet lately. It's been so hard for me to get close to you. I seem to walk in a room and you leave it. Last night I tried to hold you and you pushed me away and rolled over and went to sleep. Why are you putting up a wall between us? Is there something . . . ?"

Elaine interrupts, "It's this trip to Korea. I have so many feelings and I'm afraid if you hold me I'll relax and all the tears will come flooding out. I want to be strong for Janey."

Elaine puts her pen and paper on the coffee table and gets up. She starts pacing around the room, looking at all the family pictures on the tables and walls. "When Janey was fifteen we went with that tour group to Korea, and she met her foster mother. That seemed enough for a while. But then we put in a search for her birth mother, and didn't hear anything for five years. It seemed to really affect her. Now they have finally found her birth mother and she wants to meet Janey. Janey has waited so long for this. There are so many built up expectations. Will the meeting be good for our Janey? Will she finally get some answers?"

Elaine picks up a picture and looks at it then puts it down and picks up another picture. "For so many years I have thought of this woman who gave birth to our daughter. On Janey's birthdays I've thought about her. I see the presence of this woman in Janey's face. A woman who reflects back, like a mirror, our daughter. I want to tell her, her daughter is happy and strong. That she shouldn't worry. Janey is fine. I put myself in her place and I know what it's like to lose a child. Oh, I want to hug and thank her for giving me the gift of raising this beautiful daughter of ours. When Janey went to Camp Choson she learned the history of Korea, she learned to make bulgogi and chop chae, and she learned Korean songs and dances. But I'm aware that there are still so many missing pieces for her. Sometimes Janey will say, 'I wonder what it would have been like to grow up in Korea?'"

Elaine sits down next to Jeremy and puts her head on his shoulder. "These first two years of college have worked wonders on Janey. She has started writing her own music and finding beautiful ways to express herself. She seems so happy and content with her life and who she is now. High school seems like ages ago. I wonder how it will turn out when we all meet. Will I lose my Janey to Korea? Will she love her Korean mother more than me? Will it be too hard for her to handle?"

Jeremy turns and puts his arms around Elaine. "Elaine, you are being so silly. Janey is a strong, confident young lady now. She'll be fine. And our daughter loves you so much. Who does she go to when she is having a bad day? Who does she spend hours shopping with and talking about boyfriends and gossip about her friends with? She has always needed you and wanted to be with you. Those couple of high school years were hard, but you two found a new understanding after seeing that counselor. So now you two are attached at the hip most of the time. Just like two peas in a pod. Going to Korea isn't going to change that. You two . . ."

Elaine interrupts, "I know it's silly. But still . . . ? I think I'm going to go lie down. Thanks Jeremy."

Elaine kisses Jeremy, gets up, and leaves the living room. Jeremy picks up the newspaper and soon his mind is filled with baseball scores, golf tournaments, and soccer games.

Janey walks into the living room. "Oh, there you are. I've been looking all over for you. I need to talk to someone and Mom is so on edge right now."

Jeremy pats the cushion on the couch. "Come and have a seat."

Janey starts pacing instead. She starts talking very fast.

"I've been upstairs packing for our trip and I just keep thinking, I'm scared, dad. What if I don't like my birth mom? What if she doesn't like me? What if she decides not to see me after all? What if I look in her face and there is nothing there? And what about my birth dad? I've never really thought about him. But if I have a birth mother, I have to have a birth father. Where is he? Doing this has opened up so many more questions for me. How will it feel to see her face?"

"Janey, sit down. You are making me dizzy with all your pacing."

Janey finally sits down and is quiet.

"That's better. You've asked some good questions, Janey. I wish I had some good answers. We are journeying into a place we've never been."

Jeremy puts his arm around Janey. "But remember, my bright eyed dancer, your mom and I are with you wherever this journey takes you. I'm sure when you see her face you'll see something. I'm sure she'll be there from what the social worker said. Your birth father, we will probably never meet him. The social worker said that she does not have permission to share that information, we don't know why. But your birth mother is excited to meet you. Honey, I know this is hard. Going into the unknown is always hard. But we are doing this as a family."

Jeremy kisses the top of Janey's head. "Janey, honey, remember we love you and we will always be here."

There is the sound of the back door opening and closing. "Hey, Janey! Jaaaney! It's Katie and Lisa."

Janey calls out, "I'm in the family room!"

Lisa and Katie walk in carrying a plastic bag with a skirt in it.

They walk behind Jeremy and say, "Hey, Mr. Swanson."

"Hi Katie, hi Lisa." Jeremy gets up hastily before they can say anymore.

"I'll see you later, Janey; I told your mom I'd go upstairs to finish packing."

Jeremy leaves as Katie sits on the couch with Janey, and Lisa sees a game of Gonggi (Korean jacks) on the corner table. She picks it up, sits on the floor, and begins playing jacks.

Katie looks at Janey and says, "My mom said you were leaving tomorrow afternoon. So we thought we better come in and put in our orders from Korea. In fact, see if you can get me that dance game, Pump, and maybe some cute fans."

Lisa stops playing jacks and looks at Janey. "And you better bring me back some real authentic Kim Chi, you know I love how it smells. Not! And maybe you can get me this Korean jacks game and a CD by H.O.T."

Janey, feeling overwhelmed, says, "Slow down you guys, I'm not going to remember all that, you'd better write it down."

Katie hands Janey the plastic bag she brought in. "Oh, and here is the skirt you wanted to borrow. Oh yeah, and where are the plants you want us to water while you're gone?"

Janey looks around. "The plants are here in the living room and on the front porch; I'll show you in a minute. I have the watering instructions upstairs; you could come up and help me finish packing. I'd love the company. Plus we can catch up, I haven't seen you guys since Christmas."

Janey stands up. "So, are you coming?"

Lisa and Katie stand up. "Sure, let's go."

As they walk up the stairs, Lisa asks, "So can we listen to your new CD's while your gone? Did you bring your Play Station 2 home for the summer? I mean what a waste for it to just sit here all by itself with no one to play it . . . ?"

After the girls get the watering instructions they go home so Janey can finish packing.

Later that evening, after Janey and Elaine are in bed, Jeremy walks into the living room. He looks around to make sure the room is empty. When he's positive it is, he looks up. "Oh, Lord, it's been awhile since we've talked. My life this week has just been so busy and full of . . . I know that's no excuse. Look, I really need you right now." He walks over to the table with the pictures and picks one up.

"First I want to thank you again for giving us this child to raise. She's been everything a father could want. Even through the rough spots, she asked for what she needed. Tomorrow we're leaving for Korea, to meet her birth mother. Please protect my Janey, and have this meeting with her birth mother go well. And could you help me? I'm always the strong one for my family. I'm a little nervous about all this and I just don't feel very strong right now."

He puts the picture he is holding down and starts to turn away, then stops and looks up again. "Oh yes, could you bless the airplane and make sure we get there safely? I still have trouble trusting that big machine can fly."

Jeremy hears Elaine calling from upstairs. "Jeremy, where are you? It's getting late and we need to be up early, we need to be at the airport at least an hour and a half before our flight leaves. Jeremy!"

Jeremy calls up the stairs. "I'll be right up, Elaine, after I turn off the lights and check the front and back doors."

Chapter 7

Mai Lee and her grandmother are waiting at Gate 23 at the Daegu international airport. They are standing and watching out the window looking for flight 247. They are both dressed in their hanboks, a traditional Korean dress worn for important occasions. Sim Chung's hanbok is white and blue with small silver flowers embroidered along the bodice. Mai Lee's hanbok is pink and white with purple rose buds embroidered on the skirt. Sim Chung puts her hand on Mai Lee's arm and says, "She is almost here. I can feel her excitement . . ."

"Oh Halmoni, my knees shake. I can barely hold myself up. My heart is racing. My hands, look at them tremble. I want to run away. Will I know her when I see her? I can't wait to see her face. I wonder, will she have my face?"

The social worker from Eastern Services walks up to Mai Lee and Sim Chung. She bows to them and says, "Sim Chung, Mai Lee."

Mai Lee and Sim Chung bow to her.

The social worker continues, "I am Oori Ko. I am from the Eastern Services. The plane should be landing soon. I will bring you to a room in the airport where you can have some privacy with Jai Ling and her family. I must get the room ready. I'll be back when the plane lands."

Mai Lee turns to her grandmother and pulls something out of her hanbok. "Halmoni, here is the doll you gave me fourteen years ago. I am happy that you want to pass it on to our Jai Ling."

~

Jeremy, Elaine, and Janey are on the airplane. Jeremy has fallen asleep. Janey and Elaine are awake and looking out the window when the plane's PA system comes to life with an announcement. "We are approaching Daegu International Airport. We will be landing in approximately fifteen minutes."

Elaine pats Janey's hand and smiles. Janey smiles back.

"Mom, I am so nervous. I don't know if I can do this. My hands are trembling; my heart is racing. I don't think my legs would support me if I stood up right now. I want to run away. Do you think I'll recognize her? When I look into her eyes will I know it's her? Will she be glad to see me? Will she know me? When I see her face, will I see my face?"

"Calm down, Janey. Here take my hand." Janey takes Elaine's hand.

"We will know soon enough, Janey."

The plane starts its descent and lands at the airport. Janey feels the wheels touch down and squeezes her mom's hand. "Mom, we're here."

Elaine looks over at Jeremy who is still asleep. "Jeremy wake up, we're here."

Elaine and Janey stand up and stretch. Elaine says, "After 22 hours my feet will finally feel the ground again."

She looks over at Jeremy and sees he's awake and starting to stand up. "Jeremy, grab the carry-ons, Janey do you have . . . ?"

"Yes, Mom, I packed the gifts in my backpack."

They exit the plane, Elaine in the lead; Janey has her backpack on, and Jeremy has the carry-ons and the camera.

They walk by a window overlooking their plane. "Jeremy, take our picture. Janey, let's stand here so we can get the plane in the background."

Jeremy starts to take the picture.

"Wait! Jeremy, are you sure the memory card is in the camera?"

"Did you charge the camera battery, Dad?" Janey chimes in.

Jeremy checks the camera and mumbles not quite awake. "Yes and yes. OK, now say KOREA."

Janey and Elaine groan and say, "Korea."

Janey turns to her mom. "Here Mom, will you take my backpack? It's killing my back?"

Elaine takes the backpack and gives it to Jeremy.

Janey starts talking and pointing at everything. "Oh Mom, look at all the pictures and look at those hanboks. They look like the ones we saw last time in Seoul at the Korean market, Nam dae mun."

Suddenly Janey sees a Korean woman and her grandmother standing at a window by the arrival gate.

~

At the same time Mai Lee sees Janey exiting the jetway and walking towards her. She whispers to her grandmother. "Jai Ling. It is Jai Ling. It's you, Halmoni. She looks just like you. See her eyes, her mouth?"

Sim Chung smiles. "You have always had my eyes and my mouth. So Mai Lee she has your eyes and mouth. Her smile it is yours also."

~

Janey notices the two women are staring at her. She whispers to her mother. "Mom, that must be her. Look at how she is looking at me.

Mom . . . Mom . . . what's wrong?"

Elaine has stopped walking, tears streaming down her face. She is staring at Mai Lee. "It is you, Janey, she looks just like you. She is so beautiful."

~

As Elaine is talking, the social worker walks up to Mai Lee and Sim Chung. She escorts the women over to Janey and her family. She introduces herself to Elaine, Janey, and Jeremy.

"Ahn-yang-ah-sa-yo, welcome to Korea. My name is Oori Ko. This is Mai Lee and her grandmother, Sim Chung. They don't speak English, so I will be their interpreter."

Mai Lee walks up to Janey and looks into her eyes and smiles. She gently brings her right hand up and touches the side of Janey's face. She looks into her eyes and studies her mouth. Then she takes both of Janey's hands in her own, slowly looking at them and turning them over. She lets go of Janey's left hand and twirls her around with her right hand, to look at all of her. She says something to Janey. Oori Ko says, "She just said that you have her face and hands. You possess the fluid movement of a Korean woman and you have eyes like Sim Chung, her grandmother."

Mai Lee takes Janey's hand and leads her over to Elaine. Then Mai Lee looks at Elaine and says something. Oori Ko translates, "She said thank you for raising this beautiful daughter and asked if she may hug you."

Elaine, in tears, reaches out to Mai Lee and gives her a big, emotional hug. Together Mai Lee and Elaine turn to Janey and reach their arms out to her. The three women hug, tears streaming down their faces, with big smiles. Mai Lee turns and reaches for Sim Chung's hand and brings her over to meet Janey and Elaine. Sim Chung is carrying a beautiful Korean doll with a porcelain face. She turns to Janey and says something as she hands her the doll. Oori Ko translates her words. "She says, she is happy to meet you and has brought you a family gift. This doll she is giving you has been passed down for generations; she wants to pass it down to you, as you are her first grandchild." Janey, with tears in her eyes, turns to Sim Chung and says, "Kam-sa-ha-mida." Janey looks at the porcelain doll, tears streaming down her cheeks, as she holds the doll to her chest. She looks up at Sim Chung, smiles, and gives her a hug. "Please tell her I feel honored to be given such a precious gift, and to be her first grandchild." Oori Ko translates her words to Sim Chung, who smiles at Janey and nods her head.

Jeremy, burdened with all the things he is carrying, looks on with tears in his eyes, happy to see the smile on his daughter's face and the joy in her eyes. He looks at Elaine and sees her face; it is calm now. She has finally met the woman she has thought so much about all these years.

Elaine and Janey turn and look at him, motioning for him to come join them. He walks over and is introduced to Mai Lee and Sim Chung. Then Oori Ko says to him and his family. "I will bring you now to a more comfortable private room, where you can have your first visit."

~

Janey, Elaine, and Jeremy are sitting on the plane waiting for take off.

Their three-day visit seemed way too short. They hear the engine noise build up and the plane begins to roll. They start speeding down the runway and suddenly the ground begins to fall away. They are on their way back home. Each day they were in Korea, they were able to visit one place with Mai Lee and Sim Chung and Oori Ko. The first day they went to a baseball game at Daegu stadium, the next day they went to dinner at a Korean restaurant, and the third day they went to the Daegu Zoo. When Janey and her family were on their own they absorbed all they could from Korea, the markets, the hikes through beautiful scenery, and hearing music performances at night.

Now the plane is leaving and Janey at first is quiet, looking out the window as they take off. But once they are in the air the words begin to just flood out.

"Mom, I just don't know what to do with all these feelings inside. It was so exciting to meet the woman who gave me birth, a woman who looks like me. I just couldn't stop looking at her. I'm glad we took lots of pictures. And I love Korean food: Bibimbop, bulgogi, chop chae, and tofu soup with beef and octopus. And her gentle grandmother seems so wise and caring. No offense, Mom, but it makes me wonder how I'd be different if I had lived in Korea with them. I feel sad that I lost that part. But mixed into all that, is knowing I love you and dad so much and I can't imagine my life without you.

Then I feel what it must have been like for her. I can tell by the way she looks at me that she has thought of me over the years. I'm so glad we got to meet each other. I love the doll Sim Chung gave me. It is so precious and to think it has been given to the first grandchild over the generations. I am Sim Chung's first grandchild. I was so glad we could spend a little time with them each day. But there is still this tiny sense of loss flowing through everything. And a lot of what if's . . ."

Janey stops talking and looks out the window of the plane, deep in thought, then sighs. A tear escapes her eye and slides down her cheek.

She turns to Elaine. "But I am soooo glad we went and that Mai Lee and Sim Chung can be a part of my life. I am so glad to know we can write letters to each other through Oori Ko. It is so nice to find some pieces to the puzzle. It was nice to even talk about medical histories to find out something about my genetics. And my birth mother told me a little about my birth dad. I guess I will never meet him. I realize how much I love my home with you, my friends, my school, and my life. But now I feel more connected to Korea and where I came from. I feel a peace inside."

Chapter 8

Mai lee and her grandmother are sitting in her grandmother's living room having a little private celebration with tea and snacks.

On the table in front of the couch are bowls of sweet Korean rice cakes, candied ginger, Korean sesame candy, and a tea set. As they talk about the visit they eat snacks and drink their tea.

"Oh Halmoni, she is so beautiful. Her eyes are so bright . . ."

Sim Chung adds, "And happy. Yes, her eyes are bright and happy. They are smart eyes. I told you Jai Ling had smart eyes."

"And Halmoni, I see Jai Ling in Kim Lee and Sang Hee. Kim Lee has the same smart eyes she has. When Sang Hee smiles, she has the same little dimple by the left corner of her mouth that Jai Ling has." Mai Lee pauses a minute and sips her tea. "I have been thinking lately about Sang Hee and Jai Ling having the same birthday. I think it is to show I can have what I lost. I have Sang Hee and I can still love Jai Ling and feel the connection there."

"Our ancestors do bless you, Mai Lee. You are right. Jai Ling and Sang Hee, having the same birthday, is a way the ancestors have given for you to heal what you lost. Our Jai Ling will always be a part of us through your Sang Hee and Kim Lee. The ancestors tell us all is right with the world. And look at Jai Ling's American mother, Elaine. She loves Jai Ling so very much. And did you notice she has eyes like Jai Ling also. Smart eyes. Her father too, he is so much the teacher . . ."

Mai smiles, "Yes, my soul is quiet. After all these years I can feel peace inside. I know my Jai Ling is happy. She knows of her culture. This honors me to know she has pride in herself. And I love the gift they brought: this beautiful scrapbook of Jai Ling full of pictures and stories of her childhood."

Mai Lee places the scrapbook on the table next to the bowls of snacks and opens it. "I love this picture of Jai Ling performing at her piano recital. She is studying music in college too. Halmoni, do you have a special place I can keep this? So I can look through it when I here."

Mai Lee stops and looks at her grandmother, "Halmoni? . . . Jai Ling is like you. I think she will grow to be just like you. She will know things. She has your wisdom in her eyes. I have decided, Halmoni. When Kim Lee turns sixteen and Sang Hee is eleven, I am going to tell Hee Sauk of this daughter. I want Kim Lee and Sang Hee to meet their sister if the ancestors allow."

Sim Chung deep in thought. "Sixteen and eleven. Yes, those are good ages to learn new knowledge. Hee Sauk will be . . . what . . . forty-five? It is a good age for him to hear the truth. Your marriage roots will be deep and fertile; the news may cause a windstorm but the roots will hold."

Mai Lai smiles. "Jai Ling said she would write and send pictures. The social worker, Oori Ko, said she would translate the letters when she writes. I asked her to call you when the letters arrive. Is that OK, Halmoni? Do you mind?"

"No, granddaughter. No, I do not mind. And your scrapbook I will keep in the 'quiet room' in my special cupboard under the window. You can come and look at it whenever you want to."

~

Janey is just back from Korea, sitting at the writing desk in the living room writing a letter to Mai Lee and Sim Chung. The porcelain doll Sim Chung gave her is sitting on the table. She hears the back door open and the voices of Katie and Lisa talking to each other.

Katie walks into the living room. "Hey neighbor, your mom said we'd find you here. We want to hear all about Korea."

Lisa adds. "Yeah, Mom said maybe I can go on my eighteenth birthday. So tell us, what was she like? Everything, tell us everything."

Katie and Lisa sit down on the couch as they are talking. Katie realizes that Janey is writing. "What are you writing?"

"Oh, it's a letter to my birthmother and my great-grandmother. I can finish it later. You want to hear about my trip? Well, it was incredible. My birth mom is beautiful. And I got to meet my great-grandmother. My birth mother's name is Mai Lee and my great-grandmother's name is Sim Chung. She is seventy-eight. Sim Chung had these incredible eyes. Eyes that look right through you . . ."

Lisa looks at Janey. "Yeah, like your eyes."

Janey looks at Lisa surprised. "What? . . . like my eyes? My eyes look like I can see through you? Really? You never told me that."

Katie says, "Yes we did. Remember when you helped with my school carnival? I asked you to be a fortuneteller, because you had the look."

Janey smiles. "I didn't know you meant my eyes were . . . Well anyway, my birth mother kept touching me and smiling. She held my hand while we talked . . ."

Katie interrupts Janey. "What did your mom do while all that was going on?"

"My mom? My mom cried, I mean she had tears in her eyes the whole time and a huge smile. My mom looked happy and peaceful. Then the coolest thing happened: my birth mother and my mom hugged and smiled."

Lisa sighs. "Oh, I wish I could have been there. I wonder if I'll ever get to meet my birth mother. Mom said that we don't know for sure if I can because . . ."

Katie interrupts Lisa, not wanting her to go on talking. "So what about Mr. Protective? What did he do the whole time?"

"My dad? He just sat there looking like a fish out of water with all the hugging and crying. Look, I was just going to go upstairs and finish unpacking. My mom wants to get all my clothes washed. Why don't you guys come up and help me? I want to show you my new hanbok. Plus I got you something . . ."

Katie excited interrupts, "What? You got us something? What a neighbor."

Lisa joins in. "Come on, let's go upstairs. Did you get the CD and poster?"

Janey gets up from her seat, leaving the porcelain doll sitting on the table.

Katie, getting impatient, says, "Come on, don't keep your friends in suspense." Then Katie sees the doll. "Wow, where did you get that? It's beautiful. It looks old."

I got it from my great grandmother. It used to belong to her great-great-great grandmother."

Katie looks around the room. "So, do you have any pictures yet? I mean you did take pictures didn't you?"

Lisa joins in. "Yeah, I want to see pictures of your birth mom and your great grandmother?"

Katie looks at Janey. "Did they wear hanboks? We want to know and see it all."

Lisa says, getting excited. "When the time comes you can help me get ready for my trip to Korea. Maybe I can borrow your Han Bok? In a couple of years I'll almost be your size."

Janey looks first at Lisa, then Katie. "Slow down you guys. Come on, let's go upstairs. I'll tell you everything and show you pictures and give you your gifts."

Lisa and Katie say at the same time. "Now you're talking."

The three girls go up to Janey's bedroom.

Katie looks at Janey. "It's really nice to have you home for the summer, I miss you when you're away at college."

After the girls go home, Janey goes back to the living room to finish her letter. She starts writing. "Dear Oma, Thank you and Sim Chung for the porcelain doll. I will cherish it always . . ."

As she is writing, her mother walks into the living room talking to Janey. "Janey, did Lisa and Katie find you? I sent them in while I was weeding the garden. I thought maybe you'd want to go to the mall and do a little shopping? I need to get a gift for Lisa and Katie's mom, to thank her for watching the house while we were gone."

Elaine sees Janey writing and stops. "Oh, I'm sorry. I didn't know you were busy. Looks like your writing a letter."

"Yes, I thought I'd write to Mai Lee and Sim Chung to thank them for the porcelain doll."

Elaine sits down next to Janey. "Mai Lee is such a special person; so is her grandmother, Sim Chung. You know I think I'd like to learn more Korean. It's such a rich language. I love the hanboks we got in that open-air market, Seomun in Daegu. I think I miss the smell the most. The smell of Kimchi cooking and all those rich spices you smell as you walk along the sidewalks. And people, did you ever see so many people in one place . . . ?"

Janey joins in. "My favorite was chop chae."

Janey gets up and parades in front of her mom tossing her hair around.

"And I think I need to get my hair streaked; every woman in Korea seems to have their hair streaked."

Janey walks over to the table of pictures. "But I think what I liked most is seeing faces like mine, everywhere I looked. And Mai Lee felt so familiar to me. Like I was looking in a mirror."

Janey walks back to Elaine and sits back down. "And it made me happy to see your face throughout the trip. You seemed at peace like you found something you'd lost. Since I've been home I feel that same peace, like I found a big piece to the puzzle."

Janey looks at Elaine. "I have something I want to tell you. I met someone this year at college, I think he might me 'the one.' He is a year a head of me in school and is studying engineering and going for a Ph.D. He is blonde with blue eyes and has a few freckles across his nose; he makes me laugh.

We have so much fun together, I love being with him. His name is John. Maybe this summer you can meet him. He's from out East but he might come visit here in August. But enough talking, I think it's time to go to the mall and shop till we drop, I can fill you in on all the details about John while we cruise our favorite stores. I'll finish this letter and the unpacking tomorrow."

Elaine stares at Janey. "What, you have a boyfriend and you're just telling me now . . ."

Chapter 9

Sim Chung is her "quiet" room, lying on a day bed next to the low table; she is dressed in a nightgown and appears to be asleep.

Mai Lee walks in quietly looking for her grandmother. Mai Lee whispers, "Halmoni, are you awake?"

Sim Chung opens her eyes and looks at Mai Lee. "No need to whisper. I may be getting older but I don't sleep all day. My mind is too active to allow sleep. I have so much to ponder. Now what does my special flower want of me at this hour?"

Mai Lee starts pacing. "I had a dream last night. I dreamt Jai Ling was coming here and . . ."

Sim Chung interrupts, "Oh, my mind is slipping into old age. Here—I received this yesterday from the Eastern Services."

Sim Chung pulls an envelope out from under her pillow and hands it to Mai Lee. Mai Lee stops pacing and takes it quickly, tears it open and reads it. Suddenly she sits hard on Sim Chung's bed.

"Halmoni, it is my dream. My dream is true. Jai Ling is coming in a month. She is getting married and wants to bring her husband here on their honeymoon. She wants him to meet us. She will be staying in Seoul for a week. Then traveling to our humble town by the ocean. She wants to visit our home."

Mai Lee stands up and starts pacing up and down, then stops and looks at Sim Chung. "Oh, Halmoni, I must tell my family. This time I must tell the secret so it can be free to blossom and gain new life. It is time for my children to learn of this sister."

Mai Lee starts pacing again as she is talking. "Kim Lee will be fifteen in a month and Sang Hee will be ten. My husband too can hear of this daughter."

"You are right, Mai Lee. Hee Sauk's love is deep; he will be able to endure this wrinkle in his life. He is older and wiser and knows more about the world. He has changed with his travel to other countries, like the United States. He sees there are other ways to live."

Sim Chung motions for Mai Lee to sit down next to her on the bed. Mai Lee sits as Sim Chung continues speaking. "And Mai Lee, you must be careful how you tell Kim Lee. He is the oldest child in your family. It might rock his position to know of this older sibling. And with Sang Hee be gentle how you tell her of the shared birthdate; it might make her feel closer to Jai Ling, or it might threaten that your love is divided and she doesn't have as much as she thought."

Mai Lee looks at her grandmother. "You are so wise, Halmoni. I will take my time in how I tell them. Then I will write Jai Ling and tell her, nay, we want her to visit our home. We should meet here first, the home of my Halmoni. Then I will bring her to my home."

Sim Chung takes Mai Lee's hand. "It will honor me and your ancestors to bring her here first. Now go, let me rest. Tell the news to your family. I will tell your Omoni, my daughter."

~

Janey is standing on a chair in her living room. Her mother is sitting on the floor hemming the dress with pins stuck in her mouth. Out of the corner of her mouth she says, "My wedding dress fits you beautifully, Janey. Just a couple inches shorter and . . . " Elaine stands up and backs away, looking Janey up and down. "Oh, Janey, you look so beautiful. My little girl has become such a beautiful woman." Elaine keeps staring at Janey not speaking; a tear glistens in her eye.

"Mom . . . hey Mom . . . come on . . . I don't want to stand here all day."

Elaine seems to come to, sits down, and begins pinning the hem again.

Janey excitedly says, "Oh Mom, in just three weeks I'll be Mrs. John Langdon. No, I take that back I'll be Mrs. Janey Langdon. My name will never be John. Why do woman do that? You know, use their husband's name, like they don't have an identity of their own."

Elaine stops pinning and looks up at Janey. "That will never happen to you, princess. You have always been your own person. I know from previous discussions on important decisions like where the wedding should be and where the honeymoon . . ."

Janey interrupts her mom, "Let's not start that again. Don't worry; I'm not going to stay in Korea to live. I'm just going for a month on my honeymoon. I want John to know some of my culture." Janey looks at her mom. "Mom, what is going on with you? Why is this so hard for you to understand?"

"Oh Janey, honey, I do understand. It's just that, well, I'm . . . I mean; you're getting married. I'm so afraid I'm going to lose you. You'll have a husband; you can live anywhere.

Then you have your birth mother in Korea and I, well, I don't want to lose you in my life. In less than a month I'm watching you get married and then you'll have your own home. I've always thought that that home would be in the same city. So we can go shopping, have lunch; I can babysit your children. If you go to Korea for your honeymoon and see your birth mother—what if you stay there and she gets to go shopping with you and have lunch and . . . ?"

Janey steps down from the chair and hugs her mom. "Mom, no one can ever replace you. You are my real, forever-to-eternity mother and I love you with all my heart. I will always be your little girl, even if I did decide to live in France or Canada or Korea. We will always be close; we will always be strong in each other's lives."

Elaine takes a shirttail and dabs at her eyes. "I know Janey, you're right. It's just that, well . . . " Elaine sighs. "I am glad, Janey. Really I am. I love John. I know I'm not losing a daughter; I'm gaining a son. All this wedding stuff has just made me feel so emotional. Now, come on, let's finish this dress, then go out shopping for . . . for, whatever."

Janey gets back up on the chair and Elaine starts hemming again.

When the hemming is done, Elaine goes upstairs to get ready for shopping. Janey gets off the chair and stands in front of the floor-length mirror her mom brought down from upstairs. She starts fixing her hair in different ways to see how it would look with the wedding dress. Her dad comes whistling into the living room. "Janey, have you seen your moth . . . ?

Jeremy stops talking when he sees Janey in her wedding dress and stares. "Janey, you . . . look . . . so . . . so."

Janey turns from the mirror and looks at her dad. "Not you too. Look, I'm just wearing a wedding dress, not a sign saying I'm leaving you forever."

Jeremy is still staring. "You just look like you're glowing . . . yes, you're glowing. I guess your dress makes me realize this is for real. I mean I'm going to give you away to another man. No more late night talks or early morning walks."

"Dad, don't worry. I'm sure there will still be times I'll need your advice."

Jeremy seems deep in thought. "I really like your John. He in some ways reminds me of myself at that age. I love the way he looks at you."

"Then why are you acting like things are going to be so different? I'm still your Janey."

"But Janey, marriage is a big change. Your home with John will take priority over our home. I know, I'm supposedly gaining a son; he is a great golfer. But your life is changing. You can make your own choices without my advice. That's how it should be. But I'll miss being that person to you . . ."

"Daddy, earth to dad. Are you hearing anything I'm saying?"

"Janey, remember I'm giving you away at the wedding, I'm giving you to John. In other words I'm letting you both know you don't need me. I'm telling John I'm trusting him to be there for you in ways I have been and I'm letting you know it's OK. Oh, I'm sure we will still have our times but it will be different. Janey, I . . ."

Janey runs over and hugs her dad tightly. "Oh, Daddy I love you so much. I'm going to miss all our . . ."

Janey and Jeremy hear Elaine talking as she walks down the stairs. "Janey honey, are you ready to go shopping?"

Janey kisses her dad on the cheek and says to her mom, "I'm almost ready; I just have to change out of my wedding dress."

Chapter 10

Sim Chung and Mai Lee are sitting in Sim Chung's living room, having a cup of tea. They are both quiet for a moment. They have just spent the last week with Jai Ling and her husband.

"Halmoni, John, he is so handsome, isn't he? She has married well. He will bring her much happiness. Did you see how he looks at her? It took Hee Sauk two years of marriage to look at me that way. America is such a different place."

"Yes, this John is very handsome and intelligent too. He is a doctor."

Mai Lee laughs, "No, not a medical doctor. He has his Ph.D. in engineering. He has been in school for a lot of years."

"What did Jai Ling say? She will have this Ph.D., too?"

"Yes, in music. She plays piano. My Sang Hee is just like Jai Ling. She loves the piano too. Did you see Sang Hee sitting with Jai ling? She loved it when Jai Ling braided her hair. Kim Lee was even won over by the end of their visit. He especially liked it when they invited him to Kyungju. When he got back he seemed a foot taller. Even Hee Sauk with all his reserve became interested in Jai Ling and her husband. He even honored them by speaking in English. I didn't know Hee Sauk could speak it so well. It must be all the traveling."

"Your husband, is he fine with this new awareness?

"Yes, but when I first told him, his face became dark, then he left for the rest of the day. He came back and said he would meet her. That was a lot for him to do in such a short time. Hee Sauk is a good man, a good husband, and a good father. Jai Ling is off traveling now. She and her husband must be arriving in Hong Kong about now."

Sim Chung reaches over and pats Mai Lee's hand.

"The ancestors have guided you well, Mai Lee. Jai Ling is a happy woman with the world at her feet. I'm afraid Korean culture would not have been so kind to her. The decision so many years ago, was a decision blessed."

~

Elaine is in the living room dusting all the pictures sitting on the table. The picture frames have doubled over the last couple of years. Janey walks into the living room with an envelope full of new pictures from her honeymoon. Elaine stops dusting and looks at Janey.

"Well, Mom, we found it. The house we have dreamed of. It is perfect. Two bedrooms, two baths, a screened-in porch and best of all, it's only two miles from you guys. So I was . . . that is John and I were wondering if you and dad would come and look at it with us tonight. Before we make an offer, I'd like you to see it."

"Of course, Janey. We'd love to. Your dad should be home soon. Why don't you and John come for dinner and we'll go out after that? Now what about those pictures from the honeymoon? I've been dying to see them and hear every detail about everything . . . well, not everything . . . but most of the things you did."

Jeremy walks in the living room as Elaine is finishing her sentence. Elaine sees him and says, "Guess what, they've found a house and they want us to see it tonight."

Jeremy walks over and hugs Janey. "Congratulations! Now did I hear someone talking about pictures? Come on share your trip with your old dad. I have only heard bits and pieces since you got back. Tell me all about meeting your brother and sister in Korea. I mean every detail. And your birth mother's husband, how did he treat you? How did it feel, to you? To meet them and share them with John?"

"Oh, you guys are ganging up on me." She lifts up the envelope that's in her hand. "Here are the pictures from the trip. Let's sit on the couch. I'll show them to you."

They sit on the couch with Janey in the middle. Janey takes out the photos and begins passing them to her parents as she talks.

"I loved sharing Korea with John; I think he understands me in a way he didn't before. He sees I'm Korean. Look at this picture. See the look on his face? He's always known me as your daughter and hears me speak like any other American girl. But in Korea when I used the little Korean I knew he, well, he . . . looked at me at first like I was a stranger. Then he said it made him feel closer to me, closer than he had ever felt before."

Janey shows them another picture. Jeremy sees it and says, "He looks plenty close in that picture."

"Oh Dad, we are married. Oh, and here is a picture of my Korean siblings, Kim Lee and Sang Hee. I was so glad John was with me when I met them. He was so good with them and I was so nervous. He calmed me right down. Here is Hee Sauk, my birth mother's husband; he was very reserved at first, but then he wanted to take John golfing. Here's Hee Sauk golfing."

Jeremy looks closely at the picture. "He looks like a good golfer. What did he shoot?"

Janey laughs. "I don't know. Oh, and here is Mai Lee and I shopping with Sang Hee in the Daegu Seomun market. Remember Mom, where we bought our hanboks. It felt so comfortable there, Mom. I felt like I belonged. I didn't feel like a stranger. Oh, and here is Kyungju, the ocean village where we brought Kim Lee. Look at him and John body surfing. I don't know who was more fifteen, Kim Lee or John. Here is Sim Chung."

Elaine lets out a little gasp. "I just can't believe how much she looks like you, I mean you look like her."

Janey looks closely. "You think so? You know when I see my face in the mirror now, I see a face that belongs to my great-grandmother and my mother and my little sister."

Elaine points at the photo. "I know, Sang Hee has the same dimple."

"Does she?" Janey looks, "Oh, you're right. She does."

Janey puts the photos down and leans back with a big sigh.

"Mom and Dad, you are the greatest. You have always helped me and guided me to find myself. All the times I struggled with being different, with telling you I liked to pretend I belonged to families that we met who were Korean. You never got mad, you always understood my need to find myself. And Mom, we had all those late night girl talks, when I could ask you any question. You've always said I am the daughter of your soul. You're right Mom, our souls are one. And Dad, you've always believed in me and when Mom and I were at our emotional peaks you were always the voice of reason. And now I have John and my memories of Korea. I have never felt so happy."

Chapter 11

Mai Lee sits at the low table in the "quiet" room. She has a smile on her face. Sim Chung is kneeling at the altar. Mai Lee is sipping her tea, waiting for the right time to disturb Sim Chung. Finally she can't wait any longer. She picks up the envelope she has brought with her and takes out a letter and begins reading it out loud:

> *"Dear Oma, I am writing you today to tell you, I am pregnant. Our baby is due in seven months. We have decided to name the baby Elaine Mai Langdon, in honor of you and my mother. I hope it is OK with you. Our baby's*

due date is in June. So be thinking about me
when the robins build nests in the trees.
Love, Janey

Mai Lee asks, "Oh Halmoni, did you hear?"

Sim Chung gets up slowly saying, "I heard, Mai Lee. I have gotten used to you being here during my sacred time. I have learned to have two minds. One for praying and one for listening."

Mai Lee walks over and assists her grandmother as she walks over to lie down on the day bed.

Sim Chung smiles at Mai Lee. "Please Mai Lee, pour us some tea."

Mai Lee turns to the low table and pours a cup of tea for Sim Chung and hands it to her.

Sim Chung takes a sip. "Thank you, precious granddaughter. And soon Mai Lee, you'll be a grandmother just like me."

~

The bedroom is dimly lit, a crib with pink and white sheets, a mobile of fish dangling over it. A rocking chair is rocking slowly by the crib. The baby is crying. Janey walks into the room, picks up the baby, and sits in the rocking chair. Janey's porcelain doll is sitting in a little chair by the little table next to the crib. Janey begins humming "Rock-a-by-baby," then stops and talks quietly to her child. "It's the middle of the night, little Ellie Mai. Don't you know you should be asleep . . . don't look at me with those beautiful eyes, that see right through me. A story, huh . . . you want a story. I guess I can tell a story to those wide-awake eyes. Let's see,"

"Once upon a time a little child was born named, Ellie Mai. She was born on the beautiful day

261

of June 18th. The flowers were all in bloom. There were red roses, and pink, yellow, purple and white pansies in her garden. On the tree in her front yard were the most fragrant apple blossoms. Ellie Mai loved their smell, so sweet and pink. This little girl loved music and liked to sing. Little Ellie had a special doll." Janey picks up the doll with the porcelain face. "Her doll was named Sim Chung. Sim Chung was a magic doll and could talk. Sim Chung was also a very wise doll who knew things. This porcelain doll loved little Ellie Mai with all her heart. Ellie Mai kept Sim Chung close to her always. One day Sim Chung told little Ellie Mai the secret of Ellie's specialness. She told her that she was the luckiest girl in all the land because she had three grandmothers. One of her grandmothers lived in a land far away with people who had beautiful, silky black hair, eyes that lit up the world and dresses the color of rainbows; their homes smelled of bulgogi, chop chae, and kimchi. This grandmother loved her from afar. The other two grandmothers lived in her land, a land of love and hugs and chocolate chip cookies. Elaine Mai was a child surrounded by the best of all worlds. Her world was big and covered lots of land. When Ellie Mai is old enough, she will fly on a silver bird and visit the far away land with its cherry blossom trees. She will visit the land her mother was born in and live in the land her mother was raised in."

The baby is sound asleep, so Janey stands up and places her gently in the crib. "Good night, my little Ellie Mai."

THE CLAMSHELL

It's time to face the dragon
It's time to hear it's roar
It's time to face the dragon
And see what he's here for
It's time to tame the dragon
It's time to make him my friend
It's time to tame the dragon
And bring my fear to an end

There is a tiny girl named Reyita, who is so very young; she has long curly brown hair and eyes the color of chocolate. She hides deep in the dark, shadowy forest. Everywhere she looks there are trees and little creatures scurrying around. The trees and rocks are her home. Birds, squirrels, and deer are her friends. She loves to watch and play with all the little animals: the rabbits and squirrels, the birds and chipmunks. She huddles between her special rocks and trees; darkness flaps its wings around her ears and eyes. Sometimes she reaches up with her hands to protect herself from the onslaught of shadows. Other times she loves this dark place where no one can see her. For so long she's hidden away here. Surrounded by her favorite things: her soft mattress made of feathers, her comfy pillow made of fragrant grasses, her tiny mirror she found under a tall tree, and the tiny crown she made out of sticks, mud, and pretty rocks she collected. She feels safe among the forest things, her cries and tears muffled by the leaves and wild grasses. It is a good place to hide from the world outside. A world where people grow big and Reyita, in her forest, stays tiny and small.

One day she feels a change; she sees someone enter her forest. He is a big, scary hunter, with black hair all over his head and face; his eyes are black and cruel looking. He tries to grab Reyita, with his large hand covered with black hair. But she runs and runs and runs, until she is no longer in the dark forest, but she's in the glaring light of the sun, unprotected. The hunter sees her. The hunter shoots her with his bow and arrow; it goes in her back and through her heart. She takes the arrow and pulls it out, leaving a small hole in her heart. The big, scary hunter stays in her special forest so she cannot go back.

Reyita wanders lost in the open meadows and rolling hills. She is lost and exposed. Everyone is so big and they can see her now. They laugh at how tiny she is, how funny her voice sounds. They laugh at the tiny hole they see in her heart. She walks hunched over to hide it. They laugh at how funny she walks.

The eyes that look at her are cruel and teasing. Reyita keeps searching for a place to hide.

Suddenly there in front of her is a big clamshell, open and empty. The clam has moved out long ago. She climbs in. It is perfect, just the right size. She closes it so there is just a crack to let in the sunlight. Reyita begins to miss her favorite things. She wants to go back to her forest and collect them. But that means she has to leave her new, safe, home. Reyita builds up her courage and when the sun goes down behind the hills, she decides to go back into the forest. She hides in the shadows so the hunter won't see her. She tiptoes into the forest; her heart is pounding so hard she almost can't breathe. She sees her treasures; she hears the hunter snoring loudly. So she runs and grabs her treasures and brings them safely back to her clamshell.

Reyita busies herself and makes it a comfortable little home. She has all her favorite things: her feathers to sleep on; her pillow, made of soft grasses where she sits and sings her favorite songs; and her mirror where she can stare at herself with her little jeweled crown. She imagines that she is a beautiful, lovable, precious little princess. She also brought reminders of her animal friends: bird feathers from her birds, acorns from her squirrels and chipmunks, a piece of a deer antler from her deer friends, and some fur shed from the foxes.

She loves her new home where she feels safe from the hunter and his bow and arrow. She feels strong and beautiful. But the minute Reyita leaves the shell and walks into the sunshine, where people can see her, she feels their eyes watching her and hears them saying how ugly she is. She avoids going out in the sun. She avoids their eyes.

One day when the shadows are long and the day is ending, Reyita ventures out further than she's ever gone before. She climbs to the top of a hill and is entranced by what she sees down below; in a shaded place by a lake, she sees dozens of clamshells just like hers. Reyita quietly creeps into the shadows to watch. All the clamshells are open. Little tiny people are inside singing, writing, playing instruments, and looking in the mirror, just like she does. She can't believe her eyes. She stands there watching, afraid to come out of the shadows and be seen. She hears a voice from behind her singing the sweetest song she's ever heard:

> *You're home now little one.*
> *Your home is here with us*
> *You're home now little one.*
> *Your beauty's seen by us*
> *Come live here little one. Come be part of us*
> *Come live here little one and create here with us*
> *The world can be a beautiful place.*
> *Just find your home with us*
> *We'll heal your heart and make you strong.*
> *So please come sing with us*

Reyita turns and sees a tiny little girl with white hair and a nice smile. The little girl says, "Bring your clamshell here by the lake." Reyita instantly knows it is OK. She runs back, gets her clamshell, and brings it to the lake. After she sets up her clamshell she looks around. Down the shore a little ways, is a forest. A new forest she can visit whenever she wants to. Reyita knows this is a place she belongs.

She begins to let others hear and see her inside her clamshell. She feels safe. Reyita sits for hours in front of her mirror looking at herself; wearing her precious jeweled crown, she's a beautiful princess. For the first time in her life, she stays a princess when she leaves her shell. The hole in her heart begins to heal and soon she can stand straight and not be afraid to look in the eyes of other people.

Reyita's clamshell now sits open like the others. Her neighbor on the left is a girl whose skin is the beautiful, brown color you see in the eyes of a deer. When she plays her violin it sounds shy, haunting, and seductive. Another clamshell contains a blonde curly haired boy, who plays the piano. His music can sound like a gentle breeze blowing, or a thunderous dark cloud approaching. Further down is a clamshell where a red haired, freckle faced girl plays her flute, a light sound that bounces through the trees like a butterfly and it tickles Reyita's nose. From other shells Reyita hears voices singing. Some voices are rich and low, and rumbling; others are high and full, the voices make such exhilarating harmonies that the leaves on the trees dance and her eyes fill with tears. All the music reminds Reyita of summer nights in her forest when the crickets would come out and sing their chorus. Now when she sings, her voice rings out with all the other inhabitants of the clamshells. For the first time in her life, she feels like she is part of the incredible harmony and she is finally home.

THE EVICTION

White Powder

You came home late, you seemed so sad
Suddenly you grow, so very, very mad
You're eyes are glazed, an angry red
I feel that familiar, tingle of dread
I run up the stairs, to get away
I am so very, very afraid
I hear your footsteps; you're coming near
My heart is pounding now; the monster is near.

White powder, white powder on your clothes
White powder, white powder under your nose

Sara looks around the apartment. The dining room table is set with a white tablecloth, two candles burning, and plates set with silverware. One of the wine glasses is on its side; red wine is bleeding slowly across the white tablecloth. She takes a deep breath, exhales, and looks at James lying on the floor.

"You better not wake up, because I dare you to say another word. If you say one thing, I'm packing up my stuff and leaving right this minute and never coming back. Not one word. I can't believe I have loved and supported you for three years."

Sara stops and looks at a picture of her and James dancing, hanging on the living room wall. "I remember when we met, how you smiled with that sparkle in your eye. But most of all I loved how you looked at me. I felt my world take on meaning. I felt myself relax for the first time since I was born. We danced all night. I remember how good your body felt pressed close to mine. I can feel the tingle on my lips from that first kiss. I needed you so my life could make sense. So many years of running came to a quiet, comfortable caress. Then you asked me to marry you. How lucky could I be, I thought. You wanted me. I knew from that moment on, everyone had been wrong. I was worth something. I was valuable and worthwhile, because in your eyes I was somebody. Even through the black eye here, sprained wrist there, cracked ribs, I felt you loved me. Why would I leave someone who loved me so much, who gave me importance? I believed in you and what I saw in your eyes the first time we met."

Sara reaches up and brushes a tear off of her cheek. "I do love you, but I don't need the physical arguments. The price of your love is too high."

Sara watches as a drop of blood splashes on the rug at her feet. "Do you see the blood dripping from my nose? Can you feel the throbbing in the red lump over my eye?"

Sara looks at the floor by the couch. "Oh my God, look what I've done. Oh I'm sorry, so very sorry. Look at you just lying there. I think I broke the lamp."

Sara goes over and bends down putting her hand on his chest. "Oh good, you're still breathing."

She touches his face. "Look at your face, it looks like it did when we first met, so gentle and quiet. I remember how you looked at me, I got lost in those eyes."

She yanks her hand away and stands up. "The way you looked at me tonight, I thought I was a goner for sure. The whites of your eyes were so bloodshot. You had your mask on again. The one called 'raging monster.' I've always been terrified of that look—oh, my poor lamp. What was I to do? The blood is still running from my nose."

Sara reaches up slowly and feels her face. "My lip feels so swollen; I think my hand is broken. Why a knife?"

She looks down at him lying there in his jeans and a black tight fitting t-shirt. "Look at your arms, so strong and protective. Protective, how can I say that? I remember you holding me and swinging me around the dance floor, I was so happy back then."

Sara turns away from him. "But tonight, a knife, you had a knife. I really believed you'd use it. I can't take it anymore. Where will I go? I can't stay here."

She looks around the living room anxiously and sees their couch with a knitted blanket draped on the back and throw pillows of the same color. The two comfortable stuffed chairs sitting there just waiting for her to curl up in them, their plants, green and luscious, sitting on the table with framed photos.

"Do you remember when we first moved in here together? Everything was so new: our first dinner, our first houseplant, we had a home. I had a home. Then it became my first black eye, my first broken bone and tonight . . . oh my god, tonight you had a knife."

Sara begins to pace around the living room. "I can't stay here, where will I go . . . ? You were the only one who made me feel like I was somebody—now look at me. I'm just a gnarled and broken creature; maybe all this is my fault because I'm defective in some way."

She stops and looks directly at James' face. "I wonder if you know about the wounds bleeding in my soul. Of course you don't. You never really did. You only saw what you wanted me to be. I was your possession to do with as you pleased. You loved me only for what I could give you. Yet, I never did it right or good enough."

Sara feels a tear escape down her cheek. "Oh, I see the bump on the side of your head, I want to touch it, to nurse it, and to take care of you . . . isn't that funny, a real riot. I stand here hand swollen, nose bleeding, fat lip, torn blouse and I can still want to love you." She starts to pace again. "Boy, I need help. I've got to go. I'm leaving—now!"

Sara walks over to the dining room table and picks up the knife and the red rose. She brings them over to where James is lying on the floor. "Here, I'll leave you with the knife and the rose from our anniversary."

She bends down, puts them on the floor beside him, and stands back up. She hugs herself. "But I am taking my pregnancy with me, the pregnancy I never had a chance to tell you about."

Sara looks around, grabs her purse and jacket, and leaves the apartment. She walks blindly down the streets of New York, trying to figure out where she should go. She sees a bus bench and sits down, gripping tightly to her purse. Tears are flowing freely, tears of anger and loss. She sees an ATM across the street. Without thinking about it she withdraws money from her checking account. She takes out a thousand dollars. She quickly tucks it in her billfold as a plan forms. She takes out her cell phone and dials a number, one she hasn't dialed for a few years.

"Hello, Karen, you were right about James. I wish I had listened to you before I married him."

Sara starts crying. "Karen, I need to leave New York. I have to get as far away from him as possible. He doesn't know anything about you, so he wouldn't know to look there. So, could I please, come and stay with you? I can sleep in the barn, if you don't have any room. What? I know. I've finally come to my senses. I can? You have a guest room I could use? Thanks, Karen, you're a lifesaver. I'm going straight to the airport and get the first plane to Des Moines. I'll call you when I get there."

Sara's plane lands the next morning at 8 am. She has no luggage. So, she doesn't have to stand in front of the carousel waiting. She feels it's a little early to call Karen, so she decides to find a restaurant at the airport and have a good breakfast. She feels free; a weight is lifted off her shoulders, even though there is a deep sadness in her heart. She orders eggs and hash browns and her stomach growls. When the eggs come she takes one look at them and a sudden nausea sends her running to the bathroom. *That's right, I'm pregnant, I forgot.* The weight lands back on her shoulders. *I can't face Karen with her three children and tell her I'm pregnant. She would never understand if I decided to not keep it.* Sara checks into a Residence Inn by the airport. She uses their computer in the guest area and researches places that deal with her predicament. She finds a place that is out of town, on a quiet country road, that is staffed with competent doctors, according to the web site. Next she calls Karen and tells her, she can't get a plane until tomorrow. She calls the clinic and the only appointment available is 8:00 in the evening. She lies down on the bed and falls into a deep sleep. A couple of hours later she wakes up. She starts pacing the floor. *Am I making the right decision? I don't want any reminders of him.* As the time gets nearer, she gets anxious, not able to eat or relax. Finally she calls a cab. When they get close to the country clinic, she asks him to drop her off at the end of the road that leads up to the clinic.

As she walks, she thinks to herself. *This road is so dark. But I am on my way. I have to get it done tonight. I have been working up the courage all day.*

Sara stumbles a couple of times, and even falls once. The road isn't very well lit, or the easiest path to walk on.

A black bird swoops low and sees a woman with tears in her eyes. Sara looks up at him. *"Mr. Black bird, do you wonder why I am on this road, at this time of night, and why am I so sad?"*

The bird flies away and Sara focuses on the path she is walking on, wondering, *why for all these years, did I let it happen? Well, it's over now and tonight will make it just a memory. I will try to forget. In just a couple of hours it will be done.*

She keeps steadily walking but she never seems to get any closer. *I love the person growing inside me. I hate the reason it got there. But it keeps growing and now it must be dealt with.*

Oh, where is the clinic? I can't see a light. It is supposed to be just down this road, but there is no light, only darkness.

They say, that it's not a person until it is born, but, those pictures, the fetus looks so human.

Sara keeps walking but a little slower now. She sees two cats by the side of the road; they seem to be in the middle of lovemaking.

What happened to me wasn't out of love. It was a violent act meant to control me. He said he loved me, but too many bruises said otherwise. Didn't it? At times he could be so gentle and loving. But those times seemed to be less and less. He had so much anger. Now he is finally gone, I am finally rid of him. The only part of him that is still here is, living inside of me.

Now her steady pace is broken. She is so uncertain. *Oh, where is the building? It must be here somewhere? It is sooo dark.*

Her pace becomes even slower; eventually she sits down. She feels so torn; the wrinkles on her forehead become a network of frustrated lines. Her mind is a mass of contradictions. She looks around her and sees farmland and trees.

Her eyes rest on a piece of glass glistening in the scant light of the moon and stars. Her face grows suddenly calm, smooth, and confident. The big rock she sits on steadies her. Tears are streaming down her cheeks; she feels a small flutter from deep inside her. It makes her cry harder. There is no light anywhere, not a sound, nothing. She picks up the piece of glass and holds it in her hand. It is smooth and cool to the touch. The edges are ragged and sharp.

Suddenly there is a terrifying, angry scream, then all is quiet again. Just down the road is a building with lights on in every window, a building she will never see.

The black bird swoops down again. All he sees is a woman sitting on a rock and a fragment of glass with a stain, a dark red stain.

She sits quietly a moment and then gets up slowly, sucking the blood off her finger where the glass cut her. She knows what to do.

I want a nursery decorated with fluffy lambs, or trains and cars, or a princess dancing in a picture on the wall. Oh, I feel you flutter deep inside.

She puts her hand on her stomach and pats it. *It's just you and me kid.*

She turns away from the building that is just down the road. She takes out her cell phone and calls Karen.

THE CHOIR

Little Bird

At times I hear these words,
fluttering through my head.
Can you see me? Can you hear me?
Can you feel what I said?
Oh I want to be seen, I push out my boundaries
And fill it with the world.
I feel a little bird trapped in me

So I write ten more songs. I create another world
I write so many plays, I just want to be heard
Oh, I just want to be. I want them all to see
That beautiful bird, that's trapped inside of me

Little Bird flying high. Little Bird touch the sky,
Little Bird, Little Bird of mine

Chapter 1

Kirby walks into the chapel with her torn jeans and leather jacket. Her light brown hair is cut short and spikes up with a messy look. Her intense green eyes study the stained-glass window of Jesus walking on water. The freckles on her nose, and five-foot height, almost makes her look like she is fourteen, until you look in her eyes and see the years of pain and struggle. She walks over and stands in front of the window wondering, *what am I doing at a private Lutheran college?* She shakes her head and looks around the chapel to make sure no one is there to hear her.

Then she looks up at the stained-glass window again and says, "Hey, you up there. Look, I'm not very good at this kind of stuff, you know, praying. But right now I really need someone to listen, and since I have no one else, I thought, well, maybe I'd try this. So here goes." Kirby starts pacing back and forth in front of the window. "I've got these voices creeping in; they're louder than ever. Telling me I'm no good. Who do I think I am, going to college? I can't make it here; I don't have any talent. These voices create this thick armor around me. Metal walls that just keep everything inside. I have got to do this. I have got to make it this time. I can't let partying or anything get in the way. I have got to do this. I just hope they don't laugh at me." Kirby stops pacing and looks at the stained glass. "Oh, please, look way down deep in my heart. Can't you see the music I have in there?"

Kirby starts humming a tune. She finds a piece of paper on a table and starts writing down words, goes over to the piano in the back of the chapel, and picks out the notes she is humming. After a few minutes she has a song written down. She sings:

> *Oh please hear my plea, take this pain from me*
> *Hold my hand; help me stand by your side*
> *Oh, show me the way, to be with you today*
> *Yes, guide me on my journey.*
> *Oh, please set me free, from these shadows I see*

Kirby stops looks around. She looks back at the stained glass window and says, "Thanks!"

Then she runs out of the chapel, and goes to her dorm room.

Chapter 2

Kirby stands in front of the music building and thinks, *this is the first day of classes at this college. Don't mess it up. Last semester didn't work out so well at the University. I'm lucky they let me transfer here.* She takes a deep breath, walks into the music building, and looks for the choir room. She passes a couple of classrooms with chairs, chalkboards, and a piano in the corner. She finally finds the choir room and walks in. The choir room is large, with five rows of chairs set up on steps going up. There are a lot of students and just a few empty seats. Then she sees her new roommate, Sabrina.

Sabrina waves at Kirby and says, "Hey Kirby, come and sit here."

Kirby goes and sits by Sabrina, a pretty, tall, brown haired girl, with brown eyes. Sabrina says, "I didn't know you were in choir too."

As Kirby sits down the choir director, Dr. Paul, comes in and stands at the front of the classroom. He is short and pudgy with gray hair and a look in his eye that reminds Kirby of a televangelist. As she is looking at the choir director, a sexy, good-looking, dark, curly haired boy with a leather jacket and torn jeans comes in and sits with the tenors.

The choir director raises his voice and says, "Time to quiet down everyone."

Kirby asks, "Sabrina, who's the guy with the dark curly hair?"

"Oh, That's Zac. He loves to party. The last I heard he was going with Kendal. Have you met Kendal yet?"

"No, I have only been on campus two days. Remember I told you last night I just transferred here from a school in Colorado."

"That's right, I keep thinking you just switched majors and dorm rooms, that you've been here longer."

Kirby is still looking at Zac. "He looks like someone I should probably stay away from."

Sabrina looks at Kirby. "Why, don't you like hot guys who party?"

Dr. Paul looks at Kirby and Sabrina. "Would you two young ladies in the first row please quiet down? I read a Bible verse this morning from Proverbs; it said that it is wise to do what you are told—if you talk a lot, you are sure to sin. If you are wise, you will keep quiet. So let's everyone be wise and listen. I am your new choir director. As you know, your choir director last semester was in a car accident. He is on the mend. But he will be gone this semester."

Dr. Paul picks up a piece of paper. "It says here we have a transfer student; let's see, Kirby." Kirby raises her hand. "Let's see, you are a soprano, and you are sitting in the soprano section, so that's good. Now will you all take out the pieces you were working on last semester; Kirby you can share with your neighbor. I'll have a music folder for you at the next class."

Sabrina whispers to Kirby, "He is sooooo weird. What did he say about verbs?"

Kirby smiles. "I think he said Proverbs. You know, from the Bible or someplace like that."

"No kidding, he is actually quoting from the Bible? This can't be good."

Kirby looks up at Dr. Paul. "I know, he seems kind of strict, so like the worst teacher I had in junior high. How old does he think we are, 12?"

Looking at Kirby and Sabrina, Dr. Paul says, "Girls! Didn't I ask you to quiet down? Am I going to have to change your seats? Now where was I? Oh yes, before we start I should tell you a little about myself. Before coming here I was teaching in Illinois. My choirs won competitions on the national level. They did tell me I was far and above the best director they ever had. Well, enough of that." Dr. Paul glances at the paper again. "Oh, and class is short today because of a meeting I must attend with the college chaplain. So put your music away and instead why don't we just go around the choir quickly and everyone can tell me their name and any special music interests."

The students stand up one by one: "My name is Zac; I play guitar. My name is Sam; I sing in the choir. My name's Sabrina; I sing anything. My name's Carrie; I love to sing the Beatles. My name is Kendal; I'm a soprano. My name is Michael; I play the piano. My name is Natalie; I want to be an opera star. My name is Kirby; I play the guitar. I also love to dance and sing all night long." Sabrina joins in with Kirby. "Music is in our soul, our hearts are full of song." More students join in. "So we will sing today, sing out loud and clear. Because we want to show the world that we are here."

Dr. Paul starts clapping his hands. "OK, students, it's time to quiet down."

Everyone sits down and the room is totally quiet. "My, you young people sure have a lot of energy. Let's see if we can take that energy and sing God's praises."

Dr. Paul sees the clock. "Oh, I must leave for my meeting."

Dr. Paul rushes out. Everyone starts picking up their books and talking.

Sabrina turns to Kirby. "I think we shook him up."

"Thanks for joining me in my chant, it was cool the way everyone else joined in too."

Zac walks by looking at Kirby. Sabrina says, "Hi, Zac."

Zac smiles. "Hi Sabrina," and keeps walking.

Kirby sighs. "I sure hope Dr. Paul loosens up a little. I love singing in choirs but he just may ruin if for me."

"Did you see Zac checking you out? See you later—I got to run, I forgot something I need for my next class, and I don't want to be late, so I need to go back to the dorm and get it."

Kirby bends down to pick up her books. Zac walks in the room and grabs a book from under his chair. He looks at Kirby.

"So you play guitar too? Do you want to get together and play sometime?"

"Sure, how about tomorrow? I've got free time in the morning from 10 to 12."

"OK, Kirby, it's a date. I'll meet you in the practice rooms at 10:30. See you tomorrow."

Kirby walks out of the choir room and sees the door to the practice rooms across the hall. She notices a code box and realizes she needs the code. She goes upstairs to the music department office and gets the three-digit number, then goes downstairs and uses it to open the door to the practice rooms. It's a long hallway with rooms on either side. She walks down the hall and looks at the various rooms. The rooms are medium sized rooms and contain either a grand piano or an upright piano and three folding chairs with music stands. She opens the door to the last one and sits down to practice piano before her voice lesson.

Chapter 3

Zac and Kirby are sitting in the practice rooms playing guitar. They have been in there almost every day this week. Kirby plays a couple of minutes and then stops and looks at Zac, a smile on her face.

Zac looks up. "What? Why'd you stop? Why are you looking at me like that?"

"I heard you were running around the dorm hallway with just your underwear on. Looking for your clothes."

Zac laughs. "Yeah, that was weird. I woke up Saturday morning after a night of partying and I couldn't find my clothes, my wallet, or my car keys. Then my roommate came in and said he saw my clothes in the hall. I opened the door to look and my shirt was on the floor in front of the elevator and my pants were lying close to my dorm room. My wallet and car keys were just sitting there on top of my pants. The money was gone from the wallet but my credit cards and license were still there. The last thing I remember last night was sitting in my car trying to get the key in the ignition."

Kirby stops smiling. "It's too bad someone took your money, but at least they left everything else. Sounds like a little too much alcohol. Anyway, let's play some more guitar."

They start playing and running through solo riffs. Zac starts playing an old Beatles tune and making up a guitar solo. Kirby stops and watches him.

When he's done playing he looks up at Kirby. "I love playing this guitar. When I have my guitar in my arms, I feel like I'm somebody. I'm on top of the world. When my fingers pluck the strings, it's like I'm singing, yelling to the world how I feel. Time goes into some other dimension and pretty soon I realize two hours have gone by. It's amazing, it helps me say things I can't put into words."

Kirby asks, "When did you start playing guitar?"

Zac looks at his guitar. "A friend of mine had this old guitar he didn't want, so he gave it to me. I spent hours reading books about chords, listening to music and trying to play what I heard. I could do it too. My friend Steve couldn't believe it. He made me play at his parties. Everyone thought I was so cool. I must have been twelve or thirteen; it was the summer before eighth grade."

Kirby sighs, "I wish I could play guitar like you. Your fingers just fly over the strings."

Zac strums a couple of chords. "When did you start playing guitar?"

"A couple of years ago. My friend Skip taught me a few chords. And then I started writing my own songs. I was home a lot that summer and I . . ."

Zac looked at Kirby. "Why'd you stop talking?"

Kirby hesitates, then says, "I'm sorry, I just started thinking about that summer and, well, that was the summer my mom got sick with some weird immune stuff. Anyway, will you play that song you were playing again?"

Zac asks, "Which one?"

Kirby says, "The one you're writing."

Zac plays a few chords, then stops and looks at Kirby. "Is your mom still sick?"

"Look, I don't really want to talk about it. OK?"

Zac shrugs. "Sure. OK."

Zac leans back and starts to play his song for Kirby. She tries to copy what he's doing.

When Zac's done he looks at Kirby. "Play and sing me one of your songs."

Kirby plays and sings. When she's done she sighs. "When I play guitar, especially my own songs, I feel like a door opens and lets out something that's been trapped inside me for so long. It uncovers feelings I didn't know I had. And when I hear you play, I feel it too. It's like every note vibrates through my bloodstream and brings energy to every part of me. My heart opens and sings its own words. Music is so amazing."

Kirby looks at Zac. "It's weird, but I feel like none of the teachers here seem interested in our music. It makes me feel invisible. It's like they have all the answers and I don't know anything. It feels like jazz, blues, rock and roll are dirty words around here. Hip-hop and rap—forget it. They say that's not really music. I thought college would be different. But it feels like it did when I was growing up. I used to perform for my parents' friends. I never did it quite right. My father really didn't like it when I decided to play the guitar. He thought I should play the violin."

Getting angry, Kirby says, "God, I just hate it. How can they tell us what we should do all the time? Sometimes I feel so scared, I shake all over. I think I'm afraid I'm going to see myself fragment, and I'll watch all my little pieces scattering in every direction, trying to please everyone. That's when I get away by myself and write music. It soothes me somehow, to just let it flow out of me. It's almost like throwing up, the way it pours out of me at times. I get up at night and can't sleep until it's all written down. It feels like I'm satisfying some need that's way down deep inside me. When I write music I don't worry about all the things people want from me. The songs are just for me."

"Man, Kirby, when you talk I feel like you are singing my song. My uncle couldn't stand me playing guitar either. He always made me close the door to my room and turn my amp down. That's why I hide away with my guitar, it helps." Zac looks at Kirby, "I don't think I've ever met anyone quite like you."

Kirby sits a minute, trying to make a decision. "I heard something else about you. Last weekend and some fight?"

Zac says, "Oh, great, I'm so glad everyone's talking about me. All I did was defend my buddy who was in trouble. You know Kirby, besides you, my guitar is my best friend. Someday I'm going to show everyone, I'm going to be a rock 'n' roll star. I'll have the best electric guitar money can buy."

Kirby, sorry she had brought up the fight, says, "Show me that riff again, the one with the incredible major seven chords."

Chapter 4

A couple of days later, Kirby is sitting in the practice room with Sabrina. Sabrina is at the piano and Kirby is sitting in a chair with her guitar. Sabrina turns and looks at Kirby. "Boy, Kirby, how many times were you and Zac in the practice rooms last week? Four . . . five?"

Kirby thinks a minute. "Five, but who's counting. He told me he broke up with Kendal."

"Yeah, I heard they broke up last weekend. But it wasn't Kendal's idea. She still has it bad. He just has so much trouble . . ."

Kirby interrupts, "Well, I think he's incredible. His music . . . he is such a genius . . ."

Sabrina stops her. "Be careful Kirby, he has a reputation for . . ."

Kirby ignores Sabrina. "He is the first person I've ever met who loves music the way I do. You know, going inside the music and really feeling it. Oh, Sabrina, if you could see him the way I see him. Don't tell anyone, but I wrote a song about him called 'The Guitar Man.' When I watch him play guitar, the words just started to flow out of me."

Sabrina looks hard at Kirby. "Kirby, you're scaring me. Zac is fun but don't fall for him. He is nothing but trouble."

"But Sabrina, what we experience together feels so . . . so . . . private. No one has ever really understood me like he does. He understands that intimate place inside my soul that feels and creates and sees the world in a different light than everyone else. He writes music too and has experienced that wonderful, miraculous moment when music all comes together and makes sense."

Kirby puts her guitar in the case. "When I was a kid, my parents thought I was weird because I spent so much time in my room. But the world I created there was so much better than the one I had around me. I learned then that there is this inner world that belongs to me. An inner place only I seem to feel and understand. When I'm with Zac, I feel like I'm in that place and he's there too. I've never experienced it with someone. He can get as excited as me over a stupid seventh chord played in just the right place. Oh, it's so hard to explain, but when we do our music together it is more intimate than having sex."

"Kirby, you are talking crazy. Zac is the type that is here one day and gone the next."

"It's OK, Sabrina, I don't want anything more from him than what I've got. I probably wouldn't like him in the real world. I mean, what if I went to a party and he was a jealous, possessive jerk? Or maybe he can't dance or kisses terrible, then where would I be? It would ruin everything. Besides, he drinks and parties too much."

Sabrina nods her head. "Now you're making some sense."

"Sabrina, I know there is no such thing as a perfect guy. I learned that long ago. Every guy I've ever known has turned out to be a loser."

"Well, like they say, you have to kiss a lot of frogs before you find your prince."

"You got that right, Sabrina." Kirby looks at her watch, "Oh, no, choir started five minutes ago. We better hurry."

Chapter 5

Dr. Paul is sitting at the piano in the front of the choir room, talking quietly to a student. The rest of the choir is looking over a new piece of music. Kirby, Sabrina, and Kendal are sitting together in the soprano section.

Kirby looks at the clock. "God, this has been such a hard week. We've got to do something tonight, Sabrina. Go dancing, something. I feel like I'm just watching the clock waiting for the hand to reach the twelve."

Sabrina yawns. "I know what you mean. I think the clock has stopped or something. Maybe the power went out in the building?"

Kendal, Zac's old girlfriend, joins in sarcastically. "Yeah, right, the lights are still on. Helllooo."

All three girls stare at the clock.

Kirby is watching the hands of the clock. "There . . . it . . . goes. Finally."

Dr. Paul looks at the choir. "OK, everyone, before you go, I have a prayer for you to start off your weekend. It is Psalm 33. 'Rejoice in the Lord, O ye righteous: for praise is comely for the upright. Praise the Lord with harp: sing unto him with the psaltery and an instrument of ten strings. Sing unto him a new song; play skillfully with a loud noise. For the word of the Lord is right; and all his works are done in truth.' Have a good weekend." Dr. Paul gathers up his music and leaves.

The whole choir just stares for a moment; they can't believe what they just heard. Then Zac stands up and says, "Hey everyone. Let's do what the weird, old dinosaur says. Let's sing a new song and play it loudly, my place in an hour. I think it's time to get high and party."

There is a chorus of, "Yes."

Everyone stands up and gets ready to leave. Kendal is looking at Zac. "Oh you guys, Zac is so hot."

Sabrina looks at Kirby and rolls her eyes. "Cool off Kendal, take a breath, do you want to go to the party with Kirby and me?"

Kendal looks down. "I can't go. He broke up with me. I don't think I want to see him with another girl right now. I'm heading to the practice rooms. See ya."

Kendal leaves. Kirby turns to Sabrina. "I think I'm going to head to the practice rooms too. I don't think I want to party with Zac either."

"See you later, Kirby. I'm not missing a party tonight."

Kirby watches Sabrina leave and then says quietly to herself. "I wish I could party too. There's just too much alcohol there." Kirby walks out heading for the practice rooms to write music.

Chapter 6

Kirby and Zac are walking down the street on the way to her dorm room. Zac is talking about the Science Museum. "That dinosaur exhibit was really awesome. I have such a thing for the Tyrannosaurus Rex, the strength and power in his legs and the sheer bulk of his jaws. You can just see the energy pour out of him. He's not afraid of anyone or anything. He is the King. He doesn't take shit from any other dinosaur. He rules the world around him. He towers above it all. He can see what's going to happen before it happens. I mean he is ready for anything. He is . . ."

Kirby interrupts, "So scary. Can you imagine meeting him on the road? Or like that scene from 'Jurassic Park,' where the Tyrannosaurus Rex picks that man up off the toilet." Kirby shivers.

Zac puts his arm around Kirby. "Are you cold? You're shivering."

"No, it was just the thought of . . . " Kirby pushes Zac's hand off her shoulder. "Zac, we're just friends, remember. I agreed to go with you only because I thought it would be more fun than having to go and do the research for class by myself. Here's my dorm."

Zac and Kirby stop in front of her dorm.

"You can't blame a guy for trying."

Kirby looks at Zac. "Yes, I can. Should I tell Kendal?"

"Hey, go ahead. I heard she's seeing Brandon now. She and I are history. Well, I guess I should get going. See you tomorrow in choir."

Zac hesitates a moment, and then grabs Kirby and kisses her. After the kiss he leaves quickly, with Kirby staring after him, with her right hand touching her mouth where the kiss had been. Then she seems to come to and rushes into the dorm.

When she opens the door to her dorm room the lights are off. Sabrina is lying in bed. "Kirby is that you? How was the Science Museum?"

"It was great. I loved the dinosaurs, and the Natural Disasters exhibit was incredible. Sabrina?"

"Yeah."

"Zac . . . kissed me. I didn't want him to necessarily but he just suddenly grabbed me and kissed me goodnight. I didn't want to like it, but I did. It was just so gentle and . . ."

"Kirby, it's late, I've got to get some sleep. Let's talk about it more tomorrow, I've got this huge test in six hours." Sabrina punches her pillow and lies back down.

Kirby sits by the dorm window with a note pad and a pencil. She opens the window and lets in the fresh air. She takes a couple of deep breaths and sighs. Meanwhile Zac is sitting in his dorm room by the window drinking a beer and playing his guitar. Kirby begins writing a song:

> *The kiss on my lips lingers for you my love*
> *My hungry eyes bring your vision in my soul*
> *My kiss it trembles,*
> *until my body can't sleep anymore*
> *Oh, I wonder if you're thinking of me tonight*
> *Oh yes I wonder if you're thinking of*
> *me tonight, tonight, tonight.*

Meanwhile Zac is holding his guitar playing and singing the song Kirby wrote for him.

> *Fingers entwined in the strings of your life*
> *Let the music flow way down inside you,*
> *Then play for me; play me the song*
> *you know I want to hear.*
> *Guitar man, sitting over there, guitar*
> *nestled in your arms like a baby.*

Chapter 7

Sabrina is sitting at the piano in the practice room. Carrie, a full figured red head with an amazing voice, is standing by the piano getting ready to sing, when Kirby comes rushing in. "Oh, you guys, I am so sick of Dr. Paul. I'm so sick of teachers, period. Dr. Paul told me I have pitch problems. I take voice lessons; my teacher has never said I have pitch problems. I told him that and he said maybe I shouldn't be a music major if I can't take a little criticism."

Sabrina looks at Kirby. "What? That's ridiculous. Your singing is great. Don't listen to him. He is just a jerk."

"I know, Dr. Paul makes me feel so little. Like he is this big godlike being I could never measure up to. And those Bible verses . . . it's like he's on this journey to save us all."

Carrie speaks up. "Dr. Paul just doesn't get it. He just doesn't understand. I don't think he even sees us. He just doesn't have a clue."

Sabrina continues the rant. "Dr. Paul just likes to shame us and to yell at us. I think he must hate his job and he hates us too."

Kirby joins in. "He seems to hide behind his Jesus; I just don't know what to do. I just want to stand up and say to him 'we're not so bad'—just get to know us. You might like us if you do."

Kendal pushes open the door to the practice room. "I can hear you guys all the way down the hall. What's going on?"

All three girls say at once. "Dr. Paul."

"Oh right, I should have known." Kendal holds up a handful of tickets. "I've got some complimentary tickets to 'The Magic Flute' for tonight. Anyone want to go?"

Kirby says, "Get out! Free tickets? Hey, I'm in."

Carrie and Sabrina join in. "Me too."

Kendal hands out the tickets and then looks at Kirby. "I heard something interesting. There is a choir song competition for all the colleges in the state. You should write something and enter it."

The other girls look at Kirby. "Yeah, Kirby. Go for it. We'll show old Dr. Paul."

Chapter 8

Dr. Paul is standing in front of the choir. All the students are staring at him. He is in the middle of one of his life lesson lectures. "Look, I don't know what your problem is. I mean, you students as a whole just seem so out of touch with your classes and what has to be done. I assigned this piece of music two weeks ago.

You sound like you just opened it up. I thought you were college students. You act more like junior high students . . ."

The girls start to whisper to each other. Carrie begins, "God, he is ruining it for me. I loved coming to choir last semester. The music, the sound, and the way it filled the room. After a hard day of classes it was always so great to come and just perform and sing . . ."

Kendal joins in. "And no matter what chaos was happening in my life, choir always seemed the same. A place to come and relax and sing."

Sabrina whispers. "It always felt different here somehow. Sometimes I'd have a fight with someone outside of choir and I'd be angry. But it always seemed in choir that the anger would go away because suddenly I'm singing a duet with my worst enemy. How do you stay mad at someone you sing with?"

Dr. Paul continues, "You forget to come to classes. In my music composition class of twelve, I'm lucky if there are eight students that show up. The eight that do show up have only done half the work. How do you expect to be musicians if you can't . . . ?"

Kirby says under her breath, "Maybe because no one wants to be in your class. You're right—he is ruining the feeling I get when I sing in choirs."

Sabrina adds. "I don't understand why he has to take the fun out of everything. Remember last semester . . . ?"

Kendal looks at Sabrina. "Yeah, the way Dr. Peter described a choir piece brought tears to my eyes; when I opened my mouth to sing I . . ."

Carrie interrupts, "I felt like I was singing from my heart."

Sabrina adds. "I felt my whole body begin to shake with the beauty of the words . . ."

Kirby laughs. "The only thing in this choir that makes my body shake is laughter . . . at him and his Bible verses. He's like a drill sergeant when he teaches music. Like he's beating us over the head with the notes . . ."

Sabrina sighs. "Yeah, instead of helping us appreciate the meaning and the beauty. He punishes us for any little mistake."

Dr. Paul is getting worked up. "To be good musicians you must be able to execute the music perfectly. That means practice, practice, practice. Take Zac, who isn't here again today. He shows up to choir every other day and consequently he is usually singing the wrong notes. Yes, I can hear your mistakes from up here; I have an incredible ear. I'm rarely, if at all, wrong."

Zac walks into the choir room wondering why no one is singing.

Dr. Paul looks at Zac. "And here he comes now. Yes, our dear Zac, our rock and roller, who thinks he is too good to show up for choir on time. You know when you are late, it is inconsiderate to your classmates for it changes the tempo of the class . . ."

Kirby looks at Zac. "He is always on Zac's case . . ."

Carrie adds. "And everyone else's. The man is from another planet. He lives in his own little world."

Dr. Paul speaks louder. "When I was in college, I was by far the best student they ever had. You know why? Because I went above and beyond what was expected of me. I was always on time. I practiced my music at least four hours a day."

Sabrina giggles. "Of course he did. What else would he do? Who'd go out with him? He probably practiced to cover up for no social life."

Dr. Paul continues. "I was told many times in college and graduate school that I was far and above any student they'd ever taught. That was of course because of my talent but also I practiced. Now Zac, why don't you enlighten us with that tenor voice of yours and show us how that passage should be sung, the one on page five, starting with measure . . ."

Zac interrupts, "Sure, it goes . . . I want to party and dance and . . ."

The choir laughs but Dr. Paul's face starts to turn red. "Zac, that is just what I mean. No respect, you never take anything seriously. Zac, I would like to see you in my office after class.

Now, will all the tenors please sing that phrase I was talking about?"

All the tenors begin singing:

Lord won't you bless us with . . .

Dr. Paul stops them. "No, No, you are going flat on that B, think higher . . ."

Kirby raises her hand and says, "Dr. Paul . . ."

Dr. Paul, impatient, blurts out. "Now what is it, Kirby?"

Kirby points to the clock. "The clock. I don't want to be late for my voice lesson again. We are running over . . ."

Dr. Paul looks flustered. "Oh, this is so . . . so . . . frustrating. Look, every one of you better come prepared tomorrow . . ."

The students stand up and start gathering their things.

Dr. Paul continues, "Ah, yes, choir is dismissed."

Chapter 9

The next day Kirby is sitting at the piano in the practice room writing down music on a musical score. Zac pushes into the practice room.

He sits and puts down his guitar case. "Hey Kirby. What did you think of that music theory test? It seemed pretty easy."

Kirby doesn't look at Zac, and continues to write on the musical score. "Yeah, it was OK."

"What's wrong, Kirby?"

Kirby shrugs. "Nothing, I'm working on my songs for the choir song competition."

Zac asks, "Sure, OK. Want to play some guitar?"

Kirby looks up at Zac. "I don't think so, Zac."

Zac says, "What? Are you mad about Saturday? I'm sorry I partied too long on Friday and ended up staying at a friend's house. We didn't get up until late Saturday afternoon. Some of my high school buddies stopped over and we started partying again. By Sunday I figured you'd be mad, so I just didn't call. Look, I know I can be kind of a jerk. All my friends say so; it's not just you. I forget things, or I just blow them off. Everyone says that about me. Come on Kirby, please don't be mad."

Kirby, softening a little, says, "I don't know. I've got a lot to do. I've got a lesson in a half hour and I've got to finish writing these songs. They're due a week from Monday . . ."

"Songs . . . songs for what?"

Kirby rolls her eyes. "Zac, I just told you, for the choir song competition. If I win, I get a scholarship, and the choir performs my songs at a concert. I keep hearing a song in my head. *'Oh Lord Up above, please fill me . . . '"*

"You'll win, no sweat. So come on Kirby. Meet me here after your piano lesson. I've written a couple of new songs too. I want to play them for you . . ."

Kirby looks directly at Zac. "OK, but you'd better show up."

"I'll be here, Kirby. I promise."

Zac leaves and Kirby sings softly. *"Please fill me with love, give me hope and strength and courage."* She writes down the lyrics and then sees the time and rushes out for her piano lesson.

When her piano lesson ends she heads back to the practice rooms. She gets out her guitar and waits for Zac. Twenty minutes go by and no Zac, so she puts her guitar away and picks up her things and heads to her dorm room, angry and disgusted.

Chapter 10

Dr. Paul is standing in front of the choir looking concerned. "I've been sensing a dark cloud hanging over this choir lately. I see little arguments springing up in the music building. I think it's time we stop and hear the glory of God's words. Something that will lift us up and give us the answers we need. It is Psalm 138, a hymn of Thanksgiving. 'I will praise thee with my whole heart:

before the gods will I sing praise unto thee. I will worship toward thy temple, and praise thy name. In the day when I cried thou answeredst me, and strengthenedst me with strength in my soul."

The students in the choir start looking at each other.

In the soprano section, Kirby whispers to Sabrina. "Dark clouds over the music building . . . can you believe it? The only dark cloud is coming to this choir. We seem to hardly ever sing anymore . . ."

Sabrina closes her music folder. "I know, all we get are his Bible verses. I want music, songs, I want to be uplifted and inspired."

In the alto section, Kendal looks over at Zac. "Where the hell were you last night? You were supposed to call me and we were supposed to . . ."

"Calm down Kendal, I fell asleep . . ."

"Bullshit, Zac. Carrie saw you sitting on some rotten barstool talking to a blonde with a green top that only covered enough of her to not get her arrested . . ."

Zac says defensively, "Yeah, well I needed a few beers before I tackled my paper . . ."

"Oh, Zac, you always have some excuse. You are just so . . . so irresponsible."

In the soprano section, Sabrina looks at Kirby. "Speaking of singing and being inspired what happened earlier today with Zac?"

Kirby looks disgusted. "Who knows? He didn't show up again. That's twice now in the last week. I've had it. I called his dorm room and no one answered. God, Sabrina, guys are such losers."

Dr. Paul continues on with his Bible verses. "Though I walk in the midst of trouble, thou wilt revive me: thou shalt stretch forth thine hand against the wrath of mine enemies, and the right hand shall save me. The Lord will perfect that which concerneth me: thy mercy, O Lord, endureth for ever: forsake not the works of thine own hands."

Sabrina answers Kirby. "Tell me about it. Remember how I rushed getting my shower this morning, tripping over your shoes, bumping my knee, so I wouldn't be late for my breakfast date with Michael. Well, he never showed up."

Kirby looks at Sabrina. "Men, what are they good for? Why do we want them? Why do we think we need them?"

Sabrina answers. "Yeah, they forget our dates."

Carrie, listening in on Kirby and Sabrina, leans over and adds. "Or sometimes they come but they're two hours late. They say they're going to call us. But our phone never rings, then we see them the next day and they act like we're making it all up."

All three girls sigh and say, "Men!"

Meanwhile Dr. Paul is rambling on. "There is also the uplifting Psalm 150, 'Praise Him with the timbrel and dance: praise him with stringed instruments and organs. Praise him upon the loud cymbals: praise him upon the high sound cymbals. Let every thing that hath breath praise the Lord. Praise ye the Lord.' Oh my, I got carried away. I just love the Psalms, don't you? I mean they seem to just speak to our lives and what we are experiencing."

Kirby speaks up. "Excuse me Dr. Paul, but choir ended and I have to get to my voice lesson."

Dr. Paul looks at the clock. "Oh my, I am sorry. You're right. You're dismissed."

Chapter 11

Kirby is in the practice room practicing piano. Zac opens the door and looks in.

"Hey, Kirby. You got a minute?"

Kirby stops playing and looks at Zac standing there holding his guitar case.

Kirby says, "That depends."

"Depends on what?"

Kirby looks directly at Zac. "What my minute is being used for. I don't have time to waste on jerks."

Zac walks in and closes the door. He sits down putting the guitar case on the floor in front of him. "Kirby, please don't be mad at me. I know I'm a jerk but I've had a lot on my mind lately."

"Yeah, like Kendal. Quit playing with me, Zac. I don't have time for all your games. Why did you kiss me that night? I thought we were just friends and then you kissed me. Oh, forget it. I don't need this right now. I've got a lot to do. Just go away . . ."

"Kirby, come on. Don't be like this. We are great together. I've never met a girl like you."

"You're high again, Zac. Please, I don't need someone like you in my life. I have enough problems. All you want to do is party and have a good time. I thought you were serious about music. You are nothing but a . . ."

"Wow, man, give me a break. What is it with you Kirby? I thought we had something . . ."

"That's right, Zac. We HAD something. But now there's nothing . . ."

"Why are you so upset? Kendal and I are just friends. I haven't kissed her for over a month. She still calls a lot and we like to get high together. But we're just friends. Kirby, I have been trying to get next to you for weeks now. You just keep me at arm's length, except when we play our guitars, then I feel like we are in the same room. I feel like . . ."

"Look Zac, it can never work between us. I don't get high. And you do nothing but get high. You are no good for me, Zac."

Kirby moves the music on the piano and a picture falls to the floor and lands by Zac's feet. Zac bends over and picks it up. "Wow, who's this? She's beautiful."

"It's a photo . . . of my mom . . . before she got sick."

Zac studies the picture. "You look so much like her. You've got the same hair, the same eyes. Where was this picture taken? Was she a nightclub singer or something?"

"Yes."

"Does she still sing and . . . ?"

"No, she's in bed most of the time. Now, she'll probably never get out of bed because . . ."

Kirby takes the picture from Zac, and looks at it. It's seems to draw her to another place; her voice gets softer. "I remember how she used to light up a room when she walked into it. When we had company over she would get them all singing and dancing by the end of the night. She had this smile . . . I remember one Christmas, she was putting a star, a white star with little streamers that hung off each point, on the top of the Christmas tree. She was singing some stupid song about twinkling stars. She reached down and touched my shoulder, she smelled so good. Some perfume she used to wear whenever she got dressed up. Her fingers felt cold . . . her nails were a deep red . . . she gave me 'the' smile. She looked so happy. Her eyes were so blue, like a lake I saw once up in the mountains, almost turquoise. I wanted her to come down off the ladder and hug me in the worst way. But I was too old to want a hug from my mom." Kirby looks up and sees Zac sitting there watching her. "Zac, look I need to be alone right now. I'm not good company. I . . . please . . . leave."

"I'll leave on one condition. You'll give me another chance. We're good together."

"Zac, I don't want to do this right now. Look, I just got back from Methodist Hospital. I talked to some old, gray-haired doctor, who stood there with ketchup in his moustache, telling me my mom is dying, congestive heart failure on top of all her other medical problems. She may have one or two weeks left."

"Wow, Kirby, I didn't know . . ."

Kirby continues, "I hate hospitals. The smell, bodily fluids mixed with disinfectant. I always gag. My mom just lies there with tubes in her nose and mouth. She can't talk. All she can do is nod. Do you know what it's like to think you may never hear your mom talk again, never hear her voice? I want to get high in the worst way, but I know what will happen if I do. It is taking everything I've got to hold it together. I need to fill myself with music right now. I need to feel the notes wash over me, pour out of my eyes and mouth. I don't want this to be happening. I knew the news was going to be bad, but I didn't think it would be this bad, one to two fuckin' weeks. I don't think I can do this. Leave, Zac, please just leave. Go . . . I"

Zac gets up and goes over to Kirby. He pulls her up and holds her. She lets him, finally relaxing.

"Kirby, I am so sorry. I lost both my parents when I was in junior high school. My mom and dad had a fight one night, took off in the car and hit a tree head on, about a mile from home. I had to live with my uncle and his family. Let's just say my uncle wasn't very happy getting another mouth to feed . . . so, I know what your feeling. Like the concrete ledge you've been standing on has turned to shifting sand. Like you are living someplace between worlds and you are out of sync with the music . . ."

Kirby looks up at Zac. "Exactly Zac. It's like I can't hear the ending to the song. Just when I thought I was getting it, the key changes and it's someone else's song. I don't know how to play it or sing it, all I can do is sit by and listen . . ."

"I know Kirby, I have been sitting and listening for awhile. Then I met you and I began to hear my music again. My songs started taking shape, I . . ."

"Look Zac, I don't know if I want the job of helping you find the words to your songs. I'm still trying to find mine. And one of my songs is drug free. I can't get into partying with you, Zac. Please go now. I need to be alone for awhile."

"But Kirby?"

"Please, Zac."

Zac looks at Kirby, then reaches down and grabs his guitar and leaves the practice room. Kirby sits back at the piano. She takes a deep breath, and then releases it. She picks up her pencil and begins writing again.

Chapter 12

A couple of days later, Dr. Paul is standing in front of the choir by the piano. There are quite a few empty chairs.

"Where is everyone today? Anyone know where Zac is? He just can't seem to grace us with his presence—too many fun things to do I suppose. I just don't understand. Students today are just so lazy. Everyone lounges in their dorms sleeping, listening to music, who cares about classes, I mean, in my day if we skipped a class we were out on our ear. Now everything is so politically correct. Everyone afraid of law suits. I mean, what is this world coming to? You students get away with everything and we professors are supposed to be understanding and flexible— understanding and flexible for what? So you can stay up all night doing who knows what? Never studying, why bother? Class? Why should you go? You're tired from all the fun you're having. To you college is just one big party. No responsibility."

Dr. Paul is getting himself worked up. "Why, when I was your age, nothing less than straight A's was expected. I never had time to do all these parties. My parents would disown me if I showed just a little bit of your attitude. I mean the only way you'll make it in this world is to respect and follow the rules. And of course aspire to be perfect, or at least to do your best. But college these days is like a den of iniquity. Look at the musical the theatre performed this last weekend, all that profanity. And rules, where are the rules? I see ponytails and earrings on men. I see beautiful young ladies with pierced lips, tongues, eyebrows, noses and tattoos like the boys. Oh, what are you thinking? Ladies should be pure white petals, like on a soft, velvety lily. Not filled with thorns and graffiti. And men should be men, the strong hunter, leading and being strong. Colleges today remind me of the verse I just read last night, Joel 3 verse 12. It said the world was ripe with sin, because there is so much evil. Can't you students see the evil around you? The newspapers reek of it. Young people today must listen. Then it talks about being in the Valley of Decision, the time can be dark, no sun or moon, no stars will shine. He will be a safe place for us all. So you students can be saved from all your irresponsible ways. God will lead you."

Dr. Paul looks up at all the students' faces and becomes confused, almost like he forgot where he was. "Oh, where was I? How did I get to here? Oh, yes, you students must get to your classes and do your work. Take school seriously, it isn't just about having fun." Dr. Paul starts looking really uncomfortable. "Excuse me a minute choir. Ah, Carrie, why don't you come up here and take the choir through 'Bless Us Dear Lord.' I'll be back in a few minutes."

Carrie gets up and stands in front of the choir then sits back down.

Zac comes walking into the room. "What's wrong with you guys? Where's Dr. Paul? Someone say something, what gives?"

Kirby answers Zac, "Dr. Paul, I think he's on the edge."

Sabrina looks up and says, "Yeah, I mean, his face was so red. I thought he was going to explode."

Carrie adds. "And the stuff about sin, we are all sinners, full of evil . . ."

Kendal sighs. "Whew, that was heavy."

Kirby looks at Zac. "It started because you weren't in choir again and then . . ."

Zac answers. "Well the guy's too old to be teaching. I mean he hasn't a clue . . ."

Dr. Paul walks back into the room looking at Zac. "Well, my, my, you decided to come to class. Why ever for? You don't want to be here. And talent, maybe you have some somewhere, but I haven't seen it. Look how you dress. Leather jacket, tattoos, pierced body parts. You are a disgrace to your parents, to yourself, to this college. Now if you want to be part of this choir, you come to class, you learn your music and leave the leather jacket in your dorm room. Shape up and we'll be just fine."

Zac looks Dr. Paul in the eye. "I can't be a disgrace to my parents, they're both dead." Then Zac walks out of the choir room, leaving Dr. Paul with his mouth open.

Chapter 13

Sabrina, Kendal, Carrie, and Kirby are in the practice rooms talking about songs they are working on for an upcoming performance. Kirby is sitting at the piano writing music down. Sabrina, Kendal and Carrie are sitting on the chairs.

Carrie asks, "Sabrina, what song are you doing for Concerto Aria?"

"'Nimmersatte Liebe' or 'Insatiable Love.' You know the one about a young maiden wanting more than mere kisses. I can't believe the line in the song that goes, 'The maiden like a lamb held still, feels the blade descending, she drank kisses with the thrill of pain and rapture blending.' I'm supposed to act like I'm ready to experience 'the thrill of pain.'"

Everyone laughs except Kirby who is busy writing her music down.

Carrie, still laughing, says, "Ooooo, don't let Dr. Paul hear you talk like that."

Kendal interrupts. "Oh, forget Dr. Paul."

Kendal turns to Sabrina and says, "I'll bet you're ready for the 'thrill of pain,' Sabrina? I know I am. I wouldn't mind being 'like a lamb held still that feels the blade descending' either."

Sabrina looks at everyone. "I don't think any of us would mind feeling 'the blade?'" Everyone nods, yes. "Speaking of blades. I read somewhere when a geisha reaches the age of 14 or 15, it is time for her deflowerment."

Kendal nods. "Yeah, I read that too. It's called a Mizuage."

Sabrina gives Kendal a dirty look, and continues, "Anyway, men bid for the honor of becoming her first guy. They bid thousands of dollars. On her first night she dresses in a beautiful kimono, very expensive, and has her hair done."

Carrie adds. "Yes, and they drink some Japanese liquor."

Sabrina continues. "Sake, it's called Sake. Anyway the geisha is sent to a teahouse room to wait for her patron. When he comes she must lie down and wait for the 'blade to descend.' Can you imagine? My first time, I had on jeans with holes in them. I didn't get thousands of dollars, I got dinner at Applebee's."

Kendal laughs. "Mine wasn't much better. Everyone else talked about how great it was. So the guy I was seeing, well, we did it in the back seat of his car. I remember his zipper getting caught in his underwear. I kept hitting my head on the inside of the car door. Hey, Kirby are you with us? Earth to Kirby, are you listening to anything we're saying?"

Kirby looks around confused. "What? I'm sorry, what did you say? I keep hearing this song in my head. I'm trying to get it all written down while I hear it. Let's see—'*Lord Hear our Voices.*' She writes it down and looks up at Kendal. "There, now what did you say?"

Kendal asks, "When was the first time you felt 'The Blade Descend?'"

Kirby thinks a minute then says, "Well, I was dating this guy who was a hippie type and older. He had long hair and he drove a Buick hearse when I first met him. He was living with some friends from California, sleeping on their couch. So my first time was on their living room floor; then we ate brownies with something extra in them."

Carrie looks shocked. "Kirby, that doesn't sound like you."

Kirby smiles. "That was then and this is now. Really you guys, I need to get to work."

Kendal looks at Kirby. "Are you OK? I mean you've been so to yourself lately. What gives?"

Sabrina nudges Kendal and gives her a look.

Kendal says, "Oh, I forgot, your mom is in the hospital. How is she?"

"Look you guys, I don't want to talk about it. OK?"

Carrie looking uncomfortable says, "Come on you guys, it's time to get back on track. We're supposed to be practicing our songs. I've got class in twenty minutes."

The girls stop talking and listen; there is a lot of commotion outside in the hallway.

Sabrina asks, "What's going on out there?" She goes out into the hallway and talks to some of the students who are congregating there. She comes rushing back in looking at Kirby and says, "You guys, it's Zac. He's in the hospital!"

Kirby quickly stands up. "What? What are you talking about?"

"Zac is in the hospital. He overdosed or something. Someone said he did it on purpose."

Everyone gets up and starts talking at once, not sure what to do, or where to go.

Kirby starts pacing. "How? When? I just saw him last night."

Carrie says, "I saw him at supper last night and he was just fine."

Kendal shows them her cell phone. "I have my cell phone—should I call someone?"

Kirby sits down. "You guys, I shouldn't have left him last night. He was really down when I got there. But we talked for hours and he seemed fine when I left. I can't believe this, we need to find out what hospital."

Kirby runs out the practice room door; Carrie, Kendal, and Sabrina follow her running down the hall.

Chapter 14

Dr. Paul is sitting at the piano in the choir room looking at some music. Kirby walks in. "Dr. Paul?"

"Yes, Kirby?"

"Do you have a minute?"

"I was just looking at the songs you submitted for the competition, Kirby. You have some beautiful words in them. Do you believe the words you write?"

Kirby walks in and sits on a chair by the piano. "Sometimes more than others. Look, I came here to tell you something. My mom, they aren't sure when . . . I mean she is in hospice care now. I'll be missing a few days to sit with her."

"I just heard, Kirby. Are you OK? I heard about Zac, too. Does anyone know how he's doing?"

Kirby sighs. "Zac's going to be fine. No one's talked to him yet; they won't let us visit him, just immediate family. But I heard he'll be back Monday. As for me, well I'm hanging in here."

Dr. Paul looks upset. "Oh my . . . this is . . . this is just all so distressing. When I was in college I don't remember anyone's mom ever dying. And suicide, that was unheard of. I mean an accidental overdose once, but nothing like this. I just don't know."

"Dr. Paul, no one ever said for sure it was suicide. Right now they are saying it's an overdose. Dr. Paul?"

"Yes, Kirby?"

"I came here because I wanted to talk to you about something. Is it OK if I, well, if I ask you something?"

Dr. Paul looks a little defensive. "Well, I am kind of busy, but I guess if it's important."

Kirby hesitates a moment, then takes a deep breath and exhales. "The students have been talking and we all usually love singing in the choir. But now, it feels like a scary place to come instead of a refuge with beautiful music and inspiring words. So I was wondering. I mean, I just keep trying to figure out, why? You know, why you dislike us so much? I mean what have we done to make you so angry?"

Dr. Paul looks surprised. "Dislike you? I don't dislike you. I, it's just, that, well, I just don't understand you. I mean with Zac. Why ...? I've been reading the Bible, trying to understand what happened. I thought I was trying to lead you students to a life surrounded by God's Word. I think His Word is so inspiring and beautiful, like the words here in your songs. I've been staring at them, trying to understand how you . . . well—I can't believe you wrote these. I mean you act so irreverent at times. I thought God was the farthest thing from your thoughts. You don't talk or dress like I'm used to."

Kirby leans forward in her chair. "Dr. Paul, God doesn't feel to me the way He seems to feel to you. I mean Jesus was a rebel in His time. He didn't conform to all the rules. He defied them at times. He challenged the authority around Him with new ideas. God isn't scary and punishing. When I'm in chapel with God, I feel His warmth surround me and I relax. I feel safe. I rest in His arms and wait for His voice to guide me. I know you mean well, but I don't think you see us. It feels like when you look at us, you're looking past us seeing something that's not there. Its like we're invisible or something. We all love music; that's why we're in the choir. That's why we are music majors. Music inspires us and soothes us. It heals us. It's probably when I feel the closest to God."

Dr. Paul sits a minute looking at Kirby, puzzled. "You feel close to God? I never thought of you like that. But I know about the 'feeling closer to God when you play music'; I feel it too. It's funny, I just never thought of you that way. That you love music and God, that you feel the safety and closeness. Anyway I'm canceling choir today. I need some time to think; in fact I think we all need some time. And Kirby, I really don't dislike you. I just need some time to understand. I guess I have been going through something too. I've been having so many students not show up for class. At the other school where I taught, no one ever missed a class. I have never had low enrollment. The other school I was at was a Christian college and we quoted Bible verses in our classes when they fit. The students' response here has been disconcerting for me. I want to thank you so much for coming today and talking to me and for your music. I'll keep your mom in my prayers."

Kirby stands up. "Thanks, Dr. Paul. I'll see you later."

Kirby walks out of the choir room; Dr. Paul watches her and then turns to look at the music on the piano.

Chapter 15

A couple of days later, Kirby, with tears streaming down her face and her nose running, walks into her dorm room carrying a six-pack of beer. She sits down on her bed, taking out a beer bottle and holding it to her head; it feels cool on her hot forehead. She grabs a stuffed animal that is lying on her pillow. It's a cuddly lion, with a full mane. She hugs her knees and starts singing:

> *Mom, you died last night.*
> *There was no time to set it all right*
> *No farewells, no long good-byes,*
> *now you just closed your eyes.*
> *Mama won't you dance with me,*
> *please just come and dance with me.*
> *Won't you run and chase me,*
> *hug and hold and kiss me,*
> *Mother won't you come.*

Her phone starts to ring; she stops singing and answers it. "What? I had to leave, dad. I just couldn't stay there and look at her body . . . dad . . . you're drunk. I don't want to talk to you right now. Goodbye dad."

Kirby hangs up the phone, picks up her six-pack of beer and runs to the chapel. She is singing to herself. "*Life is going, very fast now, where it goes I do not know. Tossing me up in the air so far. Always keeping on the go. Life is going very fast now.*" She reaches the chapel, walks in, falls to her knees, and puts the beer down.

She looks up at the stained glass window. "I see you standing there, with your arms reaching out. I wish you could be flesh and blood, someone who could hold me in your arms. I don't know of any time in my life when someone reached out their arms to help me. My mom—I guess she'll be coming to see you. At least that's what the pastor at the hospital said. Take good care of her. I mean . . . oh, I don't know what I mean."

Kirby stands up and starts to hurry out of the chapel; then she stops and goes back for the six-pack of beer.

Kirby runs out onto the college quad by the music building. She sits on a bench, opens a beer, and drinks it. As she takes out another, she sees the sun starting to rise; yellow and orange colors look like they are painted on the horizon. She takes her beer, lifts it up to meet the sunrise, and says, "Cheers." Pretty soon all six bottles are empty, lying on the ground at her feet. She starts singing to herself. *"Fear and anger push me further on, running from what has to be, can't turn back the paining is catching up, now it's right behind me."*

She notices Zac standing and looking at the music building. She stands up, sways a little, and grabs the bench to steady herself.

Zac sees her and starts to turn away, but then Kirby stumbles. "Kirby? My God Kirby, you're drunk."

Kirby lets go of the bench and starts staggering over to him, slurring her words. "Hey, yer back. I'm so glad yer OK. I mean relieved, yeah, I'm relieved. Fuck, you really scared me, Zac. I mean . . . you fuckin' scared me."

Zac, afraid Kirby might fall, starts walking towards her. "You better go to your room and just sleep it off. You'll get in trouble if anyone sees you."

"Wha' . . . do I care? I mean wha' the fuck do I care about anything?" Zac reaches Kirby. She stops and looks directly into Zac's eyes. "How did it feel?"

Zac, taken aback, says, "How did it feel? How did what feel?"

Kirby says, "You know, lookin' death in the face and then coming back."

Zac is shocked at the words and starts to turn away.

Kirby grabs his arm. "Where you thinkyergoing? I got somethin' to say to you."

She lets go of Zac's arm and looks at the empty quad in the dawn's light. She feels like she is in some abandoned world, where no one exists but Zac and her. She looks at Zac. "I saw death. I saw it creep over my mother's body. I saw her shtruggle to breathe. I watched her shtruggle to swallow. I sat and fed her these ice chips because she couldn't swallow water. I rubbed her feet; they were so cold and icy as death began to take her away. I watched her fingers twist and roll her blanket as she mumbled unknown words into that place I couldn't see. I saw her eyes fly open with fear and look around and say, 'Am I dead yet?' Then she looked at my face but didn't see me. I watched her . . . yeah. I watched her for so long. She shtruggled between these two worlds; wanting to die but wanting to live. I watched her fight."

As Kirby is talking, her words seem to sober her up and she stands a little straighter. "I saw her fear. I smelled her fear; it smelled like perspiration and old clothes. We read to her . . . the 23rd psalm, to reassure her. To help her see those green pastures she could lie down in, knowing she wasn't alone. Shit, wha' the fuck was I reassuring her about. I don't know where she went."

Kirby grabs hold of Zac's shirt and looks into his eyes. "Where do you go Zac, when you die? Did you see anything, Zac? Was there a white light? Did my mom go somewhere?"

Kirby sighs, lets go of Zac's shirt, and watches a bird land on the bench. "I mean, I saw her leave, I watched her body grow so quiet. One minute she took a breath, then the next minute she was so still . . . no breath. Her body changed too. It wasn't her body anymore. It looked empty, like a shell that is left behind at the beach. She just moved out. Her eyes stayed open. Can you believe that? They don't close like they're falling asleep. They just sit open, half open. But there is nobody there. I was holding her hand. I could feel her energy, life, slip away. Fuck, Zac."

Kirby looks directly at Zac again. "Did you see anything?" She grabs the front of his shirt again. "Did you? . . . tell me you did.

Please tell me she went somewhere. Zac, please, tell me. Did you see anything? Did you see Him? Are there people on the other side waiting for you? Did you see anyone?"

Zac looks at Kirby, his eyes full of hurt and fear. "I don't know Kirby. It was just so dark. I don't remember. I don't want to remember. I gotta go, Kirby. I gotta go."

Zac tries to turn away, but Kirby still has hold of his shirt.

"Please don't leave, Zac. I don't want to be alone, not right now. I mean, I keep drinking because I just keep seeing her. I don't want to see it ... the body ... you know, lying there—empty."

Kirby let's go of Zac's shirt. She lowers her head, tears dripping, making little wet spots on the dirt by her shoes.

Zac backs up a little. "Kirby, I'm sorry about your mom, but I don't know if I can do this with you."

Kirby looks up at Zac. "You know what really pisses me off ... you. How could you do that to me? How could you just throw it all away? I saw my mom fighting to stay alive, fighting with everything she had and you, you just tried to throw it all away. How could you? Life sucks but it's our life. I don't care what happens. I'm a fighter, like my mom. I'm going to fight to stay alive. I'm going to fight; you better fight too, Zac. You better fight too."

Zac sighs, "I know, Kirby. I've been fighting for the last week. I've been trying, Kirby. I've really been trying."

Zac turns, walks over to the bench Kirby had just been on, and sits down.

Kirby watches him a moment, sighs, then walks over and sits down next to him. The sun is creeping its way over the distant trees. All the buildings stand dark and quiet waiting for the students to come. No one else is around, just Zac and Kirby sitting on the bench in the quad. After a few minutes, Kirby takes out a pack of cigarettes, and offers one to Zac.

Zac asks, "When did you start smoking?"

"I used to smoke, but I started again yesterday."

They light up their cigarettes, take a long pull and blow it out slowly, each thinking their own thoughts.

Eventually Kirby looks at Zac. "Are you OK?"

"I don't know, Kirby, I've been trying, but it's so fucking hard. I've been standing outside looking at the music building. Trying to work up the nerve to face everyone. Now they all know."

Kirby leans back. "Yeah, people are hard to face sometimes—why, Zac? Why'd you do it?"

"Kirby, you wouldn't understand."

Kirby takes another pull on her cigarette, and watches the smoke curl up. "Come on, Zac, try me. I talked to you. Now it's your turn, so come on. Try me."

"Shit, Kirby. I haven't told anyone. I don't know if I can."

"Look, I told you something no one knew about me."

"I know, Kirby, it's just . . ."

Kirby interrupts Zac. "Come on Zac, it helps, to talk, to say it out loud."

They both sit there a few minutes looking at the ground, smoking their cigarettes.

Zac finally looks up. "Pain, it's pain Kirby. That's why I did it. Pain. Sometimes the pain in my body feels like it's going to explode and hurt all the people around me. I have fantasies sometimes, weird ones, like walking into the registrar's office naked. I stand up on one of the counters and yell obscenities at everyone walking by, like those crazy people on street corners preaching at you downtown. I yell so everyone can see me. Really see me."

Zac takes a drag off his cigarette. "When I was in high school, I had days I just couldn't hold in the urge to scream. So after school I'd go home to my uncle's bathroom and get a razor blade. I'd sit on the bathroom floor and run the blade across the palm of my hand. I'd watch the red blood ooze its way out of the white cut I had just made. It would sting, but it would help the numbness. I could watch my pain trickle out onto the bathroom floor. It felt so good, like I was freeing something. I was in control of my pain, instead of at the mercy of everyone else's. It felt good. It became my own little secret. There were so many secrets. So many things I had to hide, like the knife . . ."

Zac stops, staring at the ground, deep in thought. "I was six years old. I was asleep and my mom and dad woke me up with their arguing; I heard the sound of the silverware clinking together as the drawer was pulled open. I knew my dad had taken out a knife. Suddenly I felt like I had to use the bathroom but I was too afraid to move. My father was yelling at the top of his lungs; my mom started screaming. Then everything was quiet, so quiet. The clock ticked away the minutes; the water dripped in the bathtub down the hall. I got up slowly, afraid to look. I tiptoed in and there they were in the bedroom, my mother lying on the end of the bed, crying. My father lying on the floor, the lamp broken, red blood oozing out of the cut on his head. The knife lying there, the blade looking so sharp."

Zac shook his head trying to come out of the memory. "Wow, man, I'd forgotten about that night. Anyway, there are so many secrets. So much I've never told anyone. You know we sit in choir and sing these songs. What do they mean, Kirby? Where do they fit in my life? When has God been there for me? Sometimes I wish I could feel the words, feel them way down deep in my soul. I want them to carry me and make the pain go away. I want the words to wrap around me, like a mother's arms so I can snuggle in and feel safe. I've never felt safe, Kirby, never"

Kirby and Zac sit a minute each lost in their own thoughts, finishing their cigarettes.

Zac feels a couple of tears streak down his face. "You know Kirby, some nurse at the hospital said what I did was a cry for help. Maybe it was. All I know is, it was the first time anyone ever found out about the pain. I used to walk around with my palms all carved up after a session with the razor blade. No one ever noticed my pain, never. This time someone did. It's kind of scary to be found out, but in some ways it's a relief. I also talked to a woman at the hospital, a psychologist or something. The way she listened when I talked, the way she looked at me, I think she actually cared. Maybe there is a place for the pain to go, without me having to watch it ooze out drop by drop. What are we doing here Kirby? What's this all for?"

"I don't know Zac, I guess we want to make something of ourselves."

Zac looks around. "But no one here seems to care. Everyone's always too busy to talk. The professors are always telling us what's wrong with our work, never what we do well. I've never felt like I fit in. I wonder if I ever will?"

"I know what you mean, Zac. I've decided I'm going to graduate in spite of them all. I'll prove they don't know shit."

Kirby stops talking because she hears voices, she looks at her watch. The students are starting to come to their classes. Kirby stands up. "I'd better go. I'm in no shape for class. You're going to be OK, Zac."

Zac stands up and pulls Kirby into a hug.

"Kirby, I'm so sorry about your mother. I'm so sorry I wasn't there for you."

"Yeah, well, I guess we are here together now on that shifting sand. I better go."

Zac kisses Kirby passionately; after a minute Kirby pushes away.

"I've got to go Zac, see you later."

After Kirby leaves, Zac bends over and picks up her empty beer bottles and throws them in the trashcan; then he walks into the music building.

Chapter 16

Kirby and Sabrina are sitting on their beds, Kirby with an ice pack on her head, Sabrina painting her toenails.

"God, Sabrina, I feel awful. No more drinking or cigarettes for me. I haven't used for a week and I still feel hung over. I don't want to go back to class tomorrow. I don't know how I'm going to do it. I feel so raw."

"I know, Kirby, give yourself some time. Hang around in the dorm tomorrow; who says you have to go back to class? It's only been a couple of days since the funeral."

Sabrina finishes her toenails and starts to fan them to dry the polish.

"But Sabrina, I've got to do something. I've got to feel normal. I need to feel the routine of my classes surround me and give me something to do to keep my mind occupied."

There is a knock on the door. Sabrina looks at Kirby. "It's kind of late for visitors."

Kirby yells. "Come in." Zac walks in.

"Hi Zac." Kirby looks closely at Zac. "Are you doing OK? I haven't seen you for a couple of days." Zac walks over and sits down next to Kirby.

Sabrina stands up and slips on her flip-flops. "Look, I'll see you guys later. I told Kendal I'd go over and visit for a while. I think now is a good time."

"So Zac, what's going on?"

"Look, I'm sorry I didn't come to the funeral."

Kirby puts down the ice pack. "I know, I understand."

"Kirby, I really wanted to, for you. But I was afraid."

Zac stares at his hands and then looks up at Kirby. Kirby stands up, "Zac, I don't think we should . . ."

Zac stands up and puts a finger on her lips to stop her from talking. Then he takes her in his arms, and places a kiss where his finger just was, a nice tender kiss. The tender kiss turns into a hot passionate kiss. Zac moves Kirby onto her bed and lies down beside her. He looks into her eyes and strokes her hair. Soon she falls asleep. "I'm here for you now, Kirby. I'm here for you now."

Very early the next morning Zac wakes up and sees Kirby sleeping on his shoulder. He looks around and realizes they must have fallen asleep like this last night. They are still lying on the bed, fully clothed. He feels Kirby move and looks down. Her eyes are open; he can tell she's trying to figure it out too. "I think we laid down here last night and both just fell asleep."

Kirby lies there for a few minutes.

Zac looks at her, "You're so quiet."

"Am I?"

"Is something wrong?"

"It's nothing, Zac."

They lie there for a minute or two saying nothing. Zac can feel some tension in the air.

"Come on Kirby, what gives? Something's bothering you, I can tell."

"I just don't know if this is OK. I'm scared, Zac. I don't want anything to ruin our friendship."

"What could ruin it?"

"I don't know, it could change things, if we become involved in other ways."

"What? You don't want to be my girlfriend?"

"I don't know, right now I just like having you as my best friend."

"It's my getting high, isn't it?"

"Yes, Zac, it's the getting high thing, and I can't forget what just happened to you. I grew up with so much alcohol. My parents are the type that look good to the world, pillars of the community. At home we were rudely awakened half the time with their drunken fights. Then we'd wake up the next morning for breakfast, they'd start cracking jokes like nothing ever happened. I'm so sick of pink elephant jokes to excuse their hangovers. I'd go to school on four hours of sleep, feeling crazy, and they're cracking jokes. When my mom got sick it got worse. My dad always had a drink in his hand, my mom high on some painkillers."

"Kirby, I'm not going to ..."

"Look Zac, I just can't stand the smell of alcohol anymore. I don't want to smell it on your breath. It scares me. I don't want to be like my mom and dad, not in any way. Now my mom's gone, and I, I just don't know what I'm doing. I'm stuck here in a world I don't know. I drank again, after two years sobriety, Zac. It scared me. I don't ever want to do that again. I know what can happen. Zac, I know you like partying with your friends, you like to drink. I'm afraid I'll get sucked back in. I don't want to die, Zac. I don't want to feel like that ever again. I wish you and I could just live in the practice rooms forever. I love it when we are totally absorbed in our music. The way your fingers fly over the strings, the look in your eyes when you're singing. I love your talent and your passion. I love having you as my best friend."

"Kirby, I love having you as my best friend too, but I would like more. I have never had anyone look at me the way you do or understand what I'm going to say before I say it. I know we have both been through a lot lately. So for now let's just enjoy our close friendship. I don't know what I would have done if you and I hadn't talked that morning in the quad. You helped give me the courage to face that day. And Kirby, because of what happened, I am taking a good hard look at my chemical use. I haven't used a mood altering substance since that night I was in the hospital. I know I have some things I need to work out."

Kirby sighs and takes Zac hand. "I'm glad you were there for me too that day. I don't know what I would have done, if you hadn't been there."

Zac kisses Kirby on the top of the head. They both fall back to sleep.

Chapter 17

Dr. Paul is standing in front of the choir, directing the last of the music. He looks at the clock. "Sorry, we ran over a little, good work today everyone. The piece is finally coming together."

Kirby gets her things and starts to leave; Dr. Paul stops her. "Kirby, I'm glad to see you back. If you need any help getting caught up let me know."

"Thanks, Dr. Paul."

Kirby sees Zac waiting for her. "Say Zac, do you have a minute? I want to show you something."

"Sure, what is it?"

"You'll see, come on."

Kirby grabs Zac's hand. She starts walking over to the chapel with the stained glass window. Zac stops. "The chapel? What do you think you're doing, Kirby? I can't go in there."

Zac turns to go; Kirby grabs his arm.

"Please Zac, this place is important to me."

"I can't Kirby."

"Why not?"

"After my parents died and I moved into my uncle's. My uncle made me go to church every Sunday. It was either a Holy Roller church or a Pentecostal type place where people rolled on the floor, or spoke in tongues. Once he brought me to one that had snakes. He thought I needed to be saved, that there was evil in me, kind of like how Dr. Paul thinks of me. When I left home at eighteen I swore I would never set foot in another church."

"But my chapel isn't like that, I promise, please come with me."

Zac goes with a guarded look on his face and a tension in his body that could help him run at any minute.

"My first interesting experience with church was when I was in sixth grade. I was at church camp. The front of the chapel was all big windows that looked out over the lake. On the other side of the lake was a big green hill. I was asked to sing a solo that morning for chapel. I think it was 'Beautiful Savior.' Anyway, after I sang there was a short sermon and then we sang 'The Old Rugged Cross.' As I was singing and looking out over the water, I began to feel myself being pulled over the water to the top of the hill. I was sitting in the chapel but I was also up on the hill. I started to cry, I don't know why I was crying. But I was still crying when the service ended. That was a very spiritual moment for me, but in sixth grade I didn't understand the emotions. As I grew older, I hardly ever went to a chapel or church."

Kirby stops in front of the chapel door. "Remember last night when I talked about getting high? I tried to do what you did; they called it an overdose too. I was so low. During that crazy time I found something I forgot I had. I've never shared this with anyone. I thought it would help you understand me better."

Kirby opens the door to the chapel. "Come on and sit with me—please?"

Zac hesitates, looks at Kirby then goes in. Kirby walks up to the stained glass window where Jesus is walking on water, and kneels down. Zac stands watching her, not sure what to do.

Kirby starts talking. "When I feel alone and I have all these voices pounding through my head, I come and sit here. I become quiet inside. Then I begin to hear this voice way down deep inside me. It's a voice that believes in me and gives me strength to face and do things I don't think I can do alone. When I'm crazy and wild I can't hear this voice. I have to be quiet. See that flame on the eternal candle? It's always burning and waiting for me when I'm ready. I go away a lot but when I come back it's always here. So many people in my life seem to have forgotten me, left me, but not Him and not the eternal flame. He is here just waiting for me to let Him in. When I'm here I don't feel so alone, so abandoned. It's not like that stuff Dr. Paul dished out. You know, dress right, be a good boy or girl, wear Jesus on your sleeve to prove you're a righteous person. It's a private relationship, between God and me, an intimate conversation with someone who loves me. It's these quiet moments in here that get me through those shitty moments out there."

As Kirby is talking Zac slowly walks over to her and kneels down, looking at the stained glass window and then at her.

Kirby continues talking. "With my mother dying and all, I lost this place for a while. It's not a concrete ledge but it is something to hang on to when there is so much shifting sand. I've been sitting here a lot lately. I can feel the love. I know my mom is happy now, free from pain. I can feel her love more now than I did before. I know the world can be a cruel and scary place. When

I step out of the world and into here, I feel love, I feel safe, and I feel stronger."

Zac, almost speechless, finally finds his tongue. "Wow Kirby, I never knew you were like this. This feels a lot different than the churches I went to with my uncle."

"Well, this place is personal. I brought you here because I think you and I are a lot alike. I can see it in your look—lost. When I quit using they talked about a Higher Power. I thought they were full of shit. Then I started writing lots and lots of music and I began to feel what they meant by this Higher Power. The music doesn't come from here." Kirby touches her head. "It comes from here." She touches her heart. "I feel like the songs are given to me. When I get blocked, I walk in the woods or I find a friendly chapel. In the quiet I start to hear that voice and the music flows out."

Zac looks at Kirby. "I never thought of that before. I start songs but I never can finish them. I get blocked and then I feel lost. I don't know how to get the quiet or the safe place, its been buried for so long. So I get high and sometimes when I do, I find the words. Getting high helps me release the stuff that is bottled up behind the walls."

Kirby looks at Zac. "Well, I guess being here or with nature is my natural high. Because that's where I find what I've lost."

Zac looks around, and then looks up at the stained glass window.

"You know Kirby, you're right. It does feel peaceful here, and safe. Yeah, it does feel safe. I just remembered a song I heard in church when I was a kid it went something like this:

> *Sometimes the way is dark and cold*
> *No one is there that we can hold*
> *The path is rocky, trees get in the way*
> *Guide us around them, teach us to pray.*

Maybe church isn't such a bad place after all."

Chapter 18

Kirby is sitting in the practice room writing furiously at the piano. One pencil is behind her ear, one is in her mouth, and another is in her hand writing music. Zac walks into the practice room.

"Kirby, here you are. I've been looking all over for you. Where have you been?"

"Here, Zac. I've got so much work to do. I've been trying to rewrite my composition. Also I've just needed some time to myself."

Zac sits down. "I know there is so much happening. But we're cool, right?"

"We are, it's just that, I'm still trying to deal with my mom stuff, I love being with you. But I know you are still trying to find something too. I feel like we are two lost souls looking for something."

"So, let's find that something together. I've been doing a lot of thinking lately. What's really important are you and my guitar. We can make beautiful music together, I know we can."

"You really think so, Zac?"

"God, Kirby, you're different from anyone I've ever met. At the hospital, when times felt the darkest, I kept seeing you sitting in here with your music. I'd remember things you said. It gave me comfort, a sliver of light in a very dark time. You remember the psychologist I told you about? I called her and we set up an appointment for next week."

They sit there quietly, both in their own thoughts.

"Come on Kirby, let's go out on a date tonight. Let's go out for dinner and a movie?"

Kirby looks at the pile of papers on the piano. "I need to work for a couple of hours. I guess I could . . ."

Sabrina barges into the practice room, breathless.

"Kirby! You won! Did you hear? You won!"

"I won? I won, are you sure? Where did you hear that? I won!"

"Kirby, I'd knew you'd win,"

Sabrina looks at Kirby. "Yeah, no surprise. I saw it on a sheet of paper they posted in the music department. I bet they called you. Is your cell phone on? Anyway, I've got to go, I'm late for class. I just had to find you and let you know. Congratulations."

Sabrina hugs Kirby then rushes off to class.

Kirby takes out her cell phone. "I forgot to turn it on this morning."

Zac stands up and goes over to Kirby, he hugs her. "Congratulations! Now let's go out and celebrate. Come on Kirby, dinner and a movie."

Kirby is standing there in a daze. "I won, I really won," then she seems to realize Zac is standing there looking at her. "Sure, pick me up around seven."

"OK, I'll see you then. Thanks, Kirby."

"Thanks?"

"Yeah, just thanks."

Zac leaves and Kirby turns around and starts writing furiously to get her composition finished. "I won," she says quietly to herself.

Chapter 19

Kirby, Sabrina, and the rest of the choir are in a large room in the basement of a church; there are several portable full-length mirrors scattered throughout the room. Several students are looking in the mirror doing last minute touch ups to their make-up before the performance begins. Kirby and Sabrina are standing in front of one of the mirrors fixing their hair.

"So Kirby, how do you feel? Did you see the church sanctuary? It is packed. I hear standing room only is left. Can you believe it? They are here to listen to your music, your music. This is sooo exciting."

Kirby looks at Sabrina in the mirror. "Sabrina, I didn't sleep a wink last night; my stomach is in knots."

Carrie walks over to Kirby and Sabrina. "Here you guys are. I've been looking all over for you. Did you see it upstairs? Where did all those people come from? I think it's our biggest audience yet. Do you have lots of friends, Kirby?"

"Not that many, I have no idea where they are all coming from."

Kendal runs up to the girls. "Guess what you guys? Remember that audition I went on last week? Well, I got the part. It will be my first paying job as an actress. I'm so excited."

Kirby hugs Kendal. "That's so great, Kendal. I knew someday you'd be a big star."

Zac comes rushing up to Kirby, breathless. "Hey, any of you guys know how to tie a tie? I have no clue how to wear one of these things."

Kirby looks at his tie. "Here Zac, let me. I used to tie my dad's ties all the time."

As Kirby is fixing Zac's tie he asks, "So how's our star songwriter? Did you see all the people? They're here to listen to your songs. Can you believe it, Kirby Rhodes, the famous female composer? Move over Stephen Sondheim, Leonard Bernstein."

Dr. Paul comes over to the group where Kirby is. "Here you are. It's time to line up. Zac, you look very nice, so classical, where's the rock and roller?" Then he turns to Kirby. "Kirby, are you ready to have your words and notes sung to the rafters?"

"I think so. I'm so nervous; the butterflies in my stomach are swing dancing."

Dr. Paul pats her shoulder. "I know, opening night jitters. It gets easier. In fact I know of a Bible verse for just such an occasion. Let's see . . . " He smiles at everyone. "Just kidding. But Kirby I want to give you my own blessing. To Kirby, write your music, sing your songs, create from your passions, and be alive with the energy and light God has given you." He turns and looks at the whole choir and speaks loudly. "OK, everyone, line up and let's go up there and raise the roof ten feet off its rafters."

The choir lines up and walks into the packed church and onto the four risers. They are all dressed in black with white accents. Dr. Paul stands in front facing the choir. He lifts his hands and the choir begins singing.

Oh Lord up above, please fill me with love
Give me hope and strength and courage
Oh, make me whole, yes help me to grow
In this precious life, You have given

Zac sings in his beautiful tenor voice:

Oh Lord, hear my plea, take this pain from me
Hold my hand; help me stand by Your side.
Oh, show me the way, to be with You today
Yes, guide me on my journey

The whole choir sings:

Oh Lord, set me free, from these shadows I see
Help me stand in the light You are giving.
Oh, heal my soul, Please make me full
Of this love that I know You are giving.

The audience applauds. Dr. Paul turns to the audience.

"I came in the middle of this school year, complaining how young people dress, how they talk, how irresponsible they are, all the tattoos, the body piercing, the hair of many colors. I used to see it as a sign of something negative, a deterioration of things I held dear. I thought it was my job to make the students see the light, to tell them God's story. These songs you are hearing tonight are written by one of these students I refer to. It's opened my eyes. I learned through her music that young people do see God's light. But they see it through their own eyes, their own understanding. These songs have given me a glimpse of what they see, and it's beautiful. I'm learning to listen to what they are saying. Now, before we continue the concert I would like to introduce the composer we are honoring tonight, Kirby Rhodes."

Kirby walks up to the microphone. "Thank you all for coming tonight to listen to my music. Music is the voice of my heart and soul and it is exciting for me to share it with you. This year has been a year of growth for me. So please, sit back, listen, and let us entertain you. Thanks again for coming."

Kirby goes back to her place in the choir and Dr. Paul turns to the choir and raises his hands and begins the next song:

> *Lord hear our voices, Lord hear our pleas*
> *Guide us on this journey, help us to be free*
> *Please show us the way now, show us where to go*
> *Fill us with your wisdom, Help us to grow*
>
> *Sometimes the way is dark and cold,*
> *No one is there that we can hold*
> *The path is rocky, trees get in the way*
> *Guide us around them, teach us to pray*
>
> *Pain it surrounds us into our life it creeps*
> *Sometimes it feels as though you're asleep*
> *We reach up our arms, we're on our knees*
> *Won't you help us, hear our pleas*
>
> *God we see you, our eyes are open wide*
> *We'll no longer run away, we'll no longer hide*
> *As children we bow and open our hearts*
> *Won't you guide us, please give us a start*

SNOWFLAKES

Look At the Snow

Look at the snow falling down on the street
Big fluffy flakes is all you can see
The wind sends them twirling in the cold air
Sparkling like diamonds being tossed everywhere

Where did they come from? Where will they go?
Dancing and swirling putting on a grand show
Now they're a snowman with a black hat
Then they become a ski trail, long, smooth and flat.

Oh, fly little snowflakes; make all the children smile
Riding on sleds, going down hills for a mile
Land on their noses, their faces and chins
Bring us your beauty when the cold winter sets in

Sara, the snowflake, swirls and dances her way to earth, feeling the birth of her freedom. Floating on the gentle air, falling peacefully on the ground, she sees others join her in their own unique song of rhythm and dance. Sara the snowflake marvels at the unique design of each snowflake as they fall gracefully around her.

One is "Sam" he says. One says she is "Susan"; another says she is "Jaspar."

Jaspar seems big and fluffy, bigger than the rest and when she lands she laughs. Jaspar tells us we are all snowflakes, newly born and white and pure. Jaspar has a beautiful voice and she sings to us stories about life. More of us come and pretty soon we are a pile of cold, tingly white powder. We enjoy the people as they come and shovel us, tossing us in the air till we dance and glisten in the day's sunlight. Children come and make us into different shapes to play with and sometimes they throw us through the air until we explode in a loud laughter flying every which way.

We are happy. Jaspar tells us we are snowflakes so that people can use us to build and make snowmen, snow forts, snow horses, and snowballs. It is a wonderful winter. Sometimes it snows and others join us. Sometimes the wind howls twirling us to new places.

One day the sky fills with dark dense clouds, the wind is howling loudly, and the world is full of big, powdery snowflakes. There are so many of us swirling around we can barely see anything else. Pretty soon some of us are lying on piles of snow that are more than five feet tall. It is breathtaking to look down from that height. Pretty soon everywhere we look is just snow— there are no people, no cars. The streets and sidewalks are completely empty. Jaspar tells us we are part of a blizzard. She tells us that when the snow finally stops we will see a lot of people shoveling and using something she called "snowblowers." We all laugh, "isn't that just another word for the wind?" She tells us that a snowblower is a machine people make to get the snow off the roads and sidewalks. It is even more powerful than the wind. We all say at the same time with great wonder, "Ohhhhhhhhhh," at the thought of something more powerful than the wind. Jaspar is always explaining where we are.

Then one day someone asks, "Why are we here?"

Jaspar thinks a minute and starts to sing in a crystal clear voice that seems to bless the world around us, and blows through the trees. Then she stops to listen and says, "because we have a purpose?"

"What's a purpose?" Sara asks.

"It's a reason to be. You see we cover the earth allowing it to hibernate and sleep, restoring its energy and renewing its nutrients. We help people have fun. They ski on us, play games with us. When it's time, we'll change and become what is again needed for the 'Great Order of Things.'"

All of the snowflakes start to dance and twirl around, laughing. We like feeling our importance in the "Great Order of Things." Months pass and things start to change. The sun becomes warmer and Sara notices some of the other snowflakes melting away, disappearing. She and the other snowflakes get scared. "What's happening?" We ask.

Jaspar says, "We are changing into a new form. Some call it dying."

"What does that mean?" We all ask.

"It means you will melt and become water, the ground will absorb you and you will feed the earth and grow into food. Others will evaporate into the air and eventually form clouds that will create rain. You will come to the earth as rain, replenishing rivers and lakes providing water for people to drink, feeding the soil and plants. Once again growing foods."

"What is food?" a snowflake asks.

"It is what people eat so they can grow bigger, it keeps them alive."

"Do people die?"

"Everything at some point dies, or as I like to think, it changes into another form of being. Like how we change to water, everything changes to another form."

"Does the earth die?" We ask.

"Parts of the earth die, but the part that dies brings forth new life, a new beginning. The earth adapts to what is needed. The earth continues on indefinitely and holds all of life; it is a large place for us all to live, in many forms, all together, to help each other grow and become what we are meant to be."

As the sun gets warmer more snowflakes melt away and soon Jaspar, the biggest of the snowflakes, begins to feel herself change and become what she is meant to be. As the spring wind blows, you can hear Jaspar's voice singing softly, and floating through the treetops.

MAMA

Mama, please come dance with me
Please just come and dance with me
Won't you run and chase me
Hug and hold and kiss me
Mama won't you come

It was a black thunderous night; the rain was pouring down, the bony hand with its long fingers of light reached out with its death grip. Trees were bending with the weight of the wind. Large tree branches were being torn loose and tossed into the air like toothpicks. The thunder growled its way across the sky. The wind howled outside the window. The car she was driving was being tossed around like she was in a snow globe and someone was shaking it. She wondered if the storm would ever stop. Up ahead of her she saw the wall cloud begin to rotate . . . she wondered if she would make it home.

~

She pulls her car into the garage, opens the car door and gets out. She walks outside into the cool night air. She looks at the wooden garage door as she closes it. The brown paint is peeling in spots. She notices pieces of wood are missing at the bottom of the door. She looks up at the garage and notices it is starting to slant ever so slightly to the right. The cement in the driveway is cracked and dirt and weeds are pushing their way up through the concrete. She sighs and walks up the sidewalk to the back door.

She looks around the backyard. She sees the swing set with two swings. One of the chains has come loose so one swing is on the ground. The sandbox has the beginning of a castle—a tower with a window. The kiddie pool still has water in it. Leaves are floating on the top of the water that looks a little green. Her daughter's big wheel bike is sitting on its side, like she has just jumped off it and rushed into the house. Her face glows with the memory.

She opens the back door and steps into the kitchen. The kitchen is in its usual state of chaos. Dirty dishes are stacked in the sink, crusted with day old food. The cupboard doors are partially opened, showing rows of cereal boxes and cooking supplies. The drawers are not quite closed, so food has fallen in among the silverware and utensils. Coffee rings shine like halos on the stove and table. There is dried food on the counter that will probably need a knife to scrape it up. The floor looks like a child's playground: sand here, toys there, cups and food lying under the table. The red light shines on the stove; one of the electric burners is still turned on low. She smiles to herself.

She notices the bathroom as she walks by. The faucet has the usual leak, dripping occasional slow drops of cold water on the white porcelain. Beard hairs cover the ledge and bottom of the sink. The towels are hung in their sagging position, labels half off. The bathtub wears a dark ring of dirt around the inside. The rug is no longer a soft white and blue; it is a dingy gray. Dust balls form in the corners and under the radiator. She hugs herself.

She turns and goes into the living room. The piano keys are showing; music covers the top of the piano like someone has just finished a frenzied concert. The couch is sagging in those favorite spots people sit in. The toys are picked up and neatly stacked in the corner. The carpet holds white strings, crumbs, and shredded up candy wrappers. The big easy chair is minus one of its cushions. A tear escapes from her eye and rolls down her cheek.

She enters her daughter's bedroom and looks around. Her dolls are neatly stacked on the shelf. Books are still on the floor and table, piled high, covers battered with frequent use. The green carpet has begun to get bare spots; lint can be seen in the soft beam of the night-light. Her daughter's clothes are scattered on top of the change table. Dresses, overalls, shirts, all piled in disarray. She can see her daughter asleep in her little bed, cuddled into a fetal position, hugging her teddy bear. She sits a moment watching her daughter sleep.

She looks last at her bedroom, clothes hanging haphazardly on the chair and dresser. The bed sheets are half on the floor, half on the bed. The light is on. She sees her husband sitting on the edge of the bed, hair disheveled, head in his hands. She hears her daughter wake up with a whimper in the next room. Her daughter crawls out of bed and runs crying into the bedroom yelling, "MAMA!" She sees her husband pick her up, cuddle her tightly into himself and lay his head gently on hers, kissing the top of her head. She hears him whisper, "Mama went bye bye honey, she won't be back anymore. But I know she sees us and is watching over us right now. She loves us very much." His tears glisten in her hair where they fall. He rocks her gently back and forth singing softly, "Birdies fly up in the sky" until her daughter drifts off to sleep.

She crouches down and reaches her hand out to touch her husband and daughter, wishing she could put her arms around them and experience their warmth, and feel once again, the touch of their kisses.

DAPHNE

Music Man

Oh music man, fill my heart with
the notes of your love song,
Oh music man, fill my soul with
the passion of your words
Oh music man, fill my heart with
the notes of your love song,
Oh music man, fill my soul with
the passion of your words

My body comes alive with each word that you say,
My eyes fill with visions and dreams
My heart opens up, feels the energy flow,
My head sees the beauty in my soul

My eyes open up, I see so much more,
I feel the power inside me
I see the way you opened the door
It brings me inside all the beauty

You guide me into a world I don't know,
My heart fills with awe and wonder
My soul wants to dance and twirl around,
I thrill at the sound of the thunder.

Oh music man, fill my heart with
the notes of your love song,
Oh music man, fill my soul with
the passion of your words

Oh music man, fill my heart with
the notes of your love song,
Oh music man, fill my soul with
the passion of your words

Chapter 1

Joselyn, a tall woman in her early twenties, with shoulder length brown hair, is sitting in the library with its large fireplace made of marble, and shelves lined with numerous books. While talking on the phone, she looks at the soft comfy chair and big soft couch, wishing she were sitting there instead of on this hard chair by the desk. The coffee table is a mess, with musical score paper and pencils strewn around.

Joselyn sighs. "Oh Caitlin, things are just getting so . . . so out of control. I don't think I've been shopping in a month . . . you bought a what? For how much? Can I borrow it sometime, it would look nice with my new dress . . . William? He's fine. I was with him Saturday at that bed and breakfast. He asked me to marry him. I haven't given him an answer yet . . . of course I'm excited. What do you mean I don't sound it? There is just so much to consider. There's Kenneth . . ."

Just as she says his name, Kenneth, a tall, wiry, dark-haired young man, comes running into the library. He stands in front of Joselyn, very agitated. Joselyn tries to ignore him and keeps talking on the phone.

Kenneth starts speaking very loudly. "Oh, Joselyn, have you seen my glasses? You know how badly I need them and I'm afraid Grandmama has brought them with her shopping. I'm sure she has brought them with her. You know I can't write a thing without them. Joselyn, are you listening to me? Joselyn!"

"What? Just a minute Caitlin." Joselyn puts her hand over the phone. "What, Kenneth?"

"My glasses. Have you seem them? I'm sure Grandmama . . ."

"Kenneth, they're on the top of your head. Can't you see I'm on the phone?" Joselyn takes her hand off the phone. "I'm sorry, Caitlin. What were you saying? Dinner?"

Kenneth feels for his glasses and finds them nestled there in his hair. He puts them on. "That's better. Now what WAS I going to do? Ah, yes." He walks over to the coffee table sitting in front of the couch and picks up a musical score and a pencil. He begins to write.

Joselyn, still on the phone, says to Caitlin. "I don't think I can go. Not tonight. No, Kenneth has to . . . what did you say?"

As Joselyn is talking Kenneth suddenly starts running around the library counting loudly. "1-2-3-4," He pauses then counts again. "1-2-3-4."

Joselyn covering the phone, asks, "Kenneth, what ARE you doing?"

"Oh Joselyn! This is so wonderful. I've just discovered what a whole rest feels like. When I run fast, I feel the beat as my blood pulses through my heart. 1-2-3-4. It's exhilarating! It's glorious! Oh Joselyn, you should try it."

"Yes, Kenneth. Look I'm on the phone—can you please be a little quieter?" Kenneth continues counting quietly.

"I'm back Caitlin. This afternoon? I'm busy Kenneth needs to . . . what? Tomorrow. I'll see. I will call you tomorrow."

Chapter 2

The next day Joselyn walks into the library and sees her Grandmama, a full figured, gray haired woman in her early seventies, sitting in the comfy chair by the fireplace writing a letter. Kenneth is drinking soda pop from a can, and sitting on the couch working on a musical score. She sees a jump rope sitting behind her Grandmama's chair and shakes her head. Joselyn takes a seat next to Kenneth on the couch, pulls a compact mirror from her pocket, and begins to pluck her eyebrows.

"Oh, Joselyn, must you pluck your eyebrows now? This is a serious conversation. It needs all of your attention." Kenneth sips from the soda can, clears his throat, and continues speaking. "I mean we have to decide this matter today. You know how important it is to be prepared. You must know my wishes now when I can say them. I mean, if I were in a coma, I wouldn't be able to tell you and then you wouldn't know what I want. It could be disastrous."

The telephone rings. Joselyn stands up. "I'll get it."

Joselyn sits down and picks up the phone. Kenneth sends her dirty looks. "Hello Caitlin. Yes, I know it's tomorrow. Look, I don't think I can go anywhere. It's Kenneth. You know how he constantly has to plan for everything. Right now he is wants to finish planning for his funeral . . . what? Yes, I know, he just turned eighteen. But he wants us to know his wishes for when the time comes. So far we've found out he wants a white casket with purple trim. What? I know it's strange, but what can I do? He's my brother . . . what are you getting upset about? I know I had to cancel before too. It hasn't been a month; just last week you came over to tell me about Jeffrey . . . What? . . . you're right, that was almost a month ago. William? Look I can't talk about this now. I'll call you next week—maybe we can do something on Friday. Yes, I promise, I will call. Bye."

Joselyn walks back to the couch where Kenneth is looking furious and Grandmama is writing a letter.

"OK, we need . . . we need to what? Now what was I saying before? Joselyn, where is your pen? Why aren't you writing this down? Here, you better use this rock to hold down the paper; you know how drafty this place can be. Grandmama, will you please stop writing that letter and pay attention? This is important."

Grandmama puts down her paper and pen. "Yes, dear. But you know I've got to finish this letter soon. So please, can we get this done?" Grandmama looks at Joselyn. "Who was on the phone dear?"

"It was Caitlin. We talked about dinner tonight. But I told her maybe next Friday. Let's finish this discussion." She looks at Kenneth. "So Kenneth, I have my pen and paper. Now let's see . . . you said before you want a white coffin, instrumental music featuring the piano, roses, no other kind of flowers, just roses. Now what else?"

"Well, my funeral must be on a Thursday. I mean Thursday has always been a green and yellow day for me. You know how much . . ."

Joselyn interrupts. "Kenneth please, can we get on with this? Why don't you take off that sweater? It is so warm in here."

Kenneth bats away her suggestion with his hand. "Oh, stop fussing. The funeral must be a Thursday. I want Reverend Nelson. He is my favorite minister and he understands me so well."

Grandmama starts to chuckle. "Kenneth, he is in his 60's. By the time you need a funeral he will have been gone for a good 20 years or so."

"Oh, you're right Grandmama, I hadn't thought of that."

Kenneth looks flustered; he starts looking around the room. "Where is my jump rope? You know I need my jump rope to help me think. Where is it? Where could it have gone? Oh, it has to be around here someplace."

Kenneth starts to run around the room anxiously looking for his jump rope.

"You don't think that someone came in and . . . oh, here it is."

Kenneth looks relieved when he finds the jump rope behind his Grandmama's chair. He begins jumping. His face starts to relax. Then the phone rings again. Kenneth begins to jump rope faster.

Joselyn gets up to answer the phone.

"Hello, William. What? Oh I forgot I was supposed to call this afternoon. Kenneth needed me to . . . look you have to understand he's a little eccentric. Crazy? Don't say that. Please don't be mad. Sometimes there is so much going on here . . . I have a life! Yes, I get frustrated sometimes . . . but his music, his talent . . . he couldn't do it all without our support. My talent? Grandmama says I have plenty of time. Please, William, don't pressure me. Yes, I will give you an answer soon. I do love you too. Grandmama and I have taken care of Kenneth for a long time; he is such a genius. I can't just suddenly . . . OK, let's talk next week. How about Wednesday? I promise I'll call you Wednesday. Love you too. Bye."

Joselyn sighs and walks over and sits on the couch. She picks up her paper and pen. Kenneth is still jumping rope and Grandmama has resumed writing her letter.

"Who was on the phone dear?"

"Just William, I told him I'd call him back later."

Grandmama looks up at Joselyn. "Joselyn you know . . ."

Kenneth stops jumping rope and sits down. "That's better. I can think clearly now. Where were we? Oh, yes, the minister. Let's see, when the time comes it can be any minister from that church on the corner. St. Lukes? St. Marks? Or whatever it is. The one with the beautiful stained glass window of the Last Supper."

Joselyn writes, "Church on corner. Check."

Kenneth looks at Joselyn. "Oh and Joselyn, I must get a hold of that woman. What was her name? You know, the one I was with a few weeks ago, the one with the gold-spun hair that stayed together when she moved. The one with the blue Wedgewood china eyes that looked out through those lacy black lashes. Oh, you must remember."

Kenneth gets up and starts pacing. "You must remember?"

Grandmama and Joselyn look at each other and roll their eyes.

Kenneth continues. "We made love that night. It was like writing a symphony. First I thrust inside her like a waltz, 1-2-3, 2-2-3, 3-2-3, 4-2-3.

Grandmama looking flustered. "Kenneth I don't think you . . ."

"Her breath came out like quarter notes—1 2 3 4." Kenneth begins speaking a little faster. "Then like eighth notes—1&2&3&4&," Kenneth speaks even faster. "Then like sixteenth notes—1e&a2e&a3e&a4e&a." Then suddenly she opened her mouth and a symphony exploded into the room. High notes, I'm sure it was a high C. Low notes. All the way down to low F. Throaty middle notes flew around the room. Then she laughed, then she cried, or was it I? I can't remember. Anyway, that was when I asked her to go to Israel with me. I've always wanted to go there. I love to hear the Yiddish language with those wonderful throaty, guttural sounds. Words like l'chaim, chutzpah, and tuchis. I have the tickets for Israel somewhere..."

Kenneth stops to pat down his pockets and pulls them out. "Yes, here they are. I know Joselyn, I should send her some flowers. Let's see, ones like her name. All yellow. Let's see, dandelion, no not that."

Kenneth begins pacing again. "Let's see Daisy. No. What was her name?"

Suddenly he stops. "That's it. Daffodils, yellow daffodils like her name. Daphne. That's it. That is her name, Daphne. Please Joselyn, send her some daffodils and remind her of our trip."

The telephone rings; Joselyn gets up to answer it. "Hello? William? I thought I said I'd call you next . . . this weekend . . . I can't. I'm going to Israel with Kenneth. It's his first performance of Symphony #4 and Love's Requiem . What? I have to go? You want to come with us? But you hate dressing up and sitting through . . . his music is so important. William don't hang up. William?"

Joselyn gets up and sits back on the couch.

Kenneth is still pacing. "So Grandmama. I must be at the airport by 5:00 pm Friday. I need my red-plaid suitcase. The one with the piano monogrammed in the left corner. Oh, and Joselyn I just remembered you don't have to find Daphne. It is you who is going with me to Israel. You must have forgotten, dear. I don't know why you thought I should send flowers to Daphne..."

Grandmama interrupts Kenneth. "Kenneth where will you be staying in Israel—at a hotel or at the conductor's home? You know home cooking is so much better for the stomach when you are under stress."

"I'm staying at the Conductor's, Grandmama. I found out he speaks Yiddish. Did I tell you I love the throaty, crisp quality of . . . ?"

Joselyn interrupts, "Yes, Kenneth, you told us. Can we wind up this funeral business for today? I have a headache and I'm getting hungry. It's almost time to dress for supper."

Kenneth says, "Lets see. We covered the . . ."

Impatiently Joselyn interrupts, "caskets, music, day of the week, minister, flowers, and church."

"Well good. That's fine for now. Joselyn, did you hear me say 5:00 Friday?"

"Yes, Kenneth, I know."

Kenneth picks up his musical score and begins to puzzle over a measure. Joselyn watches him a minute and then gets up and ruffles his hair.

"Yes, little brother, I know. Grandmama should we go see about supper?"

Joselyn and Grandmama leave just as Kenneth stands up and runs for two beats then stops. Runs again for two beats, stops and scribbles something on his sheet of music.

Chapter 3

A warm sun shines on Joselyn as she sits on the front steps of her home, a very large house made of big beige stones and stucco. She looks out at the green lawn that carpets the front yard for miles. She remembers rolling down the soft, emerald hills, laughing with Kenneth as he toddled down behind her. She was eight; he was four. Their closest neighbor was two miles away. She feels a soft breeze that tickles her ears. She sighs, listening to her brother at the piano in the house. He plays a few notes on the piano, stops, then plays, then stops. William is sitting next to her also listening.

William interrupts the silence. "Why does he keep stopping?"

Joselyn, lost in the music and her thoughts, almost forgot William was there. "I'm sorry, what did you say?"

William says, "Why does he keep stopping?"

Joselyn turns and looks at William. "He's writing down what he just played. He is trying to finish the first movement of a sonatina he started before we went to Israel. Israel was so wonderful. Have you ever been there? Kenneth, you should have seen him. His fingers danced over the piano. It was like the piano was just an extension of his fingers. He looked like he and the piano were one. Sometimes the piano was his lover; other times it became his enemy. He made the piano laugh, then cry. It was just, mesmerizing. The audience exploded with applause. It was deafening. They kept yelling encore! Encore! Kenneth must have played an hour of encores. They loved his music; everyone loves his music. Such passion, such beauty, it just flows out of him.

"Joselyn, I asked you a question ten minutes ago and suddenly you're talking about Israel and Kenneth again. I don't know why I keep trying."

"I'm sorry, William. It's just that . . . being with Kenneth and his performances . . . I always need a day or two to come down from the intense experience. I need to regroup."

"You always have some excuse. Look, I feel like you've been backing away from me every since I asked you to marry me. We were having such a good time at that bed and breakfast in Toronto. Maybe I shouldn't . . ."

Joselyn stops William. "I . . . it's just . . . well marriage is so permanent. I haven't done all that I need to yet. When my parents left . . . I just had Kenneth and Grandmama. And Kenneth is sooo talented and eccentric. He needs someone there to take care of the little details. Grandmama can't travel like she used to . . ."

Williams gets up and starts to pace back and forth. "Why don't your parents come back and . . . ?"

"William, they are touring. With their singing careers, they travel all over Europe. They don't have time right now in their careers to . . ."

William stops pacing and takes Joselyn's long slender hands into his. "But how about you and your life? Look at these hands, the hands of a great pianist. Joselyn, you need to get away from the family and make one of your own. Don't you see you're being consumed by . . . ?"

William is interrupted by Kenneth, who is yelling inside of the house, "Grandmama, Joselyn . . . Joselyn!"

Hearing Kenneth's frantic voice, Joselyn stands up and tries to pull her hands away. "William, I have to go to him. He's panicked. Can't you hear him? He gets lost sometimes in his music and has trouble coming back. I need to go to him. Please let go."

Kenneth yells louder. "Joselyn!"

Joselyn runs up the stairs and into the music room where Kenneth is seated at the grand piano, William is right behind her.

Kenneth sees Joselyn. "Oh, there you are. I was . . . I couldn't remember where I was. What day is it, Joselyn, what day is it? Is it Wednesday or Thursday? I remember now . . . it's Thursday because we were at the theater last night. Yes, it's Thursday." Kenneth starts calming down. "It's Thursday." Then he sighs, sits down at the piano and begins playing.

Joselyn rubs his shoulders a minute, and then kisses him on the top of his head. "That's right Kenneth, it's Thursday."

Joselyn looks up and sees William standing there watching her with Kenneth.

William asks, "Joselyn, please can we talk?"

"Kenneth, I'll just be in the next room." Kenneth continues playing while Joselyn and William leave the room and go down the hall and into the library.

"Joselyn. I don't know what to do. I can't stay around here with you and watch you lose yourself and not pursue your own talent. Why does everyone else matter but you? I need to travel, I need to go places, do things. But I want you with me. Every time I picture myself on my sailboat you are by my side. On the airplane to Rome, you are by my side I . . ."

"Look, I can't be by your side right now. My parents' careers are bigger than ever. Kenneth's career is on the way to greatness.

I just can't right now, William. Maybe in a year or two when things have steadied themselves around here. But not now."

Kenneth yells from the next room. "Joselyn, I've done it! Come quick, I've finished the first movement of Daphne's Sonatina, the one where I see Daphne sitting in a garden. She is sad and angry because her lover left her. Please come and hear it . . . Joselyn!"

"William, please, just give me some time."

"I'm leaving for Denmark tomorrow. I'll be gone a month. I'll call you when I get back. But Joselyn, please, think about us."

William leaves and Joselyn rushes into Kenneth to hear his new sonatina. She sits in a soft chair in the music room, a large room with incredible acoustics, lots of windows, and a music system set up on the shelves to record the creations of a genius. She watches Kenneth at the grand piano, sighs with pleasure and listens as the notes fill the room.

Chapter 4

Grandmama sits at a small round table sipping her tea, looking around at the garden. She loves the beautiful patio created from different colored bricks that wind around in a spiral, creating a beautiful pattern. She enjoys all the flowers: red, orange, pink, white, and tangerine roses filling the garden with color and fragrance. She admires the table with a small vase of flowers from the garden, a tea set, and a plate with croissants.

Joselyn walks out of the house and sits across from her grandmama, looking around her. "It is so beautiful out here in the garden." She sits back and sighs, pouring herself a cup of tea.

Grandmama smiles. "I know we should sit out here more often. It is so relaxing. Joselyn, I haven't heard you practicing lately. How come?"

"I don't know, sometimes I think I should forget about playing concerts. I mean I'm 22 years old and life has been so frantic around here. Traveling to Israel, then last week Italy, next week

Brazil. It was nice seeing Mom and Dad in Italy. I think it helped Kenneth to spend some time with them."

"I just wish they could find more time to spend with him and you. You know your grandfather was a lot like Kenneth and actually so is your dad. I think eccentric musical genius runs through the male genes in my family. The women, well, we just get to watch from the sidelines. But you are different; you've got musical talent from your mom without the eccentricity of your dad or grandfather. So dear, I don't want you to forget about your dreams. I mean your piano playing is every bit as good as your brother's."

"But I can't compose like him. He has become known all over the world and he's barely 18 years old."

"Don't compare yourself to him. He has his talents; you have yours. I heard you once say that when you watch Kenneth play piano it's like the piano and him are one. Do you know how I feel when I watch you play piano?"

"Grandmama, I didn't realize you even watched . . ."

"Well, I do. When you sit at the piano, place your hands on the keys and begin playing, it's like you've entered another world. Your whole body transforms and takes in the music. Suddenly you look like you're dancing and the piano is your partner. You are a woman in love and the piano is the dark stranger that brings you to lands never chartered before. Your face is lost in a reality I can't see but I can feel, through the music you spin around me. It's like you take on a glow, an iridescent glow, that stops time yet pushes it forward all at once. It's an incredible experience. I wish you'd share it with others. I feel so blessed after I've been listening to your music."

"You've never told me this before, Grandmama. I've been under the impression with all that goes on around here; there isn't any time for me. I just didn't know anyone ever noticed."

"I'm sorry, you're right. I've been wrapped up in the success of your parents and Kenneth, but at night in the quiet hours before sleep, it's you that I think about. Don't let the rest of the family dwarf what you have. Go out there Joselyn and pursue your dreams."

"But Kenneth, he needs so much . . ."

Kenneth walks into the garden and sees Joselyn and Grandmama. "Well, here you are. I've been looking all over for you, Joselyn. I've finished the 2nd movement to Daphne's Sonatina, the one where the red bird is sitting on her shoulder singing the most beautiful song, a sad, poignant song, a song that heals her broken heart. I thought maybe you'd come and listen to it. You know, be my audience, you too Grandmama. Oh and Joselyn, I figured out how to feel those ties between notes. If I breathe, then hold my breath, then stomp my foot while I'm holding my breath, I can feel the notes that are inside the hold. You should try it, Joselyn. By the way, Grandmama, did you take my glasses again? I just had them."

Grandmama smiles at Kenneth. "They are on your head. Remember they are usually on the top of your head. I've never taken your glasses yet."

"Will you come and listen? Please? And Joselyn, wear the red dress that buttons up under your chin. It feels so nice to see red when I'm playing. Like the red bird on my shoulder that visits me in the garden sometimes. I'll be ready in fifteen minutes. I've got to put on my performing tuxedo with the little piano on the lapel. Now where did I put that?"

Kenneth leaves, scratching his head and muttering to himself.

Joselyn looks at Grandmama. "I do love him, all his eccentric talent, stuffed into that wiry body, exploding out and covering us with . . ."

"Responsibility, Joselyn, yes, lots and lots of responsibility."

Chapter 5

Grandmama and Joselyn are seated on the couch in the music room, listening. Joselyn has on her red dress. The sun is shining through a window, creating a natural spotlight on Kenneth as he is playing the piano. Kenneth finishes the last chord with an intensity that seems to vibrate through the room. Then Joselyn and Grandmama begin to applaud. Kenneth gets up wearing his performing tuxedo with the piano on the lapel and takes a bow.

Grandmama says, "That was very nice dear. Very nice."

"Yes, Kenneth, I can tell you've worked hard on it. That ending is so much better. I like the combination of a sixth chord and then the ninth chord. It was . . ."

"No! No! Didn't you see them? The birds, the notes they flew around the room, first slowly, then faster. Didn't you feel them caress your face then tickle your nose? Joselyn didn't I see a tear in the corner of your eye?"

"You might have, there was this one spot that . . ."

"Might have, what do you mean might have? I saw it."

Kenneth gets up and starts pacing around the piano. "Why, doesn't anyone understand me? Why doesn't anyone see what I see or feel what I feel? It's like I reach out, I pour all of myself into the music and I pour all the music into myself."

Kenneth stops and looks out the window, lost in his thoughts. Then he starts quietly. "There is this intense moment where nothing exists but the music itself. Notes big and little surrounding me, caressing me, urging me to play louder, faster, or slower and gentler. The room disappears and it is only the music. The whole rests hanging upside down, the half rests settle peacefully on the shelf. When the music starts the story unfolds, the red bird enters in, the tears flow down the walls, the pain swells, then subsides."

Kenneth turns and looks at Grandmama, and Joselyn. "Can't you feel it? Can't you see it? There was MAYBE one, ONE spot!"

Kenneth begins pacing back and forth in front of the window. "There is never just one spot. It is always all of it, all at once encompassing you, filling you, taking over your body so that it is no longer your own. Your heart is given up to the beauty in the music. Your eyes see what's not there."

Kenneth starts walking faster. "Please, don't you see it? Please tell me you see what I see, feel what I feel? Please, do you have any idea what I'm talking about?"

Grandmama quietly stands and starts going over to Kenneth. "I'm sure we understand some of what . . ."

Kenneth puts his hand up and stops his Grandmama and turns to Joselyn. "How about you, do you see . . . ?"

"Well, I can't say that I see everything you are . . ."

Kenneth kneels down on one knee in front of Joselyn, who is still sitting on the couch. "But Joselyn, music is so much more than what's here in front of us. It changes time, like a time machine sending you to places: past, present, and then past. It's the sound that vibrates every nerve in your body taking possession of you. You are transported to places uncharted. It captures your emotions, sending them wherever it wants to. It transcends reality and the room disappears and other places, other worlds draw themselves around you. And you are no longer you, but are part of a bigger symphony. You are connected to everyone and everything. Oh, please say you understand!"

"Kenneth, calm down, I'm trying to. I experience things too when I play music but . . ."

"Things, you experience THINGS. Music isn't a thing, never a thing. Music is all that matters."

Kenneth gets up angrily and starts pacing again. "When I chew my cereal in the morning I feel what 2/2 time feels like, when I jump rope I feel the timbre of sound flow through me. When I play a note on the piano, my finger is the ivory and ebony and notes flow through me and out into the room. My heart is the pulse of life, like the tempo is the pulse of the music. When the piano hammers hit the strings my nerves feel the music pulsing through . . . my nerves . . . my strings . . . they are all one. Do you feel it? Do you understand?"

Kenneth starts pacing faster. "1-2-3-4, 1-2-3-4, 1-2-3-4, 1-2-3-4. Can't you feel it, the pulse of 4/4 time? Can't you feel it?"

Kenneth starts counting quietly to himself.

Grandmama, still standing, looks at Joselyn. "He really has himself worked up over this piece, Joselyn. What are we to do?"

Joselyn calmly smiles. "He'll run out of steam. He always does, then he'll sit down and play and we'll applaud and he'll say, 'Oh, I'm so glad you've enjoyed my piece. It's so nice to have a family who understands me.' You know he always does Grandmama. He always does."

Chapter 6

"Oh, what to do?" Kenneth says, pacing in front of the couch in the music room. He has the recording of his piano music turned up loud. "What do I do? I think I should have . . . what? Yes, in the third measure after the E-flat and before the C, I should have made them eighth notes."

Joselyn comes rushing into the music room looking around. "Kenneth, remember William is back from Denmark and he and Caitlin are going to be here any minute for our small dinner party. Are you ready?"

Kenneth looks around him. "Oh, Joselyn I just can't figure out the ending to the third movement of Daphne's Sonatina."

"Please, Kenneth, just let it go until after this dinner party, then I'll listen to the recording with you."

Kenneth, sighs and turns off the music. "OK, I think I'm ready. My pencil is in my pocket. I have score paper in my left pants pocket, just in case. Now tell me this again. Who is this Caitlin? Does she like music? Does she play piano? Sing?"

"Kenneth, I told you she's my best friend from college, she was a year behind me in school. We ended up being roommates when I was a senior and she was a junior. You met her a few weeks ago, sometime before our trip to Israel. She has blonde hair and blue eyes . . . remember?"

"Oh, Daphne, you mean Daphne . . . with blonde . . ."

"No Kenneth, that's the name of your sonatina. Caitlin is her name. You met her about the time you started writing the first movement of Daphne's Sonatina."

Joselyn says, "There's the doorbell, that must be them now. I'll meet you at the library, I'll bring them there to have a drink before dinner."

Joselyn rushes out of the music room. Kenneth says to himself, "Caitlin . . . blue eyes like Wedgewood china, golden-spun hair. You were the one . . ."

Kenneth walks down the hall to the library. Soon he hears voices, and then Joselyn comes in with Caitlin and William.

Kenneth stares at Caitlin and then runs up to her. "Daphne, I'd know you anywhere." Joselyn gives Kenneth the evil eye. "I mean Caitlin. How nice to see you again. Do you sing or play an instrument? Do you like music? Have you seen our grand piano? It's just down the . . ."

"Kenneth, why don't we sit in here and have a drink first? Can you please get the drink tray?" Joselyn turns to her guests. "Caitlin and William, why don't you have a seat."

Kenneth scratches his head as he leaves the library to get the drinks.

Caitlin sits on the couch; William sits in the big chair by the fireplace.

Caitlin looks around. "I forgot how big this place is. Do you ever get lost?"

Joselyn laughs and sits down next to Caitlin. "Only once when I was five. I ended up in the basement; I had no idea where I was. To this day I don't know how I ended up there. Anyway Kenneth seemed quite excited to see you, Caitlin. You made quite an impression on him the last time you were here."

"Why did he call me Daphne?"

"I don't know. I guess you remind him of . . ."

Kenneth rushes in with the drink tray staring right at Caitlin. "Joselyn, could you clear a spot for the tray?"

Joselyn reaches over and moves some magazines off the coffee table in front of the couch. Kenneth puts the tray down on the table, and stands up still staring at Caitlin. "It is you. You are Daphne. My golden haired Daphne with the China blue eyes." His stare is so intense that Caitlin at first looks away, but then gradually her eyes are pulled to his and they stare at each other.

Kenneth almost whispers, "I was sitting at my piano, looking out the window to the garden and saw you standing there with my sister. You began to glow and music was pouring out of you and into me and I played it on the piano. You felt so sad and angry. It was an incredible experience. That's when I started writing the first movement to Daphne's Sonatina. Seeing you again tonight, I feel that same strange restlessness stirring in my body. The notes are building up in me and they want to pour out of my hands and onto the piano keys. Will you please excuse me? I have to go."

Kenneth runs out and soon you can hear him playing the piano.

Joselyn turns to Caitlin. "I'm sorry, there he goes again. He recorded this last night and has been listening to it all day. He doesn't like the ending but he can't figure out what is wrong. I think you've inspired him. I didn't know you were his Daphne. He is trying to finish the third movement to, 'Daphne's Sonatina.'"

William speaks up. "I don't know about you but I could use a drink. I'm really thirsty." William gets up, walks over, pours himself a drink, then sits back down.

Caitlin, not hearing William, says, "I know you said he was eccentric, Joselyn, but is he always this intense?"

"Yes, very often. So how does it feel to know you've inspired his song?"

"I'm not sure, it's kind of weird but also kind of flattering."

"A few weeks back, before the day Kenneth was planning his funeral, he started composing Daphne's Sonatina. He says his sonatina is a story about a fair maiden whose lover has left her crying in a field of flowers. As she sits there a bird, a red bird, to be exact, comes and sits on her shoulder and sings her a song. A song that caresses her heart and heals its brokenness."

Caitlin turns white. "That's eerie."

William looks around. "What's eerie?"

"Joselyn, don't you remember when I came here that day? Jeffrey had just moved out and left me for someone he met in Brussels. I was so heartbroken. Then Kenneth opened the window to the music room and I could hear his music. Remember I said I felt like his music freed my heart. Like a weight had been lifted off me and . . ."

Suddenly the piano music stops and Kenneth comes running into the room. He stands in front of Caitlin, staring down at her.

"I finished it. I finished my Sonatina. The third movement completes the story. After Daphne's lover goes away, and her heart heals, she looks up and sees through the trees, a dark haired man. She thinks the man is carrying her heart but instead it's a red bird. He lays it on her shoulder and Daphne begins to sing with the bird. Notes of love and joy fill the countryside. She weds the dark man in the trees with the red bird."

Catlin stares mesmerized by Kenneth's words; she stands up and he takes her hand.

"Kenth, I mean Kenneth, if the invitation is still open I would love to see your grand piano. Would you play Daphne's Sonatina for me? I would love to hear all three movements."

Kenneth and Caitlin walk out of the room.

"William, what just happened? Did you see that?"

"I think your brother just swept Caitlin off her feet. Now, may I sweep you off yours?"

William gets up and walks over to Joselyn.

"But Caitlin is three years older than Kenneth."

"Joselyn, love wants what love wants." William takes Joselyn in his arms and gives her a long passionate kiss.

Chapter 7

Ocean waves are crashing to the shore. Sea gulls are flying overhead. The sky is a deep blue with just a few wispy clouds floating lazily by. The sandy shore has a few sunbathers scattered around on luxurious beach chairs. People are running in the water, splashing; the water sparkles in the sun like a million diamonds.

Joselyn walks up to William. "I can't believe we are here. Look William, just look at the ocean waves, and so much beautiful sun. I love the feel of the soft breeze and the sand through my toes. And we have our very own beach chairs." Joselyn sits down on her beach chair, laughing. William's chair is right beside hers.

William, watching her, asks, "How did you like parasailing?"

"William, you were right. It was so breathtaking. It was like I was a bird flying over the land feeling the wind through my hair, the sun warming my back. Oh it was glorious. I've never felt so free. I'm so glad you talked me into this vacation. The last tour I was on was so grueling and exhausting. I think I've played in every orchestra hall in Europe and the United States. It was good seeing my parents in Belgium, but with them it was non-stop, so much to catch up on."

"I'm glad I finally got you to slow down long enough to go on a real honeymoon."

William leans over and kisses Joselyn. "So talking about feeling free, have you heard from your brother? Or Caitlin?"

"Remember, yesterday, I told you . . ."

"Told me what?"

"William, I'm sure I told you about the letter. Oh, that's right, I started telling you and then you kissed me on my neck and well . . ."

"What, Joselyn? What did the letter say?"

"Caitlin quit her accounting job for good. She said she loves traveling with Kenneth on his concert tours. Now they are planning to be married. She wants to devote all her time to his career and picking up all those little details. She always did love details. I guess that's why she became an accountant."

"So they are getting married? Who would have thought . . . ?"

"Yes, who would have thought that having you and Caitlin over for dinner that night would change my life? Who knew there was a real Daphne? And from what Grandmama says, Caitlin keeps inspiring more and more music. I didn't now my brother could love . . . or I should say focus on our world long enough to see someone else. But our dear Caitlin seems to cross into his world, while still living in ours. I'm glad you were patient and waited for me."

"It's funny. I wasn't sure that night if I could wait any longer. But then I decided you were worth the wait. By the way, how's your Grandmama doing?"

"She's fine; Kenneth and Caitlin are going to keep living in that big house with its warm fireplace, grand piano and the garden outside, so she's happy. It still amazes me that Caitlin is Daphne. He seemed to change that day when Caitlin and I were in the garden. I thought it was because he had started his new piece, Daphne's Sonatina. Not that he had fallen in love. Oh William, I love you so much and I'm so glad Kenneth is experiencing what we have."

Chapter 8

Kenneth and Caitlin finish their dinner in the dining room; grandmama is out for the evening with friends. The large chandelier hangs over the center of the table that is filled with left overs from their evening meal of pheasant, with red potatoes and green beans. Kenneth and Caitlin get up from the table. Caitlin is wearing a red dress with a small bird monogrammed on her shoulder. Kenneth is wearing his performing tuxedo. They walk down the hall to the music room. Kenneth sits down at the grand piano, Caitlin walks over to the couch and takes a seat. Kenneth plays the new concerto he is working on.

When it is finished he looks up at Caitlin. "Did you hear it Caitlin? Did you see . . . ?"

"The birds? Yes, dear Kenneth, one was red and one was blue."

'That's right, and the room, did it . . . ?"

Caitlin smiles. "Fill up with notes? Yes, it did, and I actually saw an eighth note escape out the window.'"

"Did your heart become . . . ?"

"A prisoner of the music? Yes, it did."

Kenneth gets up from the piano and kneels down in front of Caitlin. "Did you feel how time . . . ?"

"No longer existed? I did. We were outside of time."

"Oh, you do understand me so well. I knew the moment I saw you in the garden, outside that window, that you belonged in my world and I yours."

Kenneth lays his head in Caitlin's lap. She begins to stroke his hair.

"Kenneth, you have opened my world and my heart to places I never knew existed. I feel the music encompassing our lives bringing us together into its loving embrace. I never knew such beauty existed."

Kenneth sighs, "Yes, music is everywhere, you can feel its pulse, see its beauty in everything. You just have to slow down and be quiet enough to hear the symphony playing."

Kenneth looks up at Caitlin and she lowers her lips for his kiss.

Together they say, "I love you."

TOMBSTONE CITY
WINS AGAIN

Life is Going Very Fast Now

Life is going very fast, now.
Where it goes I do not know
Tossing me up in the air so far,
always keeping on the go
Fear and anger push me further on,
running from what has to be
Can't look back the pain is catching up,
Now it's right behind me
Darkness it surrounds me everywhere,
swirling with confusing sights
Who am I? Where will I go?
Lost in this life's lonely fight.

As he sits in his car waiting for the red light to change, he fondles his newly bought computer game. To just look at it makes his hands clammy and his stomach get butterflies. A brand new challenge—he can't wait to get it home and try it. *But*, he thinks to himself smugly, *I'll soon master it, like I always do.*

He glances in his rearview mirror and sees brown eyes with slightly darkened circles beginning to form, and dark stubble on his face (no matter how much he shaves he just can't look clean shaven). He looks at his hair and thinks, *I've got to get a haircut soon.* He feels cramped, sitting with all six feet behind the small steering wheel.

The light finally changes and off he goes speeding home. When he reaches his driveway, he puts his car in the garage, grabs his new package, and runs to the door. But when he gets in, his wife says, "Hi, John, don't forget tonight's the night we are going to your mother's for dinner. We've got to hurry."

John's heart sinks. Dinner at his mother's means: dinner, dessert, slides, talk, talk, talk. He won't get home until late. John gets a sudden stomachache. "Julie," he says, "I can't make it tonight. I've got a bad migraine and I feel like I'm getting the stomach flu. I won't be able to eat a thing."

"John, this is the second time in the last two weeks you've gotten one of your migraines. The last time was when we were having dinner with my sister. Maybe you should see a doctor to make sure it's nothing serious," Julie says looking at him suspiciously mixed with concern. "I hate to leave you home alone if you're feeling so badly. Maybe we should just cancel altogether."

John panics. "Julie, please go and give my apologies to my mother. You know if neither of us go, we'll hear about it for weeks."

Julie looks hard at John. "Are you sure you'll be all right?"

"It's OK," John says, "I'm just going to take a couple of Tylenol and lie in bed, and hopefully sleep."

Julie sighs. "Well, all right. You do need your sleep. You've been up all month working on those silly work-related computer projects till all hours."

Julie leaves, hesitating once more, but is reassured when she sees John in his bathrobe lying in bed. She goes into the garage, starts her car, and backs out onto the street.

John lies there listening . . . glad when he finally hears the car drive away. He waits until he is sure she is gone. Then feeling the excitement he felt in the car earlier, he gets up, finds his new computer game, fumbles with the cellophane, and unwraps it. Finally it is ready to slide into the port on the computer. It goes in so easily, so smoothly. The words on the screen say, "Tombstone City." He pushes the command button. Then he chooses his method of play. He will start with beginner level, easy board, slow pace, until he figures out the game and what strategies will work.

The game appears on the monitor. There is the safety zone and lots of cacti and tumbleweed. He needs to shoot and destroy them all with his schooners. Ah, he gets his first cactus, now two, and three, now the tumbleweed. He keeps racking up more and more points: 1,000, then 5,000. Suddenly things begin to change, some of the cacti start to get his schooners. Time after time they catch him. He just isn't fast enough. He hasn't figured out how to effectively use his safety zone. All at once he has run out of schooners. The game is over.

Ah, but that is the joy of having your own game, you can just start again. This time he will try the moderate level and see what it is like. Again, there are some cacti and tumbleweed, but the cacti move real fast; he has to really be alert. Then he figures out how to use the safety zone, so the points begin to pile up—he gets 10,000, then 25,000. Suddenly he has 125,000 points and he still has three schooners left. He isn't sure how long he's been playing, but his fingers are cramping up and his left hand is numb from pushing down on the controls. His neck feels stiff. He is bracing himself on the floor so hard the chair cuts off the circulation to his left foot, so his foot is numb. His eyes are starting to burn from staring so intently at the screen. He is really getting one of those migraines he told his wife he had earlier.

Suddenly he hears the garage door opening. Like a little boy getting caught with his hand in the cookie jar, he quickly turns off the computer, runs out of his office, and jumps into bed. He pretends to be asleep when he hears his wife coming into the house. He hears her footsteps in the kitchen, then on the stairs. His heart sinks; he hears her in his office. He must have forgotten something, maybe just to turn off the lights.

But when she comes into the bedroom, he knows he's been caught because of the banging and slamming she is doing with the door and drawers. She begins calmly, "John, I think you have a problem. Your computer has become your whole life and now these computer games. I wonder now, about all those late nights you said you were working on computer projects for work. I bet those nights you were just playing these silly computer games. It's unbearable—you are even lying to get out of doing things so you can stay home and play these ridiculous games. I suppose last week when you didn't go to my sister's, you were playing your games, but just didn't get caught.

Well, this time you left the monitor on. I felt the warmth of the machine and saw some new game stuck in the slot. I have had it. You need help. Your time has run out, John. There are no more boards here, no more men left, there is no safety zone—in other words, John, the game is over."

MR. RED

I See You Standing There

I see you standing there; darkness is everywhere
You turn and look at me, your eyes are angry
You'll never see me, You'll never hold me,
You'll never know my name

Then the rain begins, dripping on my skin,
So I run and hide, to that place I have inside,
Where no one can see me, no one can hold me,
No one can know my name

Sometimes the sun peeks out,
I want to run and shout
Twirl around without a care,
arms reaching in the air
I want to see me, I want to hold me,
I want to know my name

But, You'll never touch me, You'll never love me,
You'll never know I was here

Living In the forest is a pretty little girl with legs that run so fast no one can catch her. Her long brown hair flies in tangles of movement as she bounces, runs and twists her way through life. Her nose is covered with little brown specks of "Angel Kisses." Her eyes shine like sparkling emeralds, bursting with energy and adventure. She names herself "Princess Magi" (pronounced Maggy) even though it's spelled like the wise men. She loves the sound of her name; it is magical and musical and rolls off her tongue. Her best friend is a little red squirrel that lives in a tree by her house. Some of her best adventures are following him as he runs through the forest. She has the most trouble when he climbs to the tops of trees and jumps to the next branch. The branches won't hold her weight and she is forced to climb back down to the ground. But eventually Mr. Red will come back and find her. His bushy tail tickles her ankles and toes when he gets excited because it wiggles so fast.

This morning when she wakes up, everyone else is still asleep. She goes quietly into the kitchen and finds leftovers in the refrigerator. She puts them in her pockets and then makes a peanut butter and jelly sandwich to hide in her dresser drawer with a juice box. Finally she is ready to go outside to find Mr. Red.

He is waiting for her on the bottom branch of the maple tree. His tail is swishing very fast; he seems excited to bring her to a new place in the forest. He scampers off, stopping to check and make sure she is following him. He leads her down a long path where the trees get thicker and taller; soon they come to a small pond. He shows her a path that circles around the pond. On the other side there is an amazingly tall oak tree. It is so tall the branches seem to get lost in the clouds in the sky. On the lowest branch someone has hung a swing. The seat is made out of a two-foot piece of wood and thick ropes are tied around the branch.

Maggy is so excited. Being only six years old, she has never been on a swing before. She climbs on and wiggles her legs until the swing starts to move. Eventually she learns if she straightens her legs going forward and then bends them when she goes back she can swing faster and higher. Mr. Red sits on the swing next to her, enjoying the ride. After a while, Maggy's legs feel tired, so she gets off the swing and sits down by the tall oak tree.

She takes the leftover food out of her pockets. She has four chicken wings and some carrots. She brought a couple of crackers for Mr. Red. After they eat their lunch and she buries the bones in the dirt, she notices something pink sitting next to the trunk of the oak tree. It's a pink ribbon; she picks it up and sees it is a barrette. It looks old and worn. She wonders about the girl who used to wear the pink bow. *Did she live out here in the woods?* Next to the bow, she notices a little door that fits into the trunk of the tall oak tree. She opens it and inside she finds a doll about the size of her hand. It is made of cloth and the face has two buttons for eyes and the mouth and nose are stitched in with pink thread. The doll is wearing a corduroy jumper. Maggy has never had a doll before. She holds the doll, talks to her, and puts her on the swing. She says to the doll, "I think I'll name you Sadie." Then she gives Sadie a ride on the swing, going back and forth.

Soon she notices the sun is starting to get lower in the sky, going behind the trees. It is time to go home. She reluctantly gets up, not wanting to leave her new place. She opens the little door to put the doll back where she had found it; she notices there is something else in the little tree house. She pulls it out; it is a book with lots of pictures. She opens it up and on the first page are two little girls; one girl has brown hair, one girl has blonde hair. They are smiling and waving out at her from the book. As she turns the pages she notices the two girls going on adventures like she and Mr. Red do. They go on picnics, they climb trees, and on one page they are riding bicycles.

She feels Mr. Red's tail and hears him chattering. It is time to go; it is getting dark. She quickly puts the book back with the doll and closes the little door. She is so excited for tomorrow to come, so she can come back and play with the doll, ride the swing, and look at the book. Mr. Red is standing in front of her twitching his tail to let her know they need to leave—now.

A feeling of dread makes her legs heavy and her feet drag on the way back home. Today it is totally dark by the time she reaches her house. Maggy slowly opens the front door and walks in. She sees her mother, sitting in a chair, and staring out the window. Her mother, a thin, frail woman, with wispy long brown hair, is a misty image you can't quite see. When you try to touch it, it becomes a misty vapor that swirls from your touch. Maggy gave up trying to touch her long ago. Her mother sits and mutters words Maggy can't understand. So Maggy tiptoes past her mother and ventures further into the darkness. She needs to get to her bedroom.

She will be safe in her bedroom with the big window that looks out at a beautiful maple tree that is bursting with color. She can look at the tree and pretend she lives in its branches with the birds and Mr. Red.

But first she has to get through the darkness. She can hear the TV on in the living room. The man likes to lie on the couch and watch it. It looks like he's asleep. She walks ever so lightly trying to be invisible so he doesn't wake up. She is halfway through the darkness when she trips and makes a noise.

Suddenly there is a rumbling that shakes the floor under her feet. Her whole body shakes, her teeth are chattering, and then comes a tremendous roar that is deafening. She runs so fast her shoes fly off. She makes it to the bedroom before he sees her. She can hear the growling, roaring sound still rumbling outside her door. She pushes her dresser against it and sits in the corner and gets real small. So small she is sure no one can see her.

Eventually the sound gets quieter and quieter. She can hear the voices from the TV talking through her bedroom wall. She can hear the sound of her own breathing. She feels her heart beating. She looks at the window and Mr. Red is there sitting outside it, looking in at her, swishing his tail and eating an acorn. She goes over to her dresser and opens the top drawer where she has put the peanut butter and jelly sandwich that she made early that morning. She takes the sandwich and the juice box from her dresser and goes to sit by the window. She watches Mr. Red as he runs up and down the maple tree, stopping every few minutes to look at her.

Soon she starts to yawn; slowly she gets up and climbs into her bed pulling the covers up tightly. She watches Mr. Red, eventually closing her eyes and thinking of her forest and the adventures they will go on tomorrow. She lies there thinking about the swing, the pink bow, the book, and the doll that lives in the tree. She imagines seeing another little girl, like her, who once lived here in the woods, played with the doll, and rode on the swing. Maggy falls asleep, finally, thinking about tomorrow when she and Mr. Red will go visit the little doll and ride the swing to the top of the trees.

The next morning Maggy wakes up bright and early. She needs to hurry because it is always better if she is gone before they wake up. She can't wait to go visit the swing and tree. She tiptoes into the kitchen, finds some roast beef and bread and wraps it in a napkin and puts it in her pocket. She tucks a water bottle in her shirt. She walks slowly across the living room; her mom is sitting in the chair this morning, mumbling to herself. Maggy opens the front door and runs outside.

Mr. Red is waiting for her on the path by the front door. Soon they are both running to the pond and the swing. The sun is out, the sky is blue, and the air feels warm and comforting. As they near the pond they hear someone singing quietly:

Good morning world, good morning world,

I look outside at the trees so tall
The breeze is flowing through them all
Their leaves do dance against the sky
Look at all those birdies fly

The grass glistens green with the morning dew
The air is fresh; it smells so new

The squirrels scamper up and they scamper down
Looking for acorns on the ground

Good morning world, good morning world,
Good day

Maggy stops and listens, feeling drawn to the beautiful sound but afraid at the same time. She and Mr. Red hide behind a wide oak tree and peek around the trunk. A beautiful woman with long brown, wavy hair is sitting at the edge of the pond; her hand is trailing along in the water as she sings. She seems lost in her own world. The swing is right behind her. Maggy wants so badly to swing but is afraid of the woman. She doesn't know what to do; then suddenly Mr. Red dashes over to the woman and twitches his tail.

The woman glances up and says, "Hi, Mr. Red, long time, no see." Maggy watches, not able to move. She can't believe the woman knows Mr. Red's name. And she can't believe Mr. Red went up to her and isn't afraid.

Maggy tries to feel brave enough to go to the swing. She takes a step and a branch cracks under her foot.

The woman looks around. "Who's there? Is someone there?"

Maggy comes out from behind the tree. The woman looks at her. "What is your name, you pretty little girl?"

Maggy clears her throat. "Princess Maggy."

"Hi, Princess Maggy. I'm Lilly. I used to live in these woods with my parents years ago. In fact, my father built this swing and made me the elf's house in the tree. My mother made me a doll that I kept in it. We moved away years ago. I wondered if I'd ever be able to find this place again. And here I am. Do you come here a lot?"

Maggy, still struggling with the reality that there is a woman speaking to her, says quietly, "I just found this place yesterday. When I found the pink bow it made me wonder about the little girl it once belonged to. Does it belong to you?" Maggy starts to warm up to the woman. "I love swinging on the swing. Do you mind if I swing on it now? I learned yesterday how to make it go fast. If I push my legs straight I go forward and then I bend them back to go backward. I can swing real high when I do that."

"You must be a very smart little girl, Princess Maggy. It took me a long time to figure that out when I was your age."

"I love your doll, too."

"You mean it is still in the elf's house?" Lilly gets up, walks over to the oak tree and opens the little door. She pulls out the doll. "Wow, I can't believe it. I used to play with this for hours. Oh, and here is my favorite storybook. Would you like me to read it to you, Princess Maggy?"

Maggy has never had anyone read to her. She goes and sits on the ground close enough to see the pictures without touching the woman.

Lilly begins reading, "Betsy looked out the window as a moving van pulled in across the street. A car pulled up behind it and a girl her age jumped out of the back seat. Betsy ran out her front door and across the street to meet the new girl. She wanted to have a friend so badly she didn't have time to be shy."

Maggy whispers, "The only friend I've ever had is Mr. Red."

Lilly smiles. "Mr. Red became my friend after my big sister left me."

Maggy looks at Lilly. "Will you be my friend?"

"Well, Princess Maggy, I'm only here for a couple of days. I just came here to find something. Living in a big city, full of people, has made me feel lost and lonely. I thought if I came back here I'd maybe find myself again. But I can be your friend while I'm here. I think we should start our friendship by me pushing you on the swing. What do you think?"

Maggy's eyes light up. "Yes, oh yes, please."

Maggy jumps on the swing and Lilly pushes her from behind.

Maggy asks, "Will you sing, while you push me? I love to hear you sing."

"OK, I'll finish the song I was singing earlier." Lilly begins her song:

> *Look at the children outside in their play*
> *I could watch them every day*
> *The sun is out and the rain is gone*
> *It's time to sing out my favorite song*
>
> *Good morning world, good morning world,*
> *Good day*

"Thanks Lilly, I like that song a lot."

"Princess Maggy, I need to go now. But I'll be back tomorrow around the same time. I'll see you then."

Lilly leaves and Maggy feels her stomach growl. She sits down by the elf's door and pulls out her roast beef, bread, and her bottle of water. Of course, she brought crackers for Mr. Red. They sit there quietly eating. When they are done there isn't a crumb anywhere.

Maggy brings the doll out of the elf's house and plays with her. She rocks her and sings silly songs. She puts her on the swing and gives her a ride. Mr. Red jumps on the swing too. The sun starts to feel really warm and Maggy starts to get sleepy. She sits on the ground and leans back against the oak tree, cuddling with Sadie the doll, and falls asleep. Mr. Red stands guard while she sleeps.

After a long nap, Maggy wakes up and decides to wade in the pond to cool off. After she wades, Mr. Red and her start racing on a path around the pond. Maggy puts the doll by the tree, so the doll can watch. Soon the sun starts to lower itself behind the trees. It's time to leave. Maggy decides to bring Sadie home with her, to keep her company.

Maggy likes to get home when it's almost dark because usually the man is asleep by then. When Maggy arrives home, she sees her mother sitting and staring out the window. She is still a misty image that mutters to herself. She can hear voices from the TV; there is a soft growling sound and snoring coming from the living room. Maggy walks quickly to her bedroom with her doll, grabbing a banana and a box of cereal from the kitchen on the way. Just before she gets there she trips over something on the floor. The floor starts to shake and growling fills the room. Maggy opens her bedroom door, goes in, and closes it just in time.

She sits on her bed and eats her cereal and banana as she watches Mr. Red climb and jump from tree to tree outside her window. She is not so afraid this evening, maybe because Sadie is with her or maybe it's because she is meeting the woman tomorrow at the pond. She starts wondering about Lilly; she feels like she's seen her before.

The next day Lilly is waiting by the pond when Maggy gets there. She smiles when she sees Maggy. "I've been waiting for you. Do you want to see where I used to live? It's not very far from here. We'll let Mr. Red lead the way."

"OK, if it's not too far." Maggy follows Mr. Red and Lilly down a path on the other side of the big oak tree. The trees are very thick and close together. Suddenly there is a clearing. In the clearing is a house that looks a lot like Maggy's own house, except it is painted red. Maggy and Lilly go in the house. There isn't any furniture, just a sleeping bag and a camper's lantern.

"Come on, let's go around back." Lilly leads them to the backyard. There is an old sandbox and a rusty bike next to it. "Do you know how to ride a bike, Maggy?"

"No, I've only seen them in pictures." Maggy goes over and touches the wheels of the bike.

"I know this one looks rusty, but it works great. I've been riding it all over the place since I got here. Come here and I'll give you a ride."

Maggy walks over slowly, not sure about this. But Lilly's big smile encourages her until suddenly Maggy is sitting on the bicycle seat. Her legs don't reach the pedals, so Lilly lowers the seat. Soon Maggy can feel the solid, pedals under her feet. Lilly holds the back of the seat and steadies the bike while Maggy starts to pedal slowly. They work at it for half an hour, then Lilly lets go when Maggy doesn't know it. Suddenly Maggy is riding the bike by herself. By lunchtime Maggy is riding up and down the path with Mr. Red chattering along behind her. She learns how to stop the bike and can get off without falling. Her stomach starts to growl and tells her she is hungry. Suddenly Maggy realizes she didn't bring any food.

Lilly looks at Maggy. "Are you hungry?"

"Yes, and I forgot to bring something to eat."

"That's OK, I have sandwiches and chips in my backpack." Lilly goes into her house and comes out with her backpack. She hands Maggy a tuna sandwich and a bag of chips. She has crackers and nuts for Mr. Red.

They sit down on the grass and start eating their lunch. Lilly looks at Maggy for a couple of minutes. "Princess Maggy, I need to tell you something. I know your mom. She is my older sister. She used to live here in this house too. The pink bow you found by the pond was hers."

Maggy looks at Lilly. "That's why you look like someone I've seen before. You look like my mommy. Or you look like my mommy used to look. Now when I look at my mommy she doesn't seem real. She's more like a fairy tale image you can never really touch. She doesn't talk. She used to talk a lot but now she just mutters."

Lilly picks up a rock and tosses it into the grass. "Your mom and I used to be close. Then when she turned eighteen she met this bad man. My parents didn't like him and neither did I. Just before my fourteenth birthday your mom ran off and married him. She used to call us every couple of months to let us know how she was. She called once right after she'd had a baby, and she wasn't making any sense. My mother thought your mom's mind started to not think right. There was something wrong with her words. It must have been when you were born because it was about six years ago. Then a couple of years ago, your mom's calls stopped. When my mother tried to call her, her phone was disconnected. We all wondered where your mom was and what happened to you. We were worried because your father has this darkness in him that makes him very angry and as dangerous as a grizzly bear."

Maggy sits thinking a moment and says, "The man in my house, he is my father? I didn't know that. I just know he is scary and growls so loud the floor shakes. So I stay out of his way. I don't want him to see me."

Lilly looks lovingly at Maggy. "When I saw you yesterday, I knew you were my sister's daughter. You look just like her. I didn't know she had moved back to this area with her husband until I saw you. That's why I left yesterday. I went into town to find out more about your family. You must have been born at home. No one knew anything about a baby being born from around here. I don't know how you've been surviving in that household. The grocer told me he brings bags of food once a week and there is always an envelope taped to the door with money. He said a little girl called in the order and asked him to bring it every Monday. He has been delivering the same food for two years now."

Maggie looks at Lilly. "That was me, I'm the little girl who called. There was this one day when I was so hungry and there was no food. On the TV I saw a store with food and they had a phone number you could use if you needed food. So I got the phone and pushed in the numbers I saw on the TV screen. A man answered. I told him what my favorite foods were. He asked me if I wanted him to bring them to my house. I told him I did. Then I found an envelope with money in it. The first time the man came I was outside with the envelope. He showed me which ones he needed for the food. I hid the rest in my room to pay for the bags of food that came every week. Then our phone didn't work anymore, but the man kept bringing the bags, and I always put out the same money."

"Oh, Princess Maggy, you are such a smart little girl to call and get food to your house. You really amaze me. Does anyone even cook in your house?"

"The angry man, you said is my father, sometimes cooks."

"I'm glad to hear that. I also talked to the doctor in town; he said your mom came to him once, about three years ago. You were running a very high fever. He gave her some medicine to give to you. He had trouble understanding what your mom was talking about half the time. You were just barely three and he couldn't believe how well you talked. Your mom didn't bring you back for the follow up appointment. He never saw you or your mother after that. He tried to find out where you lived. But there wasn't any record of your birth and your mom didn't put an address on their forms. So have you been lonely way out here with no friends?"

"No, Mr. Red is my friend and we have our own language we speak and we love to play games. I like being your friend too. You pushed me on the swing and you read to me and today you taught me to ride a bike."

"You know Maggy, I came back here because I felt like I'd left something important behind. I didn't know what it was. I was called back to this place. I think it was to find you. Mr. Red and I became friends after my sister left. That summer there were no other children around so he would lead me through the woods on fun adventures like he does to you. I think he purposely brought you here a couple of days ago. He wanted you to find the swing and elf's house. But most of all he wanted you to find me."

Maggy and Lilly look at Mr. Red. His tail is twitching wildly and he seems to chatter excitedly to let Lilly know she is right.

"I found some people in town who can get help for your mom and dad. I know you'd miss Mr. Red terribly but do you think you'd consider coming home with me to the city? You can meet your grandparents. They live a couple blocks from me. There is a park close by and a school; you are school age now. What do you think?"

Maggy looks at Mr. Red. She feels a sadness in her so deep, but she thinks about Lilly's voice singing songs and reading books to her. She knows this is what Mr. Red wants. She gets up and walks over to Lilly wanting to sit on her lap. Lilly looks at Maggy, pulls her onto her lap, and puts her arms around Maggy, kissing the top of her head. Maggy doesn't remember ever being touched before.

She loves the feeling of Lilly's strong arms around her, holding her. She doesn't ever want Lilly to let go of her. She wants to sit here forever in the warmth and safety of Lilly's arms. She loves that Lilly smells like sunshine and soft breezes. Maggy is so happy she doesn't have to go back to the dark house in the woods, with her mother's misty image and the dark scary growls that rumble the floors at night, ever again. Maggie relaxes and sits back. She can feel Lilly's heart beating and she realizes for the first time what home feels like.

BERT

3 o'clock In the Morning

It was 3 o'clock in the morning,
when I got your call.
It was 3 o'clock in the morning; you
were hurting and ready to fall

Are you gone? Could you be gone?
What did I do wrong? Could you be gone?

You said, "Can you come over and hold my hand?"
You said, "Can you come over I really need a friend?"
When I got there, I sat down by your side.
When I got there, I just held you while you cried.

Are you gone? Could you be gone?
What did I do wrong? Could you be gone?

We sat there for hours; we talked the night away.
We sat there for hours; there was so much to say
Then I had to go, I said good night
Then I had to go, you really seemed all right.

I wonder how long I've been sitting here? Bert thinks, as he sits on a park bench, a few trees scattered around him. He is wearing his favorite black bowler hat, and is sitting with his hand resting on a black cane that is standing between his legs. He looks around him and sees a young man running into the park. The young man's hair is dark and curly. He is wearing jeans and a leather jacket. He sees Bert sitting on the bench and goes over to him. The whole time he is patting his pockets, a cigarette is hanging out of his mouth.

"Excuse, me." The young man clears his throat and says louder. "Excuse me, do you have a match?"

Bert looks at him curiously. "Sorry son, I don't. You really shouldn't smoke, you know. It coats your lungs with black stuff. Makes your breath smell bad and your teeth turn yellow. You know Gladys used to say, Gladys is my wife, she passed away a year ago next month . . ."

The young man sits down, his left leg nervously bouncing up and down, as he looks around.

Bert continues, "Anyway, she used to say she wished no one had ever invented the cigarette. She said she saw no positive reason that cigarettes exist. I'm inclined to agree with her."

The young man growing more agitated says, "Look, I didn't ask for your life story, just a book of matches."

"That's the problem with you young people, you never slow down, never take the time to get to know who's sitting next to you. You're always looking for something else on the other side of the hill."

The young man stands up agitated. "Look man, I just want a light."

Bert smiles. "I know, I know, me too. I want a light, a light that will show me the way home. I think I've been sitting here for six hours now. Though I'm not really sure because I forgot my watch. I have forgotten where I live. I checked for my wallet but I must have forgotten that too. I don't suppose you might know where I live?"

The young man starts pacing; puzzled, he stops and looks at Bert.

Bert continues. "I mean, maybe you saw me walking somewhere? You know, you passed me on the street?"

The young man takes a good look at Bert. "I don't think so . . . you know I had a nightmare like that once where I went to the store to buy a six-pack of beer. When I came out of the store I didn't know where I was and then I couldn't find my car. I walked up and down the sidewalk and my car was gone. Then there was this man, he had a gun." The young man starts pacing again as he speaks. "He came walking toward me, I started to run but I didn't know where to go. Nothing looked familiar. I could hear his footsteps and smell his cigar. Then there was this ringing that startled me; it came from all around me. Then I woke up . . . the ringing, it was my alarm clock. But that feeling of being lost stayed with me all day."

Bert looks around him and then at the young man pacing in front of him. "Am I awake?"

"What?" The young man stops and looks at Bert.

"I said, am I awake? Could I be having the same nightmare? You don't have a gun, do you?" Bert looks concerned and anxious.

"No." The young man looks around him nervously. The trees look kind of strange, not quite real. "Where am I? What is this place? Do those trees look strange to you? Are you for real? Oh, I wish I had a match!"

The young man walks back and sits down next to Bert on the park bench. "So, do you have a name?"

Bert sits up even straighter, his white gloves gripping firmly to the top of his black cane. "Bertram Aloysius Delacroix. People usually call me Bert. Though when I was younger they teased me and told me my name was Bad."

The young man looks at Bert like he's crazy. "What?"

"The initials from Bertram Aloysius Delacroix spell bad. You know if I had matches, I wouldn't give them to you."

The young man looks puzzled. "Why not? What have I ever done to you . . . ?

Bert interrupts the young man. "Because I like you. You have a nice face. So I don't want you to die and cigarettes will . . ."

The young man gets angry and interrupts, "Knock it off. You're not my dad. I don't need a lecture, so can it, old man."

With a funny smile on his face, Bert says, "How do you know I'm old? Maybe I'm an 18 year old just dressed to look 80. Or maybe I have a rapid aging disease."

"Excuse me, but what planet have you been partying on, Bertram? How long did you say you've been here?" The young man's leg starts bouncing again.

"Bert . . . please just call me, Bert. Bertram takes too long to say. Bert feels better on the tongue, a nice crisp 'T' to end it, not that soft, mushy 'M' sound. A sound like someone is humming. No, I like the crisp 'T', don't you?"

The young man stands up and looks at Bert. "I asked, how long have you been sitting here?"

"Six hours . . . six days . . . it all feels the same since my Gladys left me. But I'll join her shortly."

The young man looks around the park area. "What direction did you come from? Maybe I can help you find your way back." The young man gets a funny look on his face and looks at Bert. "What do you mean you'll join her shortly? I thought you said she was . . . oh, wow!"

The young man starts to back away from Bert. "You're weird man, you are the weirdest . . ."

Bert sits there thinking, and finally answers the young man's question. "Let's see, I don't remember which direction. I passed some trees, no people, one duck, a robin flew by with a worm in its mouth, probably off to feed her babies . . . " Bert begins speaking to himself unaware of the young man. "Gladys and I never had babies . . ."

The young man is still puzzling over Bert's question. Bert is lost in his own thoughts.

"Bert, my man, there are trees everywhere. Don't you remember which way you came from . . . ?"

Bert continues talking to himself, "We tried, but for some reason God didn't seem to want us to have children. My Gladys loved children. A little girl who lived next door came over every day after school. Gladys always had cookies for her. I was never sure children and I would get along . . ."

The young man realizes that Bert isn't even listening to him so he speaks louder. "I said Bert . . . hello Bert . . . don't you remember which way you came from?"

Bert sighs and looks at the young man. "Maybe I just dropped in. Which way did you come from? Did you see any people or ducks or . . . ?"

The young man starts to look puzzled and goes and sits down on the park bench. "That's weird . . . I . . . I don't remember either. I think I got lost . . . no . . . it was dark. I had to get away . . . from . . . it was all way too much for me to handle. Life started to close in, school, jobs, my parents, I lost myself somewhere . . . I had to get away from my life . . . so I . . ."

The young man shivers and wraps his arms around himself. He gets up and starts pacing again, going faster and faster. "How long have I been here? Where's the path that brought me here? I don't know how to get back to where I came from. Man, what is this place?"

Bert quietly sits thinking. Then he looks at the young man. "Does it matter . . . what place this is? Haven't you ever just sat in a quiet place to . . . ?"

"Quiet place? Now what are you trying to . . . ?"

"Yes, young man, a quiet place. That place inside your soul that is quiet. When I am in there I feel like there is no place else to go. I don't want anything, I'm not pushing to . . ."

"Boorring. Bert, you are so boring. Why would I want to just sit . . . I mean there is so much to . . ."

"Run away from. When you push too hard you miss what's right next to you. If you're busy trying to go somewhere, you never enjoy the 'here'. Just sit . . . feel that quiet place in your soul. Let yourself be there for just awhile. Come on, young man, stand still a moment and close your eyes . . ."

The young man just paces faster. "I don't like that place . . . that quiet place. I've been quiet before but it scares me. I don't like the feeling . . . tired . . . no energy, that sense of not knowing where I want to go. That place is like this place. What is this place anyway?"

"Come on, young man, come and sit down. Relax."

The young man sits down on the edge of the bench and starts biting his thumbnail.

Bert looks at the young man. "I like the quiet place. It gives me time to know myself and hear my thoughts. It slows time down so I can notice every little thing around me. Each moment is a gift. I'm not exactly sure what this place is for you, but I'm beginning to think it's my 'Waiting Place'. Look up in that tree."

The young man looks up at the trees behind the bench.

Bert points at a weird looking tree. "Do you see it?"

The young man stands up again, backing away from Bert. "Hey man, YOU ARE FREAKING ME OUT! This place is freaking me out, waiting place, quiet place . . . I don't belong here. I think I'd rather be back where I was . . . anything is better than this."

"Young man, when you are ready, this is a wonderful place to be. I don't think you're supposed to be here . . . look, there it is again." Bert points up at the trees.

The young man takes another step back. "Yeah, I don't think I'm sup . . . oh my God. What is that, that white stuff that's waving in the breeze? Wait a minute, there isn't a breeze. What is that?"

Bert smiles. "I think it's my guardian angel. He's been with me all my life, but I've just been able to see him since I've been sitting here. I think he's waiting to see if I'm ready. I don't see yours though . . . it must not be your time."

The young man looks at Bert like he is lost his mind. "Must not be my time for what? Seeing if you're ready for what? Hey man! Now you're really freaking me out . . . guardian angels . . .

quiet places . . . waiting place. Where ARE we? I don't think I'm ready for this . . . I'm going back to where I came from."

The young man turns to leave, looks around, and scratches his head.

"Good, I'm glad, but Jake, don't forget the quiet place. Know . . . just know . . . it's OK to be quiet with no place to go. It won't last forever, so let it be there when it comes. Get to know and love yourself, Jake. You do that and you won't be in this waiting place again for a long, long time. I know you're not ready for this place. That's why I didn't have matches. I was hoping. Bye, Jake. Have a great life!"

Jake, looking even more puzzled, says, "How did you know my name? I never told you my name."

"Are you sure? Anyway it doesn't matter. Bye, Jake. My waiting is over; I'm ready. See my guardian angel beckons; you'll find your way back, Jake. I knew you weren't really ready for this place."

Bert stands up and walks toward the white swirling smoke in the trees. Soon the whiteness envelops him and he disappears.

Jake watches as Bert disappears. He feels a tingling; an energy starts to encompass him. Suddenly he sees the path back home; a light guides him. He can hear machines beeping and people talking. He can smell disinfectant. He is excited to be going back home. "Thanks, and good bye Bert." He runs along the lighted path.

The nurse yells to the doctor. "I have a pulse. I think he is coming around."

PURPLE SCARF
AND TIARA

The room with the darkened windows,
I look inside and see the shadows.
A sliver of light falls on a child,
She turns and sees me standing there,
In the room with the darkened windows

I go and sit down by her side,
She crawls upon my lap and cries.
I stroke her hair; I kiss her nose.
She turns and smiles up at me,
In the room with the darkened windows

Chapter 1

Her green, almond shaped eyes look out the big picture window. Outside her favorite maple tree explodes with orange, yellow, and red leaves. Her black puppy is sitting next to her, looking where she looks. She strokes his black ears and kisses the top of his head. On her head she wears a rhinestone tiara and purple scarf, for today she is a beautiful princess living high up in her tower where no one can find her. Her feet wear her magical shoes that make her feel like she is flying over the ground.

She hears her mother calling. "Elena, come here and eat your lunch."

Elena pretends not to hear and points at something out the window. "Skippy, look, do you see the magic dragon flying over that tree? I wonder where he is going."

"Elena, get in here this minute, before it gets cold."

Finally Elena gets up slowly; Skippy follows close behind her.

"Elena, I don't know what it is you see out that window. Now sit down and eat; I have to run downstairs and put in a load of laundry."

Elena sits down and Skippy sits under the table by her feet. She eats her peanut butter and jelly sandwich and chicken noodle soup, giving Skippy bites of her sandwich. She stares out the kitchen window as she eats; her tree is blowing in the wind and leaves are dripping off the branches. She sees Mrs. Daley walking down the sidewalk with a bag of groceries—Mrs. Daley, who is big and soft and cuddly. Mrs. Daley looks up and sees Elena through the window and smiles.

"Mommy, Mrs. Daley is home—can I go see her after I finish my lunch?" yells Elena.

She hears her mom coming up the stairs. "Elena, stop yelling at me when I am out of the room—now what do you want?"

"Can I go over to Mrs. Daley's?"

"No, after lunch it is time for your nap. Maybe after your nap," said Elena's mom as she puts down a basket of clothes she has gotten out of the dryer. Then the phone rings.

As her mom is talking on the phone, Elena gets down from the table and wanders into the living room again to stare out her window with Skippy.

"Skippy, later today we will have to go visit our secret cave. That one over there." She points out the window so Skippy can see it.

Elena's mom walks into the living room. "Elena, it's time for your nap. Head upstairs, I'll come and tuck you in after I clean up these dishes."

Skippy and Elena head upstairs; Elena lays down and Skippy jumps up to keep her company. She falls asleep before her mother comes to tuck her in.

After her nap, she runs over to Mrs. Daley's back door and knocks. Mrs. Daley opens the door. "Why Elena, how nice to see you, I'm just ironing. Do you want to come in and have a couple of cookies and talk to me while I iron?"

Elena thinks, *my favorite, watching her iron*! "Sure," she says, as she gets comfortable sitting on a kitchen chair. She looks around the kitchen. The light yellow cupboards and the white and yellow curtains over the kitchen sink make her smile. *Mrs. Daley's kitchen is happy,* she thinks, as Mrs. Daley brings her a plate of cookies and a glass of milk.

"Mrs. Daley, why do you need to iron clothes?" asks Elena, as she picks up a cookie.

Mrs. Daley starts ironing and answers, "To get the wrinkles out."

"But why don't you want wrinkles in your clothes?"

"Because you want to look nice and have your clothes smooth looking. By the way, don't you start school tomorrow?"

"Oh yes, I'm going to wear my blue dress and my red tennis shoes. I can't believe I am going to school, like William and

Patricia do. I do kind of worry about Skippy; he'll probably miss me while I'm at school."

Elena takes a bite of her cookie. "Mrs. Daley, what's that noise?" Elena says looking a little frightened.

"That's the refrigerator making ice cubes."

"Our refrigerator doesn't make ice cubes except when we put water in a tray. How does yours make ice cubes?"

"I'm not sure how it works. I think Skippy will be fine. It's only three and a half hours and you'll have the whole afternoon to play with him."

Elena climbs off the kitchen chair and says, "That reminds me, I should go home now. Skippy is probably wondering where I am. Bye."

Elena opens the back door and walks into the house. "Mom, Skippy, I'm home!" yells Elena. She stops short; an uneasy feeling comes over her.

"Your mom went to get something for supper," says her dad. Skippy runs up to Elena, wagging his tail, wanting to be petted. Elena pets him and then runs upstairs to her bedroom and gets out a couple of books to look at. Skippy follows her and lies down next to her, putting his head on her lap.

A few minutes later she hears the front door open and close. She runs downstairs and sees her mom; relief floods through her. Her mom is saying, "Now where are Patricia and William? They know it's dinner time."

Skippy and Elena resume their position at the big picture window. She is safe in her tower. She is so pretty and special when she wears her purple scarf and tiara. When she looks outside she sees her whole kingdom; everyone out there loves her.

A few minutes later, William and Patricia come in the back door talking about something funny; they both start laughing.

Elena's mom says, "It's about time you got home; supper is almost ready. Go and wash your hands."

At the supper table Elena's mom asks, "Elena, what do you want to wear for your first day of kindergarten? Your new green dress or the blue one?"

"I think I'll wear the blue one."

"Now remember you are not wearing those new tennis shoes."

"Mom, I have to. They are magic and fast. I'll need them tomorrow."

"We'll talk about it tomorrow, now finish up your dinner."

Elena's father says, "Yes, Elena, you want to belong to the 'Clean Plate Club'; your brother and sister are already members."

Elena looks at everyone's plates. They are all empty except for hers. She has some broccoli left; she doesn't like broccoli. When no one is looking she takes her broccoli and feeds it to Skippy who is lying under the table.

Elena's mom looks at her plate. "Good, now that you are done eating and have cleaned your plate you can help your brother and sister clear the table."

Elena starts thinking about the first day of school as she brings a dish to the sink. She isn't watching carefully and trips over Skippy and drops and breaks the plate.

"Good going, clumsy," says her brother. "Mom, Elena broke a dish."

Elena sneaks away before her mother has a chance to reply. She goes upstairs to her bedroom and plays with her doll; Skippy is the horse.

That night after her mother tucks her in and says, "Don't let the bed bugs bite," Elena lays awake for a long time thinking about school. She has watched her older brother and sister go to school for years. She can't believe that now she is old enough to go too. Suddenly she hears the door open downstairs, and the stairs creak under the black shadow as it climbs up to her in her bed. She stares out the window at the darkness beyond. She panics; she can't see her tree, it is too dark. The night has swallowed it up. The shadow comes nearer and she can feel its breath on her arm as it sits by the bed. "Are you asleep?"

Elena doesn't answer. She realizes Skippy isn't on the bed anymore. He must have gone downstairs. Her heart races; she is alone with the shadow, she can feel its touch. She closes her eyes and tries to picture the tower she lives in at the picture window. She knows she looks pretty in her tiara and purple scarf. She hears the shadow whispering. Her tower starts to get dark and the window gets darker. Skippy is gone. She is afraid. Then the shadow is gone and she goes to sleep feeling her legs tingle like someone just took their hands away.

Chapter 2

The next morning Elena is up bright and early. Skippy is sitting at the end of her bed. "It's almost time to go to school, Skippy." She bends down and holds Skippy's head between her hands. "Now, don't worry, I'll only be gone for three and a half hours. Then we'll have the whole afternoon to play. We can go outside and play catch with your favorite ball." Skippy licks her face in response. She stands up with a smile on her face and puts on her blue dress and red tennis shoes. She runs downstairs, eats her cereal and says, "Bye Mom," and runs out the door.

Her sister, Patricia, is waiting with a friend on the sidewalk. Elena follows behind her sister as she walks to school. Suddenly Skippy runs up and starts walking beside Elena.

"Skippy, you can't come with me. Remember I said I'll just be gone for three and a half hours; then we can play. You can't come with me to school." When they stop to pick up Judy, Elena asks Judy's mother to keep Skippy in the house until they have left because she doesn't want him to follow her.

After her first day of school Elena runs home feeling proud to be old enough to go to school. She is excited to tell Skippy all about it. She runs the two blocks, bursts into the house, radiating with energy and yells, "Skippy!" He doesn't come. She yells louder, "Skippy!" He still doesn't come. She runs up to her bedroom; he isn't there. She runs down the basement. "Mom, where is Skippy?"

"I don't know—how was school today?"

"Fine, but where is Skippy?"

"I haven't seen him all day, Elena, don't worry he'll be back."

Elena grows scared. "Where could he be?"

"Maybe he found a girlfriend or a playmate," says her mom to soothe the panic.

But Skippy isn't home by suppertime. When bedtime comes, Elena has to go to bed alone. She lays in the darkness of her bedroom and shakes with fear and the pain of losing her precious companion. *Where has he gone?* She thinks. *He has never left and been gone this long before.* When she wakes up the next day her stomach is in a knot and she has a headache. She runs downstairs; no one else is awake. She looks all over the house, she looks out her window, and she looks out both doors of the house. No Skippy! He still isn't back. Elena starts to cry, her whole body shakes with the tormenting sobs. Her mom hears her and gets out of bed.

"Elena, stop crying, there is no reason to cry. He'll turn up sooner or later."

Elena doesn't want to go to school; she wants to drive around and look for Skippy.

She throws a tantrum and won't get dressed until her mother says, "Elena, I promise I will drive around and look for Skippy while you are at school."

Reluctantly Elena leaves for school. At lunchtime she runs all the way home. There is no sign of Skippy. By suppertime everyone is worried.

"Tomorrow we'll put an ad in the paper and call the pound," says Elena's mom.

Elena makes her mom call the pound twice a day. After the ad is put in the paper Elena jumps every time the phone rings. She watches her parents' faces to see any sign of news. There is none.

When she falls asleep at night, she dreams about the black phone. It turns a sickly gray and the receiver bangs up and down, the phone sprouts legs and starts coming after her. She is afraid the phone is going to get her. She wakes up with her heart pounding. Three days go by with Elena staring at the phone waiting for it to ring or come alive. Every time it rings she gets anxious, wanting to hear her parents say, "Oh, you found him," but afraid to hear that something has happened to him.

On the fourth day, when her mom calls the pound, she hears her mom say, "What? You have a dog fitting Skippy's description at the pound?"

Elena starts jumping up and down. "Mom, get the car keys, let's go now. Please Mom, let's go." Elena's heart is dancing. *Skippy, Oh, I will see you again. I'll pet your black fur and you'll lick my face. I'll throw your favorite ball for you to catch. You'll sleep on my bed. Skippy, we're coming.*

But when they get there and see the dog, her heart stops and lays down to die. It isn't Skippy. Elena cries all the way home. She doesn't eat any supper and goes to her bedroom to hide. Elena starts staying in her room or going to her special window to watch for Skippy. She just can't believe he hasn't come back to be with her. He's her best friend and she thought she was his best friend too.

Chapter 3

Elena starts a daily vigil of watching out the window, hoping she will see Skippy run up to the house.

One day her mom asks, "Elena, where are your purple scarf and tiara?"

"I don't know."

"Elena, this is ridiculous, he was only a dog. We'll get you another one."

"I don't want another dog. I want Skippy."

Soon a month has passed and there is no dog. Elena stops her vigil at the window and stays in her room all the time. She knows she will never see Skippy again. Her mother hears her upstairs playing, but she doesn't hear the hidden sobs of abandonment and loss.

Mrs. Daley stops by one day looking for Elena, but Elena won't come down to see her. She pretends to be asleep when her mother calls her.

That night Elena is laying in bed, staring out the window into the darkness; tears are streaming down her cheeks and her aloneness encompasses her. She hears the stairs creak and she can feel the coldness of the approaching shadow. Fear grips her. She knows it is no use; no one loves her now that Skippy is gone. She knows she can't tell anyone how she feels because she knows it is her fault. Skippy wouldn't have run away if she hadn't left him at Judy's house. He must think she abandoned him so he ran away. She doesn't know how, but she knows that she can cause bad things to happen by talking about them. The shadow tells her that. The shadow is near. She tries to see out the window but it is too dark. She feels the shadow touch her. She realizes she is alone and no one can help her.

The next morning she dresses slowly for school. Her mom yells, "Elena, hurry, you'll be late for school!"

Elena comes downstairs and sees her older sister, Patricia, is all ready for school. Elena sits at the breakfast table and looks out the window; her tree is covered with snow.

"Elena, you have got to eat something. You are looking so pale, do you feel all right?"

Just then William charges into the room. "Mom, I'm in a hurry, what did you do with my science project? The one I had in the bathroom."

Elena slips from the table as her mother's attention turns to her brother. She gets her coat on and leaves for school without saying goodbye.

After school she dawdles home, ignoring friends as they pass by. When she arrives home, it is empty. Her mom is gone. Then she hears the back door open and close. It is Mrs. Daley.

"Elena, your mom had a doctor's appointment. I guess you left for school before she could tell you. So you are coming to my house for lunch."

Elena feels a butterfly in her stomach and then her heart. *Mrs. Daley, big, soft, cuddly Mrs. Daley, I'd forgotten about Mrs. Daley.* She follows her next door. Mrs. Daley has made her favorite, creamed tuna fish on toast. Suddenly she feels hungry. She eats two pieces of toast covered with tuna.

Mrs. Daley stares at Elena for a few minutes as if she is deciding to say something. She takes a big breath and begins. "Elena, I haven't seen you for a while. Not since Skippy left. How come?"

Elena looks at Mrs. Daley. She doesn't know why she hasn't come.

"I bet you miss your puppy. I had a dog once that ran away. I cried a lot; he had been my best friend."

Elena stares at Mrs. Daley and suddenly big tears are streaming down her cheeks. "Skippy was my best friend. We did everything together. I loved his black fur and the white star he had on his chest. He was always with me. I thought I was his best friend too. Why did he leave me? Where is he now? Is he OK? Did he find another family? Did he leave because I wouldn't let him come to school with me? Did he think I wasn't coming back? Did he think I didn't love him anymore?" Elena breaks down into heartbreaking sobs. Mrs. Daley sits down next to Elena and puts her arms around the little girl. Elena cries and cries; her whole body hurts with the pain. Mrs. Daley kisses Elena on the top of her head and keeps telling her it is going to be all right and Skippy knows how much she loves him. Finally the tears stop coming. Elena for the first time in a long time can feel her heart beating in her chest. It feels happy.

There is a knock on the back door.

"Hi, I'm back from the doctor's. Elena, are you OK?" says her mother when she sees Elena.

"She's fine, we just talked about Skippy and missing him."

"Oh Elena, we'll get another dog someday. It's nap time, we should go home now." Elena's mom seems uncomfortable.

Elena gets up slowly looking at Mrs. Daley. Mrs. Daley is staring at her mom with a funny look on her face, like she is mad at her.

Chapter 4

Elena starts going to Mrs. Daley's whenever she can. She finds an excuse almost every day. Elena's mom feels relieved; she doesn't have to look at Elena's long face staring out the front window all day.

Then Elena finds out that she is going to Mrs. Daley's for a whole day. Her mom and dad are going somewhere and her brother and sister are staying at friends' houses. When Elena wakes up the next morning she feels strange, like she does after the shadow comes to visit her. She suddenly doesn't want to go to Mrs. Daley's. She throws a temper tantrum when her mom wants her to get dressed.

"Oh Elena, why do you have to be so difficult? Now get dressed!"

Finally Elena is dressed and is sent to Mrs. Daley's back door. Mrs. Daley is washing dishes when Elena comes in. Elena sits for a long time and watches and asks a million "why" questions. "Why do you use a sponge when you wash dishes? Where does the water go when it goes down the drain? Why does the clock tick?" Mrs. Daley answers all her questions patiently.

Then Mrs. Daley stops washing dishes, and asks Elena if she wants to help make lunch. After they have cooked the hot dogs and chili and set the table, they sit down to eat their lunch of Coney Islands. Suddenly Elena has a strange urge—she wants to tell Mrs. Daley about the dark shadow that visits her at night sometimes. The thought makes her anxious; she knocks her glass of milk over. She has never told anyone about how scared she is at night, no one but Skippy. She wonders if Mrs. Daley ever has a dark shadow visit her at night. Suddenly she wants to know in the worst way.

"Mrs. Daley?" Elena whispers.

"Yes, Elena."

"Mrs. Daley? Do you ever? I mean have you ever, oh never mind." Elena feels so uncomfortable, like the world will stop if she says anymore.

Mrs. Daley seems to understand and doesn't push the matter.

"Would you like me to read you a story, Elena?"

"Maybe later. Can we play that card game you taught me the last time I was here? I think it's called 'Slap Jack.'"

"That's a great idea, Elena." Mrs. Daley gets a deck of cards out of the kitchen drawer. The rest of the day goes so fast that Elena can't believe it when her mom comes to get her.

"Mom, Mrs. Daley asked me to help her make Christmas cookies next weekend. Can I Mom? Please? Oh please, say yes."

"I don't see why not," says Elena's mom looking at Mrs. Daley.

"Which day do you want her?"

"Saturday, if that's OK?" says Mrs. Daley.

"Saturday it is then. Thanks for taking her today."

"It was my pleasure," says Mrs. Daley as she winks at Elena.

Chapter 5

Elena's week seems to fly by. Her mother can't believe it; Elena is wearing the purple scarf and tiara again and playing at her favorite window. Elena is so excited. She likes Mrs. Daley's kitchen. It is so cozy and safe.

A couple of nights before Elena's going to make cookies, she is visited by the shadow. She hears the steps creak. She tries to picture Mrs. Daley's kitchen. The shadow seems to be everywhere and then the shadow does something it has never done before, and she can't breathe, she thinks she is going to die. Then the shadow whispers something in her ear and is gone. Elena trembles and cries. She can still feel the shadow's touch. When she falls asleep, she has terrible dreams. In her dream she feels someone grabbing her ankles and pulling her down the bed; she tries to kick her legs loose but she can't. She feels a weight on her body; she can't breathe. She is choking, gasping for air. Her mouth opens and she tries to scream but no sound comes out. She wakes up; her nightgown is wet with her own perspiration. Her legs are tangled in the sheets. She looks out the window; the sun is shining. Her maple tree, still covered in snow, is standing tall outside her window. She can hear her mother downstairs making breakfast. She gets out of bed slowly, trying to shake away the nightmare.

When Elena goes downstairs and sees the breakfast on the table, she throws up. Her mother keeps her home from school. That night she has trouble falling asleep. She keeps seeing the shadows and monsters and hearing strange noises. Saturday morning finally comes and she can go to Mrs. Daley's. She runs downstairs.

When her mom sees her, she says, "Elena, I was just going to call Mrs. Daley and tell her I thought it best we cancel making cookies for today."

Elena panics, "Why? I'm fine, really I am. Please don't cancel, Mom, please!" Elena's voice has risen in pitch and is almost a scream.

"All right, if you're sure you feel OK."

Elena sits down and eats a big breakfast to prove to her mom she is fine. Then she runs upstairs, gets dressed, and flies next door to Mrs. Daley's.

After two hours and six-dozen cookies later, Elena and Mrs. Daley take a break to eat some of their creations. Elena's night shadow sweeps through her thoughts suddenly. Mrs. Daley sees her face change.

"Are you OK? Elena."

"I'm fine." Elena starts to fidget in her chair.

Mrs. Daley says, "How about a story, Elena?"

Elena feels relieved. Once again Mrs. Daley seems to know how she is feeling. "Oh yes, I love stories," she replies.

Mrs. Daley gets her book about Little Red Riding Hood and sits in the rocking chair by the kitchen window. She begins to read to Elena. Then she comes to the part where Little Red Riding Hood is afraid walking through the woods, because it is dark, and there are shadows, scary dark shadows. Elena doesn't hear the rest of the story. Suddenly she feels the nightmare from a couple nights ago, the hands on her ankles, the weight lying on her. She looks at Mrs. Daley. *Mrs. Daley knows about shadows, she knows about fear, she knows about the darkness.* When Mrs. Daley finishes the story she looks at Elena searchingly because Elena has such a haunted look on her face.

"Elena, what is it, what's wrong?"

"You know about the shadows, you know about the darkness, you know about the fear. I thought you knew, because you knew about Skippy too."

"Slow down, Elena, what are you talking about?"

"The shadows, you know about the shadows that come at night, the ones that whisper, the ones that scare you and touch you . . . " Elena is talking so fast, she is gasping for air.

Mrs. Daley looks at Elena with shock and disbelief at what she is hearing. From deep inside she feels the little girl's terror and loneliness. Suddenly she wants to protect her and love and help her more than anything else. Elena is crying now, big tears flooding down her cheeks, hanging onto her chin and nose. Mrs. Daley asks, "Elena, why don't you come and sit on my lap."

Elena slowly goes over and sits down laying her head on Mrs. Daley's shoulder; the tears are still flowing freely, unencumbered. Her fear begins to relax and let go of her. The words keep coming.

Mrs. Daley just listens and rocks Elena. Elena no longer feels alone. The shadow seems less scary. She feels the warmth and love, sitting in this kitchen smelling of six dozen cookies she has just helped bake.

Soon Elena falls asleep in Mrs. Daley's arms. As Elena sleeps Ms. Daley thinks about what Elena has told her. She thinks about Elena's father and his drinking and anger problems she has witnessed over the years. She never in her wildest dreams would have thought him capable of what she has just heard. She feels tears rolling down her own cheeks, after hearing the secrets this little girl in her arms was forced to keep. She sighs, reaches for the phone sitting on the table next to her, picks it up, and calls information.

"I would like the phone number for Hennepin County Child Protection Agency." She dials the number, and listens to it ring as she feels Elena's breath going in and out, smells the shampoo in her hair, watches her heartbeat in the soft part of her neck . . . "Yes, hello. I would like to report a case of child abuse . . ."

Music

I have written and produced two CD's. They are "Reflections of the Inner Pond" and "Got to Keep on Going." At the beginning of each story and inside the stories of Mr. Red and The Choir are original songs I've written. If you are interested in hearing the songs, listed below are four places the CD's are sold.

The songs you see throughout the book can be heard on Amazon.com http://www.amazon.com/Got-Keep-Going-Helen-Lapakko/ dp/B00320J7YA/ref=sr_1_1?ie=UTF8&qid=1449545366 &sr=8-1&keywords=got+to+keep+on+going+CD

Overstock
http://www.overstock.com/Books-Movies-Music-Games/HELEN-LAPAKKO-GOT-TO-KEEP-ON-GOING/4982403/product.html

CD baby
http://www.cdbaby.com/cd/HelenLapakko

I Tunes
https://itunes.apple.com/us/artist/helen-lapakko/id334801136

If you would like sheet music of the songs, or if you would like more information about the songs you can contact me at mericapalen@hotmail.com

Printed in the United States
By Bookmasters